The
Sacrificing of
Thomas Cranmer

C. A.
HOPE

CRANTHORPE
— MILLNER —
PUBLISHERS

To the one and only Colin, with love

A Note from the Author

I first came across Thomas Cranmer when studying A-level history. My favorite era was, and still is, the era of the Vikings, although I also loved the Plantagenets, whose reign ended in 1485. The Tudors were new to me, but I quickly discovered that this period of history was not only well documented, but also brimming with events and interesting characters. One such character was Thomas Cranmer. He just kept popping up; at every significant event, there he was! Most of my textbooks said very little about him: some briefly recorded him in a good light, others in a negative light, but he was invariably mentioned. He even appeared in a television series called The Six Wives of Henry VIII, alongside Thomas Cromwell. His seemingly constant presence fascinated me. I soon learned he was in attendance at every historical event during that period, from when he was first summoned to Court to assist with the divorce of King Henry VIII from his first wife, Catherine of Aragon, to the time when Queen Mary ascended the throne.

As time went on, I began to dig around, and collected a substantial amount of information about him. He was not some dry, boring priest, nor was he a gung-ho, swashbuckling hero. He has been accused of being timid and lacking in courage by many historians, but he was only human. When the possibility of being burned at the stake for your faith is a constant threat, I can imagine it is impossible not to feel permanently afraid. For him, that threat was, for the most part, a permanent presence in his life. Regardless of this, he was certainly dutiful. His entire life was dedicated to serving God, serving his king, and reforming what was, at that time, a very corrupt Church. Then, as now, the world of power and politics was full of ruthless, self-seeking people, who would stop at nothing to gain their own slice of power; plus, of course, the wealth that accompanied it. Thomas Cranmer had his own bête noire in the form of a man named Stephen Gardiner. Execution was considered the norm, and Stephen Gardiner wanted Thomas Cranmer executed. He was a persistent, dangerous foe, who ensured that from the moment Cranmer began working for King Henry VIII, he could never sleep peacefully.

It seems tragic that, when he was eventually executed, Thomas Cranmer perished thinking his work had been in vain. He had worked selflessly to reform the Church in England, but when Mary Tudor became queen, she immediately reinstated Roman Catholicism. He must have found this devastating. Yet, just a few years after his death, Elizabeth I ascended the throne, and reestablished the Protestant Church. This is his legacy, and that of those who also perished.

Having researched the life and times of Thomas Cranmer for nearly thirty years, on 23rd March 2020, came the first Covid 19 lockdown. So, if I was ever going to do anything with my research, now was the time.

I have to say, it kept me very well occupied, gave me a number of sleepless nights, but I was never bored! Throughout this period, I was encouraged and supported by a number of friends and relatives, whom I am grateful to. It's a long list, therefore, I will only name four and send sincere groveling apologies to everyone else! They were outstanding, and exceedingly patient when I asked questions (often at an inconvenient time) such as, 'seriously, how long do you think it will take a human body to burn?' So, to my wonderful cousin Diane, and friends Delia, Chris and Wendy, many thanks.

Also, sincere thanks to Kirsty at Cranthorpe Milner, for her enthusiasm for this era in history, and for recognizing Thomas Cranmer's unique contribution to it. Likewise, my gratitude to Victoria for her stoic editing, which must surely have taken many hours.

God bless all of you.

<u>Chapter One</u>

It was late spring, in the year 1515. The sun was setting, sending golden rays over the sparkling water of the River Cam, and the air was rich with the heady scent of flowers and the evening chorus of birdsong. But this beauty went unnoticed by the lone figure on the grassy riverbank. He simply sat, staring at the ground, his knees pulled up beneath his chin, tears trickling slowly down his cheeks, his dark eyes red rimmed from weeping. Wispy strands of dark brown hair poked from beneath his scholar's cap, and his young face was thin and clean shaven. Whilst it could not be described as handsome, nor was it unpleasant. It was a gentle, sensitive face. The visage of a compassionate person. His name was Thomas Cranmer and, half an hour ago, his wife, Joan, had passed away.

Dabbing his eyes with the hem of his shabby mantle, he took a long, deep breath. There was no grief in his heart, only deep regret, for he and Joan were ill-suited. Everyone had known. Indeed, when he had first expressed an interest in her, his closest friends had advised him to stay away - but he had not heeded their words. Joan had never been easy to ignore.

Thomas' life had begun on the second of July 1489, in Aslockton, Nottinghamshire. His parents were well-to-do

1

farming folk, but only his eldest brother could expect any inheritance, as the land owned by the Cranmer family was modest at best. Thomas and his younger brother were, therefore, expected to forge a career somehow, somewhere. A scholarly child, his early education had been blighted by a bullying and abusive schoolmaster, and despite his pleas, his father, who was also named Thomas Cranmer, had insisted upon his son remaining at the school, in the hope that the strict schoolmaster might knock some spirit into the lad. Unfortunately, the schoolmaster's physical and verbal beatings had the opposite effect, though in retrospect, Thomas suspected he would have been timid no matter how gently he had been tutored as a child.

Following the death of his father, his mother, Agnes, had the foresight to suggest that the young Thomas, then fourteen years old, should be despatched to a university, for he was gifted academically and would surely prosper in such a climate. His oldest brother, now in charge of the farm, acted accordingly, and within weeks, young Thomas arrived at Jesus College, Cambridge. Immediately, he realised that this was where he belonged. Such a wealth of knowledge, all at his fingertips! Studying for a degree was the most joyful pleasure he could imagine, and he progressed effortlessly from Bachelor of Arts to Master of Arts, began teaching, and in due course, was elected to become a Fellow of Jesus College. Books became his most precious possessions, and he collected numerous tomes during his time at Cambridge, filling his room with piles upon piles of academic texts. Unfortunately, a couple of years later, he encountered a distraction... a distraction named Joan.

Her nickname was Black Joan, on account of her raven hair, foul moods, and unpredictable temper. Yet somehow, for some unbeknown reason, she mesmerised the quiet, scholarly

2

teacher. She was a barmaid at the Dolphin Inn, and although he and his friends mostly frequented the White Horse Inn, sometimes, for variety, they would visit other hostelries. After months of barely acknowledging his existence, one day, whilst serving ale and food to him and his friends, she singled him out. Suddenly, he felt the full force of her personality – when she was in a good mood, Joan was irresistible – and she quickly became his mistress.

As yet he had not taken priestly vows, but it was anticipated he would one day do so. It was not unusual for a member of the clergy - or someone preparing to become a priest - to take a mistress. It was frowned upon, but rules were lax; as long as the relationship was discrete, it was acceptable. It was even deemed acceptable for those who had actually taken their vows. Even Thomas Wolsey, the king's almoner, was known to have a mistress and, according to rumour, Wolsey was soon to become a cardinal no less.

Joan was a fine-looking woman, but as a serving girl, she was far beneath him socially; serving girls were regarded as little better than prostitutes. Yet he continued to visit her; indeed, he found her hard to resist. Their trysts were far from romantic, taking place in her cramped, grubby room above the Dolphin Inn. There was something almost sordid about those visits, for the duration of which her roommate was instructed to make herself scarce.

Perhaps it was the excitement that made him keep returning to her? Certainly, in his lifetime, he had never come across such a high-spirited person. Her wit was quick and, when in a good mood, she was entertaining beyond anything he had ever known; sometimes he ached with laugher at her novel comments and opinions. But love itself did not enter into their relationship, and he rarely mentioned her to his friends. For their part, they avoided the subject, believing – and hoping – that he would come to his senses and ultimately end his relationship with such an unsuitable, unstable woman. Then, one day, when he was visiting her room, she informed him she was pregnant.

Those words nearly knocked him to the floor; he collapsed heavily onto the only chair in the room, whilst Joan, her long black hair in disarray, informed him of her condition, sobbing all the while about her reputation being ruined. Stunned, he turned and walked from the room, seeking out his closest friend, Hugh Latimer, who was also a Fellow of Jesus College. Latimer, nearly as scholarly as Thomas, was far wiser, or at least, he was wise enough to avoid distractions of the Joan variety.

"I'm going to marry her," he had informed his friend.

Latimer, a thin, forceful, energetic man, stared at him in horror. Later, when Thomas informed his other friends of his decision to marry, their reactions were much the same. Marriage would mean the loss of his fellowship; a fellowship, once removed, would never be restored. His career would be ruined. Joan was not a woman of good repute; the baby might not even be his! Of course, he could continue to teach, but Joan was hardly the most sensible choice of wife for an academic. But despite his friends providing him with copious reasons not to marry her, he could see no other option. After all, to desert the woman would be a heinous action; in the eyes of God, marriage was the only way forward. Eventually, albeit reluctantly, his closest circle of friends agreed, and a simple ceremony was arranged. He chose not to inform his mother of the news, deciding to await the birth of the child before he did so. After all, what mother would be anything but delighted by the arrival of a grandchild?

4

Once wed, he and Joan moved into a set of rooms not far from Buckingham Hall, where Thomas had acquired employment as a reader. He had reasoned that the rooms would delight his new wife, for though they were small, they were a vast improvement upon the room she had lived in above the inn. They had a bedchamber, just big enough to hold a bedstead with a straw mattress, plus a chest for their admittedly meagre belongings. In the main room, furnished by a simple table, a couple of chairs, and a settle, Joan had ample space to prepare and cook meals. Admittedly, it was a somewhat gloomy place, but he could afford little else, though it was entirely possible that Joan believed him to be more affluent than he actually was.

Prior to their marriage, he had been warned of Joan's volatile temper; according to her fellow serving girls at the Dolphin Inn, the slightest incident could provoke her. But, thus far, he had managed to avoid being on the receiving end of one of her rages, and he had convinced himself that he would be spared. However, as her pregnancy progressed, and her body became cumbersome, Joan's temper grew more unpredictable. He had requested that she stop working at the Dolphin Inn – it was, after all, not an appropriate profession for the wife of a scholar – but her work had provided an outlet for her dark outbursts. Once separated from it, her husband became her only distraction. As was expected of any wife, she kept their rooms clean and cooked his meals, but their relationship was far from affectionate. Instead of welcoming him home after a long day at work, she would scream at him, kicking and punching him, all without provocation. She even took to throwing objects at him, any objects, his precious books included. Simply saying 'hello' was enough to cause an outburst. He dreaded going home, and his friends, concerned at his evident distress, hardly knew what to say, or how to help him. But now, it was all ended.

The child was delivered, stillborn, after nearly two days of torturous labour. Joan, her voice hoarse from hours of screaming, her body broken from pain, had begun to bleed uncontrollably, soaking the bedding and straw mattress with sticky, red liquid. Thomas had immediately been summoned to her bedside, having already been informed that the child had perished. He had held Joan's hand tenderly until her angry spirit was finally silenced. Feeling her hand grow limp as the priest delivered the Extreme Unction, he had been flooded with relief, followed instantly by shame. After all, relief was not an emotion one should feel after the death of one's spouse. It was wrong. Undeniably wrong.

Stumbling from his home, he had ended up sitting on the riverbank, without knowing quite how he had come to be there. Just as his tears began to dry, he sensed the presence of someone behind him, and heard a gentle cough. Turning, he saw the ascetic face of Hugh Latimer, eyeing him with concern.

"Friend Cranmer." There was kindness in Latimer's voice.

Being greeted with such sympathy nearly triggered another uncontrollable bout of tears, but Thomas managed to calm himself, wiping at his eyes to stem the flow. He felt the brief pressure of Latimer's hand upon his shoulder, as his friend settled onto the grass beside him. Both were silent for a while.

Once able to speak with some semblance of control, Thomas murmured, "She is at peace now."

Latimer, forthright and honest, again laid a hand on his friend's shoulder. "As are you. Perhaps the university will take you back? You could have your old room... be with us again..."

6

Thomas shook his head vehemently. "That would be more than I deserve."

"Nonsense, my friend. You are a great asset to the university, and well-liked by all." He was only telling the truth. Thomas Cranmer was a popular man; his marriage to Joan had not changed that. "Come." Latimer stood, briskly brushing the grass from his clothes. He was never one to prevaricate; his life was one of perpetual bustle and motion. "Let us to the White Horse, where our friends await us. Let us eat, drink, and enjoy an energetic debate. Ridley has just recently read one of Erasmus' latest essays; that should keep us entertained."

Reluctantly, Thomas rose to his feet to stand beside his companion. Taller by two inches, Latimer was only considered of average height at best, meaning Thomas was undeniably short, though this fact did not particularly perturb him. He gave a nod of assent to Latimer's proposal.

"To the White Horse," he agreed. It was certainly better than returning to his home... if it could be called a home. A battleground was probably a better description, not to mention that when he did eventually return, he would be faced with the corpse of his late wife. No doubt by now the midwife would have prepared her for burial, with the infant enclosed in her arms, as was customary in such situation; but still... he had no desire to deal with Joan's dead body just yet.

At a steady pace, the two men headed towards town, a journey which took them past a gibbet, from which dangled a cage holding the remains of what had once been a man. His carcass had been coated in pitch then left to rot, so that everyone could behold his fate: the fate of a lawbreaker. The bones, with strips of pitch-coated skin still clinging to them, were lying in a heap at the base of the cage: the ribs had collapsed into the pelvis, whilst the skull, minus the lower jaw, rested below the collar bone, grinning obscenely at passers-by, its white teeth gleaming. A few strands of blonde hair, which had missed being coated in pitch, fluttered in the light breeze. The lower jaw was lying somewhere beside the dead man's feet. The teeth were white and in good condition, suggesting this had once been a young man.

Thomas and Latimer, familiar with such grizzly sights, were too preoccupied to take notice.

"Maybe it would be best if you returned to my rooms tonight," Latimer suggested.

Thomas felt a surge of gratitude; it was as if his friend had read his mind.

"I have a spare mattress you can use," Latimer offered. "It's only a straw one, like mine, but it is clean, and comfortable enough." Hugh Latimer was not one for reckless spending. Though he could have afforded a softer, more luxurious barley mattress, he chose not to spend money on unnecessary luxuries.

Thomas did not need persuading. He would take any opportunity not to return home. "I am sure the mattress will be perfect," he smiled weakly.

*****

For him, it felt as though his life began afresh on the night of his wife's death. Joan had been a wild, winter storm, and a welcome tranquillity followed her passing. To his infinite pleasure, his fellowship was restored to him, and he returned to his studies with gusto. He was already well-versed in both Latin and Greek, but continued to add to his extensive vocabulary, and picked up two additional languages – French and German – driven by his desire, his need, for knowledge. Next, he was ordained a priest and beneath his scholars cap he bore a priestly tonsure. Then, a year later, he achieved a doctorate, and his life became one of constant productivity, lived entirely within the realm of the academic world. Even when not teaching, he dined and drank with his fellow academics. As far as women were concerned, the memory of his nightmare marriage tormented him to such a degree that a liaison was totally out of the question. Besides, he was now too focused on his work to consider such a distraction.

A few years after Joan's death, news filtered down the university grapevine of a German monk, called Martin Luther, who was said to be challenging accepted beliefs, and turning the established religion of Roman Catholicism upside down. His writings, though forbidden, had somehow been smuggled into the country, despite the threat of imprisonment should one be caught reading them. Indeed, books and pamphlets written by Luther, if discovered, were promptly burned by the authorities, in an attempt to destroy the evidence of his blasphemy.

Unsurprisingly, being a renowned scholar, Latimer possessed several pamphlets written by Luther, as did Nicholas Ridley and Thomas Bilney, who were part of Thomas Cranmer's close inner circle of friends. Thomas himself was too nervous to actually own any, but he eagerly borrowed his friends' copies, and had read most of Luther's work. After a time, the people who followed Luther's philosophy came to be known as Protestants, on account of their protests against Catholicism. As for the White Horse Inn, it became a hub of sorts, with individuals coming from far and wide to immerse themselves in Luther's work and discuss his teachings, to the extent that the inn was nicknamed 'Little Germany.' A certain Robert Barnes was one such individual. After training to become a priest, he had come to Jesus College to study for his doctorate, and met Cranmer, Latimer, Ridley and Bilney in the

White Horse Inn one evening. An avid reader of Luther's work, Robert's insight and way with words all but set their discussions alight, and they swiftly became friends.

Most evenings, the five of them would gather at the White Horse to eat, drink, and discuss the Protestant movement. For many years, even before Luther's work had been published, Thomas and his friends had been secretly building an argument against the Church of Rome. They all felt that change was long overdue, as did many others, though they would never dare say so in public. Tales of corrupt monks and nuns were rife, and it was well accepted that the monasteries fleeced people out of their money.

"I have witnessed this thievery more times than I care to count," Barnes informed his audience one evening. "Some poor soul will be shown an empty vial, supposedly containing the blood of a saint, which they have been told can only be seen by those absolved of sin. Miraculously, when they pay the requested sum of money to the monk, the blood becomes visible." An excellent orator, Barnes enjoyed expounding his views to an enraptured audience. "You see, once the money has been paid, the monk will press on a tiny spring, allowing a small amount of real blood – usually that of a freshly killed cockerel, or some other such creature – to flow into the container."

Barnes never shouted, for it was dangerous to speak too loudly, but his voice possessed a certain resonance that drew people in; that made them want to listen. Indeed, Thomas had noticed various customers at the inn visibly straining to hear what Barnes was saying.

The inn was filled with a variety of people, but scholars and other occupants of the college were inevitably in abundance. It was easy to spot those who were scholars, teachers, or lawyers, as they tended to wear long black gowns; clothing showed status, and a long gown could only be worn by a person who did not undertake manual work. Even if a manual labourer could have afforded such an item of clothing, the length of such gowns made them impractical. Instead, manual labourers opted for shorter, knee length versions. The younger gentry also tended to wear shorter gowns, as such attire was more suited to riding, though their gowns were of finer fabric than the manual labourers' and were often wonderfully embellished. There was no way a person of status, in his expensive and colourful short gown, could be mistaken for a humble manual worker. Older, high-status individuals, whose athletic days were over, might also favour a long gown, but the rich tended to select finer, more luxurious fabrics, unlike Thomas and his companions, whose gowns were all made from simple, woollen cloth.

Not long after Barnes had finished his tale, a serving girl arrived, placing bowls of soup in front of them, along with a platter of bread and a jug of ale. None of them asked what kind of soup it was; there was wisdom in ignorance sometimes. At least it smelled appetising. With his customary grace, Nicholas Ridley thanked her for her kindness, prompting the girl to offer him a beaming smile in return. Ridley had that effect on people.

As was customary, the five men all produced spoons from their belt pouches, or pockets. Most eating houses did not provide spoons or knives; indeed, The White Horse was well regarded amongst most professional people, as it provided not only mugs for ale but also wooden bowls for soup. Ale houses were often simply a place where ale was brewed and served, with patrons providing their own drinking vessels. Ale houses that did serve food often used bread as a dish, pulling the middle out of a rounded loaf – leaving the base and sides intact – before pouring soup or stew inside. Patrons were expected to devour the stew, then the bread.

11

"I have heard tell of similar scandals," Latimer mused, resting his chin on his thin hands. Everything about Latimer was thin; he rarely gave himself time to eat a decent meal. "Change is most certainly needed, but I suspect it cannot occur with someone so strict and orthodox as Cardinal Thomas Wolsey in charge. He is ambitious and powerful... and a servant of the Pope. For the structure of the Church to change, his authority must diminish, and I can say for certain that he has no intention of allowing that to happen."

"I entered Holy Orders because I felt God called to me. Many priests enter orders for more selfish reasons, believing that wearing a priest's robe will protect them from hellfire." Barnes paused, taking a moment to swallow a couple of spoonfuls of soup before resuming. "Luther admits this was the reason he initially became a priest: to obtain protection from divine displeasure. So many priests, and nuns too, are immoral; they live loose lives, yet berate others for doing likewise."

The five men huddled together around their table. Night had just fallen, and the candles had been lit inside the inn. Though they provided some illumination, the cheap tallow used to make them smoked heavily when lit, making it impossible for any light to travel more than a few inches. Meanwhile, the smell of burning fat drifted into the room from the kitchen, accompanied by wisps of smoke from the hearth every time the kitchen door was opened. No one paid any attention, being either accustomed to the thick atmosphere, or else so busy talking that their thoughts were otherwise engaged.

"Not only are they immoral, but half of them are illiterate too." Ridley, a quiet but eloquent scholar, spoke with fierce passion. "I ask you, gentlemen, how can an illiterate priest give guidance to his flock? If the priest is ignorant, his flock shall be doubly so." His amiable, round face was flushed, and his voice rose with indignation.

"I agree that Wolsey is orthodox," Thomas ventured. "But if you recall, he did befriend and encourage Erasmus. There must be hope in that, surely? Erasmus spoke of corruption within the Church long before Luther."

Latimer gave a snort of disgust. "Desiderius Erasmus is basically a Humanist. He wants reform without changing the rules." He attacked his soup with venom, took a gulp, and nearly choked. After Barnes had delivered a hefty thump to his back, causing him to bounce forwards, Latimer took a deep draught of ale and continued as if nothing untoward had occurred. "In my opinion, Erasmus will always be Catholic. He wants the clergy and the Church to be improved, but not changed. For instance, my own vision is to see the Bible translated into English — I have heard talk that Will Tyndale is working on such a thing — but Erasmus would never agree to anything so progressive. Even if Erasmus does have influence over the king or the cardinal, we cannot expect him to instigate positive change."

Bilney gave a beaming smile, his expression rapt. "I tell you, my friends, when I first read Erasmus' translation of the Hebrew New Testament into Greek, I knew... I knew that the voice of God was speaking to me personally through the text. There was such a comfort and quietness within me that my very bones jumped with joy!" The gentle scholar's face flushed with delight at the memory.

Bilney's outward gentleness belied a fierce inner strength. He had already been imprisoned by Cardinal Wolsey for his Protestant inclinations, but had since been released, on the condition that he abjure his beliefs. Agreeing to the cardinal's demands had left him deeply ashamed; after all, he had denied his God. But he had known that agreeing to such a request was his only means of escape, and took comfort in the knowledge that Peter, one of Jesus' closest disciples, had once acted in a similar way. After his release, he had been more determined than ever to stand fast to his beliefs and was now the most boldly spoken of all his friends. Indeed, it was he who was responsible for the conversion of Hugh Latimer.

"By all the saints, Bilney, you can speak Greek!" Latimer argued. "Those who are not scholars… they haven't got a clue what the Bible is telling them."

Bilney maintained a serene expression, unruffled by Latimer's outburst.

"At least, thanks to our friend Cranmer here, there are more educated clergymen than there used to be," Barnes interjected, wafting a piece of bread towards Thomas, before dunking it into his soup. A stocky man, Barnes enjoyed both food and conversation, and was happiest when combining these two pleasures. "It did not take me long to discover that our Dr Cranmer has been teaching local friars, priests, and members of the clergy the Greek language, instructing them with the utmost thoroughness, and ensuring that they are well-versed in the various interpretations of the Bible." He gave Thomas a grateful smile and nodded in approval.

Wishing he could accept compliments gracefully, Thomas shrugged and muttered, "I'm an examiner now… I cannot permit poorly informed priests to venture out into the neighbouring towns and villages, there to teach and preach their misinformation to the public. It just wouldn't be right. Many of them dislike me for it, but I'm the one assessing them, so they have no choice but to comply." He smiled wryly, shaking his head.

"Come now, Thomas. Your work is invaluable; it is a great shame that there are not more scholars who are willing to follow your lead." Latimer had now forgotten his soup. It lay before him, stone cold. "If you recall, gentlemen, even the great Desiderius Erasmus himself was impressed with our Dr Cranmer's excellent work." He smiled mischievously as his friend's sallow complexion, already flushed, became bright red with embarrassment.

Thomas shuffled in his seat, taking refuge behind his mug of ale. He always omitted to mention that although some of the candidates he taught did dislike his strict teaching and high standards, the majority thanked him for it, praising his tuition to such an extent that he had garnered a reputation for himself far beyond Cambridge. A few months back, Cardinal Wolsey himself had personally written to him, promising him a higher salary if he agreed to resign from his current position and move to Oxford to teach. Wolsey had also promised that, should Dr Thomas Cranmer give his services to Oxford, he would ensure that Thomas was considered for a position in the king's Court. This he had politely declined. After all, Cambridge had supported him in his time of need; he owed them his allegiance. Besides, why should he move when he was content? Everything he desired and needed was here.

These were the reasons he had given the cardinal. In reality, his decision to reject Wolsey's offer had also been influenced by his own reservations concerning the cardinal, which had nothing whatsoever to do with differences in religious doctrine. He had heard it said that Wolsey ruled the land, not King Henry VIII. The king allegedly spent all his time playing tennis, hunting, jousting, and generally making merry, whilst the cardinal attended to day-to-day royal business. Thomas, having been brought up to revere the monarch – both his parents had insisted that a king ruled by God's own grace – felt this could only be a falsehood, in which case, Wolsey should ensure that such rumours were quashed. But though it would be easy for him to deny these rumours publicly, he had failed to do so, leaving Thomas with no choice but to mistrust him.

After enjoying another round of drinks, Ridley and Bilney both declared that they were ready to retire to their beds. Thomas and Barnes concurred, whilst Latimer, suddenly remembering his neglected bowl of soup, realised that the serving girl had long since removed it from the table.

Emerging from the inn onto the street, the friends were hit by a rush of clear air. Finally free from the smoky atmosphere of the inn, Thomas took a deep breath, enjoying the fresh, coolness of the night. Barnes laid a restraining hand upon his arm and shook his head.

"Don't do that, my friend. I've heard that the plague is carried on the evening air. Whilst we are in the tavern, the smoke protects us, but once outside, we are all vulnerable."

Summer would soon arrive, almost certainly bringing the dreaded plague with it, and everyone had their own theory as to what caused the deadly disease.

"My mother always told me the plague was carried in droplets of dew," Thomas reminisced. "When I was a child, she used to boil vinegar on the stove, telling everyone that the fumes would counteract it."

Nicholas Ridley was standing with his head bowed, his lips moving silently. Raising his head and realising that his friends were watching him, he explained. "I felt moved to pray to the Almighty, to beg him to spare us from the plague this year." His kindly face was a mask of concern.

"Amen," his companions chorused, bowing their heads in reverence.

16

*****

More than a decade after his wife's death, on a cold, bright morning in the spring of 1526, Thomas woke with a start. Dreaming of Joan was such a rarity these days; the picture of her face in his mind had shocked him into consciousness. He seldom took time to ponder over what would have happened had Joan survived, or indeed the child, though the latter scenario was easier to predict. The infant would more than likely have been sent to one of his relatives, to be reared as one of their own. He would have paid a sum towards the child's care, no doubt, but that would have been the extent of his involvement. Joan was another matter entirely, for he knew that he could not have endured living with her forever. Celibacy was not always easy, but it was preferable to the ghastly alternative of living with a harridan. Of course, he knew that very few women were as belligerent as Joan, but he saw no point in taking the risk. He was in his late thirties now – no longer young – and his life was one of contented fulfilment. He had no desire to change it for the sake of a woman.

King Henry, on the other hand, was far more interested in female company. Many rumours were now arriving from the Royal Court, one of which suggested that the king desired to divorce his wife, Queen Catherine of Aragon. No one could say for certain why this was, though most reckoned that a certain young woman the king had recently been seen with was to blame for the monarch's change of heart. Thomas, however, disregarded this rumour. The king was said to have enjoyed several illicit relationships during his marriage, therefore he was convinced that this was simply another lapse in fidelity - it was likely that nothing would come of it.

More interesting to him than the rumours surrounding the king's marriage, were those concerning the growth of Protestantism. More and more people were embracing the Protestant cause, or 'The New Learning' as it was sometimes called. His friends Latimer, Bilney, Ridley and Barnes were totally converted, and he himself was certainly interested. Martin Luther's most recent text, *The Babylonish Captivity of the Church*, which could only be described as a direct attack upon the orthodox Catholic faith, had been a fascinating read. The king's response, *Assertio Septem Sacrmentorum Aversus Martinum Lutherum*, a heated defence of the Church of Rome, had been equally eloquent, proving that the king was an excellent scholar and theologian. Indeed, the Pope had been so pleased with King Henry's defence that he had given him a new title: Defender of the Faith. Neither Thomas nor his unworldly scholarly companions realised that this title, which very much delighted the king, was nothing more than a consolation prize. The Pope had recently made King Charles of Spain (nephew to the queen, Catherine of Aragon) the Holy Roman Emperor, a title Henry had dearly wanted for himself. Knowing this, the Pope had been astute enough to compensate Henry for his loss.

Thomas, having read and analysed the King's work, found he could not agree with the king's defence, eloquent though it was. This fact sat uneasily on his conscience; Henry was the king, and as one of his subjects, surely it was his personal duty to support and obey the king?

One hot summer evening, as he and Latimer strolled towards the White Horse Inn, Thomas chanced to praise the king's education.

"I might not agree with his opinions, but he does possess a profound volume of knowledge." Thomas turned to his friend, expecting a response, only to find Latimer frowning pensively.

For a moment, the only audible sound was the slapping of their shoes on the cobbles.

In a low voice, Latimer finally remarked, "I have heard it said that Sir Thomas More wrote it, the king's work, I mean." His voice was almost a whisper. "Our friend, Nicholas Shaxton, agrees."

Shaxton was another reformist, whom they frequently met with at the White Horse, and Thomas was not surprised to hear that he believed in this rumour. The Protestant community despised More, and for good reason: an ardent Catholic, More was rumoured to keep Protestants imprisoned in the gatehouse of his home in Chelsea. If Sir Thomas More had his way, the Roman Catholic Church would remain the same, with the Pope at the helm and his cardinals and priests below him. The Virgin Mary would retain her place of veneration; services would continue to be held in Latin, and confession would be made to the village priest. These were all things the Protestants wished to abolish, yet with More in the way, there was no chance of such change occurring. Thomas was on the side of the Protestants – he believed radical change was needed – but he refused to dismiss the king and his beliefs altogether.

"The king is learned, or so I have heard," he defended the monarch.

"No one is going to say otherwise, are they? It's funny how convincing the threat of death can be," Latimer remarked dryly.

As they walked into the White Horse Inn, they found Ridley and Bilney already chatting eagerly, each with a mug of ale in hand.

"Mutton stew tonight, we have the luxury of meat!" Ridley beamed. "Why the serious faces?"

"We have just been discussing the news from Court." Latimer seated himself, gladly accepting a mug of ale from

Bilney. "I have a fearsome thirst; it's warm tonight," he gasped, taking a deep, satisfying draught of fluid.

Thomas followed suit.

"Where's Barnes?" Bilney asked, looking around. "He had better not be up in his room, writing an essay and forgetting to come and eat again."

At that very moment, Barnes appeared, looking distressed. "Bad news," he whispered, sitting down heavily.

Bilney proffered yet another mug of ale. "Here, take a drink," he instructed. "You look like you could do with some sustenance."

Barnes took the mug in his trembling hand but did not drink from it. "Will Tyndale is dead. Burned at the stake, in Brussels."

His four companions looked at him in horror as they considered the awfulness of such a wonderful man being burned alive.

"Apparently, they strangled him first, so at least he was spared the pain of the flames..." Plucking at the fabric of his long robe, Barnes dabbed at his eyes with it. "It was reported that his last words were, 'I wish that the King of England's eyes might finally be opened'."

"How did you come to hear this?" Latimer demanded, shock and sadness adding additional brusqueness to his usually dry, crisp voice.

"A letter, from Luther himself." Barnes knew Martin Luther personally and had often shown his friends letters from the man regarded as the leading reformist. In fact, he and Luther had belonged to the same order, Augustinian Canons.

Thomas remained silent, quelling a wave of nausea. Burned at the stake! Most people were not spared the pain of the flames. The prospect of such an untimely death acted as a strong deterrent to many would-be Protestants, including

Thomas himself. Were he more open about his beliefs, he too might follow in Tyndale's footsteps, whilst his four companions were certainly at risk of facing the same consequences. They were all convinced of Luther's theories, including the abolition of using money to be absolved from sin by a priest. Paying money for such a sacred thing as absolution from sin did not sit right with him, and his companions were in total agreement. They recognised that absolution came from being sincerely penitent, and laying the burden of guilt before Jesus Christ Himself, who had died to absolve mankind from sin. To pay money for absolution was wrong, indeed, it endangered the souls of those who parted with their money. People truly believed that they had been pardoned, there was no need for penitence, and ascending to heaven was a surety for them. Whilst the reality was, their fate was far from certain.

"What are you thinking, Cranmer?" Latimer shot a keen glance in his friend's direction.

"I think we should all quietly pray for safety. Safety from the plague, and safety from those who choose to harm others for the opinions they hold," he replied softly.

"Amen to that," Ridley agreed, as the five men solemnly bowed their heads. No one took much notice. In the White Horse Inn, prayer was a common enough sight.

"The death of Will Tyndale is a timely reminder that, sometimes, God demands the ultimate sacrifice," Barnes said solemnly once they had finished. "It makes me uneasy."

"Yes, just look at what happened to John the Baptist," Latimer remarked, glancing with repulsion at the bowls of mutton stew that the serving girl had just placed on their table. His appetite, meagre at the best of times, had all but vanished upon hearing of Tyndale's death. "He devoted his entire life to

21

preparing the way for the coming of Our Lord, and then he was beheaded."

"For us, the Lord made the ultimate sacrifice, so now we too must be prepared, no matter how uneasy the thought makes us." Barnes took a large spoonful of mutton stew and gulped it down, his hunger only amplified by the anxiety they all felt.

'We, who believe in God and his most blessed Son, know that we have the promise of eternal life," the gentle Thomas Bilney's face glowed with religious fervour.

The ultimate sacrifice. It was a lot to ask, Thomas silently reflected.

None of them knew it, but that was the last time they would all sit together in the White Horse Inn.

Chapter Two

Within two days of learning about Tyndale's death, Thomas found himself travelling to Waltham, dressed in plain, simple clothing, and carrying an excessive number of books. The annual plague had arrived in Cambridge at terrifying speed, and he had no desire to wait around for it to kill him. Unlike the Bubonic Plague, with its characteristic black buboes, the Sweating Sickness was swift, and less easy to identify, manifesting itself as uncontrollable shivering, followed by headaches, dizziness, and a sense of exhaustion. After a few hours of this, the characteristic sweating began, accompanied by delirium and intense thirst, a racing heartbeat, and a desire to fall asleep, though doctors recommended against allowing the sufferer to sleep, for fear that they might never wake up. The Sweating Sickness was wildly contagious, and although some people – usually the young and fit – survived, many did not.

For Thomas, escaping the plague gave him the perfect excuse to accept an invitation from the Cressy's, the parents of two of his students, who coincidentally were distantly related to the Cranmers. Aside from periodic trips to his family home, he barely left Cambridge, and had no desire to do so. Since first arriving there as a young man, he had felt comfortable and at peace. Even his journeys home were only undertaken when it was necessary for him to leave the city, for he disliked having the peaceful tenor of his life disrupted.

His family, though proud of his achievements, often informed him of their concerns that his years of study had rendered him staid and serious. He would always protest, insisting that he was not a serious person at all, enjoying jokes and laughter as much as any man. Years of dwelling with learned people had not robbed him of his humour, it had simply given him a different appreciation of what was funny. He blamed this need to engage in intellectually stimulating conversation for his inability to communicate with the youngest of his nieces and nephews. Older children were not a problem, after all, he taught youths as young as twelve at Cambridge. But with the very young, especially his infant nieces, he found it took him the majority of his stay to get used to their inane chatter.

The Cressy's had invited Thomas to their home in Waltham several times, not only because they were related to his mother, Agnes, but also because the two boys, who were aged fifteen and thirteen respectively, always wrote such complimentary letters, telling their parents how wonderful Dr Cranmer was, and how stimulating his lectures were. The boys' father had sent a steady stream of letters over the past months, urging Thomas to grant them the pleasure of his company, and with the arrival of the plague, he had finally accepted.

After two days of riding, it was early afternoon when Thomas and the two Cressy boys arrived outside the Cressy's home, to find Master and Mistress Cressy standing in the forecourt, ready to welcome them. They were agog with the news that King Henry himself had arrived at Waltham Abbey, just a few days previously, to escape the Sweat. Furthermore, his mistress, Lady Anne Boleyn, lay sick at her own family home of Blickling Hall in Norfolk, afflicted by that very illness.

"Some say that she is not the king's mistress at all," fussed Mistress Cressy, a plump, kindly lady whose cap remained constantly askew.

"Of course she's his mistress," Master Cressy robustly objected. "A red-blooded man like the king would not suffer to chase a woman who does not submit to his wishes."

Mistress Cressy raised her eyebrows at her husband, then proceeded to lead the new arrivals into the hall, her belt jangling cheerfully with a vast assortment of household keys.

"She cannot creep up on anyone," one of the Cressy boys whispered, nudging Thomas mischievously.

"Thank you, this is most welcome," Thomas said gratefully, as he accepted a mug of spiced ale from Mistress Cressy, all the while wondering whether or not he was expected to reply to the boy's jest.

Mistress Cressy came to his rescue. "Oh, ignore them!" She pinched the cheeks of both youths, using enough pressure to leave reddened blotches on each of their faces.

"Come, be seated," Master Cressy invited. "Terrible thing, this plague," he muttered, taking a hearty gulp of spiced ale. "As soon as we heard the Sweat was raging, we sent for our boys." He shook his head ruefully. "It hits the grand folk as well as the ordinary." He took another enthusiastic drink of ale, held his cup out for his wife to refill, then proceeded to discuss the academic progress of his sons.

The Cressy's home was large and comfortable, but by no means grand. Like the Cranmers, they were hard-working farming folk, though their house and lands were more substantial that those owned by the Cranmer family. Mistress Cressy's days were filled with the duties of an efficient farmer's wife: she began at dawn, supervising the milking of the cows, then proceeded to tend to the buttery, make cheese, assist with the cooking, brew ale, and ensure that the house was as clean as possible, regularly replacing the rushes on the floor to keep vermin at bay. After eating dinner in the company of her family, their servants and farmhands, her evenings were spent using a drop spindle to make yarn out of sheep's wool. She was rarely idle, and her respectable, modest clothing reflected this, comprising of a green kirtle with a gown over the top, dyed in a sensible shade of brown, complete with fitted and undecorated sleeves. Women who wore elaborate, colourful gowns, with long, trailing sleeves, were likely to be too grand to undertake domestic duties.

A homely, maternal woman, Mistress Cressy had taken an instant liking to the scholarly visitor, though his thinness did give her cause for concern, and she vowed to herself he would return to Cambridge with more meat on his bones. Socially unobservant as ever, Thomas did not recognise this motherly affection. He saw only a kindly woman of modest demeanour, who did not expose a shameful amount of bosom, for which he was immensely grateful, for he found such a manner of dress extremely embarrassing. He could not help but warm to her, and to her brusque but hospitable husband.

"Did your colleagues manage to escape the plague as well?" Mistress Cressy asked, with genuine concern.

"Yes, my companions, including my closest friends, left Cambridge with haste." He smiled wryly. There had been just enough time for him to clasp hands with Latimer, Bilney, Ridley and Barnes, and utter promises to pray for them regularly, before they had all been forced to flee the city.

Cressy extended the hand which clutched his mug. "I need more ale, wife, as does Dr Cranmer. The man must be parched after his long journey!"

She obligingly proceeded to pour ale for everyone, just as a young serving girl arrived, bearing a platter of bread and meat, which she promptly laid on the table.

"Eat as much as you wish, there are still several hours to fill before supper," Mistress Cressy instructed, noting the pale complexion of their visitor, who clearly spent most of his days indoors. Though clean shaven, he was somewhat shabbily dressed, his black gown was well-worn in several places, and she accurately suspected that he took little notice of his outward appearance. His dark hair was cut short; his priestly tonsure concealed by his cap. His face, however, was radiant when he smiled, revealing a full mouth of sound, even teeth. Having expected to feel in awe of such a scholar – she could not read or write – she found herself charmed instead. His voice was melodic and strong, yet also soft, and when he spoke, she could not help but listen; he was gentle, but there was an authority about him. It was little wonder her sons enjoyed his teaching.

"Have you ever met the king?" she enquired. It seemed to her very likely that such an educated man would be associated with royalty.

"No, despite my best intentions," Thomas confessed apologetically. "The king once came to Cambridge and rode through the streets with members of the Court, but I did not see him, for I had become so immersed in my work that I completely forgot about the procession."

Cressy slapped his thigh and gave a roar of delighted laughter. "Now there's an example for you boys to follow," he informed his sons, whilst helping himself to some bread and a slab of meat. "Work should always come first."

The boys nodded and exchanged amused glances. They were intelligent and scholarly; learning was not onerous for them. But they would never choose books over enjoyment, or the excitement of seeing the king and his courtiers riding through the streets.

After a pleasant afternoon and evening spent eating and talking, Thomas eventually decided that it was time to retire. As Mistress Cressy handed out lighted candles to illuminate their way to the upper regions of the house, her husband made a welcome suggestion.

"I was thinking, Dr Cranmer, that we might head into town tomorrow, so that I may show you our magnificent abbey. Unless, of course, you are too weary from today's travels?"

Thomas gave an eager nod of agreement. "I would dearly love to see the town of Waltham, and it's famous abbey. I have read so much about it." The abbey was said to have a remarkable library, including a Bible dating back to the thirteenth century, which he would dearly love to see. Furthermore, it was alleged to be the burial place of Harold II, his body having been taken there after the Battle of Hastings in 1066. Joseph of Arimathea was also rumoured to have been buried there, attracting pilgrims from all over the country. Although Thomas believed that the bones of many great kings of old, and religious figures too, lay beneath the flagstones of the abbey, he doubted any of them belonged to Joseph of Arimathea. More dubious still, he had heard that the 'Waltham Cross' was stored there. This crucifix had supposedly been found in Montacute, Somerset, and was claimed to be powerful enough to cure paralysis, amongst other things. Given his inclination towards Luther's teachings, he was sceptical when it came to relics, and did not believe that such a thing existed, let alone that it was capable of curing the incurable. Only God Himself could do that.

"We are proud of the abbey," Mistress Cressy told him fervently, her eyes shining. "It is such a holy place, visited by pilgrims throughout the year."

Not wishing to cause offence by reminding her that many such places, whilst providing comfort to travellers and infirmaries for the sick, were riddled with corruption, he simply nodded and smiled.

The following morning, after about an hour of riding, he found himself standing beneath the magnificent abbey walls and gatehouse, accompanied by Cressy and his two sons. The king was currently residing in the abbey itself, an Augustinian priory which dated back to the eleventh century. After Henry II had served penance there, for the murder of Thomas Becket, the status of Waltham had been raised to that of an abbey, becoming one of the most important monastic houses in England.

As the four of them stood there, admiring the majestic building before them, the gates were flung open, and a noisy cavalcade on horseback emerged. The horses were splendidly caparisoned and were led by two burly outriders.

"Make way! Make way for His Majesty the king!" the riders bellowed.

Gasping, Thomas and his companions doffed their caps, bowed their heads, and looked up just in time to see a man who could only be King Henry himself, mounted upon a horse which was the most splendid of them all. As for the king, he was dressed in a short coat made from cloth of gold, which could only be worn by royalty, and his cap was studded with gems, as was the jerkin visible beneath his open coat. Seeing him in person, it was evident that he was long of limb and

29

strikingly handsome, with red-gold hair and eyes that sparkled nearly as brightly as his jewels.

The king, noticing Thomas and his companions, gave them a cheerful wave as he rode past. Bowing again, Thomas felt overwhelmed with emotion. The king, the man who ruled by the grace of God, who had been placed on the throne by the divine intervention of God Himself, had noticed him and had waved to him. If he had not been convinced before, he was convinced now: the king was to be honoured and obeyed.

Some hours later, hungry and thirsty, the small group entered an ale house in search of sustenance, and Thomas heard a voice calling his name. Looking around the crowded tavern, he spotted a man waving at him enthusiastically. It was Edward Fox, formerly a Cambridge theologian, who had been interested in The New Learning, and who now worked for Cardinal Thomas Wolsey. With him was another man, of average height, with a prominent nose and a ruddy complexion. Thomas immediately recognised him as Stephen Gardiner, another of Wolsey's men who had formerly studied at Cambridge. To be reunited with Edward Fox was a pleasure. Stephen Gardiner... less so. He had previously found Gardiner abrasive, ruthlessly ambitious, apt to be domineering, unscrupulous, and irritatingly sarcastic.

After Thomas had politely introduced his two former colleagues to the Cressy's, he asked them what their business was here in Waltham. Apparently, they had arrived with the king.

"Alas, only the important members of the Court are permitted to reside in the abbey itself," Fox explained jovially. "Us lesser mortals had to find our own accommodation in town, hence you find us here in this tavern."

Gardiner shot a black look in Fox's direction, presumably angered at being lumped with the 'lesser mortals'.

"You must dine with us one night, my friend," Fox urged. "And your company too, if they so wish," he added, nodding politely to the Cressy's.

"No, no, you scholars must enjoy an evening together," Cressy insisted. "I can only talk of sheep and crops, hardly topics of conversation to stimulate such learned minds. That is why I want my sons educated." He nodded towards his two boys, who were openly ogling one of the serving girls and her immodestly low-cut bodice.

An evening was selected for later that week, and after enjoying a brief meal of bread, cheese and ale, the four of them bade farewell to the two scholars and returned to the Cressy's home. Regrettably, Thomas had not managed to see the ancient Bible at Waltham Abbey, and whilst the king was lodging there, he doubted he would be able to gain access. But still, it had been a wonderful day; he had met the King of England, and what a glorious sight he had been. He was quite certain that his brief glimpse of His Majesty would be a memory he carried with him to his death bed. After all, it was unlikely that he would ever meet the king again.

*****

A few days later, as arranged, Thomas rode into Waltham to spend an evening with his two former colleagues. He knew that Fox would be excellent company. He was erudite and enthusiastic, and like himself, Fox was quietly fascinated by Luther's work. If they had any time alone together, he knew they would have much to talk about. In contrast, Gardiner was Catholic, orthodox to the depth of his being, and Thomas knew that he and Fox would have to tread carefully. At Cambridge, Gardiner had been open about his beliefs, regularly remarking that all Protestants should be imprisoned, at the very least, and that Luther should be burned at the stake. He was not a man whom one wished to cross, especially now that he was working for Wolsey.

As he neared the inn where they were to meet, Thomas anxiously considered what might happen were Gardiner to learn of Fox's inclinations, and his own, for that matter. Surely, if he was in Wolsey's service, working with Fox on a daily basis, he must have guessed that the man was interested in Protestantism? He could only pray that Gardiner remained blind to Fox's leanings, and his likewise.

The evening began with the usual exchange of personal news. His two companions, both ambitious men, had left Cambridge over a year ago, at almost the same time, in search of a more colourful career. Gardiner, in possession of an uncontainable volume of energy, had been especially eager to escape the dull monotony of scholarly life.

After they had finished their meal, the topic of conversation shifted to the king.

"He is seeking a divorce," Gardiner stated crisply.

"It has become known as 'The King's Great Matter'," Fox cut in, smirking.

Gardiner shot an irritated glance in his direction.

"I take it Mistress Boleyn is the woman he desires to wed?" Thomas queried.

"Indeed, yes," Fox leaned forwards, whispering confidentially. "The king is frightfully worried about her current condition; he fears she may die of the Sweat. He has sent his own physician to Blickling Hall to tend to her, and sends her love tokens several times a day."

32

"He has already taken his case to Rome, to the Papal Courts," Gardiner said solemnly, steering the conversation back to the subject of divorce, though inwardly he was beaming, gratified to know that his career was taking him to greater heights than Cranmer's. At Cambridge, Dr Cranmer had been regarded as a great authority on most matters, and his opinion had always been considered the most important. This favouritism had always irked Gardiner, who desired status more than anything. He was himself an able scholar, and now, here he was, privy to information that the learned Dr Cranmer would never know, in the service of Cardinal Wolsey, the man who had been guiding the king for years; the man who ruled the realm from the shadows. It was deeply satisfying, and he was determined to enjoy having the upper hand while he still could. Unfortunately, the great cardinal was no longer so great; he was rapidly falling out of favour with the king, so it was likely that his triumph would be short-lived. Indeed, both he and Fox intended to cease working for Wolsey within the next few months; serving a fallen master would hinder their career progression.

"But why Rome?" Thomas asked, baffled. He was feeling increasingly uncomfortable. Gardiner's cool and appraising stare reminded him of the chilling, judgemental stare of his former schoolmaster, the man who had so terrified him as a child.

"Because Rome is the only court the queen will acknowledge," Gardiner, astute enough to know the religious leanings of his two companions, spoke slowly, as if to a simpleton. "And besides, only the Pope has the power to grant a divorce."

Thoughtfully, Thomas took a slip of ale, then proceeded to pick at the material of his sleeve, a habit he always fell into when thinking deeply. Eventually, he looked up, to find two pairs of eyes gazing at him, waiting for him to speak. "It seems strange that the Pope is so unwilling to grant a divorce in this case. After all, the king and queen are as good as brother and sister; she was married to his older brother, Prince Arthur, before the prince's death…"

"We know," Gardiner sneered, rolling his eyes. "The late Pope, our current Pope's predecessor, issued a Papal Bull, remember? A document of permission, allowing the marriage to go ahead."

"But the Bull should never have been allowed," Thomas argued. "There should have been no certificate of permission. The Bible clearly states that marriage between a man and his brother's wife should not be permitted." He spoke quietly, though there was really no need. They were sitting together in a private room. No one would overhear them.

Placing his long fingers together, in the shape of a steeple, Gardiner was eager to air his knowledge. "The Bull was permitted for several reasons. First and foremost, to strengthen the ties between England and Spain, to promote peace." He paused.

Thomas said nothing.

"The king, having agreed to these terms at the time, now objects," Gardiner continued. "He argues that England and Spain were already on peaceful terms, so this reason was not valid. He also insists that, since the Bull was issued during the reign of the late king, Henry VII, it should have become invalid once the old king died." Gardiner paused, expecting Dr Cranmer to speak. When again no argument was forthcoming, he resumed. "Campeggio, the Papal representative involved in this matter, disagrees. He claims that maintaining strong ties between England and Spain is crucial, and that the concept of the agreement being invalid after the late king's death is quite preposterous. The Bull must remain valid. You've been awfully quiet, Cranmer. What are your thoughts on this matter?"

Both Gardiner and Fox were looking at him expectantly. Taking a deep breath to calm his nerves, he repeated his former argument. "The book of Leviticus sates plainly that a man may not marry his late brother's wife." He picked nervously at his sleeve.

"But the book of Deuteronomy states the opposite, insisting that a brother can marry his late brother's wife," Gardiner argued testily. "So, you see, there is a contradiction."

"Indeed, yes." Thomas looked up, abandoning his sleeve. "But Leviticus states that it is forbidden, which is a non-negotiable statement. On that premise, it is best considered as such, don't you think?" His voice was soft but compelling, and his companions unconsciously leaned forwards, hanging onto his every word. "It is always best to avoid offending God, so I would argue that, in this instance, no marriage should have taken place. Therefore, since the marriage is clearly invalid, the king is a free man. A divorce is unnecessary."

Gardner and Fox were eyeing him keenly.

"But what of the emperor?" Fox enquired.

"Perhaps you are not aware of this, Cranmer," Gardiner was keen to maintain his superiority. "The Spanish Emperor, Charles, the Holy Roman Emperor no less, is the uncle of Queen Catherine. He will be offended if his niece is cast aside. He might seek to invade England."

"I may not be a politician, but I do know scripture." Thomas took a deep breath. "Since the king is, according to scripture, a free man, I think this business should be conducted swiftly, for the satisfaction of the king's conscience. The frustrating delays of the courts, in both England and Rome, will result in unnecessarily lengthy divorce proceedings, which may not even reach the desired conclusion. In contrast, if this matter were left to the theologians, whose opinions and verdicts may sooner be known, it would be promptly brought to conclusion with little industry or trouble. His Majesty, his conscience satisfied, may thus determine for himself whether all is well in the eyes of God. After all, what matters more than God's blessing?" Having delivered his opinion, he suddenly became flustered. He had not intended to speak at such length.

"So, Cranmer, you believe the matter needs only to be placed before the judgment of learned men? Persons such as yourself?" Fox questioned, his intelligent face alight with interest.

"Exactly. If the matter were left to the universities, I do believe it would be sorted within the week."

Gardiner eyed Cranmer speculatively. Whatever Cranmer's leanings, there was sense to what he had just said. "Hmm..." he mused. "Putting it to the universities will not please the Pope; he is not fond of his authority being undermined."

Thomas was convinced that the Pope had no authority, as was Fox, though neither of them would voice such an opinion aloud, not in front of Gardiner. Catholicism was the only thing Gardiner would ever adhere to; his faith was even more important to him than wealth and power, and that was saying something.

Thomas thought quickly, trying to change the subject to something less contentious. "Shall you see the king at all, whilst you are here in Waltham?"

"Who knows." Fox rolled his eyes. "Since we are still in the cardinal's service, there is nought to do but take refuge from the Sweat and await orders."

36

Thomas thought nothing more of Fox's comment until he was riding back to the Cressy's home an hour or so later. Fox had said 'since we are still in the cardinal's service'. Were they intending to desert the man who had served the king for so many years?

*****

He saw no more of Fox or Gardiner during his stay at Waltham; a week after he had dined with them, the Court left for Greenwich. Though he was disappointed to have missed the opportunity to catch another glimpse of the king, he did succeed in viewing the ancient Bible that resided within the abbey, which more than compensated. Furthermore, the Sweat appeared to be abating, and he hoped he would soon be able to return to Cambridge. However, unbeknownst to him, his brief reunion with his former colleagues was about to change the peaceful tenor of his life forever.

Just over a month after their meeting with Cranmer, Fox and Gardiner were summoned to the Palace of Placentia, commonly known as Greenwich Palace, to attend to the king. Thomas' suggestion of allowing theologians to adjudicate over The King's Great Matter had deeply impressed Fox, and after a few weeks of contemplation, Fox had decided to discuss the possibility with His Majesty. His request for an audience with the king was duly granted; His Majesty would speak with him after attending Mass.

That day, the service was being led by the Bishop of Rochester, John Fisher, an ardent supporter of Queen Catherine. A thin, ascetic man, Fisher was fearless; not only had he openly criticised the king's divorce plans, but he had also once compared Henry to Herod, much to the king's fury. He had even added that he was ready to lay down his life for the sake of matrimony, just as John the Baptist had done, a barbed reference which King Henry would neither forget nor forgive. The king, having heard Mass, swept from the chapel without so much as a nod of thanks to the man who had led the service.

Fox had informed Gardiner of his decision to make Cranmer's opinion known to the king, and Gardiner had thus ensured that he was present at the requested audience with King Henry. He could not help but feel disgruntled, for it had been deviously lurking within his mind that he might offer Cranmer's suggestion to the king and pass it off as his own. But, in the small chamber beside the chapel, Gardiner could only stand and listen as Fox delivered Cranmer's suggestion. Also present was yet another of Wolsey's servants, one Thomas Cromwell, an ambitious and promising young man who was totally behind The King's Great Matter. He was a common man, in Gardiner's opinion, as was Wolsey: the latter, the son of an Ipswich butcher; the former, the son of a Putney blacksmith. Gardiner considered himself far superior, being a descendant (admittedly illegitimate) of Jasper Tudor, one of King Henry's forbears, and the first Duke of Bedford.

The king listened intently to Fox's report, then contemplated the matter in silence. No one dared speak until the king delivered his opinion.

"What do you think, Cromwell?" Henry demanded, turning to the fast-rising young man. "We think this man has the sow by the right ear." As always, Henry referred to himself in the plural.

"I think so too, Your Majesty," Cromwell agreed. "It makes me wonder what other opinions this man has stored in his learned head."

"Send for him, Master Cromwell. We desire for him to attend to us as soon as possible. Our thanks to you, Fox. You did well in reporting this." Grinning broadly and giving Fox a powerful but genial thump on the back, which nearly winded him, the king swept briskly from the chamber.

*****

He was a frightened man. He had returned to Cambridge but had not even had time to unpack his bags or refresh himself before a messenger arrived, wearing what he recognised as the royal livery. Initially, he had thought the messenger was mistaken when he had pulled a letter from his sleeve and handed it to him. But no, it was definitely addressed to Dr Thomas Cranmer. He read quickly. The letter instructed him to accompany the servant to Greenwich Palace, to meet with the king. Immediately. Without delay. The words could not have frightened him more if they had leapt off the scroll of paper and slapped him in the face.

Hugh Latimer, who had himself just returned from fleeing the Sweat, heard voices coming from his friend's room. Curious, he poked his head around the door to greet him, and found Thomas looking pale and shocked, along with a man whose mantle bore a regal looking insignia. Unlike Cranmer, he had never seen a royal crest, and understandably failed to recognise it. However, the huge seal attached to the document indicated that the letter had come from some very important person.

"I am summoned to Court," Thomas gasped, trying to subdue the panic which threatened to rise within him. Taking a deep breath, he clarified, "To the king's Court, at Greenwich."

"Without delay," the messenger reminded him.

Latimer read the letter. "It says His Majesty wishes to speak with you. He simply seeks your opinion. I see nothing amiss with that," Latimer reassured his friend, aware of the thoughts that must be galloping around Thomas' head. It was no secret that Cambridge was a town where many residents held meetings to discuss The New Learning. It was also known that many of the theologians owned forbidden books. But if the king suspected Cranmer of saying or reading anything unlawful, he would have simply had him arrested. The king would not personally summon him to Court for that.

"Why is the king so desperate to see me? My companion here says he has no idea," Thomas looked beseechingly at the messenger, hoping he would suddenly say something useful.

The messenger merely shook his head. "We must leave now, Dr Cranmer. It is the king's wish to see you as soon as possible."

"I'm sure I shall only be gone a few days," he told Latimer, reassuring himself as much as his friend.

Latimer nodded in agreement. "Keep your mind fixed upon the fact that the king seeks your learned opinion. You are not being arrested." His tone was deliberately reassuring.

"Yes…" Thomas took a deep breath. "It seems I must leave directly."

"Farewell. God speed, my friend. I shall be praying for you." Latimer clasped his friend's hand firmly. "God keep you safe."

Clutching a satchel filled with the few items he thought he would need, he departed, unaware that he was about to begin a new life; one that he would never have imagined possible.

*****

40

Three days later, he found himself about to enter the presence of King Henry VIII. He had arrived at Greenwich late the previous evening and had been allocated temporary quarters in the palace itself, sharing a chamber with a man called Thomas Cromwell. Cromwell immediately gave him a lesson on the etiquette of entering the king's presence.

"When approaching the king, you must bow three times: as soon as you enter the room, as you reach the halfway point, and when you are just a few feet away from His Majesty." Though their chamber was small, Cromwell managed to demonstrate the necessary obeisance's with an air of confidence.

"I don't believe I can be as polished as your good self," Thomas told him, his voice anxious.

"I have had time to practice. Now, approach me and bow three times, in succession. Remember, when you depart, you make the same obeisance's, and on no account must you turn your back."

"You mean, I must walk away backwards?" Thomas clarified.

"Exactly. You must face the king at all times. To turn your back is a grave insult. When you gauge that you are halfway to the door, bow." Cromwell walked backwards, then gave a sweeping bow to demonstrate.

"I am certain I shall fall over, bowing and walking backwards at the same time," Thomas fretted. "I can be clumsy sometimes, especially when I am anxious."

"If it's any consolation, you would not be the first, and you will certainly not be the last," Cromwell grinned impishly.

Cromwell was of average height, clean shaven, stocky, and wore an air of supreme self-confidence. His attire was of good quality, but plain – brown, black, and grey were his colours of

41

choice – and he favoured a short coat over his companion's long, scholarly gown. Financially, he was no more well off than his new acquaintance, but this was more or less the only thing they had in common, apart from one very important and desirable gift: they were both highly intelligent and eager to learn.

Unlike Cranmer, Cromwell was fiercely ambitious, a quality he very quickly revealed to his new acquaintance. "Work hard, whether you are in the service of King Henry or Cardinal Wolsey, and you will go far. They both appreciate servants who are willing to go that extra mile for them. Though, perhaps don't rely too much on the cardinal. He is something of a falling star." Cromwell gave Thomas a solemn look. "You see, Lady Anne Boleyn is the king's favourite; he wants a divorce, but so far, Wolsey has failed to procure it. I promise you, this is not gossip, I have heard these words from the king himself," he assured the quiet little man who looked, in his opinion, like a startled rabbit. Cranmer's dark eyes were huge and wary; he appeared overcome with terror. "Come now," he urged. "His Majesty is pleased with you! Master Fox told the king of something you said when the Court was at Waltham, and he has been desperate to meet you ever since. You have no need to worry, for I shall escort you into the royal presence. Do you perchance have a better gown to wear?"

Thomas studied his gown. It looked presentable to him, at least, as presentable as a gown could be after enduring a lengthy journey on a horse. "I have brushed the mud from the hem, so it is as clean as it can be," he explained, as Cromwell's words sank in. So that was why he was here: the king had appreciated the suggestion he had given to Fox. But why had he been required to come to Court? He had nothing more to offer; the king was going to be bitterly disappointed.

42

"I am sure the king will not mind. You look like an unworldly theologian who does not care for outward show. His Majesty will respect that, as I do." Cromwell was at ease and cheerful; very little phased him. "To tell you the truth, I care not for frivolous costumes and outward displays of wealth, but there are many at Court who love to strut about like peacocks. In fact, many courtiers consider such outward displays to be obligatory." There was an edge of contempt in his voice. He intended to rise through the ranks and make himself indispensable at Court, but for the moment, he must look and dress according to what he was: a lawyer, whose knowledge of his subject was equal to that of the great Sir Thomas More. But despite his ambitions, there were plenty at Court who were keen to keep him down, unwilling to allow the son of a blacksmith to rise to a position of power.

Thomas nodded sympathetically, and Cromwell smiled in response.

"Now, come. Let us discover what the king has planned for you."

He found himself being led through a labyrinth of corridors, whilst sincerely hoping he would be guided back to his room afterwards. How anyone could find their way in a place such as this was a mystery to him; it was totally bewildering.

After a while, Cromwell stopped abruptly. "There is something you need to know; something you may not be aware of."

"Nothing terrible, I hope?" Thomas enquired nervously.

"No, no." Cromwell gave a reassuring smile. "I simply thought it would be wise to inform you that the king always refers to himself in the plural. As 'we' and 'us'."

"I see... has he ever explained why?"

Cromwell shrugged. "He is the king. He represents England. He *is* England, in a way. I assume that is the reason. You'll get used to it." He gave another reassuring smile.

"I doubt I shall be staying here long enough to do so." There was an edge of determination in Thomas' voice. He was eager to return to Cambridge as soon as possible. "But I thank you for the information," he added.

Cromwell's smile became a knowing grin.

A little while later, Cromwell paused before a set of large double doors, flanked by two heavily armed men. Thomas could not help but notice that they both looked very capable of using the weapons they held.

"Dr Cranmer, to see His Majesty, King Henry," Cromwell announced, as the doors were pushed open.

Thomas found himself entering a massive chamber, and his immediate impression was that it was flooded with light. On either side of the room was a series of tall windows, hence the wonderful illumination. As for the brickwork, it was covered in colourful, richly detailed tapestries. But the person who commanded all attention was the king himself. Tall, broad-shouldered, athletically built, his auburn hair gleaming in the sunlight, the king looked even more magnificent than he had when Thomas had first seen him in Waltham. Indeed, he was so overawed that Cromwell had to nudge him to remind him to perform the necessary three bows.

King Henry, quickly assessing the newcomer, was pleased with what he saw. The man looked unworldly, he decided, unconsciously echoing the thoughts of Thomas Cromwell, plus he looked fearful. But beneath that fear, Henry – an astute observer of men – recognised honesty and sincerity. Qualities he valued in his servants.

"We have been informed of your opinion regarding our divorce, Dr Cranmer," the king announced without preamble, presenting his hand for Thomas to kiss.

Bemused by the whole situation, he hardly knew what to say. Clumsily, he managed to kiss the royal hand, though the gems adorning the king's thumb and middle finger were of such a size that he wondered whether he was supposed to kiss the gems or the king's flesh.

"You are most welcome here," the king proclaimed, before seating himself upon a magnificently carved chair with luxurious velvet padding. "Pray sit, Dr Cranmer. You too, Cromwell."

The latter had been hovering, wondering whether to stay or leave.

"You see, though we are king, we are still a man, and need the support of a good wife, whose life has been joined to our own through a union blessed by God. Sadly, our union with Princess Catherine of Spain was not blessed; it troubles our conscience."

Thomas, feeling the force of the king's direct gaze, realised that he must actually speak. In a voice hoarse and strained – unlike his usual mellow tone – he reiterated everything he had said to Fox and Gardiner. According to the Holy Scripture, the king was a free man.

Cromwell, his chin resting upon his hand, managed to hide a cynical smile; he was of the opinion that the king's conscience had probably never troubled him until he had met Lady Anne Boleyn, though he would never say such a thing aloud of course. He observed the newcomer with speculative interest. Though he was an intelligent man, Cromwell's knowledge of theology was comparatively meagre; but this man, Thomas Cranmer, was undeniably well-read and well-versed in the ways

45

of the Church. He could only imagine the wealth and power that would be within their grasp were they to join forces… though Cranmer seemed the type to have no desire for either… which meant it would all be his for the taking. Furthermore, though he fully intended to exploit Cranmer's intellect, he found himself taking a liking to the studious little man.

"We need the woman we love by our side," the king continued, plaintively. "Even our late father felt such a need, and he was not a man who showed his feelings readily. When our beloved mother died, he was most distressed, but soon decided to make overtures to wed Queen Juana of Spain. However, once he discovered that she carried the corpse of her dead husband around with her everywhere she went, his enthusiasm for the match cooled somewhat, and he decided to remain single." The king observed the scholar before him shrewdly. The man was finally beginning to relax… a little.

The anecdote was clearly intended to amuse, so Cromwell – who had heard it before – gave a chuckle of laughter.

Thomas felt his lips give an involuntary twitch.

"Do we amuse you, Dr Cranmer?" The king gave a sunny smile.

Utterly charmed, he gave brief nod. "Yes, sire. Forgive my awkwardness. I never thought I would find myself seated beside the King of England."

"Wine!" the king bellowed, beaming approvingly at Thomas. A door that had previously been hidden behind one of the tapestries swung open, and a pageboy rushed in, bearing a tray laden with goblets and a flagon of wine.

King Henry possessed a massive amount of charisma and an ego to match, characteristics that Thomas was not accustomed to dealing with. Indeed, now that the king was moving rapidly away from the influence of Cardinal Wolsey, the king was discovering just how powerful he was. The rumours concerning the king's lack of involvement in the decisions made at Court, and Wolsey's control over him, both of which Thomas had heard and promptly dismissed, were not far from the truth. Yet though the king had spent much of his youth and early reign indulging in pleasant pastimes, he possessed an excellent grasp of affairs of State, and was well-versed in theology and canon law.

"What do you think of the fact that Princess Catherine of Spain insists that the marriage between herself and our late brother was not consummated?" Henry enquired eagerly. "Some would say that their marriage was thus invalid." He eyed the scholar keenly.

"But, sire, they took vows, did they not?" Thomas' response was swift.

"Indeed," the king nodded eagerly. "You say that you hold fast to Leviticus, which claims marriage between a brother and his late brother's wife is unlawful?"

"Yes, sire." Again, his response was swift and confident. "However, Deuteronomy states otherwise. Since there is a contradiction, I believe it would be wise to avoid such a marriage, for the sake of your immortal soul."

The king banged his now empty cup on a nearby table, leaned back, and gave a loud guffaw of laughter.

Thomas nearly jumped out of his chair in surprise.

"We are grateful to you for your wisdom, Cranmer. We feel more at peace than we have felt in months. Years, even. You must remain at Court; you shall join the household of my lady, Anne Boleyn." The king's small mouth twitched with amusement; he could not fail to observe the expression of dismay which flitted over the somewhat long features of the scholar.

Thomas forced himself to speak. "As Your Majesty wishes." His voice sounded unnaturally strangled. As soon as the divorce was procured, he would make his case for returning to Cambridge. He only hoped that the king would agree.

Chapter Three

Whilst he struggled to come to terms with what had just occurred, the king beckoned to one of his many pageboys and despatched him to request the presence of Lady Anne.

"You shall meet her," the king boomed cheerfully, his voice echoing around the chamber. "But you do not seem overly delighted about remaining with us here at Court."

The king's shrewd gaze was upon him, as Thomas searched for an honest but inoffensive response. "Forgive me, sire," he said at last. "I am accustomed to a life of quiet study. Life at Court is something I shall find difficult to adjust to."

"We understand, master scholar. We too long for quietness and uninterrupted study on occasion. To gain knowledge from worthy writings is worth more to us than material wealth," King Henry declared, not altogether truthfully. "But God has placed us in this position, and therefore we must act according to His will."

Impressed by the king's show of sincerity, Thomas nodded. "Indeed yes, sire. You have set an example of obedience, and I am glad, therefore, to serve you as Your Majesty sees fit." He pushed aside his disappointment. "I shall send for my books and other possessions within the week."

"Good," the king beamed jovially. "And fear not, you shall not be lonely. Your friends Fox and Gardiner are here at Court, and I see you have already made the acquaintance of Cromwell." The king shot a searching glance at Cromwell's tidy but sombre figure. Cromwell was a clever man, as skilled in the field of law as the little Cambridge theologian was in theology and classical studies, and he was totally ruthless. Yet, behind the ruthless streak, which the king had quickly identified upon first meeting him, lay a fierce loyalty. Wolsey had failed his king; thus he was no longer needed, yet Cromwell had not deserted Wolsey's service, unlike many others. Only a couple of days ago, both Fox and Gardiner had resigned from Wolsey's household, yet Cromwell still wore Wolsey's badge. Admittedly, he was now taking orders directly from the king, but he still showed outward respect to his former master and gave his services when required. It was a trait that the astute King Henry respected. A loyal servant was invaluable.

A short while later, there was a commotion outside the chamber, and the tapestry covered door opened. It was at that moment that Thomas beheld Lady Anne Boleyn for the first time. She was accompanied by two of her ladies, who, after curtseying to the king, stood some distance away. Following Cromwell's example, Thomas doffed his cap as she swept up to the king, her wide skirts stirring the rushes as she walked. Less than three feet away from the king, Lady Anne dipped into a deep, graceful curtsey. Her only curtsey. Clearly Court etiquette did not apply to her. The king seized her hand and kissed it tenderly, before inviting her to sit beside him, all the while keeping her hand held tightly in his.

The name 'Anne Boleyn' had been on the lips of everyone in the land for months now, and here he was, finally looking upon her. Thomas was somewhat disappointed by her physical appearance – though she was not unattractive, he had seen far prettier ladies – but her attire was another matter. He was certain she was the most stylish, sophisticated woman he had ever beheld. Her gown was the height of fashion, made of velvet in a rich red hue. Velvet could not be worn by anyone below the rank of a knight, so even without the king's favour, she could wear it, being the daughter of a knight. But the fullness of the skirts and the flowing sleeves required many yards of material, revealing that her outfit had almost certainly been a gift from the king. Her headdress was, in his eyes, different to anything he had ever seen. He was familiar with the standard, gable headdress worn by most women, which hid all but a small piece of hair at the front of the head. His own mother had worn such a headdress. But Anne wore something far more daring, revealing much of her hair at both the front and back. Her long, black, silky locks cascaded beneath her veil, all the way past her waist.

"My lady, Anne Boleyn," the king announced unnecessarily, his eyes alight with affection.

Anne stood, dipped a very small curtsey – to be shared between Cranmer and Cromwell – and sat down again.

"Dr Cranmer here has just arrived from Cambridge…"

"Oh, so you are the man who has found a solution to our dilemma." She shot an intimate glance in the king's direction. Turning her graceful head towards the newcomer she added, "You are most welcome, sir."

He began to see why the king found her attractive. Her neck was long and graceful; her large, dark eyes seemed to glow, and when she smiled, her usually tight, prim little mouth became warm and luscious. She was one of those women whose personality was sufficiently attractive that they could make anyone consider them beautiful.

"You are to be attached to Lady Anne's household," the king reiterated to Thomas. "You shall act as her chaplain." Taking Anne's hand, he kissed it again, prompting her to shoot a flirtatious glance in his direction. "The Earl of Wiltshire, or one of his staff, will direct you regarding your duties."

Anne realised that the newcomer might not know who the Earl of Wiltshire was, and promptly added, "The Earl of Wiltshire is my father."

Throughout this conversation, Cromwell, who had not said a word, was watching closely. Like Thomas, he considered Anne to be no great beauty – in his opinion, she was no better than any of the other young women at Court – but he knew her to be clever and cunning. She knew how to enhance her attributes; how to display herself to capture the attention of men. For instance, her headdress was a French Hood, named after its country of origin, designed to display one of her greatest assets: her hair. Anne had spent many years as a lady-in-waiting to the French queen, during which time she had learned how to be the sophisticated young woman that she was today. It was this experience that made her stand out from the other ladies at Court, a number of whom were definitely more beauteous than she.

Her ambition and intellect fascinated Cromwell, therefore he had decided that he was prepared to support this woman in her quest to become Queen of England. Not only would he almost certainly benefit from backing Anne over Catherine in the long run, but he also knew that Anne had recently taken an interest in The New Learning, a subject which he himself was also curious to learn more about, though he had not yet admitted as much to Cranmer. Cromwell was of the belief that Catholicism was outdated, and that Queen Catherine, like Cardinal Wolsey, would soon be forced out. Whilst he owed loyalty to Wolsey, he owed nothing to the Spanish princess, and thus registered no regret at the sudden deposition of this woman who had considered herself the Queen of England for the best part of twenty years.

Cromwell's thoughts were interrupted by the king, who continued to regally inform Thomas of his duties. "We also require you to write a thesis in support of our divorce, and to visit the universities to debate upon the subject. We anticipate that you will still have time to enjoy reading and studying."

Thomas was speechless. Visit the universities; act as chaplain to Anne Boleyn; write a thesis... it was a lot to take in!

"I am quite sure that the Earl of Wiltshire will enjoy your company." Cromwell spoke at last, covering for the speechless newcomer. "He is a man who enjoys learned discourse." Noticing the look of relief and gratitude on Thomas' face, Cromwell smiled warmly. This man, Thomas Cranmer, was truly likeable. There was a wholesome honesty about him that was seldom seen among those who flocked to the king's Court, which was nothing more than a hotbed for back-stabbing and treachery. Everyone wanted the king's favour because the king's favour could lead to riches and power. He himself wanted the king's favour for those exact reasons. But Cranmer... Cranmer desired neither wealth nor power. He only wished to read, study, and pass on his knowledge to others. The man was a rarity, and Cromwell suspected that the king had recognised this; Anne too, for she was no fool.

"My father is currently lodging at York Place, my home, thanks to the king's kindness." Anne shot another intimate glance towards her doting royal admirer. "You do look after me, Henry," she purred, before turning to her new chaplain. "Arrangements will be made for you to be taken there by barge later today, when the tide is right."

Having just made the acquaintance of Cromwell, and having found himself able to converse and enjoy the man's company, Thomas would have preferred to remain at Greenwich. He had never heard of York Place. Although admittedly, until recently, he had never heard of Greenwich either.

Unbeknownst to Thomas, York Place was one of the many palaces owned by Cardinal Wolsey. The king had discovered that his cardinal owned far more properties than he did himself; as a result, in an effort to regain some royal favour, Cardinal Wolsey had given his two favourite residences to Henry, namely Hampton Court and York Place. The latter was promptly given to Anne, though the king intended to give her Hampton Court also, when he had finished making magnificent alterations to it. He was currently having the chapel and great hall totally gutted and refurbished, whilst the gardens and courtyards were being redesigned beyond recognition. Plus, the state rooms needed renovating. At least, he thought so. Wolsey had been perfectly happy with them as they were.

"I… I don't know what to say," he murmured. "I find myself overwhelmed." But not so overwhelmed that he had failed to notice Anne referring to the king by his Christian name. This lady was most definitely not some fleeting liaison. A mere liaison would have addressed him formally.

The king stood, signalling that the interview was over. "No need to say anything," he announced cheerily, giving his new servant a hearty thump on the back, causing Thomas to pitch forward and almost fall flat on his face. "We like your opinions, Cranmer, and your loyalty. We believe you will be a great asset."

Utterly dazzled, he replied, "I shall certainly try to be," before following Cromwell's lead and bowing low as he exited the room. To his infinite relief, he successfully remained upright.

"My, you are in favour," grinned Cromwell.

"I... I don't know what to say... or think," Thomas whispered. "I hope I did not make a fool of myself."

"You conducted yourself very well and presented your case for the king's divorce most succinctly. We shall meet often, you and I," Cromwell informed him, his smile as smug as that of a cat who had just been presented with a bowl of fresh cream. "Messengers are constantly travelling back and forth from Greenwich to York Place, so be sure to keep me informed of your duties and of your progress. I suspect you will find favour with the Earl of Wiltshire."

"I sincerely hope so." Thomas sounded dubious.

"I will take you back to the room we shared last night, so that you may gather up your belongings," Cromwell offered. As they walked, he gifted his companion the benefit of his knowledge regarding the Boleyn's. "Lady Anne's mother is the sister of the Duke of Norfolk. It was an advantageous marriage as far as Sir Thomas Boleyn was concerned. I am uncertain whether this is true or not, but I have heard tell that the Boleyn's name was originally Bullen. Apparently, when the earl visited his daughter in France – Lady Anne served the French queen for some years, you know – he discovered that the French struggled to pronounce 'Bullen'. They said 'Boleyn' instead, which I am sure you will agree sounds far nicer. So, he had the family name changed... allegedly. At Court everyone takes pleasure in trying to belittle the Boleyn's you know. As you may have already heard, Lady Anne is not the earl's only daughter. She has an older sister, Mary, who for a time was the king's mistress; she even bore him a child, a daughter. There is also a brother, George, Lord Rochford. The family fortunes all depend upon Lady Anne's relationship with the king. I believe she is not yet his mistress; she has already seen her sister cave

55

in to the king's desires and be cast aside when he tired of her. Fortunately for Mary, she had a compliant husband to return to, though he has since died of the Sweat, leaving her a widow." They had arrived at Cromwell's quarters and Cromwell stopped, clasping Thomas' shoulder. "In short, the family have something of a history with the crown." He grinned jovially. "And that, my friend, marks the end of my oratory!"

Once inside Cromwell's room, Thomas began to repack the few items he had brought with him, hoping that it would not take too long for his books to be despatched from Cambridge. How would he cope without his books?

"Where is this York Place?" he asked dejectedly.

"Beside Westminster Palace," Cromwell replied swiftly, then shook his head and laughed. "You don't know where Westminster Palace is either, do you? It's downriver; the tide will soon be ready to take you there."

"The tide?" This was all so very new and mysterious. "Why the tide?"

"The Thames is tidal, so it is easier and faster for the oarsmen to row with the tide, rather than trying to battle against it," Cromwell explained.

"I see." Thomas smiled and gave a self-deprecating shrug. "It seems so obvious once it's explained. I suppose I shall soon get used to it. I have never travelled anywhere by boat or barge before... I've never even set foot on a boat." The very thought made him anxious. "All of my journeys have been on foot, or by horse. Is it not possible to reach York Place by more conventional means?" His tone was plaintive.

"The streets of London are not pleasant to walk or ride through. Many are nothing more than open sewers. Because the ground consists of some sort of clay substance, the streets are damp and muddy even when the weather is dry.

Furthermore, all manner of animals are driven through them, so there is an inordinate amount of dung, not to mention the smell permeating through the streets from the tanneries… I believe I have said enough. Whenever the king processes through the streets to meet with his subjects, he always rides; a horse is the best means of preserving your footwear," Cromwell laughed wryly.

"I remember there was a slight odour when I arrived, but it was not too dreadful. Well… it was no worse than Cambridge," he amended.

"It depends very much upon the direction of the wind. The great houses and palaces are all situated on, or near, the riverbank, so the scent is less pungent. I shall call upon you at York Place soon. I am well acquainted with the Earl of Wiltshire. He and I… well… we are of similar minds; I suspect you share our opinions on certain matters," Cromwell speculated. "But before you leave, permit me to recommend an excellent tailor. Forgive my plain speaking, but you will need a new gown, preferably two, in addition to a jerkin, sleeves, cap… all manner of garments. You are at Court now. You must look the part!"

Thomas wished he felt as relaxed as his companion, who seemed to always be at ease, regardless of the situation. But what Thomas did not realise was that Cromwell's easy manner did not come naturally, having been cultivated after years of uncertainty, spent travelling constantly from place to place.

Cromwell had received very little formal schooling and had taught himself Latin at a young age; he had always had an eye for self-advancement. He and his father, a blacksmith, had clashed violently, prompting Cromwell to flee the country as a young man and begin working abroad as a mercenary soldier in Spain. He had also worked as a merchant in Florence for a short time, before moving to the Netherlands. Upon returning to England, he decided to turn his talents to studying law, and soon became a brilliant lawyer. His status increased when he joined the Honourable Society of Gray's Inn, one of the four Inns of Court, which brought him to the attention of Cardinal Wolsey. Soon afterwards, he became part of the cardinal's household.

Though he had not chosen or intended to travel, Cromwell's experiences, and his time spent in foreign countries, had been most advantageous at Court. Not only did he have first-hand knowledge of foreign affairs, but the experience had also given him time to broaden his mind, and he had read the Bible, many of the works of Luther and Erasmus, and the writings of Machiavelli. Furthermore, he knew how to make people like him, having been forced to make new acquaintances on a regular basis during his travels, and he knew how best to extract information. He hated having gaps in his knowledge, and on this occasion, he knew that the quiet and unworldly Thomas Cranmer was just the man to fill them.

*****

York Place was comfortable and luxurious, more so than anywhere Thomas had ever been before. Not only was his room and his bed more sumptuous than anything he had ever encountered, but the food was rich and plentiful too. Sir Thomas Boleyn, recently titled the Earl of Wiltshire, explained that it had to be of a high standard, for His Majesty's sake. Since Anne officially resided at York Place, and spent much of her time there, the king was a regular visitor. They never knew when he might arrive, and since His Majesty could not be

58

served an inferior dish, they had no choice but to serve food that was fit for a king at all times.

The earl had been a most welcoming host and had swiftly arranged the services of a tailor to fit Thomas with the clothes he would require to attend the king at Court. The tailor had duly arrived, and two brand new academic gowns were soon to be delivered, alongside a number of other necessary items of clothing, including a new pair of shoes, which had been made by one of the many royal shoemakers. Though Thomas was most grateful for all this fuss, he could not help but fret over how he was going to pay for such luxuries, since he had yet to receive any payment for his services. Furthermore, his savings were meagre, for he spent most of his money on books and saved very little. He made a mental note to ask Cromwell about this dilemma when he next saw him.

Soon his life began to follow a routine. His books had arrived quickly, so he spent most of his days working on his Thesis for Divorce and preparing for his visits to the universities. During that first week, he saw little of Lady Anne Boleyn; she was at Court, in her official capacity as a lady-in-waiting to Queen Catherine. He found himself wondering how the two women could tolerate being in the same room as one another. It was a strange and uncomfortable situation: a queen, who apparently refused to leave Court, living in close proximity to a woman whose desire was to step into her shoes. As he sat pondering upon this in his room early one morning, Sir Thomas Boleyn knocked on the door.

It was the first time Boleyn had actually visited the theologian's room, and the volume of books took him by surprise. "You appear to have your own library," he noted, impressed.

Thomas stood up politely. "One day, I would dearly love to possess one," he admitted, hoping that his forbidden books – by Luther and other reformists – were well tucked away. Not that he had much to fear from Boleyn; he had soon learned of the man's inclination towards The New Learning.

"I have come to inform you that my daughter shall be residing here for a few days; she will be arriving later this morning. This evening, the king will be joining us for dinner, and you are expected to be present," Boleyn announced. "You have met my daughter, I believe?"

"Briefly," Thomas affirmed.

"Anne will have heard Mass with the king already, but she may require you to administer the Holy Sacraments to her immediately upon her arrival. After all, you are officially her chaplain." Boleyn changed the subject abruptly. "What do you think of Warham, the Archbishop of Canterbury?" he asked.

"I have never met him," Thomas replied. "But I do know that he is aged, and traditional. He will never advocate any programme of reform within the Church."

"Sir Thomas More, whom I would find most likeable if he would only consider becoming a Protestant reformist, is aware that the Church is a mess. But he is currently campaigning for heresy – in other words, The New Learning – to be stamped out. This obsesses him more than turning his attention to a programme of reform. Certes, he even has Protestants imprisoned within his own home." Boleyn was clearly outraged.

"Yes, I have heard as much," Thomas sighed.

"There is a wave of anticlericalism moving through the land," Boleyn continued. "All because of that fool Wolsey. His grandeur, pomp and splendour has outraged many, and I do believe that, if Wolsey had only set his mind to it, the king could have been divorced by now."

"It is a fact that people are dissatisfied with the clergy," Thomas agreed. He was careful to avoid commenting on Wolsey. "There are tales of immoral nuns; badly educated corpulent priests, and so forth. But you must be aware, although More and Erasmus both want change, they are Humanists. They wish the Church to remain Roman Catholic."

Boleyn gave a snort of irritation.

Thomas eyed his piles of books and pamphlets thoughtfully. Should he give some of them to Boleyn to read? He owned a pamphlet by Simon Fish, dedicated to the king, called *Supplication of the Beggars*. It was a commentary on the greed of the clergy, which criticised the over-fed monks. There was also a work by Jerome Barlow, called *Burial of the Mass*. Both of these had been responsible for fuelling the anticlerical feeling of the population.

As if reading Cranmer's mind, Thomas Boleyn seated himself in a chair next to the desk, then leaned forward confidentially. "I am not an academic, and though I lean towards The New Learning, I know that I have a lot still to learn. But I suspect that you may be able to help me with this predicament?" He eyed his companion with a keen, forthright stare.

His honesty made Thomas feel comfortable enough to find the appropriate works and offer them to Boleyn, who seized them with alacrity.

"And now," Boleyn declared, glancing out of the window where a barge could be seen pulling up to the landing stage. "Come with me. My daughter will arrive shortly." He regarded the works of Fish and Barlow with an air of reverence, which Thomas found touching. "Maybe I had best leave these here with you. Perhaps you will permit me to come here to read them… I assure you, I will not disturb your work." He nodded towards the sheaves of paper lying on the desk. "You see, I am uncertain where to hide these items. Here, in this room, you have many books – no one will pay any undue attention to them – whereas I have no books at all; they will stand out like blazing beacons."

"I understand what you mean," Thomas smiled sympathetically, preparing to follow his host downstairs and once again meet with, Lady Anne Boleyn.

*****

They found Anne pacing the floor of the main room, clutching a small book in her hand, her expression fretful.

"Ah," Anne declared, upon seeing her father and chaplain. "Greetings, Dr Cranmer. I am pleased to see you here. Forgive me for being so brusque, but I need to show you this." She thrust the book into his hands.

Thomas looked at the book curiously. There was no title on the front cover, but when he opened it, he found himself looking at an obscene picture of a cow, mounted upon a bull. "Where... how have you come across this?" he enquired gently.

"It was amongst my belongings, in one of my chests. It was most certainly not there last night; it must have been placed there while I was attending Mass this morning," she replied.

Her voice was husky but pleasing; there was certainly a charm about her. As before, she was wearing the style of headdress he had found so unusual, and about her neck she wore a velvet ribbon, from which hung a magnificent gem. He would eventually discover that she chose to wear wide, close fitting necklaces in order to hide a small, strawberry coloured birth mark on the side of her throat.

"Clearly someone must have wanted you to see it," he murmured. "Certainly, there is something repulsive about the picture." He turned the page and found a couple of lines of writing. "Hmm... 'when cow doth ride bull, then priest beware thy skull'... I do not comprehend the meaning of this," he admitted.

"The badge of the Tudors is the dun cow; the badge of the Boleyn's is a bull," Anne explained.

"Oh, I see I have much to learn." He flicked through the remaining pages of the little book. There was nothing else written, although there were three other drawings, powerfully executed, for each person was easily recognisable. They featured the King Henry, Cardinal Wolsey, and Anne herself.

"It is a prophecy, surely," the earl speculated, looking over Thomas' shoulder.

"I don't like it though," Anne replied tetchily. "It's crude. Vulgar. You agree, don't you my lady mother?"

Lady Boleyn nodded agreement.

"If someone is predicting the downfall of Wolsey, then it is too late. The cardinal has fallen; he has little authority now," the earl declared, his tone soothing. "If it is his death they are predicting, well..."

"It appears to be predicting his execution," Anne interrupted. "After all, it does say 'priest beware thy skull'..."

"Time will tell," the earl shrugged. "There is little else to say about this book, though I do wonder how it came to be placed amongst your possessions."

"I don't like it," Anne repeated irritably, seating herself elegantly upon a settle.

Closely watching his daughter and Thomas Cranmer, the earl astutely realised that, of the two, the new chaplain was the most affected by the contents of the book. He came from a

63

world where no one placed such malign items into other people's chests; he looked shocked, both by the lewd nature of the cow and the bull, and by the fact that the book had been placed deliberately where it would be found. He has much to learn, the earl mused silently to himself. Much to learn indeed.

*****

During the following weeks, he corresponded regularly with his Cambridge friends, completed his thesis for the king, and prepared himself for the sessions of debate in the universities, which were due to commence in the late autumn. He was not overly enthusiastic about the travelling, for if the weather was wet, as it often was in autumn, the roads would be muddy, and riding would be miserable. But, if the king commanded that he should commence debating… well, he had no choice but to oblige.

He also spent a great deal of time with Anne Boleyn's father, the Earl of Wiltshire, and the two of them became firm friends. The earl was ambitious, a fact he made no effort to disguise. He was also committed to The New Learning, though Thomas was uncertain whether the earl's commitment was for spiritual reasons, or because it suited his own aspirations.

Thomas had visited Court regularly since moving to York Place, and as a result, he was now familiar with the fashions and jewels that were flaunted amongst the courtiers. Thankfully, it was unnecessary for him to attire himself in anything other than the robes of a theologian. His new attire – identical to his old garments, just considerably less shabby – had long since arrived, and he had managed to pay the tailor for his services, thanks to Cromwell. The latter visited York Place at least three times a week and had promptly burst out laughing when

Thomas had told him of his financial dilemma, before unbuttoning the pouch which hung from his belt and presenting him with a handful of sovereigns.

"Your wages," Cromwell had explained.

Thomas had never seen so much money. Flustered, he had plucked a couple of sovereigns from Cromwell's extended hand, explaining that this was more than sufficient for his needs.

"No, no," Cromwell had laughed afresh. "These are your wages, from His Majesty. You must take them."

His immediate thought had been that he could buy more books, which he duly did, rapidly expanding his collection.

When he was at Court, it was obvious to Thomas that Anne was the true queen of the Court. There was something about her which set her apart from the other ladies; even though they were all magnificently clad, she always succeeded in eclipsing everyone else. She would glide through the corridors, followed by a procession of lively young ladies, and the wittiest of male courtiers. Some of them he had come to know by name, including the poet Tom Wyatt, and another young man, whom he feared was dissolute in his habits, named Francis Bryan. All the men were vying for Anne's attention. Their conversation was amusing... at least, he assumed it was amusing, for everyone seemed to be laughing uproariously. Indeed, even the king seemed eager to join in with their revelry, whenever he was able.

As for Queen Catherine, now that Thomas had seen her in person, he felt a deep pity for her. She was all but shunned by those at Court. On two occasions, he had attended a formal banquet, where it had been necessary for the crowned queen to be present; she had cut a sombre but dignified presence, and had spoken very little. The queen looked older than her years, her figure thickened by numerous pregnancies, though all her children had died apart from her beloved daughter, Princess Mary. Compared to Lady Anne Boleyn, Catherine looked dull and weary, and no one standing near her wished to divert her with merry talk. Pitying her, Thomas had bowed to her, hoping to perhaps to be invited to speak a few kind words. Etiquette forbade that he should address her first. He knew she was devoutly attached to the Church of Rome, but that was no reason for him not to offer some scriptural, Christian solace. But the queen had merely inclined her head abruptly and dismissively, her eyes akin to chips of ice. Afterwards he reproached himself for not realising that she would not wish to converse with a man who was attached to the Boleyn household, but such had been his compassion for her neglected state, that he would have gladly tried to cheer her.

During his weeks at York Place, whilst writing his thesis, his own commitment to Protestantism, which had already been deep, had strengthened to a depth he had never thought possible. Recently, he had managed to obtain one of the late Tyndale's books, titled *Obedience of the Christian Man*, which advocated caesaropapism: the belief that the ruler of a country ought to be Head of the Church in whichever country he ruled, and should thus be responsible for the souls of his people. Upon reading this, he felt a surge of delight. This was truly how it ought to be. Why should the Pope in Rome exert power here, in England?

Eager to share his findings, he gave the book to the earl, who in turn requested that it should be passed on to his daughter, Anne. Anne was intelligent, and an avid reader of Protestant literature, so Thomas gladly agreed to share Tyndale's work with her. He had already enjoyed a number of interesting discussions with her, for her mind was as quick and

66

challenging as any scholar. Why, just two evenings previously, she had spoken of the Virgin Mary, a subject he usually avoided, for his true view could be constructed as heresy. But Anne's view, he had soon learned, was most definitely Protestant, which gave him the confidence to confide in her.

"My view of the Virgin Mary..." His voice had trailed away thoughtfully after she had first questioned him, as he tried to determine how to make his opinion seem less heretical without telling a lie.

"Marry, it is best I should tell you what I think," Anne had interrupted boldly. "I am anticipating that you will treat this as a confessional, and therefore as confidential information," she had stated quietly, observing him with her intense, dark eyes. Once he had given a brief nod of assent, she had continued. "I believe the Virgin Mary was indeed a holy lady, but I do not believe she should be idolised, as she is in the Catholic Church. The Church places her on par with the son of God, which is far too high a position, in my opinion."

Exactly! He had wanted to shout the word aloud. Anne's frankness had given him confidence. "I agree," he had responded solemnly. "Christ died for our sins; he died for us. His sacrifice and infinite love for mankind cannot be contradicted. The Virgin Mary did not make such a sacrifice. She was a good and holy lady, certainly, otherwise she would not have been chosen to bear the saviour of mankind. She is to be respected, as all saints should be. But she should not be idolised."

Anne had been quick to detect another point of interest. "So, you do not believe in the worship of saints?"

"No. I believe in reverence. Respect. They are close to God. But Jesus Himself sits at God's right hand; He is intercessor for us. He belonged in heaven yet walked this Earth. He knows what it is like to be an ordinary human being. Everything we feel, He understands, because He has been here and knows what it is to be poor, hungry, alone, cold, weary, and so forth. He lived among men and gave us lowly sinners an example of the perfect life. The saints are now with God, but they did not live the perfect life. They were culpable, as we are." Thomas had stopped, suddenly realising that he had become carried away with enthusiasm. "My apologies, Lady Anne. I sound as though I am lecturing you."

"No, I am glad you have spoken with such honesty, Dr Cranmer." Anne had looked thoughtful. "You have given me much to think about. I believe you have spoken truly of the things I ought to hear." She had been seated on a low stool, her skirts elegantly arranged about her person. Rising, and thus subtly displaying that their discourse was at an end, she had smoothed the folds of her gown. "I am sure you will be curious to hear what happens tomorrow, when the king's new reformed Parliament is opened?" She had smirked impishly. "I do think... I hope... that it will set matters in motion for my own situation. One day, I shall be queen, and I will no longer have to endure the sorrowful, pained glances I receive regularly from the Princess Catherine of Spain, who continues to insist that she is the true queen." A tinge of frustration had crept into her voice. "She makes it intolerable for me to be at Court. But you know something, Dr Cranmer? Henry tells me that he intends to send her away. Very soon, I won't have to see her ever again."

Poor woman, Thomas had thought to himself. Catherine sincerely believed she was queen; it would be heart-breaking for her to lose that position after all these years. At least, given her kinship with the Holy Roman Emperor, she would be well treated by King Henry, and would be given a degree of respect.

68

"I shall be attending the reformation of Parliament session with Cromwell," Thomas had admitted. "It is a historic occasion; I shall be honoured to be there to witness it."

*****

The king's desire to divorce Catherine and marry Anne was unwavering, but he had reasons other than this for decreeing this reformation of Parliament. Yes, he wanted a divorce, but he also felt that the clergy held too much power, something which he intended to do something about - immediately. He was planning to subdue and overawe them, and since the laity were dissatisfied with the Church, he was going to make good use of this anti-clerical feeling that rumbled amongst his people. A king ruled by the approval of his people, so by subduing the Church, he would gain common approval.

Sir Thomas More was the first lay person to hold office as Chancellor, and on this occasion, he was also the first lay person to open Parliament. Henry had received a petition from the Commons, stating that they wished for members of the clergy to hold no more than one benefice each. Under the current system, many members of the clergy held numerous benefices, and usually neglected those that delivered the least money into their pockets. Furthermore, many of the priests failed to properly conduct services, as they had too many parishes to serve, and many benefices reported not seeing a priest for months.

The lay people also felt that the clergy were buying and selling for gain. Surely, the petition stated, it was wrong for people who were serving God to seek to be tradesmen too? As for funerals, some of the clergy demanded such a high price for conducting a funeral service that those who were poor could not afford to pay. Indeed, many would locate a vacant spot in a churchyard, then hastily bury their deceased relative under the cover of darkness. It was not unusual for startled grave diggers to dig in what they believed to be an empty plot, only to find a decomposing corpse lying there. This was a felony, but some were desperate enough to do it, such was the unrivalled financial power of the Church.

*****

Anne, once she had received Tyndale's book from Thomas, presented it to the king, conveniently opened at the page which advocated caesaropapism.

The king read the text carefully, then reread it, before heartily slapping the cover of the book in delight, exclaiming, "This is a book for all princes to read!" Tyndale's book had placed a seed of an idea into Henry's mind, a seed which, one day soon, would grow to become an unstoppable force.

Chapter Four

In late November he found himself thankful for the fact he was an excellent horseman. He always had been, few horses were too spirited for him to handle. He was travelling back and forth between Oxford and Cambridge, each journey through the rain, frost, and icy winds, tested his horsemanship to the extreme. His task was to set up a commission, whereby scholars and theologians would debate upon whether the king should be permitted to divorce and remarry. There would be a series of debates, then, in January, the theologians would make their final decision. After the final vote, a report would be submitted, to declare whether or not the universities agreed with the king's proposal.

Stephen Gardiner was also involved in garnering support for the king's cause within the universities, though he somewhat resented the task, for he had recently lost his benefices of Taunton, Norfolk, and Worcester as a result of the king's new parliamentary ruling, regarding members of the clergy having affiliations with multiple benefices. His ambition, however, was greater than his discontent, so he continued to begrudgingly serve the king in the hope that he might gain favour, and be granted a more important position in the near future.

During the weeks leading up to his visits to the universities, Thomas had sent a stream of correspondence to the theologians and scholars, in the form of letters and pamphlets which supported the king's proposal. He had always suffered from low self-esteem, which he preferred to regard as modesty, but during the debates, he found his self-confidence boosted by the discovery that his learned discourse had persuaded a number of eminent men towards his own opinions.

Despite the dismal travelling conditions, it was a pleasure to be reunited with his former colleagues in Cambridge, though, oddly enough, his visits were not as nostalgic as he had thought they might be. He felt comfortable with the familiarity of the place, and would often gaze fondly at his surroundings whilst debating, amazed that he had been fortunate enough to have lived there for so long. Even the horror of his brief, nightmarish marriage no longer pained him, the passage of time having blurred the remembrance of that terrible era in his life.

His time at Cambridge had been one of contentment, that much was certain, but though he still had a great fondness for the peaceful, studious life he had led as a scholar, his new life at Court was challenging... exciting. He had never felt so alive, or so mentally stimulated. Cromwell and the Boleyns were certainly partly responsible for making his new life so invigorating, but the king was undeniably the one who had made the greatest impact. Once a frightened schoolboy, Thomas was now one of the king's most trusted advisors, and Henry's unreserved faith in him had done wonders for his confidence and self-belief. The king dazzled him, which was to be expected. After all, God Himself had placed Henry on the throne; it was Thomas' duty, as well as his pleasure, to obey and to be of service to this monarch. He knew that if the king released him from service, and permitted him to return to

72

Cambridge, he would be content to resume his former studious existence. But for the time being, he was enjoying the excitement of life in the king's service.

*****

After what had felt like an eternity spent travelling, Thomas was granted a few weeks of respite, in order to celebrate Christmas with the king and His courtiers, at Hampton Court. Unsurprisingly, it was a Christmas unlike any other. As a child, he had only known this season to be a time for worship and a modest feast. There had been no exchanging of gifts, for his mother had deemed them an unnecessary extravagance; though his parents had been far from poor, they had not been wealthy either. At Cambridge, the season had been even more austere; a time for worship and contemplation, not frivolity. But in the Court of King Henry, Christmas was a season of magnificent indulgence.

The king distributed gifts lavishly, as did his courtiers, who tried to outdo each other with the magnificence of their offerings. Cromwell had forewarned him of this, and the two men had agreed not to exchange gifts with one another, focusing instead on purchasing gifts for those at Court who would expect to be indulged. Mercifully, Thomas was able to delegate, leaving the acquisition of gifts to the servant who was temporarily acting as his secretary. In keeping with the holiness of the season, he had instructed his secretary that these gifts should take the form of illuminated prayers, which were not only appropriate but were also easy to purchase.

Never had Thomas seen such colour; such magnificent food; such revelry as he saw during the twelve nights of immoderate feasting that began with Christmas Day. Mummers and minstrels entertained the king's guests during each banquet, and once the food was dispensed with, it was time to dance, an activity which he was content to simply observe. Fox and Gardiner, he noted, were far from reluctant to take part, indeed, Fox appeared eager to display his dancing skills. There were games too, Blind Man's Buff being a favourite; the more boisterous the games were, the more the king and his Court enjoyed them. Again, Thomas avoided taking part, thankful that Cromwell was also not a man for games, and was happy to keep him company outside in the crisp winter air, where they could chatter freely, without the fear of being overheard.

By this time, Queen Catherine had been sent away from Court, so Lady Anne became the undisputed, albeit uncrowned, queen of the season. It was apparent then that she had firmly secured her new position, and if any were still in doubt, the king's most recent alterations to the great hall revealed his intentions. Though the work was yet unfinished – the king's plans had turned out to be far too extravagant to be completed before the Christmas period – there had been time for the initials H and A to be prominently and decoratively carved into the wood panelled walls.

*****

In January, Thomas once again mounted his horse and rode to Oxford, to determine the results of the commission. He was tense; after weeks of campaigning, he would finally discover whether his words had made an impact. He was more confident of the verdict in Cambridge; he knew the people there and felt that he had managed to sway the majority to vote in the king's favour. Oxford was another matter, for the scholars there were far more inclined towards the Church of Rome. Most of the theologians there believed that the Bull, issued by the Pope, had voided Catherine's marriage to Henry's brother, thus making Henry and Catherine's marriage binding in the eyes of God. Thomas had debated with them energetically, trying his upmost to convince them otherwise, but there had been no way of knowing whether his attempts had been successful, until now.

Upon arriving in Oxford, he was ushered into the Chancellor's study and handed two tightly bound scrolls: the first pronouncement. Hands trembling, he unrolled the first of two scrolls, upon which was written the results of the vote. He sighed with relief. The majority of scholars and theologians had voted that the king should be permitted to divorce and remarry. Hands still trembling, he unrolled the second report. Again, relief flooded though him. The parchment stated clearly that the union between King Henry and the Princess Catherine of Spain was unlawful. As far as Oxford University was concerned, King Henry VIII was a free man, and could marry Lady Anne Boleyn, or any other lady of his choosing.

His spirits lifted, he travelled to Cambridge, where he was met by his good friend Latimer. His stomach lurched with sudden fear as he was handed the reports. The result was not a totally foregone conclusion, he knew that. But surely his colleagues at Cambridge would have made the right choice? As he opened the first report, then the second, he sighed with relief. The king's marriage had been deemed unlawful by the majority, and they had voted for him to be permitted to remarry. As he looked up from the reports, he found himself staring into the forthright and honest blue eyes of Hugh Latimer.

"The king is free to remarry." Thomas' voice was shaking.

"I am glad to hear it. Shall you return here to work now?" Latimer enquired.

"Not yet." He shook his head. "You see, I am to travel to Rome with the Earl of Wiltshire, Lady Anne Boleyn's father. Once there, I must debate with the Pope himself." He had been informed of this task by the king only a week ago, and the very thought of a sea voyage filled him with terror.

"But you are staying in Cambridge until morning." Latimer took his friend's arm. "Come, let us dine together. You know something…" His voice trailed off as he scrutinised his friend. "You know something… I do believe you are not the man you used to be. You have grown, Cranmer."

"I think you will find I am as short as I ever was." He smiled as Latimer laughed in response. "Though certainly, at this moment, I feel at least a foot taller with relief. The outcome of this commission has eased my mind."

"No, my friend, you *have* grown," Latimer insisted. "You have grown within yourself. There is a sense of purpose; a sense of fulfilment that was not there before."

The two of them stepped out into the darkness and walked towards the welcome noise of the White Horse Inn. There, they sat together companionably, totally at ease with one another, their food and drink sitting on the table in front of them.

"So," Latimer enquired, pausing to swallow a piece of bread. "Do you think the king will wed Mistress Boleyn very soon?"

"I don't see why not, though it is possible the Archbishop of Canterbury, William Warham, will be requested to authorise their divorce." Thomas looked thoughtful. "Warham is firmly orthodox, as you well know, and is obedient to the Pope. But now that the universities have declared His Majesty's union unlawful, Warham should acknowledge that the king is a free man and agree to conduct a marriage service between His Majesty and Mistress Anne."

"Can you see Warham doing that without putting up a fight?" Latimer asked in his direct manner.

Thomas sat in silent contemplation for a long time, before eventually giving a reluctant shake of his head. "I don't think Warham will do anything without the Pope's assent."

"So, the king will not be able to remarry any time soon."

"Regretfully, I think you are right. I believe the king thinks likewise, which is why I have been asked to board a ship and accompany the earl to Rome. I hate ships," he voiced plaintively.

"Nonsense, you've never been on board a ship in your life. You'll love it. The bracing sea air…" Latimer stopped, letting out a guffaw of laughter at the sight of his friend's anguished face.

*****

The king was so pleased with Thomas' work, and the verdict of the universities, that he made Thomas Cranmer Archdeacon of Taunton, a position recently vacated by Stephen Gardiner. Though he was, of course, delighted with this turn of events, it had also come at rather a bad time, for despite thoroughly disapproving of absent clergy, he now found himself having no option but to be absent from his own benefice, whilst he travelled to Rome upon the king's errand. Wanting to ensure that the spiritual needs of his beneficiaries were taken care of during his absence, he ensured that a substitute priest was installed – one who was inclined towards The New Learning – to take his place until he returned.

Unbeknownst to him, he was to remain abroad for longer than he had envisaged; when boarding the ship towards the end of January, he had no way of knowing that he would not see

England again until September. Thomas, the earl and their retinue, boarded at Ramsgate on a bitterly cold day. The ground was thickly covered with snow and was frozen so hard that it looked likely to remain thus until at least March. Initially, their brief had been to simply debate with the Pope and convince him of the decision made by the universities, but by the time they set sail, Thomas had also been instructed to visit Bologna, to attend the coronation of the Holy Roman Emperor, Charles of Spain, as a representative of His Majesty King Henry VIII. The Pope himself would be placing the crown upon Charles' head, so once the ceremony and celebrations were finished with, Thomas and the earl would accompany the Pope to Rome. Thomas had also been asked to visit Paris, after his stay in Rome, to debate with the scholars there and seek their opinion on The King's Great Matter. It made him dizzy just contemplating the hectic schedule ahead of them.

To his gratification, he discovered that he was a good sailor; it would have been humiliating to have been forced to languish in his bunk, suffering from sea sickness, whilst the earl and most of the crew went about their days as normal. But although he experienced no ill effects during their voyage, he found life aboard the ship most distasteful. Their quarters were cramped; writing and studying was challenging, if not impossible, due to the constant pitching of the vessel, and the food was foul. Fortunately, the wind was favourable, and they steadily journeyed towards the coast of Italy without any delays.

After they had gladly disembarked, they travelled ponderously towards Bologna, for many of the roads were less passable than those they had left behind in England. Thomas felt much more comfortable now that they were on horseback, and was beginning to actually enjoy their journey. The opportunity to travel had been given to him, and although he would never have chosen to venture abroad, he reasoned that it would be wasteful not to learn from the experience. He was fortunate that the earl was such an insightful and interesting travel companion; having someone interesting to converse with did wonders for reducing the tedium.

The earl thought likewise, and was thankful for Thomas Cranmer's companionship; so much so that he wrote a highly complementary letter to the king, following the coronation of King Charles.

"Here, this is what I have written to the king." The earl thrust a sheet of paper into Thomas' hands. "You may as well read it; it tells His Majesty of yesterday's coronation, and of our journey thus far."

Thomas began to read, thankful that it was his companion, and not himself, who was required to describe the pomp, colour and ceremony of such an occasion. He would have personally found it very difficult to describe the event in adequate detail; but the earl had done so with ease, writing for some considerable time, his pen scratching rapidly across the page, only pausing when it was necessary to sharpen the tip, or else change to a new pen.

After his description of the coronation, the earl had written a segment commending his travelling companion. Flushing with gratification, Thomas read: 'I am well pleased with my companion, Dr Thomas Cranmer, a man of subtle wit who conducts himself with dignity, and whose demeanour has been most pleasant throughout our journey'.

"I am undeserving of this," he murmured, willing his flushed countenance to return to its usual, sallow colour.

"You need to learn to accept compliments, my friend," the earl chuckled.

Handing the letter back to his companion, Thomas deftly changed the subject. "I have been giving the matter at hand a great deal of consideration. Both the emperor and the Pope leave tomorrow, and the king has asked us to speak with them both. Instead of the two of us accompanying the Pope, then doubling back to visit the emperor, I suggest we separate. Our retinue is large enough to be shared between us, so neither of us shall be travelling unprotected or unattended."

The earl nodded slowly. "Good idea." Throughout their mission, the earl had been glad of Cranmer's wisdom. Though he himself was well-educated, his companion was by far one of the most learned men he had ever met. Cranmer spoke French, German, Latin and Greek – he was particularly fluent in the latter two languages – and would have no problem conversing with Pope Clement, whereas the earl would have required an interpreter. But he would be able to communicate with the emperor, since they were both fluent in French. Yes, Cranmer's suggestion made sound sense.

"This way, we should also be able to return home more quickly," Thomas stated hopefully. He would miss the earl, for they had grown close during his time at Court and were now firm friends. But splitting up was by far the most efficient way to complete the king's mission. A year ago, if the king had been declared free to marry Anne Boleyn, Thomas would not have understood why His Majesty did not just wed her immediately. But during his time at Court, he had learned that the situation was not that simple. As the King of England, Henry was certainly powerful enough to marry the woman he loved, but he would not be able to control the repercussions of such a complex political statement.

The king had to look further than domestic politics; he had to take account of foreign politics as well. The Emperor Charles was powerful, and was currently strongly allied with King Francis I of France. Queen Catherine was the aunt of Charles, so if Charles were to become offended by the king's new marriage, there would be Spain's alliance with France to consider; fighting a war against the combined forces of France and Spain was something King Henry was keen to avoid. However, if Catherine herself were to admit that her marriage to Henry was unlawful... well... that would change matters. But she had, thus far, stubbornly refused, hence King Henry's desire to convince the Pope and Charles of the unlawful status of his union. If that failed, Henry would be forced to find himself another powerful ally, to keep France and Spain at bay.

As for Pope Clement, he was terrified of the Emperor Charles, whom he perceived to be the dominant force in the Catholic Church. A few years ago, Pope Clement had thought it a good idea to ally with King Francis of France, in an attempt to frighten Charles, but quite the reverse had happened. Charles and his army had promptly marched into Italy and defeated the Italians and the French, after which both countries had swiftly allied themselves with Spain and the Holy Roman Emperor. This was, of course, the reason why the earl needed to gain the support of Emperor Charles.

"It would be a great relief to get home sooner," Boleyn sighed. "For I must oversee the wedding of my son."

Thomas nodded sympathetically. The earl's son, George, otherwise known as Viscount Rochford, had recently become (unwillingly) engaged to one Jane Parker, a former lady-in-waiting to Queen Catherine, and an heiress, hence the eagerness with which the earl had pursued the match. Unfortunately, the future bridegroom could not tolerate Jane Parker, so whilst Jane Parker had initially been happy to marry George, his blatant coldness towards her had eroded her enthusiasm.

"Do you think they may refuse to wed?" He enquired.

"It could happen," Boleyn shrugged helplessly. "George can be a hot-headed fool sometimes." His voice rose in frustration. "He wrote to me not so long ago asking if I could find him a different heiress. He seems to think heiresses just sit there, waiting to be picked like an apple from a branch."

Thomas nodded, having already been informed of this numerous times.

The earl continued anyway, exasperated by his son's incomprehension. "Honestly, the youth of today! Why, my eldest daughter, Mary, she recently married Will Stafford, a mere knight of no particular fortune, and I do believe he expects me to provide for them! If he does, he shall find himself deluded."

He had heard this, too, though he could understand the earl's frustration. His own parents would probably have been equally outraged had they known of their son's marriage to a tavern girl of dubious morals.

Fortunately for the earl, he arrived home less than a month after the two friends parted; his meeting with the Holy Roman Emperor had been brief, but final. Thomas had assumed that his visit to Rome would be equally as brief, but after a month and a half, he had still not left Italy.

At first, the splendour of the Vatican had been dazzling. Though the scars of the violent battle with the Emperor Charles and his troops, plus the looting in the aftermath of the conflict, remained - many buildings still awaited repair - the air of dignity that exuded from the very cobblestones of the city made even the most disfigured of buildings seem regal. Well aware of the need for a peaceful negotiation with England's neighbours, it occurred to Thomas that the ravages evident in Rome could well become evident in London, should the

82

emperor decide to make war with Henry. Unfortunately, the Pope's fear of offending Charles prevented him from declaring the English king's marriage to Queen Catherine unlawful; no matter how energetically Thomas debated with him and his cardinals, the Pope consistently refused to risk affronting the Holy Roman Emperor. Frustrated but defeated, Thomas had promptly written to King Henry, requesting permission to leave Rome, given the Pope's intractability regarding this matter. But the response from the king had been an instruction to remain for a while longer, and to keep trying to convince His Holiness the Pope.

Disappointed by King Henry's command, he gazed disconsolately from the balcony of his chamber. A brightly dressed young woman waved and blew him a kiss, then stood staring at him, obviously anticipating an invitation to enter. Hastily, he retreated, stepping back into his room. There seemed to be a large number of courtesans in Rome, far more than he had ever seen in London, though perhaps those in London were simply less visible. On one recent occasion, he had accompanied a group of cardinals to the Coliseum, as they had been eager to show him this splendid symbol of ancient Rome. To his intense surprise, the Coliseum had been swarming with prostitutes, who had clearly gathered there to take advantage of the popularity of the great monument. As for the cardinals, they had been rather taken aback by his surprise, indeed, they saw nothing wrong with the presence of these young women.

Trying to forget the beauty of the courtesan who had gaily waved to him, he distracted himself by writing a letter to the Earl of Wiltshire, but barely had he put pen to paper when someone knocked upon his door. For a wild, anxious moment, he thought it might be the beautiful courtesan, but to his relief, he discovered it was simply a messenger, holding a scroll bearing the seal of Thomas Cromwell. So far, he had written several letters to his friend, but this was the first he had received in return. To his satisfaction, it turned out to be lengthy and full of gossip.

'Permit me to tell you what is happening here', Cromwell began. 'The king has decreed that all forbidden books must be burned, and the houses of those known to be interested in The New Learning have been searched. Fortunately, thus far, no one from the Court has had their lodgings disturbed'.

Thomas gave an audible sigh of relief; his own precious books were safe.

'There have been many outbursts in the streets, and many bonfires. I do believe the Archbishop of Canterbury, Warham, is mostly to blame, for he has been complaining to the king lately about the amount of Protestant literature that has been flooding into the country. Warham looks ill now; when you see him next, his appearance will shock you. He looks as if death is close. Well, that is my opinion, at least'.

The letter continued chattily. 'As for my lady Anne Boleyn, she rules at Court, and is much disliked by many. She has argued publicly with both the Duke of Norfolk – her own uncle, and a senior member of the Privy Council, to boot – and the Duchess of Norfolk, though one might argue that her anger is valid, for the Duchess publicly mocked the new family tree that the Boleyn's have had drawn up. As you know, the earl's wife is sister to the Duke of Norfolk, hence why Mary, George and Anne are considered at least partly aristocratic. The earl hails from a line of wool merchants, a wealthy background to be sure, but not as illustrious as his wife's. However, his new family tree tells a tale of him being descended from a Norman Lord. Anyway, the Duchess of Norfolk was most scathing, so Lady

Anne snapped back at her by publicly asking after the health of Bessie Holland, the Duke's mistress, who happens to be a laundress. This sort of behaviour will not bring her support, though I believe her temper had flared as a result of her delicate position'.

The letter took on a more serious tone. 'Her future depends totally upon retaining the king's good grace, which she seems to manage very well. His Majesty dotes upon her, but she is no longer young – I am certain she must be heading towards her late twenties – and if he should tire of her, or cast her aside, I doubt she will find a noble husband at her age. The Duke of Suffolk, the king's brother-in-law, has tried to spread a rumour about Lady Anne being the mistress of Tom Wyatt, the poet, but since Wyatt is currently in Calais, I think that rumour will be swiftly scotched. I must also inform you, for when you return home, that you must now refer to the former Queen Catherine as the Princess Dowager, for such is her official title these days'.

The letter continued to be informative, revealing that the Archbishop of Canterbury had been summoned to Hampton Court, where the king was currently residing, and had, not for the first time, refused to sign the king's divorce papers. Also, much to Anne's chagrin, Wolsey was his way back into the king's favour.

Having finished reading, Thomas leaned back against his chair, feeling the roughness of its intricate carving pressing against his spine. Cromwell was right; Lady Anne's position was fragile. The king was in love with her, that much was evident, but should that love turn sour, what would happen to her? Having known the love of the king and the power and authority that accompanied his affection, it would be very difficult for Anne to look elsewhere and find someone

85

comparable. Lady Anne was doing herself no favours whatsoever by alienating powerful people. She ought to be making friends, but instead, she was making enemies. Powerful enemies.

It was nearly two weeks before Thomas received another letter, this time from the king himself. From it, he learned that the earl was now back in England, and that the king desired for Thomas to complete his work in Rome as soon as possible, travel to Paris for a short sojourn to debate in the universities there, then return to England. His relief at the prospect of returning to England was short-lived, for the king went on to say that the earl's glowing commendation of his diplomatic skills had convinced him to send Thomas on another embassy abroad later that year. Still, at least for the moment, he had plenty to occupy himself with, including the prospect of paying a visit to his benefice in Taunton, to ensure that his beneficiaries had been spiritually supported and educated to a suitable standard during his absence.

*****

He returned to England to learn that Cardinal Thomas Wolsey had died. Though he had never managed to regain his former favour with the king, his death was still a huge shock to the Court; he had been a master statesman for so many years that it was difficult to accept he was gone. Cromwell, who had been released from Wolsey's service, had become an official advisor to the king, and wasted no time in visiting York Place as soon as his friend had returned.

"Are you rested yet?" Cromwell demanded cheerily, taking stock of Cranmer's appearance. His friend looked weary and dishevelled, and his usually sallow complexion had become an unflattering shade of brown after months spent outdoors and upon the deck of a ship.

"I am indeed. I slept more soundly last night than I have in a long time. I am glad to be home again, although His Majesty requires my services for another diplomatic mission, so I doubt I shall be here for more than a few months." He sounded resigned.

Cromwell was amused. Many a man would be only too glad to go abroad and serve the king. It was a good way to earn a promotion.

The two friends headed downstairs to join the earl, his wife, and Lady Anne, who was also present, though she was mostly at Court these days. Her regular appearances had prompted those at Court to speculate that she might now be the king's mistress, but those closest to her knew otherwise. They knew that she continued to resist becoming Henry's mistress in order to ensure that she would one day become queen; if she surrendered herself to her royal admirer, it would be unnecessary for him to marry her.

"Cromwell here has been amusing himself by tormenting the clergy," the earl observed drily.

"Persecuting the clergy?" Thomas enquired curiously. What was Cromwell up to now?

"Not exactly persecuting then - just tormenting them a little! I have placed them under a writ of praemunire," Cromwell enlightened, his eyes gleaming with mischief.

Anne, who looked tense and uptight, was seated on a low chair. It had taken Thomas some time to realise she had a preference for low chairs or stools, because she fancied that they showed off her wide, sweeping skirts to a greater advantage. There was a brittle restlessness about her that had not been there all those months ago when he had left for Italy.

"Praemunire?" Anne exclaimed. "Marry, what does praemunire mean?"

Thomas blinked, then explained gently, "A writ of praemunire is a law that was made... oh, sometime in the fourteenth century, I believe. It forbids papal jurisdiction, or any other foreign jurisdiction for that matter, to claim supremacy in England against the supremacy of the monarch." Inwardly, he was marvelling at how quick and subtle Cromwell's mind was. He knew about this law, but it would never have occurred to him to apply it.

Anne shrugged and continued to look at the two men, her expression questioning.

"The clergy are mindful of Wolsey's fall," Cromwell explained gleefully. "It is almost as good as a jest: the clergy, threatened with praemunire, because their courts function independently from the Crown Courts. I tell you, Warham looked devastated when I delivered the news."

Anne still looked uncertain.

For a moment, Thomas felt sorry for the aged Warham, who was much too old to adapt to change. Personally, he had always disagreed with the fact the clergy answered to their own court of law, and not to the Crown Courts. It was wrong, he reflected. A priest could commit a crime, theft for example, but instead of being dealt with severely by the Crown Courts, he would be sent to the Clerical Courts and receive a much more lenient sentence. "It means the clergy must submit to the same law courts as everyone else," he clarified, for Anne's benefit.

Anne gave a nod of satisfaction.

"I have also fined the Church one hundred thousand pounds," Cromwell continued, more seriously. "Which they have agreed to pay, though Warham has stressed that he wishes the principles and liberties of the Church, stemming from the

88

Magna Carta, to be confirmed in return. However, the king has refused to bend to Warham's wishes. Indeed, His Majesty wishes to be more than simply Defender of the Faith, the title given to him by the Pope; he wishes to be Protector and Supreme Head of the English Church, and to become responsible for the Cure of Souls. There is hope that we may soon be heading towards a break from Rome."

Thomas, listening gravely, turned to Lady Anne, thinking she might perhaps require an explanation for this also. "The Cure of Souls is a term used to refer to the spiritual well-being of the king's subjects—"

"I know what the Cure of Soul's means," she snapped, ignoring the glance of rebuke from her mother.

Abashed, Thomas turned to Cromwell. "Do you really think this could lead to a break with Rome?"

Cromwell was shaking his head solemnly. "Don't be too optimistic yet, there has been a setback. Bishop Fisher, always a thorn in the king's side, has spoken publicly against this, not that anyone expected any less from the old fool. The clergy are still strong; thus far, they have unwillingly accepted the king's proposal to have responsibility over the Cure of Souls and have ambiguously said that they will allow the king to be their head 'as far as Christ allows', which could be taken in several ways. But despite this potential progress, the king has taken a backwards step, and has applied for a Papal Bull to permit him to ordain Stephen Gardiner as Bishop of Winchester. It seems to me His Majesty does not yet believe in his own authority." He gave an exasperated sigh.

"If Henry keeps going back and forth in this way, I shall be past child-bearing age before we get married. I never did imagine this divorce would take so long, or be so convoluted," Anne pronounced tartly.

The earl spoke up. "When the king addressed Parliament, he said, 'well beloved subjects, we thought that the clergy of our realm had been our subjects wholly, but now we have perceived that they are but half our subjects, for all prelates at their consecration make an oath to the Pope, which contradicts the oath they make to us. If anything, they are his subjects, not ours', and I wholly agree. The clergy should belong to the king, not to the Pope."

Anne laughed. "Do you recall Chapuys, the Spanish Ambassador, complaining afterwards? He was distressed that the clergy might end up becoming 'of less account than shoemakers, who at least have the power of assembling and making their own statutes'. I ask you, what would be wrong with that? I fail to understand how Chapuys cannot see that the Church needs a good shaking."

"Like my feather pillows," her mother murmured, speaking for the first time that morning.

Anne shot an impatient glance in her direction.

Thomas could not share his own thoughts, not even in the company of these people, whom he considered friends. One day, in the not-too-distant future, he knew that Archbishop Warham would die, and that his likely successor would be the vigorous Stephen Gardiner. Surely that was why Gardiner had been made Bishop of Winchester? Unfortunately, Gardiner was most assuredly devoted to the Church of Rome, and if he were to be made archbishop, Thomas knew that there would be no change to the structure of the English Church. England would forever be shackled to Rome, deferring to a man who lived hundreds of miles away, and whose theology was totally alien to the scriptures. Without realising it, he gave a deep sigh.

"What troubles you?" the ever-observant Cromwell asked.

"The embassy I have just returned from has hardly been of any use," he replied. "There has been no progress whatsoever as far as I can see, with the divorce or the reformation of the Church."

"Come now, we have made some progress," Cromwell protested stoutly. "Take heart, King Henry just needs some persuasion, that is all. After all, it is a huge decision for him to make. We just need to keep chipping away, dripping reformist viewpoints into the royal ear."

"Then, when it is all decided and we break from Rome, we must convince Henry that it was all his idea in the first place," Anne added waspishly.

Thomas shot a quick glance of surprise in Anne's direction, then quickly lowered his gaze. Yesterday, when he had returned, she had rushed to him, demanding that he should hear her confession, without giving him the chance to freshen up or rest. Naturally, he had conceded to her demand, but it had turned out that she had simply needed someone to confidentially vent her rage upon. Of course, as her chaplain and confessor, anything she said to him had to remain confidential, despite neither of them believing that one could receive absolution from a priest. Absolution – in any reformist's mind – came from repenting to Christ alone and was automatically given to any penitent soul.

He had seen the change in her as soon as he had returned to England, and the more he looked upon her, the more he noticed. She was thinner; her features were sharper; her general air was one of stress and anxiety, and her temper more volatile. He had already witnessed her speaking sharply, not only to himself and the servants, but to her mother and father as well. She was brittle and bitter, though he assumed she restrained herself when in the king's company. No doubt she was witty, flirtatious, entertaining and charming in His Majesty's presence, putting on a display of smiles and good humour to keep the king enchanted. He was disturbed to realise that, when in the presence of those she did not need to impress, her acerbic nature reminded him very much of someone he would rather forget. His late wife, Joan.

Chapter Five

Towards the end of that year, Thomas found himself attached to the Holy Roman Emperor's Court in Nuremberg, Germany. Nuremberg was a breeding ground for reformist ideas, and he was quickly admitted into the Protestant fold, albeit secretly. Prominent amongst the scholars was a man named Andreas Osiander, who had publicly declared himself Lutheran, in spite of the fact he and Martin Luther were known to disagree over certain theological dogmas. A former priest, Osiander took a huge liking to the little English theologian, who was obviously clever despite his reluctance to voice his views, and he was swift to invite Thomas to dine with him. Charmed by the kindly yet earnest manner of Osiander, Thomas readily accepted his hospitality.

Upon arriving at the German reformist's home, he was introduced to Katarina, Osiander's wife, and his two children, for whom it was now approaching bedtime. Judging by the fullness of Katarina's figure, Thomas suspected another child would be arriving in the not-too-distant future.

"This seems a happy home," he observed aloud, accepting a mug of ale from his host. They were seated at a well-worn table, the number of chairs indicating that there would be four people dining, in a large room clearly designed for eating and socialising. As he glanced about the room, he wondered fleetingly who the fourth person might be. The house was simply furnished, but comfortable. A large, shabby settle stood against one wall, whilst a fireplace, the fire as yet unlit, stood against another, a basket of logs beside it. A steep flight of narrow stairs took up the third wall, leading towards what Thomas assumed were the sleeping quarters. Katarina was currently negotiating the stairs with the children, who kept looking back at Thomas inquisitively. From somewhere nearby – the kitchen, he assumed – drifted an appetising smell, reminding him that he had not eaten for some hours.

"It is, praise God,' Osiander replied cheerily. 'It is a Protestant household. I agree with Luther most of the time, though not always. I see no reason to always agree with friends. Without criticism from our closest companions, we cannot grow."

"I made a close circle of friends when I was at Cambridge University, and we often disagreed," Thomas revealed.

The two men were conversing in Greek, as although Thomas knew some German, he had not spoken the language regularly enough at Cambridge to be fluent, since most of the translating he did was in Greek or Latin. As for his host, he spoke no English at all.

"But despite this, our friendship never faltered," he continued. "Indeed, I would argue that the ability to engage in rousing discussions cemented our friendship, though certain persons would regularly storm off in a hot-headed rage, only to return the next evening as though nothing had happened." He was principally referring to Latimer.

At that moment, a young woman entered the room carrying a platter of freshly baked bread. She was small; slender, without being too thin, and her head was modestly covered by a linen

94

coif, allowing only a small amount of her fair hair to show at the front. Her air of modesty, combined with her demure attire, struck Thomas immediately. As for her eyes, which he later discovered were pale blue, she kept them primly lowered.

"Allow me to introduce my niece, Margaret Hosmer. She lives with us," Osiander explained.

"Ich spreche nicht viel Englisch," Margaret blushed, whilst simultaneously dropping a curtsey.

To his surprise, Thomas found himself boldly replying, "Keine Sorge, ich spreche ein bisschen Deutsch."

Her face flushed a deeper red as she waved a hand towards the platter of bread. "Das ist für dich. Das Abendessen ist noch nicht fertig." Bobbing another curtsey, she headed back into the kitchen.

Understanding enough German to realise she was inviting him to eat, he managed to reply, "Vielen danke."

"She and my wife know a little Latin and Greek. I have been teaching them. So, providing the conversation is kept very simple, they will understand what is being said tonight," Osiander explained. "I do not believe women should be left to fester in ignorance. What is the point of a marriage where a husband cannot converse intelligently with his wife?"

Indeed, Thomas found himself thinking.

"Katarina and my niece are also Lutheran in their beliefs," Osiander continued. "Why, only last night, the three of us were discussing Luther's theory that the Pope has no authority to release people from purgatory. If he had this ability, surely he should have already freed everyone?"

"That is exactly what I believe!" Thomas felt the familiar thrill of excitement that accompanied the discovery of finding a kindred spirit. Meeting someone with similar opinions inevitably led to stimulating discussion.

"A local man called Johann Tetzel, a friar, used to sell indulgences in exchange for forgiveness of sins, and it really used to irk Luther and myself. In my opinion, it is ridiculous to contemplate that the soul can be released from purgatory simply via the exchange of money. Does this outrage happen in England?" Osiander asked, taking a vicious bite out of a piece of bread.

"Oh yes," Thomas confirmed, nibbling delicately at his bread. "There is a great outrage in England because of such practices. I long to see them purged from the realm, but the king, so far at least, does not seem inclined to abolish them."

They chatted comfortably until dinner was finally ready, and Katarina and Margaret came to join them. Blushing yet again, and keeping her eyes primly lowered, Margaret pushed a bowl of what looked like some kind of stew in Thomas' direction. During the course of the evening, his attention was continually drawn to the modest young woman, who was seated directly opposite him. He was, of course, being foolish, he reprimanded himself. He was over forty years old now, whilst she looked to be only around twenty. She was most probably engaged to be married already.

"Transubstantiation is something else which we are against. I suppose you, Thomas, concur with this?" Osiander enquired, as the women both nodded in agreement.

"Yes, indeed, I do," Thomas replied sincerely.

According to the Church of Rome, when the priest blessed the bread and the wine at Holy Communion, the bread and wine became the body and blood of Christ Himself, without changing substance. But the Protestants believed that, at the Last Supper, Jesus had merely stated that the bread and wine should be taken in *remembrance* of Him. They still considered taking Holy Communion to be a sacrament, but believed that

96

the bread and wine acted as a symbol, and did not become the body and blood of Christ.

"To be honest with you, at first, I was not so sure," he admitted. "I agreed with most Protestant doctrines, but I found this particular concept very difficult to immediately accept, most likely due to all the Catholic teaching I have been exposed to over the years."

"I understand. But once you take time to accept a doctrine, and that acceptance takes deep root, then it becomes entwined with your heart." Osiander vigorously thumped his chest. "From then onwards, you will never change your mind."

"I do deeply believe that the bread and wine do not become the body and blood of Christ and are instead symbols taken in memory of Christ's great sacrifice," he earnestly assured his host. "Once I had carefully studied the gospels, it suddenly became clear to me that transubstantiation is an error which leads people astray."

The women beamed in approval, as did Osiander.

"Unfortunately, I think it is something the Church of Rome and the Protestants will continue to argue about for years to come," he added.

"I am inclined to agree." Osiander nodded gravely. "Alas, so many people combine faith with superstition." Seeing the bemused look on his guest's face, he quickly explained. "It is because most cannot read and write, and even those that can do not know Latin. With such a limited education, how are they supposed to understand the Latin Vulgate Bible?"

"Exactly!" Thomas exclaimed enthusiastically. "The Bible needs to be translated into the language of the common man. How can someone who only speaks German or English ever hope to understand the words of the Vulgate Bible?"

97

The women were again nodding eagerly in agreement, and quietly exchanging excited comments with one another.

"In England, so many priests are illiterate, and I found it bizarre that people thought I was eccentric for insisting that the priests I trained were able to read, write and understand Latin. Surely, no priest who cannot read the Bible is fit to go out into the community and teach the common man?"

Osiander had leapt from his chair and was now energetically pacing around the room. "It is obvious, yet so many people do not seem to see it. An ignorant priest means the souls of the common man are in danger." He sat down suddenly. "That is why we, as reformists, must be prepared to lay down our lives for the cause. The very souls of our fellow men are at risk," he stated gravely.

He felt a sudden chill. He was not sure he was willing to lay down his life. When reformists were punished with death, it was never a quick, clean end; all too often, execution was preceded by torture. Then came the flames. Tyndale had been strangled prior to his burning, as a gesture of kindness, but it was said that the pain of his flesh being incinerated had brought him back to consciousness. He didn't know whether this was true or not, but either way, death by burning was horrific.

"In truth, I believe the position of 'Pope' is to blame for many of these lost souls." Osiander had resumed his pacing. "When Jesus asked Peter to feed his sheep, he was not telling Peter that no one could feed them without Peter's permission, and he was certainly not telling Peter to become a Pope!" His face was flushed with indignation.

Once again, Thomas wholeheartedly agreed.

"How dangerous is it to be Protestant in England?" Osiander enquired seriously, returning to his seat as Katarina and Margaret began to clear the empty platters and bowls from the table.

"If my faith were discovered, I would be charged with heresy, and thus imprisonment. Then, if I refused to recant, I would be burned at the stake."

"The same is true here, as you no doubt know by now." Osiander gave a deep sigh. "The emperor would love to bring the Spanish Inquisition into Germany; one day I suspect he will succeed. It is dangerous, certainly, to be anything other than Roman Catholic. But he has spent much of his reign so far asserting his authority over the French and the Pope, and has not yet given us his full attention, for which I am sincerely thankful, for The New Learning is taking root and spreading rapidly. I rejoice in that."

"Likewise," Thomas agreed. Though it was unsafe, he knew in his soul that they had to continue spreading the truth.

The evening passed quickly, and after a few more hours of discussion, Thomas suddenly realised the hour was late. Feeling embarrassed, he apologised for outstaying his welcome, but to his pleasure, he was urged to visit again very soon. Preferably tomorrow.

"We have much to discuss," Osiander assured him heartily. "I have enjoyed this evening very much."

"As have I," he replied earnestly.

During the next few weeks, Osiander began to take it for granted that, after debating and talking with various scholars and dignitaries during the day, Thomas Cranmer would come to his home to spend the evening. He was becoming increasingly fond of the articulate and intelligent theologian. As for Thomas, if he were honest enough to admit the truth, he was finding the quiet, gentle, Margaret Hosmer, very attractive indeed, though he supposed that she probably regarded him as some sort of uncle, rather than as a potential suitor.

The time was fast drawing near when he would leave Nuremberg, and despite having initially dreaded being sent on another foreign assignment, he was grateful for the experience. He had learned so much more about the Protestant faith, and had met many scholars, including a close friend of Luther's called Philip Melanchthon, who often debated with Osiander. Not long before Thomas was due to depart, Melanchthon accompanied him to dine at Osiander's house. Melanchthon was afflicted by a speech impediment, and one shoulder sat higher than the other, but neither of these hindered his work. His mind was sharp and his oratory brilliant, despite his stilted speech.

"I've heard that yourself and Luther have suggested to the king that he should consider taking a second wife... as in, polygamy," Thomas addressed Melanchthon gravely. After all, it seemed a ludicrous suggestion from two such undoubtedly devout Christians.

"It depends how you look at it," Melanchthon explained, as the three scholars sat gathered around Osiander's table with Katarina and Margaret. "First of all, the king is not truly married, so it would not be polygamy per se. Secondly, you have to look at this as a unique case. He is the ruler of a realm and must think of both the safety of the line of succession and the security of his kingdom. Catherine has thus far failed to provide him with a male heir, so it only natural that he should consider a second wife."

Thomas was silent for a moment, digesting this. "So, what you are suggesting is that, as the King of England, and being a free man according to the Bible, Henry does not require a divorce, and should simply marry Lady Anne?"

"Precisely," Melanchthon declared. "I do not know what is stopping him. He should just get on with it."

"He is fearful of offending the emperor," Thomas explained. Out of the corner of his eye, he could see Margaret, quietly seated at the table with Katarina. Both women were leaning forward, their elbows on the table, listening avidly to the conversation. His mind kept drifting. Soon, he would be saying farewell to the calm, gentle young woman whom he had become so fond of.

As the evening wore on, Katarina lit several oil lamps, and Margaret's smooth features became rosy and softened by the mellow glow. The women had both pulled shawls around their shoulders, enhancing their modest appearances and creating a homely scene, which reminded Thomas of an image from his distant past: his mother, sitting at their table with her shawl wrapped around her shoulders, passing food around, anxious to ensure that everyone had dined to their satisfaction and would not retire to their beds hungry.

Both women gave every appearance of enjoying the exchanges between the scholars, indeed, every time Thomas had visited the household, they had joined in as much as their limited knowledge of Greek and Latin would allow. It was an accepted fact that women's brains were unable to learn as effectively as men's, yet the two women present seemed to cope tremendously. They reminded him very much of some of the rare, educated ladies at court, Anne Boleyn included. His acquaintance of women was insufficient for him to draw any fully formed conclusions, but as far as he could tell, the female sex were quite capable of assimilating knowledge.

A mere twenty-four hours later, he was again dining at Osiander's house, partaking in a discussion with his host about his imminent departure to France with the rest of the Holy

Roman Emperor's Court. He sincerely hoped that his stay there would be brief, and that he would swiftly be given permission to return to England, but the emperor's plans often changed abruptly, so he could not be certain of anything.

His host's tone suddenly became more serious. "I have not failed to observe that you are much taken with my niece." Osiander was never afraid to cut straight to the heart of the matter.

The two men were seated outside in the small garden, enjoying some mild evening air together. Thomas had a feeling that his companion had deliberately manipulated the situation, so that they were able to talk alone.

"She is a good and virtuous young woman, but I am so much older than her..." He was quick to make his host aware that he had no intention of behaving in any untoward way.

"A man should always marry a younger woman," Osiander swiftly interrupted. "They age so much more quickly than men. A man needs a young, energetic wife to run his household, and to see to his needs. I would never have married a woman the same age as myself."

Thomas picked at the sleeve of his gown. Osiander's advice was nothing if not practical. Certainly, it was not sentimental. He found himself saying, "so, if I were to propose to your niece, you would be agreeable?" Mentally, he was trying to work out what would happen if he did marry Margaret Hosmer. His fellowship would be withdrawn, again. Except, this time, it would definitely not be returned. He would also lose his position as Archdeacon of Taunton, but he would still be permitted to teach, so they would be able to live comfortably – if modestly – on his earnings. Certainly, marrying Margaret would not be anything akin to his former marriage. Of this he was confident. Margaret and Joan had absolutely nothing in common.

"Of course I would be agreeable," Osiander declared. "Katarina tells me that the maid has been weeping these past two days because you are leaving. You must speak with her, the sooner the better." He was regarding his clearly astonished companion with almost comic surprise.

"This has come as something of a shock. I never expected to take a wife at this point in my life."

"You are no longer young; you have no time to waste," Osiander pronounced logically. Then, standing up, he instructed, "Remain here. I shall find my niece and send her out to you."

By the time he left Nuremberg, Thomas Cranmer had married for the second time.

*****

During the next few months, the emperor's Court travelled south-east, eventually meeting with reformists at Regensburg. The reformists were understandably cautious about speaking with the emperor – after all, he had recently declared, in public, that he would punish the Protestants for their heresy against the Church – but before any meeting could take place, Charles' mind was diverted. It was reported that Muslim Turks were set to invade Hungary, and the emperor's immediate response was to begin to muster an army, to drive the Turks away from land he considered to be Christian soil. Instead of heading to France, he decided to head towards Mantua, instructing the Pope to meet him there, to discuss strategy for a new holy war. Consequently, Thomas had to accept that it would be months before he and Margaret would be permitted to set sail for England.

During Thomas' time at Court, the emperor had taken a liking to the English theologian, choosing to overlook the rumours he had heard regarding his theology. He had also turned a blind eye to his female companion, for it was not unusual for priests to have a secret mistress. Unfortunately, despite his favour with the emperor, Thomas felt he was making about as much progress as he had made with the Pope over a year ago. It seemed to him that neither of them would ever agree to King Henry's divorce.

He and Margaret had decided to keep their marriage a secret for the moment, until the king decided to summon him back to England. He wanted to be able to explain himself before he tendered his resignation, on the grounds that being married meant he could no longer be a member of the clergy. He sighed. He would miss Cromwell, and he sincerely hoped that his friend would at least write to him sometimes. That would be gratifying. He would miss the king too, and his charismatic, larger than life personality. But life would be fulfilling in a much simpler way. The Court of King Henry VIII, with its plots and intrigues, was no place for him. He knew that. Soon, the Court of the Emperor Charles would be moving again, and he was weary of travelling. He wanted nothing more than to be summoned back to England and to resume a peaceful life. There came a light tapping on the door and Margaret's head appeared.

"Is time you eat. Abendessen?" she asked, smiling.

"Abendessen," he nodded. His once neglected German had vastly improved.

"English, please," she scolded fondly, leading the way into their small kitchen; one of the three rooms they were sharing during this visit. Since she was now the wife of an Englishman, and would be living in England soon, she insisted that they spoke as much English as possible. She would one day be running a household – a small one, admittedly – and she needed to be able to communicate, especially with the servants, else they would not respect her and would take liberties. When her English failed, she reverted to German, and hoped that Thomas could understand what she was saying. Usually, he could, but on those rare occasions when he could not, their misunderstandings afforded a source of rich entertainment.

Watching Margaret serve their simple meal, Thomas felt a deep contentment. Some men coped well with celibacy; certainly Latimer, Ridley and Bilney had never appeared to suffer for it. But he had always found unmarried life a struggle. For over a decade, he had endured celibacy because of his ghastly experience with Joan, but now, with this young woman, he had found someone who possessed a deep faith in God and a belief in the Protestant movement, combined with a kind and gentle spirit. He was content, and he had even ceased shaving the crown of his head, where his priestly tonsure had been, so confident was he that he would no longer be a priest once he returned to England.

They had only just finished eating when they heard a sharp knocking coming from the main room. Motioning for Margaret to remain seated, Thomas rose from his chair and hurried to open the door. It was a messenger, with a surprisingly brief letter from Cromwell. He began to read, and quickly discovered that one of his friends, Robert Barnes, had been incarcerated in the Fleet Prison, and would likely be charged with heresy, having been discovered vociferously preaching Protestant teachings. There was worse news to follow: Thomas Bilney had been burned at the stake in Norwich, also for heresy. He had been loudly proclaiming, in public, that the bread and wine were only symbolic of Christ's body and blood.

'I am sorry to be the agent of such terrible tidings', Cromwell wrote. 'But I wished for you to be informed swiftly, lest you hear the news elsewhere. It has to be said, there was an outcry over his sentence. He was universally loved. I very much suspect that Bishop Nix and Stephen Gardiner are behind it'.

He felt a wave of nausea. Bilney, the most innocent and gentle of them all, burned at the stake. According to the date on Cromwell's letter, Bilney had died over a month ago. Leaning forward, Thomas clutched his stomach, and Margaret gave a cry of dismay as her husband promptly parted company with his dinner.

Later, in bed, Margaret, her head nuzzled against his shoulder, asked, "Fühlst du dich jetzt besser? Dein Gesicht hat eine bessere Farbe."

"Yes, I feel better, though my sadness lingers." He rubbed his chin against the top of her head. "You're speaking in German... what has happened to your English?"

She looked thoughtful. "I think it disappeared wann your Gesicht war so pale. I think you feel better. Your Ges... face is a better... Farbe." She managed to smile. "I cannot remember the word in English."

"Colour, I think? Farbe means colour, doesn't it?" Thomas suggested.

"Ja, Farbe. Colour. You have the colour now. Not so pale."

"Well, I do feel less queasy," he reasoned. His wife's long, fair hair was draped over his bare shoulder and arm; looking at it, he regretted that women were not permitted to show their pretty hair in public.

"Vat are you thinking now, my Thomas?" she asked.

"I'm wishing you could wear your hair like this all of the time, instead of having it tucked away." He managed a faint smile.

"Nein!" She was horrified. "I cannot! It is not… it is not gut for a woman…" Again, she searched for a word and failed to find it.

"You mean, not respectable?" he mumbled into the top of her head.

"Re-spect-able," she pronounced slowly. "That is it. Not respectable. Only vicked vomen wear it so."

He wrapped his arm tightly around her. England was becoming a dangerous place for reforming Protestants. What would become of her if anything happened to him? Cromwell believed Gardiner had been involved in Bilney's death; when Gardiner became Archbishop of Canterbury, there would be even more deaths. Archbishop William Warham was over eighty years old now; his health was poor, and it was unlikely that he would live much longer. He tried to console himself with the notion that he might acquire a teaching position somewhere so obscure that no one would be concerned about his Protestant faith, but the chances of him finding such a safe position were unlikely at best. All he could do was pray to the good Lord that Stephen Gardiner would not be made Archbishop of Canterbury, and hope that whoever took the position would be more lenient towards his fellow reformists.

*****

In England, both Cromwell and Gardiner were attending upon the king. The Archbishop of Canterbury was unwell to a point beyond recovery, and it was generally accepted that he would not last very much longer. Gardiner, Cromwell gloomily realised, was the most likely man to be chosen to replace him, which was unfortunate as far as he was concerned, since Gardiner was a man whom he intensely disliked. Certainly, many others disliked him too: he was domineering, ruthless and sarcastic, but his clever mind and quick thinking made him useful to the king. However, Cromwell knew his friend Cranmer was also much admired by the king, and that there was a chance – a slim chance, but a chance nonetheless – that Cranmer might be selected in Gardiner's place. As was Cromwell's way, he began to ponder on how he might make this possibility a reality.

He and Gardiner were in the midst of listening to the king, who was voicing his desire for his clergy to be kept in their place. In His Majesty's view, the Church should be controlled by the sovereign of the realm and should obey his commands. Cromwell was nodding in agreement. This, in his opinion, was as it should be. But before he could speak, Gardiner frankly delivered his own opinion.

"Forgive me, Your Majesty, but I disagree. The Church should stand apart from the Crown," he declared in his brisk, dry voice. "The Church belongs to God and should therefore only answer to God. We should not need to seek external approval."

Cromwell had difficulty hiding a smile. This time, there had been no need for him to intervene. The king was furious, and his face reddened as he rose to his feet and ordered Gardiner out of the room. The matter was settled. There was no chance of Gardiner becoming   Archbishop of Canterbury now.

*****

Some weeks later, in mid-August, Thomas and Margaret found themselves in Matua, along with the rest of the emperor's Court. The summer heat was almost unbearable, and Thomas could not help but sentimentally recall the cool dampness of autumn in England; watching the leaves turn from green to brown and feeling a cool breeze blowing over his face. On the plus side, at least there was no plague in Mantua at this time of year.

Another letter had arrived from Cromwell, this time far longer, in which he informed Thomas that two academics had been despatched to Rome, having been instructed to search the Papal library for information which could be used to validate caesaropapism. Naturally, their task was gargantuan, for the library was huge, and neither the Pope nor his cardinals had offered to help them find the appropriate books. The academics had also been forbidden from copying anything down, and had been informed that a large collection of the library's books had been lost in transit, after the sacking of Rome. Cromwell revealed that the two of them had since written to the king, saying they felt despondent and that their mission was a failure. Thomas was saddened but not overly surprised to hear of this outcome, and he could not help but feel somewhat glad that he was not the only person to have failed to be successful in his mission. The progress towards a royal divorce was frustratingly stagnant.

Cromwell ended his letter by gleefully announcing that he had just secured a place on the king's council. It seemed the king had finally rewarded Cromwell's knowledge and talents. Thomas was pleased to know that things were going well for his very capable and very ambitious friend.

That evening, he and Margaret sat outside to eat their meal; the heat was so intense that neither of them had been able to contemplate the thought of eating until dusk, when the air was less heavy and stifling. Their lodging was comparatively luxurious compared to what they had been given previously, featuring both a ground floor and upper floor. The ground floor opened out onto a small, enclosed courtyard, and it was here that they had elected to dine and enjoy the cool of the evening.

"You must find it boring, my love, all of this travelling; spending time alone whilst I am meeting with people," Thomas remarked, once they had eaten their food.

"Sometimes," Margaret concurred candidly. "But not always. Mostly, I am practicing my English. I think I am improving." She looked to him for affirmation.

"I agree. Your English now far exceeds my German. You would make an excellent scholar." He patted her hand fondly.

"And I meet people too, so I am quite happy, my husband. When we get to England, I shall make a nice home for us. Plenty of good food and, God villing, children too."

The prospect of children was often in his thoughts, and he knew Margaret longed for them. He too wished to have children, but the prospect was terrifying. Childbirth was dangerous; he could not help but remember what had happened to Joan. He kept telling himself that some women did survive; after all, his own mother had given birth numerous times. But the sound of Joan's screams and the sight of her sightless eyes staring blankly up to the ceiling still haunted him.

"In God's own time, my dear." He patted his wife's hand again. The sky had grown dark, and the only illumination came from a lantern on the courtyard table. There was a sweet fragrance coming from a nearby climbing rose. "The air is so still," he remarked. "Yet it is not heavy, as when a storm is brewing…"

110

At that moment, there came a sudden, authoritative knocking upon the door. Laying a hand upon Margaret's shoulder, to indicate that she should remain where she was, he approached the door cautiously. Could it be a messenger from the emperor? A twinge of fear passed through him. Was it a summons? Was he to be accused of heresy? Unbolting the door, he opened it carefully to discover two messengers standing outside, wearing the royal livery of King Henry VIII.

"Dr Thomas Cranmer?" one of them enquired, in what could only be described as a peremptory tone.

"Y... yes," he stammered, feeling a surge of terror. Were they here to arrest him?

"For you." The other pulled a scroll from his sleeve and thrust it in Thomas' direction.

Managing to gather his wits, he opened the door fully. "Please... come in for some refreshment," he invited, his voice hoarse with relief. It appeared that no one was going to arrest him tonight.

"Thank you, but we have plans to go elsewhere for refreshment." Both messengers bowed before stepping back. They had spotted a suitable tavern nearby, which seemed a far more exciting establishment than the lodgings of a scholar.

Clutching the scroll, Thomas walked back into the courtyard, where Margaret was now standing, her eyes wide with anxiety. "Is all vell?" she whispered.

"Yes... well, I hope so. I need to read this." He waved the scroll aloft. Henry's personal royal seal glinted in the lantern's flickering light. "It is clearly something of importance." He began to unroll it, holding it as close to the lantern as was possible without setting it alight.

Margaret rushed into the house to find another lantern. Returning, she held it over the scroll.

Having read the contents, Thomas sat down heavily.

"Vas ist falsch?" Margaret asked, her English now entirely forgotten.

"What's wrong?" He laughed humourlessly. "Everything is wrong. The Archbishop of Canterbury, William Warham, has died. He died a few weeks ago." He took a deep breath, trying to assimilate the news he had received. "I am informed, by His Majesty the king, that I have been appointed as Warham's successor. I am the new Archbishop of Canterbury."

Taking a deep breath, Margaret digested this. "Aber es ist eine Ehre... it is an honour, my husband. Warum bist du verzweifelt?"

"I am of insufficient status to be archbishop. I am only Archdeacon of Taunton. The Pope made me Penitentiary for England last year while I was in Rome, but that is nothing compared to..." He nearly choked on the word. "... archbishop. So many others are better—"

Margaret firmly interrupted. "Nein. No one vill do better than you."

"It's not as simple as that." He shook his head. "You see, apart from my being ill-suited, I am also married. It was my intention to resign my fellowship once we returned to England, obtain a teaching position, and have done with the matter. I will never regret marrying you," he assured her earnestly. "But the Archbishop of Canterbury simply cannot be married." Thomas read the letter again, hoping he had misunderstood the contents.

He had not.

"Can you not just tell king you are married?" It seemed very simple in her opinion.

"No." He shook his head vehemently. She did not know King Henry. "If our marriage were discovered, I could be imprisoned, or even executed. The Archbishop of Canterbury cannot be a married man, it is forbidden. A mere priest cannot marry, let alone the Archbishop of Canterbury!" He began to pace around the courtyard, thinking rapidly and running his fingers through his hair.

Margaret sat silently beside him, trying to think of something helpful to say and failing miserably, fearing this good and kindly man regretted marrying her. Even worse, he might wish to divorce her. Taking a deep breath, she tried not to weep.

"This is what I shall do," he finally spoke. "What we shall do," he amended, allaying her fears. "If we delay leaving Mantua long enough, the king might change his mind, and consecrate someone else as archbishop."

She nodded, watching him expectantly, her eyes fixed upon his face.

"Yes, we will delay returning to England. Then, if that fails…" He looked at his wife with an uncertain expression. "Would you find it very humiliating if you were to join my household and pose as… I don't know… a housekeeper, perhaps? No." He shook his head. "That is far too much to ask—"

"No, I vill do anything!" she exclaimed, leaping up and flinging her arms about his neck, nearly knocking a lantern from the table in the process. "I am just happy you do not regret marrying me."

He held her tightly. "I could never regret marrying you. But the king might regret making a man such as myself Archbishop of Canterbury."

Leaning back in his arms, Margaret studied him thoughtfully. "I think it is God's vill," she suggested calmly, her earlier panic subsiding rapidly. "Have you not thought of that?"

113

"No," he admitted, smiling softly. "You see? You were destined to be my wife, to remind me of that." He drew her towards him, resting his chin upon her head.

"Yes, I was," she agreed, giving a deep sigh of relief. "Remind me, what does this word 'destined' mean?"

*****

The following day, the messengers returned, expecting to receive a reply. They had no idea what the contents of the scroll had been, but since the king had sent them to Mantua in search of Dr Thomas Cranmer, it seemed likely that a reply would be in order. However, to their surprise, there was no reply, only another offer of refreshment before they set out on their journey back to England.

"What exactly do ve do now?" Margaret asked curiously.

"The same as we have been doing for the past few months… well, over half a year now," he amended. "We remain with the emperor's Court, and I shall continue to try and persuade him to agree to the king's divorce. Hopefully King Henry will forget about me."

"If this is what God vishes you to do, your English king, he vill not forget about you," Margaret cautioned.

"If the king does not forget about me, I shall accept it as the will of God," he sighed. The king ruled through God's will, so it was unthinkable not to obey him. If King Henry wished for him to be Archbishop of Canterbury, then Archbishop of Canterbury he must be.

Chapter Six

Thomas lingered, delaying his departure for as long as he dared, but King Henry did not change his mind. Thomas Cranmer was to become the next Archbishop of Canterbury. He reckoned he must be the most unwilling person to ever occupy such an exalted position; he knew that Stephen Gardiner would have gladly accepted the role. With no option left but to return to England, he arranged for Margaret to travel back to Germany and remain in Osiander's protection for the time being. He optimistically calculated that perhaps, in a few months' time, she would be able to join him. With much weeping, and a promise to arrive speaking English more fluently than the English people themselves, she departed. He did not doubt her. She was gentle and sweet-tempered, but tenacious, and he had quickly learned that if she set out to do something, she did it.

He was replaced in the emperor's Court by a man called Nicholas Hawkins, to whom he sold most of the linen, bowls, and culinary utensils that he and Margaret had accumulated. He wished to travel to England unencumbered by a pile of worldly goods. Unwilling to overcharge Hawkins, he sold the items for far less than they were worth; as for the books he had purchased whilst abroad, they were another matter entirely. Most of them would be travelling with him.

It was painful parting with Margaret, therefore his return journey to England was utterly miserable. It was late February when he finally returned to York Place, where he would stay until Lambeth Palace, the London seat of the Archbishops of Canterbury, was ready for him. He was grateful for the delay, for York Place was comfortable and familiar.

Unsurprisingly, upon his return to his homeland, his first visitor was Cromwell, who arrived beaming with delight and offering him hearty congratulations. In fact, everyone had been loud in their congratulations, especially Sir Thomas Boleyn and his family. Thomas was well aware that his first duty as Archbishop of Canterbury would be to proclaim King Henry VIII a free man, able to marry his sweetheart, who was residing at Court. According to Lady Boleyn, Anne's temper had improved of late, though Thomas had yet to see for himself whether this was true.

"You certainly took your time returning to England." Cromwell restlessly paced around the room his friend had been using as a study since first arriving at York Place. "Just think, soon you shall be installed in your own palace. You must visit directly and take a look at it. Personally, I've never been over the threshold – I never had cause to visit poor old Warham – but I predict you will have room aplenty for your books." He glanced around the room his friend currently occupied. It was clearly inadequate; there were books piled upon every available surface, including the floor.

"That's one good thing about it, I suppose," Thomas muttered gloomily.

"So, why the long delay?" Cromwell demanded. "You delayed six weeks by my estimation. I would have set out straight away, lest the king should change his mind." Unhooking his cloak, Cromwell flung it over a chair. As always, he was conservative in his attire, though his clothes were clearly of good quality.

"I don't doubt it." Thomas managed a faint smile. He and Cromwell were complete opposites, at least, when it came to certain matters. So far, he had not informed his friend of his marriage; in fact, he had informed none of his friends of his marriage. For a fleeting moment, he longed to confide in Cromwell, but after a brief moment of hesitation, changed his mind.

Seating himself and leaning back against his chair, legs splayed out comfortably in front of him, Cromwell helped himself to a mug of ale, since his companion seemed incapable of performing his duty as a host. Smiling mischievously, lowering his voice he asked in a staged whisper, "so, when will your wife be joining you?"

"My wife?"

Cromwell tried not to laugh. His friend's eyes looked about ready to pop out of his face, and his sallow skin was suddenly deathly pale. "Yes, your wife. Oh, don't worry, Cranmer. I am the only person at Court who knows, and I just happen to be an expert at keeping my mouth shut. Your secret is safe with me." He laid a reassuring hand upon his friend's arm, though he had not been entirely truthful. His spies had informed him that the new archbishop was married, so it was more than likely that the king himself was also aware of the situation, having been informed by his own spies. "But I do sympathise. What a difficult situation to be in." There was genuine compassion in his gaze.

How on Earth had Cromwell discovered his secret? Thomas anxiously picked at the sleeve of his gown, loath to speak aloud of his marriage.

"Come now, why so surprised? I have spies everywhere." Cromwell's expression switched from sympathy to amusement. "It is my business to know things. Why, I knew Lady Anne to be with child even before the king himself heard the glad tidings."

"With child?" Thomas gasped.

"Pregnant," Cromwell clarified.

Thomas was torn between surprise and curiosity. "How on Earth did you manage to discover that? And before His Majesty?" It was surely not possible.

"Very simply, my friend. I bribe her attendants on a regular basis, and they have always kept me informed about the regularity of her menstrual cycle." Cromwell explained this as if it was a perfectly ordinary thing to do.

"Cromwell!" Thomas rebuked, appalled. Why on Earth would anyone wish to know about such an intimate matter?

"Anne finally surrendered herself to the king, in the knowledge that His Majesty is now so desperate for an heir that he will not hesitate to marry her if she becomes pregnant. You see..." Cromwell leaned forward confidentially, resting his elbows on his knees. "Once the king informed her that you would become Archbishop of Canterbury, she instantly agreed to become his mistress. She is no fool; she is well aware that you will pronounce the king free to marry and will perform a ceremony between her and King Henry." Examining his fingernails with sudden intensity, Cromwell added, with exaggerated casualness, "of course, I might also have dropped a few hints in her direction that now would be a good time to produce a royal heir to the throne. A couple of months later, one of her ladies informed me that her monthly cycle had abruptly ceased."

"You're incorrigible," Thomas gasped, marvelling at his friend's audacity.

"Be that as it may, it has all worked out well," Cromwell replied breezily. "Anyway, enough of my schemes. I am here to escort you to His Majesty. He wishes to meet with his new Archbishop of Canterbury. I would suggest you don't refuse the position..." His voice trailed away.

"I fear I would be imprisoned, at the very least, if I were to refuse," Thomas muttered. "But I have no intention of doing so. After much thought, it eventually occurred to me that it may have been God's own will that led me to this position. Perhaps He wishes for me to rescue the souls of England's people from the heresy of the Church of Rome?"

Cromwell nodded. "It could well be so." He recognised his companion's sincerity and respected it. He too supported the Protestant cause, but his support came secondary to his own ambition. He became brisk. "The king wishes to see you as soon as possible, and though the barge waits, the tide does not. We must go to Court, now. I suggest you change your gown; the one you are wearing looks as though it has seen better days. In fact, it looks as though it has seen better years."

After a short journey downriver, they arrived at Hampton Court, to find the king looking pleased with himself. Standing beside him was Lady Anne Boleyn, who looked calm and serene; her sullen discontent had been erased. The king had recently honoured her by making her Marquess of Pembroke, a rare gesture, since women were seldom given a title in their own right.

After the initial greetings and congratulations, the king approached the matter at hand. "We have already sent the necessary Bulls to Pope Clement, so that your consecration may take place as soon as possible," he announced. "We must marry the Marquess without delay." The king shot a proud, doting glance towards his lady.

Thomas was silent. Papal Bulls? He was less than keen to become archbishop, but if he must be Archbishop of Canterbury, then he wished to be consecrated according to the Protestant faith.

"What is wrong, our good archbishop?" the king demanded.

Aware of Cromwell's solid, stocky frame standing beside him, Thomas felt strengthened. If he must offend the king, then it would be better to do it now. That way, there would still be time to appoint another archbishop. Speaking his thoughts might mean disgrace, or worse, but he felt he had no choice. He refused to go against his faith. Taking a deep breath, he managed to rally both his thoughts and his courage. "Your Majesty, I cannot accept this position from the Pope." His voice seemed to be coming from far away.

"Why not?" Henry's voice was clipped.

"I thank Your Grace for bringing me here, in spite of my humble status," he replied slowly, choosing his words carefully. "However, because I can only accept you, my king, as Head of the English Church, you alone have the authority to appoint me as the next Archbishop of Canterbury. My conscience cannot acknowledge any other authority; certainly, I cannot take it from the hand of the Pope." There, it was said. The king would recognise the Protestant theology, and he would be escorted from Hampton Court and placed in the Fleet Prison, from which Robert Barnes had recently been released. It occurred to him he might even be given Barnes' vacated cell.

While speaking, Thomas had kept his eyes firmly lowered, his gaze directed towards the king's feet, fixed upon His Majesty's crimson shoes, adorned with gems and slashed to display their white silk linings. They were magnificent shoes.

Impractical, of course, but magnificent. Until he had come to Court, he had never realised people could adorn their feet in such a way. Eventually, after a moment of silence, he cautiously raised his eyes upwards, only to find the king grinning delightedly.

"We understand your concern, and we will do all we can to soothe your conscience," said the king. "But, as king, we must also consider the stability of the realm. Unlike some rulers, we must take care not to rouse the common people with a sudden change, lest we give them cause to revolt; and we must also be wary of our foreign neighbours. We cannot give cause for our enemies to invade us."

Cromwell was silent, finding himself altogether surprised by his friend Cranmer's sudden display of sheer bravery. He had clearly underestimated not only the man himself, but also his devotion to the Protestant faith. The man had spoken out in front of the king. It was something he could never have imagined Cranmer doing.

"What say you, Master Cromwell?" the king demanded.

"I would say that, at this moment, the emperor is too busy sending troops to drive the heathen Turks out of Hungary to worry about what is happening in England. I cannot vouch for the King of France as of yet."

"We have also taken the precaution of appeasing the emperor by sending men to accompany his army and support his cause," Henry mused aloud.

There was no better time than the present for the king to announce himself as being free to marry. The emperor would certainly be angered, but for the time being, his attention was diverted. As for Thomas' own first task as archbishop, it would at least not offend his conscience. As he saw it, the king had never been married in the first place, so declaring him a free

121

man, and therefore able to marry Lady Anne Boleyn, would not trouble him.

"Regarding my desire not to accept Papal authority, I can show Your Majesty the relevant pieces of scripture which support this," Thomas murmured, wondering if this was the point at which the king would grow angry. But once again, as he cautiously glanced at the royal visage, he saw nothing but approval.

"We would gladly see these writings you speak of." Henry smiled benignly. "As you all know, we are guided by scripture." His small mouth became prim. "Did we not cast aside the woman whom we believed we had married, once we realised it was a sinful liaison?"

Cromwell kept his gaze decorously lowered. The king was such a master of self-deception, it was almost impossible keep a straight face sometimes. Queen Catherine was ageing, and past the age of childbirth. Anne Boleyn was glamorous and fertile. It was pure lust which had ended his first marriage, but the king was determined to dress it up it as virtue, so all his courtiers sycophantically applauded the king's sacrificial decision to end his union with Catherine.

"Indeed, Your Majesty," Thomas replied, totally accepting the king's statement.

For some time, they discussed the application for Papal Bulls, along with the consecration ceremony, which would be held in due course. After a while, the king demanded that some of his theologians should be summoned, to address the problem. The fact was, he was looking to make a break with Rome, but it was a unique situation. No monarch had done it before, and he was uncertain how to go about it, without upsetting the Pope, the Emperor Charles, and King Francis of France. He might be able to garner support from the Protestant

German princes, but they were not as powerful as Charles and Francis. He also liked the idea of being Head of the English Church; even more, he liked a suggestion Cromwell had recently made to him. The monasteries were a source of wealth, and he had already gleaned a lot of money from some of them by issuing fines to the abbots and abbesses for their lewd behaviour. But Cromwell had suggested closing them in their entirety, as the money rightly belonged to the king anyway - so said the devious Cromwell. It was exceedingly tempting.

Many hours passed, and it was almost evening before any agreement was reached, an agreement which Thomas was not altogether happy with. Wishing to appease the Pope for the time being – Pope Clement could easily arrange for an army to invade England if he so wished – Papal Bulls were a requirement. Then followed the problem of the Consecration Oath. Traditionally, this was made to Rome, but Thomas Cranmer was adamant that he could not make it.

It was the theologian, Dr Oliver, who proposed a solution. Thomas Cranmer should take the usual oath, then, after this, he would take a second one, stating that he would not admit papal authority any further than the word of God allowed. Furthermore, it would be lawful for him at any time to correct papal errors when the occasion demanded.

Thomas was unhappy, but everyone else was heaving sighs of relief. This was the nearest to a perfect solution they had come to, and everyone was ready to retire for the night. He sighed, ruffling his hair and setting his cap askew. It seemed dishonest to make the traditional oath when he had no intention of adhering to it. Plus, as far as he could see, the second oath did not correct matters.

The king was radiating delight, and the Marquess of Pembroke, who had long since quit the room out of sheer boredom, returned to find the situation was now resolved to everyone's satisfaction, apart from the new archbishop himself.

The following day, Anne visited York Place, and without being formally announced, entered the study of the new archbishop. The room was crowded, as ever, with books, and she spent a few moments simply staring, her face a mask of astonishment. Regaining her poise, she declared, "You were once my chaplain."

"And I shall always be so," he assured her, smiling as he beheld her expression. "I have yet more books in my bedchamber. When I move to Lambeth, I shall have plenty of space to arrange them." Rising, he bowed, offering her his seat; the only one which was not decorated with a pile of books.

"Have you read all of them?" she enquired in wonderment, accepting his chair.

"Most," he admitted. "There are some I have just skimmed through; others I have dipped into for information. But mostly, they have all been read."

Anne continued to marvel at his impressive collection of literature for a moment, before remembering that she had come with a purpose. "I wish to ask your advice on something, my lord Archbishop. You see, I am confused about confession. It is so much part of the Church of Rome, but I am soon to marry the king, and I seek to take my vows with my sins forgiven," she solemnly informed him.

"We should retire to the chapel," he suggested quietly. "People often enter this room to speak with me; we may be interrupted."

In silence, they walked to the chapel. Whilst he had long ago discounted the requirement of making confession to a priest, and also of receiving absolution from a priest, he was more than willing to listen to people who wished to unburden themselves of their troubles. Lady Anne glided ahead of him in total silence, her pregnancy totally invisible beneath her tightly corseted bodice. Was this lady troubled? Surely not. She was about to achieve her dearest wish: marrying the king.

Once they arrived at the small chapel, they made their way to the corner furthest away from the door.

For a moment, Anne sat in silence. Then, fixing Thomas with a direct, penetrating stare, she asked, "do you find it strange not to make confession to one of your fellow priests?"

"No, my lady," he replied, his voice low. "As soon as I accepted that confession need only be between oneself and God, I was at peace. I instantly ceased confessing to a priest. Sometimes I feel a need to talk or seek counsel, but that is another matter entirely."

"It must be a habit... I am about to commence a whole new life, and I want to begin it absolved in the eyes of God." Her voice had risen slightly, and she quickly lowered it. "For some strange reason, even though I know it is not necessary, I need to hear from you that I am absolved by God."

"If you are repentant, God has forgiven you." He gave an encouraging smile. "You see, Jesus left heaven and came to Earth for you. He gave His life for you - such is His love. He is longing for you to speak with Him, to confess your errors, and He longs to forgive," he assured her.

His smile was always gentle and kind; she had often noticed that. It encouraged her to be honest. "That is the problem, my lord Archbishop. I am not repentant. I have not committed adultery; you have made it clear Henry was never married to that Spanish woman. But clearly..." She patted her outwardly flat abdomen and left her hand lying there protectively. "Clearly I have lain with Henry and conceived his son."

125

"You do not wish to repent of engaging in a sexual union outside of marriage?" he clarified.

She was silent, reflecting upon her situation for a moment, wondering how to explain what was happening to the new archbishop, though she did not doubt he was already aware of it. She was to marry the king; it was all arranged. Yet, in just over a week, there was to be a Court, held in Paris, where Pope Clement and the French king, Francis, would declare whether they believed Henry's marriage to Catherine was invalid. Henry had falsely led them to believe that he would abide by their opinion.

If it were announced that Henry's marriage to Catherine was legitimate, Pope Clement would certainly refuse a Papal Bull permitting his new marriage. Henry desired not only for the English theologians to proclaim him free to marry, but also the Church of Rome. Anne seethed inwardly. Life was so complicated. But she was now certain of one thing: Henry was determined that the son she carried would be born in wedlock, so that no one would be able to query his legitimacy.

Finally, she replied to the archbishop's question. "No, I do not. I had to lie with Henry. I wanted him to marry me, but he kept worrying over the Emperor Charles invading; the Pope invading; the French invading... he worried over everything. As soon as we knew Warham was about to die, Henry decided you should be the next Archbishop of Canterbury, so I gave myself to him; praise God, I conceived quickly. Thus, here we are, in this chapel. I am troubled in spirit, because I want forgiveness, yet I am glad I acted the way I did. What am I to do?" She shot a challenging glance towards her companion. "And what shall happen to my soul if I die in childbirth, still unrepentant?"

"First of all, God does not judge as we judge," he explained. "You worry because you are unrepentant for this sin, and it is a sin. But it could be that you have committed other, worse transgressions. You see..." He leaned forward confidentially. "During your prayers, you need to peacefully sit with God, searching your soul for the sins you have unwittingly committed. These are every bit as serious," he explained earnestly. "God is a communicating God; He longs for you to talk to Him, and to tell Him everything."

"How easy it was when I believed in just paying for an indulgence." She gave a wry smile. "Just pay the priest, and you are cleared of all blame. But you helped me to realise the falseness of such a practice; I am indebted to you for that."

"And I am grateful to you for your open mind, my lady. It pains me that this practice still happens within the Church," he murmured. "I used to know a marvellous man named Thomas Bilney, whom I doubt you ever knew..." It was difficult to speak of Bilney without choking up; the pain of his passing remained a raw wound.

Anne shook her head and gazed at him expectantly.

"Bilney did much to convince me of The New Learning. He once told me of the moment he realised forgiveness comes from God alone. He said to me: 'my vigils; my fasts; my pilgrimages; my purchases of masses and indulgences... they were destroying me instead of saving me'. I knew then that all God desired from us was repentance to Him. I suggest you take some time to be quiet and contemplative. Talk exclusively to God; tell Him all you have told me. Then, listen to what your heart is saying. I sense you *are* repentant, otherwise you would not feel such a need for absolution."

"You have read my soul, my lord Archbishop," she rose, indicating that their interview was over. "As you have always done. It is as though you can see straight through me."

He hardly knew what to say. "That I cannot do, my lady, but I shall always be here to help you unburden yourself, both now and when you are queen."

She extended a hand for him to kiss, then swept out of the chapel, walking as though she already wore a crown upon her head.

Just a few days later, at Hampton Court Chapel, in the grey light of dawn, Thomas performed a marriage ceremony between King Henry VIII of England and Lady Anne Boleyn, Marquess of Pembroke. There were few witnesses, just a couple of Anne's ladies, and two of Henry's gentlemen, one of whom, inevitably, was Thomas Cromwell, who seemed to be included in all things these days.

"He's putting the plough before the horse," Cromwell remarked to Cranmer, whilst they awaited the arrival of the bride and groom. He was alluding to the fact that the king's divorce had not yet been publicly announced.

"Hmm… I don't think so," Thomas murmured. "Since His Majesty has never been lawfully married, there is no actual need to declare him divorced, is there?"

"But the king wishes for you to announce his divorce anyway," Cromwell persisted.

"Yes," Thomas shrugged

Cromwell chuckled. "His Majesty is a true example of a man who believes he can have his mutton and eat it." Cromwell's voice became hushed as the king and Anne entered the Chapel.

Exchanging fond glances, the couple proceeded to kneel upon two newly made, lavishly padded stools. Anne looked tense, pale and wan; she had been sick twice before leaving her chamber, and the smell of tallow from the nearby candles was not helping matters. Her leather stays were also laced far too tightly, for she wanted no evidence of her pregnancy to be visible as of yet. Henry considered it wise to hide her condition for the time being, and to delay the announcement of their marriage until after the Papal Bulls for the consecration of the new Archbishop of Canterbury had been signed. He also clung optimistically to the hope the Pope might, at the same time, also sign Bulls granting him permission to wed Anne.

The ceremony was brief, and as Henry heartily kissed his new wife, Anne felt a surge of triumph, which eliminated her earlier tension. She was queen. Queen of England. No one could say this marriage was anything but legal; Cranmer himself had assured her of his belief that Henry was a single man. After a six-year courtship, she was finally queen.

Offering his congratulations, Thomas decided against bringing up his opinion that the king really should have waited until after he had been consecrated as Archbishop of Canterbury, and had publicly declared Henry free to marry. Following this, a public announcement could have been made, stating that Henry would be marrying the Marquess of Pembroke. That would have been the most dignified way to go about it. What really irked him – and the new queen, for that matter – was that the king was still persistently hoping to obtain a Papal Bull from Rome. King Henry had explained that he wanted to ensure that no one could cast doubt upon his new marriage, or the legitimacy of his unborn son, but Thomas wished that the king would cast aside his fears and have confidence in the Protestant faith.

Watching the departing couple, Cromwell gave his friend a conspiratorial nudge. "The king wishes this to be a secret and wants no one to know she is pregnant. Some hope." He gave a snort of laughter. "Yesterday, Anne was telling Tom Wyatt, the poet, that she has an uncontrollable desire to eat apples, and that the king had told her she must be pregnant. She then went on to laugh off Henry's claims, telling Wyatt that it could not be. A man with Wyatt's lack of discretion will not permit such a juicy item of gossip to slip through his fingers without passing it on."

Discretion was also not in Anne's nature, even Thomas could see that.

"You know how Luther once remarked that the king should be allowed two wives, for the sake of providing an heir," Cromwell whispered.

"Yes, of course," Thomas replied, wondering where this was leading.

"Well, once this is made public, we have to accept that certain Catholic adherents will perceive that His Majesty has committed bigamy," Cromwell continued.

Thomas was silent, still wondering where this was going.

Cromwell's brow was furrowed in thought. "I was just contemplating how we might best deal with them…"

*****

By April, he was installed in Lambeth Palace. The king had been kind enough to lend him some money to furnish the place, and also pay for other commodities, whilst he waited to receive revenue from his new position. It was immensely gratifying to be treated in such a familiar manner by the king; he felt a great deal of admiration and respect for His Majesty, so to be treated as a friend was a great honour. God willed that he should love and serve his king, but where King Henry was concerned, it was a joy to do so.

His days were busy, far more so than they had ever been previously, but sometimes he received a break from his work, in the form of an invitation from the king to go hunting with him. The king's companions, usually including the Duke of Suffolk, who was the king's robust and energetic brother-in-law, were initially startled by the horsemanship of the new archbishop. He suspected they had anticipated he would be a timid companion, clinging timorously to his horse's mane - but had been confident in the saddle since childhood.

He felt that, at least as far as hunting was concerned, he had gained a small degree of respect, though that feeling was accompanied by a sobering thought. How much longer would the king continue to treat him in this way? Perhaps there would come a day when the king no longer looked to him for advice? After all, he assumed that the king had once approved of his predecessor, William Warham, yet by the time Warham died, the king had been seriously considering imprisoning the old man. Thomas knew the depth of his own loyalty to the king, but would the king be loyal to him? Probably not. He very much doubted his ability to continue to constantly please his master.

The consecration ceremony was to take place tomorrow, in the Chapter House of King's College, situated near to the Palace of Westminster. Thomas had written a protestation that evening, which he was determined to deliver, having deliberated for some time over the formality of the actual wording. He intended to deliver it at the very beginning of the ceremony, to explain that the vows he was going to make would merely be a matter of form. He also wanted to stress that, in his opinion, the true Head of the English Church was King Henry VIII. By doing this, his conscience would be eased regarding the vows. Peace of conscience came before everything else. He was anxious – terrified, in fact – about the outcome of his

131

protestation. To be viewed as a Protestant was dangerous; despite the measure of support coming from the king, The New Learning was still seen as heresy.

After a sleepless night, he was taken to the Chapter House, to be robed in readiness for the ceremony. All too soon, the two great symbols of his position would be bestowed upon him. The pallium – a Y shaped strip made from white lamb's wool, newly sheared on the twenty first of January, the feast of St. Agnes, in accordance with tradition – would be placed around his neck, over his robes. Then, the crosier, or pastoral staff, would be placed in his right hand. This held more significance to him than anything else pertaining to his regalia, for it symbolised the role of the Lord Himself, according to the gospel of St. John, wherein He identified Himself as The Good Shepherd. As Archbishop of Canterbury, however reluctant he might be to assume the role, he must also assume the role of a shepherd, who must follow Christ's example and lead his flock along a path to salvation.

As he walked into the Chapter House, he caught a glimpse of Stephen Gardiner, whose fury at not being selected was evident in his expression. According to Cromwell, when Thomas had first returned to England, Gardiner had looked as though he had just swallowed a wasp's nest. Even now he was looking sour, his gaze fixed straight ahead, instead of being turned towards the procession of clergy ponderously making their way down the aisle.

Until this moment, he had felt relatively calm; only a mild flutter of anxiety had been lurking at the back of his mind. But now, he felt breathless, his heart pounding in his chest like that of a frightened rabbit. He could feel the beads of sweat forming on his palms, and he was struck by a sudden fear that the crosier, when he received it, would immediately slip from his grasp. What sort of message would that send out to the watching bishops and clergy? Collecting himself, he managed to deliver his protestation, much to the surprise of John Longland, the Bishop of Lincoln, who was officiating the ceremony. Such events usually followed the same traditional pattern, and it was most unusual for that pattern to be disrupted, especially by the soon-to-be archbishop. Thomas could hear an astonished murmuring from the observing clergy echoing around the room.

Next, he took his oath to the Pope, and holy oil was placed on his head and fingers. The pallium was then placed about his neck, and the crosier was handed to him; to his infinite relief, it remained firmly clasped in his damp hand. Another oath was then required, also to the Pope, and once again, prior to delivering it, he made another protestation. Following this, he made an additional oath to the king – the wording of which he had already discussed with His Majesty – declaring that his allegiance was, and always would be, to King Henry VIII.

Suddenly, his heartbeat slowed, and he felt calm again. Resuming the tone that he had used throughout his career as a teacher at Cambridge, he coolly addressed the assembled clergy. "I, Thomas Cranmer, renounce and utterly forsake all such clauses within the oath I am about to make which are, or may be, hurtful or prejudicial towards His Majesty, his heirs, estates, or royal dignity." He glanced around the Chapter House, and found everyone's gaze fixed upon him, each face a mask of astonishment. "I also henceforth renounce all financial ties with the Church of Rome, and acknowledge myself to take on the archbishopric immediately, and only, for His Majesty, King Henry. I promise to be a faithful and obedient servant to His Majesty, his heirs and successors, for as long as I shall live. So help me God."

There, it was said. His clergy now knew where he stood. He would accept no income from the Pope, only from the diocese of Canterbury itself, a decision which no doubt his predecessors would have baulked at. He was set to become the poorest Archbishop of Canterbury England had seen in a long time, but having never sought wealth, this did not trouble him.

After making his final, if somewhat unnecessary, oath to the Pope, the consecration was over, and Thomas was finally free to return to the peace of his own personal library in Lambeth Palace, sit down with a book, and ignore the outside world for a while. After the stress and intensity of the morning's events, it was well needed.

*****

His first task as Archbishop of Canterbury was to present a Bill of Restraint of Appeals to Parliament, which forbade anyone from making an appeal to the Pope in Rome. This included the Princess Catherine, who wished to contact the Pope to complain about her new title: the Dowager Princess of Wales. The king insisted that referring to his brother's wife by any other name was treason, though she stubbornly continued to call herself 'the queen'. The passing of the Bill was no mean feat, and it took all of King Henry's charm and authority to push it though.

Unsurprisingly, the requested Papal Bulls, permitting the king's new marriage, had not arrived. The French king and the Pope had firmly decided that Henry was not permitted to divorce his first wife, and was, therefore, not free to remarry. Following the archbishop's consecration, the Pope had sent a nuncio to England, a man called de Borgo, whose thankless task was to present King Henry with a brief, instructing him to separate from Anne until his case for divorce was tried yet again. Somehow, King Henry managed to persuade de Borgo not to present him with the brief, though no one knew how. Cromwell informed Thomas that it was through bribery, which Thomas conceded was the most probable explanation. The king could be exceptionally charming in manner, and when handing out bribes to dignitaries and ambassadors, he could be very difficult to resist.

Almost immediately following his consecration, Thomas issued a document pronouncing the king to be a single man and free to remarry. This was followed five days later by an announcement that the king was now lawfully married to the Lady Anne Boleyn, Marquess of Pembroke; an announcement which was taken in sullen silence by the people of London. Anne had never attempted to cut a popular figure with the Londoners, whereas Catherine had been widely loved for her grace, dignity, and compassion for the weak and poor.

Following his declaration regarding Catherine's title, the king also declared that his daughter, Mary, formerly known as Princess Mary, should be referred to as nothing other than Lady Mary. In retaliation, mother and daughter insisted that their household staff should address them only by their former titles, and Catherine ordered new liveries for her servants, embroidered with the intertwined letters H and C.

Furious, Anne, not to be outshone by her predecessor, walked to Mass attended by sixty ladies in waiting; Catherine had always made do with thirty. Her gowns, already sumptuous, were even more so now, and Henry uxoriously indulged her every whim, even designing a new crown for her coronation. All the carvings and tapestries, in every Royal Palace, that had not already been altered were immediately changed. Each building echoed with the cacophony of stone masons and

135

carpenters, hammering and chiselling at the initials on the walls, whilst embroiderers strained their eyes in the gloom as they undertook alterations to the hangings.

This likewise applied to the Royal Barge, which now featured the letters H and A on all its curtains and banners, as well as on the woodwork. Inevitably, when the Londoners saw the barge passing, they jeered and laughed, even though tongues could be removed for such mockery. Indeed, Anne demanded this punishment, but no one came forward to condemn anyone for such disrespect.

"She is greatly disliked," Cromwell remarked one evening, as he and Thomas were walking though the gardens of Lambeth Palace.

Thomas nodded contemplatively. Anne was no fool, so he found it strange that she had not attempted to endear herself to the common people. King Henry recognised that his subjects were the ones who kept him on the throne, and his genial, bluff manner endeared him to everyone. But Anne seemingly believed she was above them.

"I wish she would do more to make herself loved… or even just respected," Cromwell added. "And not only amongst the common people. She offends courtiers left, right and centre. She flaunts her condition too, which offends the more matronly ladies. Even her sister in law, the Duchess of Suffolk, who is no prude, confesses to being disgusted by her behaviour."

"The duchess told you that?" Thomas enquired, raising his eyebrows. Cromwell's network of spies was growing by the day.

"No." Cromwell gave a shrug. "That particular duchess does not deign to speak with me."

Thomas sighed. He liked Queen Anne, and always had, but he knew others found her fiery temper intimidating. Strangely, he seemed to possess the ability to calm her outbursts, which he found rather odd, since he had certainly not been able to do the same with Joan's fits of rage. "Now that she is securely married to His Majesty, she will no doubt be as gracious a lady as I have heard Queen Elizabeth, the king's late mother, to be."

Cromwell could not visualise Anne being as deeply loved as Elizabeth had been, nor could he imagine her being gracious, but he kept these opinions to himself.

"Is everything now arranged for the coronation?" Thomas enquired. His companion had been given the task of arranging everything, including the processions to and from Westminster Abbey, the banquet afterwards, and the entertainment. "I am relieved that I only have the task of saying a few prayers and placing the crown on her head," he added.

"It is organised," Cromwell replied complacently. "The queen is to be carried on a litter to and from the ceremony, given her delicate condition. She has a new musician in her retinue, a boy called Mark Smeaton; he has such nimble fingers and plays the lute remarkably well. I have requested for him to play some of the king's own compositions while everyone is feasting. I have also arranged other entertainments, which I believe will ensure no one is bored."

Silently, Thomas applauded his companion's astute mind. To have a musician playing the king's own compositions was a master stroke; King Henry would be delighted. The king adored his compositions being lauded. Cromwell knew exactly how to flatter the king without being obsequious.

"And for the common folk, there shall be free wine flowing in the conduits, plus a whole plethora of banners bearing the queen's emblem, the White Falcon, as well as her chosen motto: The Most Happy," Cromwell continued.

"Free wine," Thomas mused aloud. "There is nothing like free wine to keep the people happy."

"Indeed," Cromwell agreed optimistically. "It might even make them cheer for the queen."

*****

On the day of Anne's coronation, the Londoners remained sullen, despite the free wine. As he travelled to Westminster Abbey, Thomas could not fail to sense the mood of the people. There was an air of disinterest, and though many people had lined the streets to watch the procession, there was little joyful cheering. As for the king himself, he was not attending. He wished his wife, the woman who would soon bear him a son, to enjoy her moment of glory alone. The one person who could have prompted the crowds to cheer, was absent.

Having never performed a coronation before, Thomas sincerely hoped that he at least appeared confident. Anne herself, according to the tradition of previous monarchs awaiting their coronation, had spent the night in the Tower of London. Today, however, as he watched her gracefully progressing down the aisle, he noticed she looked out of sorts. He hoped this was due to her condition, though more likely she was disappointed that the people had barely acknowledged her. When she had arrived at Westminster Abbey, and the great doors had ceremoniously been opened to receive her, there had been no roars of applause and shouting from without. He had personally felt chilled by that silence; there was something sinister about it. No wonder Anne felt disturbed, he thought sympathetically, as he carefully placed the newly made crown on her glossy black head.

At the banquet following the coronation, Anne appeared to revive herself, though Cromwell believed she still felt fragile; her laugh was just a little too loud, and too frequent. As for the king, he was ebullient, taking Cromwell and Cranmer aside to inform them that the Emperor Charles was now entirely uninterested in the affairs of England, not only because he was much taken with waging war against the Turks, but also because he was now fully intent on ridding his own realm of all Protestants. Henry's marriage had occurred at just the right time, and he felt smugly secure in his position. Had he tried to plan it thus, it could not have been more perfect. It was clearly a sign of God's blessing.

"Well, we are happy for Your Majesty's contentment," Cromwell congratulated the king warmly, despite having known about the emperor's disinterest for many months now.

Thomas managed to nod agreement, but inside felt a tremor of concern. Some of those heretics the emperor was so intent on 'purging' from his realm were his close friends. Indeed, one of them was his wife's closest relative. God keep them safe, he silently prayed.

"All we require now is for my son to be delivered safely," beamed Henry.

Nodding yet again, Thomas wondered how the king could be so certain that the baby was going to be male? What if Queen Anne delivered a girl? He supposed the solution would be that she must become pregnant again, as soon as possible. After all, she was the Queen of England now; her duty was to provide heirs. Whatever the gender of the child she carried, her position was totally secure.

Chapter Seven

The following months flew past in a whirl of meetings and visits, with Thomas spending much of his time travelling through his new diocese. He also managed to visit Taunton – where he was still Archdeacon – and several other dioceses, which brought approval from some bishops but offended others, who accused him of interfering. For the most part, he ignored their criticisms, knowing that he could not possibly please everyone. King Henry, so far, was pleased with his work and approved of his diligence, which was all that mattered.

To his great relief, Margaret had finally joined him in England, and had settled herself discreetly in Lambeth Palace. Her presence was peaceful and soothing, whilst her English – true to her promise – was much improved. Her behaviour and demeanour, when anyone was present, was polite and respectful, but despite this, both of them knew that the general opinion was that she was more than a mere servant. He was also well aware that the worst gossips in any establishment were the servants themselves.

One of the most obvious signs of Margaret's special status was her behaviour regarding his library. None of his servants ever disturbed him when he was writing in his library, at least, not without due cause. Margaret, on the other hand, would enter simply to rebuke him because he had missed a meal, or was overworking. He had discussed this dilemma with her after hearing the servants whispering about it, but she could not be persuaded to alter her behaviour. As his wife, his wellbeing was her primary concern, and she took this duty very seriously. In all honesty, he invariably enjoyed her interruptions, and did not push the matter further. It was comfortable to be fussed over by a well-meaning, doting wife, even if it did invite speculation.

He sighed. It was likely the punishment would be severe if his marriage was discovered. Certainly, he would be stripped of his office; imprisonment was a certainty, and death a possibility. At the moment, the king favoured him, so perhaps imprisonment might be his only punishment. But if he lost the king's favour... he preferred not to consider what would happen then. Years ago, when ordained a priest, he had taken vows of celibacy, but had still married Margaret, in light of Martin Luther's view that those men who could not handle celibacy should marry, and remain faithful to one wife, rather than risk their souls by indulging in lewd practices. The Bible was clear that marriage was a holy bond, and he hoped one day to persuade the king that, given the sacred nature of marriage, members of the priesthood should not be barred from taking wedding vows.

Cromwell, having met Margaret numerous times, approved of her. He also thought it hilarious that a rumour was going around the Court, suggesting that the Archbishop of Canterbury was not only married, but that he had smuggled his wife into Lambeth Palace in a packing case. This rumour was far from amusing to Thomas; indeed, it was a source of great unease. He knew the king was aware of the rumour, because His Majesty frequently made a reference to packing cases whenever his archbishop was present, much to his embarrassment and confusion. He always found his face flushing, and could never think of a suitably witty riposte to cap the king's remarks.

August soon arrived, and Queen Anne was taken to Greenwich for her lying in. Notices had already been written to send abroad, announcing the arrival of a baby prince, and Henry was in high spirits, still supremely confident that the babe would be a son.

"Just feel how active he is," he had often declared, laying a bejewelled hand over Anne's swollen abdomen.

Thomas, aware that the babe was equally likely to be a girl, continued to find the king's confidence unsettling, but remained silent on the subject. The Court was quiet for the next month, as they all waited in limbo for the birth of the infant prince. Then, on September the sixth, a messenger from the king arrived at Lambeth Palace. The king required the attendance of his Archbishop of Canterbury, for the queen had been delivered of a baby. A girl. Both mother and baby seemed likely to survive.

He was swiftly rowed to Greenwich, flanked by a joyful chorus of Te Deum's, resounding from both sides of the riverbank, as the churches welcomed the new royal arrival into the world. The Londoners, always ready to celebrate a royal birth, were already on the river, with bearbaiting and cockfighting taking place on a series of floating wooden rafts. An oarsman informed Thomas that the streets were full of mummers and minstrels, as well as people dancing. They might not like the queen, and the baby was only a girl, but the common folk were more than eager to make merry regardless.

He found the king in a serious mood, clearly disappointed, but resigned. With him was Cromwell, naturally, whose constant attendance was making him the most disliked person

142

at Court. The king seemed unsure of why he had summoned his archbishop.

"We require some spiritual counsel," he eventually mused aloud, in a voice much lower than his usual, exuberant tone. He looked totally dispirited.

"Have you a name for the infant?" Thomas enquired, after offering warm congratulations.

"Elizabeth, after my lady mother," the king replied tonelessly.

"Your Majesty, I do believe Princess Elizabeth is a gift from God. He knows what He is doing in our lives, even if we sometimes feel ourselves to be in turmoil."

"Now we know why we sent for you," Henry managed a weak smile. "You remind us that we are subject to God as much as the humblest ploughman."

"Amen," Cromwell piously agreed. "As are all men."

"What about the baptism?" Thomas enquired. A massive state affair had been organised, and he assumed it would go ahead. After all, why not celebrate?

"Oh, just a small private thing, we think, archbishop," the king declared airily. "Just a few guests. No need to make a celebration for a girl. We desire for you to be one of her godparents," he added, as an afterthought.

And so, a few days later, as per the king's command, Thomas performed the baptism of the little Princess Elizabeth in a small, understated ceremony.

*****

Not long after the baptism of the little princess, a strange incident occurred, involving a woman named Elizabeth Barton, nicknamed the Holy Maid of Kent. For the past two years, she had been making outrageous predictions, claiming that she could hear the voice of God Himself. She had powerful supporters, including Sir Thomas More and Bishop Fisher, all of whom considered her saintly. She was allegedly a Benedictine Nun, but from what Thomas had heard of her predictions, he was dubious. As far as he could deduce, she was a fraud; a peasant woman, prone to fits and hallucinations.

Unfortunately, she had suddenly come into considerable prominence, after loudly claiming that the saints had instructed her to tell the king that if he did not cast Anne Boleyn aside and return to Queen Catherine, both he and Anne would meet an untimely death. Of course, predicting the death of a king was treason, so Henry decided it was time to address the problem. Once she had been arrested, and the books and pamphlets containing her prophecies had been burned, the king handed the case over to his Archbishop of Canterbury and, naturally, Thomas Cromwell.

Having openly admitted to Margaret that he was fascinated by this case, Thomas had Elizabeth Barton brought to Lambeth Palace, where he could examine her in the presence of Cromwell.

"I shall lurk in the background, for want of a better description," Cromwell declared, as they waited in the library for the heretic's arrival. "I think you are best qualified to question the woman, for you are far more open-minded. I am already certain she is a fake, and I have yet to set eyes on her. Indeed, from what I have heard, she is being manipulated by a certain Edward Bocking, a member of the clergy who is also imprisoned."

"I would not describe myself as entirely open-minded. I have my suspicions," Thomas confessed. "And I have also heard of this connection with Master Bocking, whom I fear will

144

turn out to be a rather unsavoury character. But I shall not permit my suspicions to prejudice me."

"I don't doubt it." Cromwell was pacing around the library, restless and eager to prove Mistress Barton a fake. "I believe your natural delicacy might prevent you from asking some, shall we say, personal questions. If necessary, I shall interrupt," he added bluntly, as a noise outside heralded the arrival of the prisoner.

Also present with the archbishop and Cromwell was a man called Ralph Morice, the newly appointed secretary to the Archbishop of Canterbury. An earnest, studious man, who was as sombrely attired as his two companions, Morice sat with a pen, ink and parchment, ready to record everything that was said during the interview.

There was a sharp knocking on the door, and two rough-looking gaolers entered, standing on either side of a thin, haggard-looking woman, who appeared to be no older than twenty-five. She was clad in a shabby, grubby, nun's habit, and an unsavoury smell emanated from her person.

"You may leave. Wait outside, please." Thomas addressed the gaolers, who were holding the woman more roughly that he thought necessary. Turning to Elizabeth, he indicted to a chair. "Please, be seated. No one here shall hurt you. You are merely required to answer my questions with total honestly."

Silently, the young woman seated herself.

He could not help but notice that there was an air of assurance about her; she had clearly become well-used to public attention. "Tell me about your early life," he invited gently.

"Little to tell." The woman spoke with a strong regional accent, and it took very little coaxing for her to reveal that she had been born of lowly stock and had gone to work as a servant at Aldington, in Kent. Then, aged sixteen, she had suddenly started becoming uncontrollably hysterical, and going into strange trances.

"You had been in good health up until that point?" Thomas asked.

"Aye, sir," she replied. "People asked the Blessed Virgin to intercede for me, and the fits stopped. But since then, I have continued to have visions, but because they is holy visions, I was allowed to enter a nunnery."

She seemed perfectly at ease, he noted, , leaning back in her chair, her hands folded quietly in her lap. Just like Margaret looked when they sat peacefully together. "Tell me about Master Edward Bocking," he requested, trying to cast aside his preconceived suspicion that Bocking was, very likely, a scoundrel of a man; he was surely manipulating this woman and using her to obtain money. People were paying him to meet with her and listen to her while she pretended to communicate with the saints.

"I met him at the nunnery," Barton replied. "He is a member of Christ's Church, Canterbury." She announced this with huge pride, her face lighting up, making her look much younger. "He's heard of ye, sir."

"And I have heard of Master Bocking." Thomas paused. "Tell me about your messages."

"I hears from the Holy Virgin, and she does tell me how wrong the king is to marry Mistress Boleyn. I sent messages to the late cardinal, and to the Pope." Her voice rang with pride.

"I take it you do not write your own letters," he clarified.

"No sir, I cannot read or write. Master Bocking, he does most of em."

"I also understand you have been in contact with the Bishop of Rochester and Sir Thomas More," he encouraged gently. She was beginning to become distracted, looking around the room

146

in awe, which was hardly surprising. She had probably never seen so many books in all her life.

"Oh yes, sir. But they is not in touch now. They stopped replying to my letters," she assured him.

This did not surprise him. More was no longer in the king's good grace, having opposed his marriage to Anne, and the Bishop of Rochester was threatened with praemunire, for being in contact with Barton. Since her imprisonment, her influential friends had evaporated. "Describe your visions to me," he invited, listening to the sound of Morice's pen energetically scratching away in the background as he recorded the interview.

The gentleness of the interrogation now seemed to confuse the woman, jolting her out of her previous calm demeanour. She had expected harshness, perhaps even physical violence; she knew how to deal with those. She found the archbishop's kind and soothing voice unsettling, and soon began contradicting herself. Her description of her visions lacked any conviction, and it soon became apparent to her listeners that, as they had suspected, she was merely a simpleton, who'd had the misfortune to fall into the path of Edward Bocking.

As they were nearing the end of the interview, Cromwell finally stepped forward, and proceeded to ask the same questions as his friend, only couched differently. Her answers became even more confused, and she ended up admitting that her visions were not really visions at all. She also stated that she was obedient to Bocking's instructions, but refused to admit that it was Bocking who had encouraged her to create these false visions. Eventually her gaolers were summoned, and she was returned to her prison cell.

A few days later, Elizabeth Barton was formally tried. Not only was she accused of heresy, as anticipated, but she was also accused of lechery, theft and various other crimes.

147

"I doubt she is guilty of anything other than deception," Thomas remarked to Cromwell, as they sat listening to the trial. "If it were up to me, I would have her merely confess her mistakes in public. Bocking is the one who should be imprisoned."

Cromwell, predictably, was less lenient. "I know she is a woman, but she must be made an example of. As for Bocking, I agree that his punishment should be more severe than hers. I say hang him."

"His crime is surely not…" Thomas faltered. Cromwell was right, Bocking's crime was classed as treason, and therefore worthy of the death penalty. "I just wish Mistress Barton could be dealt with lightly. She is a simpleton, a tool in the hands of a manipulative person. She did not intend to commit treason."

"Ah, but by allowing herself to be instructed by a greedy man, she has herself committed errors. She is accountable and must be tried and punished according to the law." Cromwell's time as a lawyer had made him merciless. "If you had your way, my friend, no one would ever be hung, or otherwise executed. It is necessary to make an example of felons, else everyone would be out there committing crimes."

The following day, at St. Paul's Cross, both Barton and Edward Bocking publicly confessed to their crimes. They were both found guilty of treason, as were several others who had been complicit with them, and all were sentenced to death by hanging. Although he had not been in touch with Elizabeth Barton for some time, the Bishop of Rochester was also sentence: but to perpetual imprisonment rather than death. However, after agreeing to pay a three hundred pound fine, he was promptly released; his wealth permitted him to avoid punishment. Sir Thomas More was found to be innocent of conspiring with Mistress Barton and was acquitted forthwith.

Whilst walking back to the river, Thomas happened to come across one of his clergymen, John Capon, who was in the midst of spontaneously preaching sermons to groups of passers-by, telling them that the words of Elizabeth Barton were not to be trusted, and guiding them towards the ways of The New Learning. Thomas was informed that Capon had been doing this on a regular basis, and that the unrest appeared to be abating as a result, so effective was Capon's message. Thomas duly reported this to the king, who was greatly impressed, and promptly suggested to Thomas that Capon should be made Bishop of Bangor in recognition of his support. Capon, bemused by his sudden elevation, duly promised to enthusiastically continue with his sermons.

"Uphold the break with the Church of Rome, and the king will be even more pleased, as will I," Thomas solemnly advised.

*****

Since Elizabeth Barton's demise, Cromwell – always eager to turn a situation to his advantage – had let it be known,, throughout the Court, that he had been busy creating a list of persons whom he suspected to be secret supporters of Barton and her rhetoric.

"You are a true follower of Machiavelli," Thomas commented, as they both headed towards a meeting of the Privy Council at Hampton Court.

Cromwell smirked. He was now Master Secretary, a position which had formerly belonged to Bishop Gardiner, but to Gardiner's chagrin, the king had seen fit to remove him and give the position to Cromwell instead. "Come, Cranmer, you must recognise the genius of this plan? Not everyone supports the break with Rome and the reforming of the Church, but if they think their name is on my list, they are likely to prove less… well… opposing."

"Where do you keep this list hidden?" Thomas was curious. "What if it were to fall into someone else's hands."

"It won't." Cromwell was smug.

"You keep it under lock and key, I assume?"

"I keep it in my head. It changes by the day, you see. Actually, it changes by the hour, depending upon who irritates me, and when."

Thomas shook his head as they were joined by other members of the council. It was easy to be overawed by the powerful, august members of the Privy Council, people such as the Duke of Norfolk, the Duke of Suffolk and Sir Thomas More. He tried not to be, but it was very much a work in progress; sometimes he wondered whether he would ever feel comfortable amongst them.

Cromwell, by contrast, was perfectly at ease, as he was when it came to dealing with most things in his life, including the king.

"Your Majesty," Cromwell stated matter-of-factly. "Our alliance with France is uneasy…"

"Fox-nosed Francis practically licks the feet of the Pope," Henry grumbled, alluding to his French rival's long, thin nose.

"Because they are a Catholic nation…"

The king interrupted again. "We are also a Catholic nation, Master Secretary. I am Head of the Church, not the Bishop of Rome. Nothing else has changed, as of yet." The king's speech was clipped, and his tone held a warning.

King Henry was alluding to the fact he had recently been declared excommunicate by the Pope. Thomas had also been excommunicated, though this did not trouble him in the slightest, since he did not consider the Pope to have any power anyway. Unfortunately, although those bishops who were

150

inclined towards the Protestant faith were equally unfazed, most of the clergy he commanded were Catholic, and regarded his excommunication as a serious issue

Unlike his own situation, Thomas viewed the king's excommunication with a certain degree of apprehension. After all, Henry was not a committed Protestant at present, and it was possible that this might convince him to return to Catholicism. Fortunately, thus far, Henry had only demonstrated feelings of outrage at the Pope's decision, announcing angrily that it mattered not. In his view, the Pope was merely the Bishop of Rome, whereas he, King Henry VIII, was Head of the Church in England; how dare the Pope imagine he held any authority over the monarch or the Church in England.

The king's anger had relieved Thomas, for it signified that the Church in England was now severed from Rome. Even though services were still at present conducted according to the Catholic format, God willing, in the near future, Protestantism would take over. Still, listening to the king and Cromwell, Thomas could not help but sigh internally. The king was slowly coming around to Protestantism as a concept, but there were many aspects of the Catholic Church that he still clung to. Whilst the king had recently removed four of the seven sacraments, by passing an Act of Ten Articles of Faith, he still insisted on upholding his belief in transubstantiation, which Thomas and his fellow Protestants so longed to dispose of.

Thomas had recently been involved in writing a pamphlet on the king's behalf, entitled *Institution of a Christian Man*, designed to explain the Ten Articles of Faith to the common man. The king also hoped that the pamphlet would promote 'unity and concord in opinion,' and 'stop so much bickering amongst the clergy'. In truth, Thomas saw very little point in releasing the pamphlet. Theologically, not a lot had changed:

the Mass was the same and was still spoken or sung in Latin; the Bible was still written in Latin; the status of the Virgin Mary remained unchanged. People were also still expected to confess to a priest, in addition to confessing to God, for though the king accepted that God alone had the power to absolve one's sins, he felt it best that things should remain as they were, just to be safe. Yes... there was still much that needed to change.

Cromwell, despite the king's tone, continued to argue his case in his usual calm and urbane manner. "Your Majesty, I desire to merely suggest forming an additional alliance. The Emperor Charles' empire consists of an alliance between Spain and Burgundy, and certain German states. France and England are allied, but France appears to have been drifting towards Charles in more recent times, ever since we separated from Rome—"

"Just spit it out, man!" Henry demanded testily.

"As you wish, Your Majesty. I propose that England becomes allied with the Protestant German princes: the Schmalkaldic League," Cromwell announced, bracing himself for the king's wrath.

Henry, however, looked intrigued. "Hmm... English trade with the Low Countries has been declining since Charles took control..."

"If we were to join with the Schmalkaldic League, we might be able to trade with the Baltic." Cromwell's tone was seductive.

"What do you think, my lord Archbishop?" Henry suddenly demanded.

Taken aback by the suddenness of the question, Thomas wished he could be truthful. Joining forces with the Protestant German princes seemed excellent to him; it might hasten a true Reformation in England. But, of course, an opinion could not be said aloud. "Your Majesty, I see nothing amiss in dealing with the princes, if it increases trade. Our sheep farmers have been unable to export fleeces to the Low Countries for some time now, so why not send their fleeces to the Baltic States?"

"Well said," Henry concurred. "You make a good suggestion, Master Secretary."

"There is more, Your Majesty," Cromwell continued, ignoring the dark looks he was receiving from other members of the council. "I believe it would be sensible for everyone, whether they be nobility, the clergy, or a common man, to take an oath of... allegiance... of support; an oath that acknowledges the validity of Your Majesty's marriage, and also the path of succession. Until the queen provides Your Majesty with a male heir, I believe your successor should be the Princess Elizabeth."

Thomas blinked. Trust Cromwell to think of such a thing. He had become more politically astute over the past few years, but he was nowhere near Cromwell's level. Though he sincerely hoped that the queen would give birth to a son, God willing, it was wise of Cromwell to anticipate what might happen if the king should die before he produced an heir. After all, life was uncertain, and many people still believed that Princess Mary was the rightful heir. If, God forbid, the king died before this was resolved, there would almost certainly be a civil war.

Sir Thomas Boleyn was looking well-pleased with the suggestion, but other members of the council exchanged uneasy glances. Meanwhile, the king was wondering at Cromwell's apparent mind-reading abilities. The issue of succession was one he himself had been mulling over since the birth of his daughter. If he should die, the country would undoubtedly descend into chaos, and he had no guarantee that Elizabeth would be crowned queen. Also, unlike his

153

archbishop, he fully understood Cromwell's thinking regarding his subjects swearing an oath in support of his marriage. With such a rule in place, he could easily determine which members of the nobility and council supported him, and which members did not.

"Proceed with both your suggestions, Master Secretary," the king commanded. "And ensure that the Lady Mary also signs an oath, dictating that she will accept her legitimate sister's place as immediate heir to the throne." His tone was ominous. "We shall have no denial from her, or her mother."

As they departed from the Privy Chamber, Cromwell nudged Thomas with his elbow. "I understand that you will soon be departing to Canterbury for a while, to settle into your official residence."

"I find myself very pleased with the Manor of Ford," Thomas admitted. "It is a lovely place, and one I could become seriously attached to. It is not too large or too grand and is homely and comfortable. But alas, my visit will mostly be spent seeing to the needs of the diocese. I must attend to the education of my clergy, especially those attached to Canterbury Cathedral itself. His Majesty has also asked me to write a treatise on irregularities in marriages, along with a treatise against Cardinal Reginald Pole."

Cardinal Pole had recently been banished from the realm; ardently Catholic, he had been loudly supportive of Queen Catherine, and had written a book, *De Unione Ecclesiastica*, in support of her marriage to King Henry. Naturally, King Henry desired for this matter to be dealt with as quickly as possible.

Cromwell nodded sympathetically. "Rather you than me. It sounds as though you have some complex tasks ahead of you."

Thomas smiled calmly. "Oh, it is only a matter of drawing attention to the corruption of the Catholic Church and its

154

institutions. Believe me, it is much simpler that some other works I have written..." He was about to continue when his companion stopped walking, peered out through a window, and laid a hand upon his arm.

"Apologies, my friend, but I must interrupt." Cromwell was looking out onto the gardens of Hampton Court. "Do you see that young lady?" He indicated towards a small, slight young woman, walking alongside a young man.

"I do indeed. Is she not Lady Jane Seymour? Catholic, I believe." The Seymour family were all said to be Catholic, though one of them, Sir Edward, the young man whom Lady Jane was currently walking with, had apparently shown an interest in The New Learning.

"Yes, she is devoutly Catholic." Cromwell lowered his voice to a whisper. "But mark her well, my friend. The Seymour's are ambitious, and she has attracted the king's eye."

Thomas stared at the young woman. "Surely not?" he exclaimed. Lady Jane did not have the poise or sophistication of the queen, nor was she reputed to possess any great degree of wit. Certainly, he had never beheld anyone laughing at her jests, whereas the queen was constantly surrounded by laughing admirers, all enjoying her lively repartee. He had seen Lady Jane at close quarters, and though she was not plain, she was not remarkably attractive either. "His Majesty is married; she could never be anything more than his mistress, though for the queen's sake, I hope His Majesty will not be unfaithful."

"From what I have heard, the king tires of Queen Anne," Cromwell hissed, keeping his voice low. "A few days ago, one of her ladies informed me that the queen publicly berated the king for flirting too enthusiastically with Lady Jane. The king replied, 'you must close your eyes and endure, as those who are better than you have done'."

155

Taken aback, Thomas stared at Cromwell in silence, trying to gather his scattered thoughts. Eventually, he whispered, "Poor Queen Anne. I pray His Majesty will behave kindly to her. He has torn the structure of the Church apart to marry her. His feelings are still strong, I am confident of that. This flirtation will surely pass. Besides, if he were to take a mistress, it would endanger his immortal soul. It is barely a year since he vowed to remain faithful to his wife."

The worldlier Cromwell was less sanguine. Anne was brittle, her temper uncertain. Now that she was queen, and in what she felt was a stable position, she was less than respectful towards her husband, and apt not to disguise her feelings. If she was angry or upset, she showed it; and she never held back from being derogatory towards Henry, no matter who was present. Cromwell was not surprised that the king had grown tired of her. "We shall see what transpires," he shrugged. "As you say, Anne is queen. Nothing can alter that. And having just divorced one wife, he cannot possibly divorce another."

"He has no grounds for a divorce from Queen Anne," Thomas stressed. "You can be assured of that."

*****

Upon arriving in Canterbury, he immediately set about completing the tasks he had set himself. He had known that the standard of education amongst his clergy was poor, but it was not until he began to examine each individual that he realised just how little they knew. To have, in his own diocese, such a vast number of uneducated clergymen was nothing less than an outrage. How were they supposed to teach the wisdom of the Bible to the common man when most of them could not read and write themselves? The scriptures were written in Latin; if

156

they could not even read English, how were they supposed to interpret Latin? Some were able to quote passages of scripture in Latin, having learned orally by repetition, but they had no idea of what they were saying. If a lay person approached them in need of spiritual counsel, their advice came entirely from their own minds, not from the scriptures.

His only comfort came in the form of his brother, Edmund, who was also a member of the clergy. Like Thomas, he had been educated at Cambridge, and whilst he was not as academically inclined as his brother, he had sufficient theological and linguistical knowledge to teach the individuals whose knowledge was lacking. Since Edmund was also based in Canterbury, Thomas enlisted his help in executing his educational programme.

He had decided that the best solution to this travesty, was to personally deliver theological lectures to the clergy in his diocese, and to send for theologians from Cambridge to act as mentors, to help the clergy further their learning. Unfortunately, this did not go down well with the clergy of Canterbury, who simply wanted to proceed in the comfortable way they had always lived. Though he was used to such resistance – his former students at Cambridge had been much the same – he still felt somewhat disheartened. But instead of dwelling on the negative, he tried to focus on those who did thank him; those who were grateful to him for enabling them to discover and understand God's word by teaching them to read and speak Latin.

"If only we could get an English Bible," he sighed to Margaret one evening. "It would make my task so much easier. I would only have to teach them to read in English, instead of Latin also. Everyone ought to be able to read the Bible in their mother tongue."

"I can't believe some can neither read nor write." Margaret was busy mending the cuff of a shirt and had paused to look for her scissors. Unable to locate them, she bit off a length of thread with a fair amount of venom. "It makes me so angry," she announced. "I don't like it when they criticise you."

"Don't worry, my love, I'm used to it." Margaret's support warmed his heart; even her reprimands about him working too hard were undertaken out of concern for his welfare. Fortunately for his wife, Thomas was making excellent progress with his written tasks, having already begun his treatise for the king on the subject of marriage, and his reply to Reginald Pole's book. "Besides, I enjoy teaching. It is rewarding to see people acquiring new skills and new knowledge." He paused for a moment, a thoughtful expression on his face. "You know... Cromwell tells me he is intent upon closing all the monasteries in the very near future."

"Is that why he has sent all of those commissioners to the monasteries, to establish their wealth?" Margaret asked.

"Yes," he replied. Very little happened in his life that his wife did not know about. "But there is so much wealth, you can hardly imagine it. I've been thinking... what if I were to ask His Majesty to use part of that wealth to promote education? To build more schools and universities, not only for the clergy, but for the common man also. All men should be taught to read and write, and all women for that matter."

"Now that, I agree with." Margaret beamed. "I love to read; it would be wonderful to be able to share my joy with the other women I know."

Later that evening, a messenger arrived at the Manor, bearing a missive from Cromwell. Now that the Pope had been demoted to Bishop of Rome, it was down to the Archbishop of Canterbury to deal with dispensations for marriage, hence why Cromwell had contacted Thomas. He desired a dispensation for two of his friends to marry and hoped that Thomas would grant it to him.

"Oh no," he groaned, having read the letter.

"Was ist los?" Margaret demanded anxiously, unconsciously reverting to her native German. Her husband appeared troubled.

"I'll reply to this tomorrow, it's not urgent. Cromwell wants me to agree to the proposed marriage of one of his friends, whose wife died some months ago. But this man now wishes to marry his wife's niece. Her niece, Margaret! I cannot allow such a marriage; it is not lawful." His voice was sharp. "Cromwell is my friend, but he cannot ask such requests of me. I cannot grant him favours when his demands are not only unlawful, but also immoral. I must be honest with him."

"I agree, but how will you convince Cromwell?"

"I shall have to be tactful. He may be angry, but I trust that he will respect my judgement. Come, let us to bed, it grows late. I will deal with Cromwell in the morning."

After a restless night, Thomas finally plucked up the courage to respond to his friend's request. 'Master Secretary, I commend myself to your lordship', he began formally. 'You know I would gladly agree to your request, if it were possible for me to do so, and if the word of God permitted it. However, this is not the case'. That sounded well enough, he decided approvingly. 'It is not expressed in Leviticus that an uncle might not marry his niece, but it is stated that a nephew cannot marry his aunt. So, by the same process, we can understand that a niece cannot marry her uncle. They are within the same degree of consanguinity.

'Also, touching on the recent Act of Parliament concerning the decrees of union prohibited by God's law, they are not set out as clearly as I would like them to be. I did speak my mind at the time of the law being made, and consider it worthwhile that forbidden degrees of matrimony should be put forward more clearly, otherwise there is ample room for misinterpretation. I have no news from Canterbury at present, but I long to hear about what is concurrent with you; if you have any good news, I pray that you will send me some. I heartily bid you farewell, your lordship's own, Thomas Cranmer'.

The letter completed, he quickly placed his seal upon it and summoned a messenger to despatch it to London. A week later, a letter from Cromwell – who thankfully appeared to be totally unruffled by his friend's refusal to permit the marriage – informed him that Sir Thomas More had resigned the Great Seal, and that he, Cromwell, had been appointed Chancellor in his place. He also informed Thomas that the king demanded his presence at Court – immediately.

"But why so quickly?" Margaret protested.

He explained that it was mostly to do with the two recent Acts that had been introduced following the last meeting of the Privy Council. Cromwell had initiated both of them. The Act of Supremacy declared that King Henry VIII and his successors were to replace the Pope, and become Supreme Head of the Church; the Act of Succession decreed that the throne would be inherited by Princess Elizabeth, should King Henry die without producing a male heir. All members of the Privy Council were required to sign these documents, to show their support.

"According to Cromwell, Sir Thomas More was happy to sign the Act of Succession, claiming that the king can leave his throne to whomsoever he wishes, but he refused to sign the Act of Supremacy. He has since resigned as Chancellor of the

160

realm and has retired to his home in Chelsea. Cromwell, naturally, has been appointed to that that position in his place."

Margaret was tearful. "But we are happy here," she murmured.

He could not help but agree with her. They were happy. But there was more to this situation than the passing of the two Acts. Bishop Fisher had become increasingly troublesome, having both verbally expounded his views on the Acts and refused to sign either of them. Furthermore, he had even written to the Emperor Charles, suggesting to him that he should invade England. Fisher had since been committed to the Tower of London and had been informed that he would stay there until the archbishop arrived; apparently, the king hoped that Thomas would be able to convince Fisher to reconsider.

"We must go," he informed Margaret gently. "But we shall return here as soon as is possible." Taking her hand, he kissed it gently. "You must pack your belongings, my dear."

"No." She shook her head, tears still pouring down her cheeks. "You must go, my Thomas, but I... I cannot. You have had so much on your mind... I did not wish to add to your worries. But I am pregnant, my Thomas. The baby is still small, but soon... soon I will not be able to hide it. I cannot return to London with you, people will talk..... "

He stared at her in astonishment. Pregnant? He had assumed that her recent weight gain had simply been due to her thriving in their new home; that life in the country was suiting her well. But now it seemed there was another explanation. He battled with the emotions swirling inside him. He wanted to be overjoyed, to wrap her in his arms and celebrate the new life they had created, but his fears tormented him. All he knew of childbirth was what Joan had been through, and he was terrified of what might happen to Margaret. Would

161

she survive? Would the child? And even if her pregnancy went smoothly, what would happen if it were discovered that the child was his? Would he lose his position, or worse? He could not leave Margaret to care for the child alone while he languished in prison.

Taking a deep breath, he tried to quiet his mind, and focus on the present. Margaret had spoken wisely; she could not live at Lambeth Palace once she looked visibly pregnant. He forced himself to speak calmly. "Do not worry, my love. When the baby is due, I shall return here, and when you are ready, we shall all return to Lambeth Palace. I am sure we can come up with an explanation for the baby's presence."

Her lips quivered as she attempted to smile. "Perhaps we can say he or she is a findling... ach, I do not know the English word."

"A foundling." His lips were also quivering as he too attempted a smile. "It's almost the same."

"At least I am under no pressure to produce a son." She held his hand tightly.

"Whatever God gives us we shall praise Him for His blessing." He wrapped his arms around her and held her close. "May He keep you safe."

"We are in His hands," she whispered.

*****

Upon arriving at Lambeth Palace, he was greeted with the news that Sir Thomas More had been arrested and was being held in the Tower alongside Bishop Fisher. As for Cromwell, he had been busy, but that was to be expected. He was never anything other than busy. During the archbishop's absence, Cromwell had prepared a Treason Act, which decreed that treason could

162

be committed by words alone. It also stated that any plot which had the potential to harm the king, queen, or any of their offspring, was constituted as treason, and that anyone who aided and abetted any such plot was equally culpable. Cromwell knew that this Act would destroy Fisher and More, along with many others, and since Sanctuary had now been abolished, none of them could escape by rushing into a place of worship. The Church could no longer protect criminals from prosecution, a change which Thomas wholeheartedly approved of, for he had long since believed that the claiming of Sanctuary was too easily misused.

Whilst devising the Treason Act, Cromwell had also been solving the king's financial difficulties. When Henry had inherited his throne, he had also inherited a huge fortune, because the royal coffers were full to overflowing, thanks to his frugal father. However, unlike his father, Henry was hugely extravagant, and had quickly spent all his inheritance. Cromwell knew of this, and whilst organising the closure of all the monasteries, it had occurred to him that the First Fruits and Tenths – the money given to the Church by any newly appointed member of the clergy – should not be sent to Rome, as tradition had always dictated. Instead, Cromwell decided it should be sent to the king. After all, the monarch was now Head of the Church, so why should the Pope receive the money? Henry, naturally, was delighted by this suggestion, and Thomas was, as ever, amazed by his friend's creative and devious mind.

One of the first things he noticed when he returned to London, was the change in the atmosphere at Court. Whereas previously the king had spent much of his time in Queen Anne's chambers, His Majesty now avoided the queen, unless Lady Jane Seymour happened to be in attendance upon her.

Cromwell had already informed him that Queen Anne kept Lady Jane inordinately busy, because if she had an idle moment, she always ended up talking with King Henry.

"The king seeks her out," Cromwell murmured, referring to Lady Jane, as he and Thomas walked through the palace gardens – always the best place to discuss anything private.

"Yes, it does appear that way." Thomas wondered what else there was to say about this matter. Jane could be nothing more than the king's mistress. However, she was Catholic, and as a mistress, she could be a powerful influence. She might persuade the king against becoming more active in promoting The New Learning, which would be problematic. "I note someone else who is new to Court." Thomas nodded subtly towards a man who was approaching them. "Richard Rich. I know him from Cambridge," he whispered.

"Outwardly Protestant. Outwardly anything that will bring him into prominence." Cromwell's tone was scathing. "Until a few weeks ago, he was attached to Sir Thomas More's household. Now it appears that he hardly knows who Sir Thomas More is. Useful man though; totally without sentiment. Will do anything for power or money… as will most people at Court, apart from your good self." He gave his companion a friendly nudge with his elbow.

Thomas said nothing. At Cambridge, he and Rich had not had much association with one another.

Rich was well within speaking distance now. Like the archbishop and Cromwell, he was clean shaven, but any similarity ended there. For a man who was not yet eminent at Court, he was frivolously clad, his clothing brightly coloured and clearly as costly as he could afford.

"My lord Archbishop." Rich gave a bow. "I trust you are in good health." He was warmly obsequious.

There was something about this man that made Thomas cringe, and after providing a polite reply, he awaited the reason for Rich's arrival.

"The queen desires to speak with you," Rich revealed. "Shall I accompany you?" he added eagerly.

"No, thank you," Thomas replied quickly. "I am well acquainted with the location of the queen's apartments."

After bidding farewell to Cromwell, he obediently hastened to the queen's rooms, wondering what the purpose of this summons might be. He found Anne seated with her retinue of ladies-in-waiting, with, as always, a group of young men. Under normal circumstances, they would all have been vying for her attention, eager to entertain her; but today her attendants seemed less exuberant than usual. Bowing, he kissed her hand as she extended it out to him. She was stylish as ever, but there was a weariness about her, as though she had won a great prize and found it to be a cup of poison.

"Leave me," Anne demanded, clapping her hands. "You may retire to the other end of the room. I wish to speak with my lord Archbishop." Waving a hand in dismissal, she offered a fleeting glimpse of the small protuberance on her right hand, a deformity she usually kept carefully hidden beneath her long, flowing sleeves. It had been there since birth, it looked nothing more than a small callous upon her smallest finger, but its presence offended her nearly as much as the strawberry mark on her neck.

"Are you in need of spiritual counsel?" Thomas enquired gently, once she had invited him to be seated. She looked brittle again, much as she had done prior to her marriage. But that could also be because she was pregnant again. "I am glad to help in—"

"No, not spiritual counsel," she interrupted. "Though I wish you were my chaplain again." The words all came in a rush.

"You know I am always available, my queen," he assured her.

"You see that woman, Lady Jane Seymour?" She nodded pointedly towards her ladies, who were all seated together, and being unusually attentive towards the woman in question. "She wants my place. She wants to be queen."

"She cannot," Thomas assured her. The queen was obviously feeling unnecessarily anxious, a symptom, he had been told, that was common during pregnancy. He wondered whether Margaret was similarly afflicted, though he could not imagine her being so paranoid. "You are lawfully queen, Your Majesty."

"The king does not care for me anymore," Anne whispered desperately, her eyes brimming with tears. "He ignores me for days on end, and rarely shows affection. He always makes a great show in public, but I can tell that he only tolerates me now. Even if I flirt with other men when he is present, he is not jealous; he no longer rushes to me to end the flirtation. He used to do that... before we were married. He knows Lady Jane is here with me, archbishop. Trust me, before long, he will come to my chambers, under the pretence that he has come to see me. In reality, he will have come to see that woman."

Thomas wondered what she expected from him. Advice? How could he possibly advise the queen on how best to reignite the king's once intense passion? He could not advise her on what womanly wiles to apply - he knew nothing of such things. He began to wonder what he would do if Margaret decided to flirt with other men. That was something else he could not imagine happening. His wife was so totally unlike the queen.

166

Eventually, he produced some appropriate words of wisdom. "My lady, you hold a high position, and are bearing the king's child. I advise you to be patient. God has placed you here, as queen, therefore you must resign yourself to His Majesty's whims, hard though it may be at times. There is no evidence that the king is doing anything more than perhaps flirting with Mistress Seymour. Once your child is born, he will be so happy, and filled with such pride for you, that he will never so much as glance at another woman."

"Only if I give birth to a son," Anne retorted wearily.

As Thomas walked along one of the vast corridors, having been dismissed by the queen, it occurred to him that the king might be experiencing a similar change of heart to that which Thomas himself had experienced, albeit under very different circumstances. Anne was strongly opinionated, temperamental and fiery, not unlike Joan had been, whereas Lady Jane was demure and had a certain tranquillity about her, much like his own Margaret. Could it be that the king was now falling for Lady Jane because she was the complete opposite of Anne, just as he had fallen in love with Margaret, who was the very antithesis to the tempestuous Joan?

He was dragged from his thoughts by a commotion at the end of the corridor, and he quickly stepped aside as the doors opened. As Anne had predicted, the king, followed by a retinue of courtiers, had come to pay his wife, and Lady Jane, a visit.

Chapter Eight

A few days after his conversation with the queen, Thomas was saddened to hear that she had miscarried; to make matters worse, the midwives were certain that the foetus had been male. Anne was wild in her grief, and he could not help but wonder whether she might be less hysterical were the king to go to her and assure her of his continuing affection. But Henry did not, indeed, he did the opposite, furiously blaming his wife for taking insufficient care of herself and the baby.

"We gave her a gift, a precious son to nurture," he bellowed, the day following the premature loss of Anne's baby.

There was a stunned silence as the king's closest courtiers waited to see who would be brave enough to speak first.

Finally, Gardiner piped up. "She will soon become with child again," he predicted. "It is a sorry situation, but such things happen to women sometimes."

"We wonder at how you can be so wise," Henry snapped. "You have never suffered the loss of a male child, a prince no less."

Thomas wished he could utter something wise, to calm the king's fury, but could think of nothing. Even Cromwell, who was rarely lost for words, was silent.

Eventually, Thomas summoned up the courage to murmur, "My prayers are with Your Majesties. This news is truly terrible, but sometimes we are strengthened by grief, though we do not realise it at the time. The queen needs cosseting during this time, Your Majesty, and no one can comfort her the way you, her lord and husband, can." He expected an explosive response, but it did not arrive. Emboldened, he added, "Only Your Majesty can command the queen to take rest. When she does carry another child, perhaps your good counsel and authority will convince her to conserve her strength."

The king took several heavy gulps of wine from his cup. "We are being advised by two men who clearly do not have wives to command." Calmer now, he eyed his Archbishop of Canterbury with a surprisingly mischievous expression. "We must wait a while before the queen can become pregnant again. After all, babes do not arrive in packing cases. If they did, things would be so much simpler."

There was a ripple of sycophantic laughter. Relieved to have lifted the king's mood, he impassively took the jibe about packing cases without flushing in embarrassment. Much as he loved the king, the only thing he could do to help him was to recommend that he be compassionate towards his wife, and hope that he acted upon the advice.

Shortly afterwards, Thomas visited the queen, and found her lying on her bed, looking pallid, depressed and unkempt. Her skin was greasy and blotched with weeping, whilst her hair, usually lustrous and flowing, was scraped back from her brow and tightly plaited, to keep it out of the way. It was a practical style, but not one likely to impress her husband. There was also a stale odour about her which would likewise not attract him.

As soon as Thomas entered the room, Anne dismissed her women, then immediately begged him to pray with her. This he was glad to do; faced with such a portrait of misery, he knew no other means of giving her solace.

"He no longer loves me." Anne hastily rubbed the persistent tears away from her face. "As soon as I turn my back, he is with that Jane Seymour." A note of resentment crept into her voice. "She is a viper! I am sure she drips poison against me into his ear."

"You must stay strong, my lady. You are the queen, and His Majesty's lawful wife. Mistress Seymour cannot bear him an heir to the throne, but you can." He hoped his tone was encouraging. "Madam, no one knows better than you how to attract the king's attention. I suggest you summon your ladies and your tiring women, so that when His Majesty visits, you look as radiant as the woman he was so eager to marry."

Anne sat bolt upright and stared at him for a moment. "You men are all the same!" Her voice was harsh with resentment. "I am in agony; my body is broken; I have not stopped weeping for days on end; I have lost a child!" She flung herself back on her pillows. "But regrettably, I hear what you say. He shall not see me looking like this." Her voice had suddenly dropped from a screech to almost a whisper. She proceeded to call for her women, and as Thomas departed, she called out to him, "I pray you will visit me again, my lord Archbishop."

Bowing, he assured her that he would gladly visit her again in the very near future.

*****

Thomas was uncomfortably aware that Stephen Gardner was becoming an implacable enemy. Gardiner was totally opposed to any sort of change within the Church, and whatever he proposed, he knew that Gardiner would be opposed to it.

170

Matters were not helped when Thomas decided to address the subject of the Winchester Geese: this was the nickname of the prostitutes who worked in the stews near Winchester Palace, Gardiner's London residence. These brothels fell under Gardiner's jurisdiction, and he made the most of them, extracting lucrative rents from his clients, and thus providing himself with a substantial income. As for the prostitutes, because they came under Gardiner's diocese, and because of their manner of trade, Gardiner could, and did, refuse them burial in hallowed ground. Instead, they were buried in the nearby un-consecrated Cross Bones Graveyard. It was believed that being buried in un-consecrated ground denied a soul access into Heaven. Although Thomas did not agree with this theory – souls who repented of sin and believed in Christ would be saved, wherever they were buried – he knew that many people did; it gave them comfort to believe they would be buried in holy ground.

Cautiously, he spoke with Gardiner about this matter, arguing that it was incongruous for a bishop to receive rents from brothels, and that he had no right to refuse those women Christian burials.

"The rent I charge is not within your remit of authority," Gardiner hissed waspishly. "It has gone on for centuries. No one has criticised any Bishop of Winchester for receiving rent from the stews until now. I see no reason why anything should change."

"The stews should be closed," Thomas suggested. "I believe—"

Gardiner was quick to interrupt. "If one were to close the stews beside Winchester Palace, they would simply move elsewhere. You cannot eradicate them, archbishop," he sneered. "Since the dawn of time, every city has had its brothels;

London is no different to anywhere else." Giving a brief nod, Gardiner walked away.

Thomas sighed. The list of grievances he had against this troublesome bishop seemed to be growing by the day. It was rumoured that Gardiner discretely kept several mistresses at Winchester Palace, and Thomas had also heard that one of his flunkeys was really a woman, dressed in male clothing. If this was indeed the case, the woman's apparel was against the law; it was illegal for women to dress in male attire. Regrettably, it was impossible for Thomas to address these issues, since his own situation – his marriage to Margaret – was not yet acceptable for an archbishop... or any other member of the clergy, for that matter. As things stood, he was unable to remonstrate with any immorality Gardiner was indulging in. He gave a deep sigh. This was an issue he must discuss with Cromwell, whose spies would soon discover whether or not the rumours were true.

Fortunately, Thomas' mind was swiftly diverted away from Stephen Gardiner, after being requested by His Majesty to informally interview Thomas More at Lambeth Palace. It appeared that the king still held some lingering regard for More, and he wished for Thomas to try and persuade him to sign the Act of Supremacy, so that he could be freed from the Tower and return to Court. Thomas had no great admiration for More – he was, after all, vigorously opposed to The New Learning – but if the man did not sign the oath, he would surely be executed for treason. He reasoned that this interview could be an opportunity to save the man's life, and perhaps persuade him to cast aside his Catholic leanings.

Bearing this in mind, he sat in his library at Lambeth, with his secretary Ralph Morice – his quill poised to record everything which was uttered – and Sir Thomas More. No one

172

else was present. More faced the archbishop cheerfully. His beard had grown ragged whilst in prison, and he had lost some weight, but his air of dignity remained. More assumed that the learned archbishop was hoping to persuade him to cast aside his Catholic faith, but as an equally learned man, he saw no reason why he should not do the same and try to persuade the archbishop to cast aside his Protestantism.

Thomas greeted More cordially, offering him refreshment, which was gladly accepted. The atmosphere between the two men was amiable; both were at ease in one another's company, despite having always disapproved of one another.

Thomas spoke first, his tone persuasive. "I know that you are fully aware of what is required of you, More. You are bound to obey your sovereign lord, the king, therefore you are bound to leave off the doubt of your unsure conscience in refusing the oath, and take the sure way by obeying your king, who commands you to swear."

Listening to that melodious voice – which in itself was convincing – and taking a sip of wine, More mentally saluted his companion. "My lawyer's brain has stood me in good stead until now, and I trust it shall continue to do so," he assured the archbishop. "Whatever other individuals may believe, whose consciences I will neither condemn nor judge, my own conscience perceives the truth to be otherwise." He was seated in the chair opposite the archbishop and kept his candid gaze upon him. "Whilst in the Tower, I have had time to diligently examine my conscience."

Meeting More's steadfast gaze, Thomas felt a surge of sadness. This man was clearly intractable, but not wishing for More to die, he was determined to persist. "I know you have studied the Bible, as I have. Surely God's word has revealed to you that the Pope has no position within the Church. He is the

Bishop of Rome, and as such is to be respected, but for him, as Pope, to hold such power and authority... it is not in accordance with God's most holy word."

"Surely then, the king cannot be Head of the Church? He is not even a member of the clergy," More promptly retorted.

After half an hour of debating with More, Thomas was buzzing with adrenaline, his body responding to the debate as though he were fighting a physical duel. More was an excellent orator and greatly learned; debating with him was truly stimulating. Before today, he had been wary of him, and had even purposefully avoided him on occasion. After all, More was bent upon imprisoning the Protestants. But now, well, he found himself rather enjoying the man's company. It was a great shame that they were such opposites theologically, for had they not been, he was convinced that they would have worked well together.

As the interview progressed, More repeated that the Act of Succession was one he had gladly approved. "As you know, I have often stated that a king may leave his throne to whomsoever he wishes. But I cannot agree with the Act of Supremacy, my lord Archbishop."

There was a moment of quiet; the rapid scratching of Morice's pen was the only sound in the room.

Casting theology and law aside, Thomas attempted to tempt More by speaking of his wife and family. "What about Lady Alice, your wife. I pray you consider her. I know you are a loving family man; you are close to your children, especially, I hear, your daughter Margaret. I understand she is very dear to you." At the mention of his wife and family, a look of sorrow crossed the prisoner's face, but Thomas could see that even this was not enough to change More's opinions. He was dealing with a very determined man.

174

The two argued for another two hours; had the circumstances been different, Thomas would have thoroughly enjoyed his time spent with More. He had been required to think deeply; to delve into his stores of knowledge in order to cap every quote or opinion More had thrown at him. He wished that More was not a prisoner; he would have made such an excellent debating companion. But there was nothing he could do, and eventually, he was forced to wearily dismiss the prisoner. Standing, he shook More's hand firmly, as they eyed one another with regret.

"Archbishop, I thank you for your kindness and hospitality. I deeply regret that we never conversed much in the past. I pray that, God willing, we shall oppose one another again."

"I too pray that we may meet again one day," Thomas sincerely replied. "May God keep you safe."

As he watched More being escorted from Lambeth Palace, an unusual surge of depression washed over him. It seemed brutally unfair that a man of such intellect and talent should be executed simply for believing in false theology. He needed to get away, to free his mind from this injustice. It did not take him long to decide the best cure was to travel to Canterbury for a few days, his excuse being that he needed to review the situation there. His spirits immediately lifted when he thought of seeing his wife again. Whenever she had not seen him for a few weeks, Margaret fussed over him endlessly, insisting that he looked pale and weary, and was not taking care of himself. Though some might find such pampering annoying, Thomas rather enjoyed it, and he was certain that her care would make him feel a thousand times better.

He was not disappointed, though given how much she had increased in girth, he protested that it was she who needed pampering. Margaret, however, ignored his protests; never one to complain, she insisted that she was in good health, and continued to fuss over her husband. As they sat together one evening, eating a hearty meal, he informed her of the real cause for his visit: his interview with Sir Thomas More.

"But you were always so wary of him... why are you now so compassionate? He is a Catholic who believes Protestants should be burned, my Thomas."

"Yes, but he is clever, and wise too. I knew he was an excellent orator, but I had never spoken to him at length before. He has such a wealth of knowledge, and yet is prepared to waste it all. I want him to understand the truth of the Protestant faith and thereby save his immortal soul. I want him to accept King Henry as Head of the English Church, so that he may be saved from the executioner's axe." He tried to explain his feelings. "If he signs the Act of Supremacy, he will be a free man, after which I would dearly love to convince him of the Protestant faith. If he would only embrace it, he could be such an asset to our cause."

"Maybe you can interview him again?" Margaret leaned back in her chair, her hands resting comfortably upon her sizeable stomach.

"Maybe. I would certainly like to speak to him before he is formally tried for treason." Thomas stifled a yawn. "I am going to write to Cromwell before I go to bed. He of all people will be able to intercede, and perhaps even convince the king not to bring Thomas More to trial. I shall ask him to intercede for Bishop Fisher as well, for though he has committed acts of treason, he is an old man. He deserves some sort of reprieve; perhaps he could just be kept in close confinement."

"Will they burn?" Margaret gave a shudder.

"No, probably not." Reaching out, he squeezed her hand reassuringly. "I do believe they shall either be beheaded or hung."

"Bad enough, but better than burning," Margaret replied solemnly.

Going to his desk, Thomas wrote to Cromwell: 'I commend myself to your good lordship. Fisher and More have both agreed to sign the Act of Succession. In my judgement, I would be satisfied with that. If it is made public that they have signed the Act of Succession, it will act as an example to others in the realm, who are in doubt. It might also finally convince the Emperor Charles that his aunt and her daughter are no longer part of the line of succession. As for the Act of Supremacy, could you intercede, and ask that these two men be spared from signing it? At least give them more time to consider the matter. If they are not given time, I fear they will shortly be sentenced to death and executed. The deaths of two such men – staunch supporters of the old order – will make a bloody beginning for the new. Your friend, Thomas Cranmer'.

A few days later, he received a reply. Cromwell had shown the letter to the king, but as far as Bishop Fisher was concerned, the king refused to change his mind. Pope Clement had recently died and had been replaced by Pope Paul III, a firm supporter of Fisher. During his first few weeks as Pope, Paul had decided to make Fisher a cardinal, an action which had thrown King Henry into a rage. As a result, Fisher was to be tried for treason within the next couple of days. By the time Thomas returned to Lambeth, Fisher had been tried, found guilty of treason, and sentenced to be beheaded that very day, on Tower Hill.

Hastily he journeyed to the Tower to visit the aged bishop prior to his execution. He found Fisher looking pathetically gaunt and weak. He was so frail that he could hardly walk, and a chair had been brought in so that he could be carried the short distance from the Tower to Tower Hill.

"I gave a letter to Bishop Gardiner following my trial," Fisher stated, his voice surprisingly firm and strong given his frail physical condition. "He will probably show it to you."

"What did you write?" Thomas prompted, doubting if Gardiner would divulge the contents of the letter.

"That I do not condemn any other man's conscience. Their conscience may save them, and mine must save me," Fisher replied. "I know we disagree theologically, my lord Archbishop, but just as I am about to face God, one day, you shall do likewise. I therefore ask you to search your soul and make peace with Him who is the ultimate judge."

Thomas noticed that Fisher was lovingly clutching at a well-worn copy of the gospel of John. He watched as the old man opened it at random.

Fisher's gaze fell upon chapter seventeen, verses three to five, and glancing towards his companion, he stated, "there is enough in this to last me to the end of my life." Straining to read the words – his eyesight was failing – he read aloud, translating from the Latin, "Now this is life eternal, that they might know Thee, the only true God, and Jesus Christ whom Thou hast sent. I have glorified Thee on the Earth; I have finished the work which Thou gravest me to do. And now, O Father, glorify me with Thine own self, with the glory which I had with Thee before the world was."

Thomas searched for the right words to say. "God be with you, Bishop Fisher," he managed, his voice unsteady.

"God has always been with me." Fisher reached out and took the hand of the archbishop. "I pray He shall always be with you, and that you shall heed His voice. May He bless you and keep you."

178

They could both hear the sound of footsteps approaching. Fisher's rheumy, faded eyes were dry, his face calm.

Thomas felt his own eyes welling up with tears. Biting his trembling lip, he watched the dignified old man being carried from his cell, still reading aloud from the gospel of St John. Half an hour later, he learned that Bishop Fisher had died, courageously and with dignity. As for the watching crowd, they had been sympathetically and respectfully silent. A tribute to a remarkable man.

He returned to Lambeth Palace, and a few hours later, received a brief letter from Sir Thomas More, which read: 'Regarding Bishop Fisher, I reckon that no one man possessed such wisdom, learning and virtue; no one can be matched and compared with him.' Thomas agreed. Fisher had lived selflessly and had served God as he saw fit. The pity of it was, his and Fisher's theological views had been too diverse to permit them to work easily together. They had each believed the other to be misguided. It was much the same with More, whose trial would be held the following day, at Westminster Hall.

Thomas was already present at Westminster Hall when More arrived by barge. Having always been popular, More was greeted by a large, noisy crowd of well-wishers. With halberdiers on either side of him, he was marched into the hall without preamble, and the trial proceeded immediately. When asked, More, his voice firm, declared himself innocent, and proceeded to ably defend himself as the trial continued.

Richard Rich, the newly made Solicitor General, having once been a servant in the More household, was called upon to give evidence. He revealed that he had visited More in the Tower, not to ask after his wellbeing – which might be expected, given he was a former servant – but to remove More's writing materials from his cell. When he heard this, Thomas felt his already low opinion of Rich descending lower still. How terrible, how cruel, to deprive such a man from his writing materials. Rich proceeded to describe a conversation he once had with More, claiming that the prisoner had openly denied Parliament's authority to make the king supreme Head of the Church in England.

Thomas took a deep breath to prevent himself from gasping aloud. He may never have been close to Sir Thomas More, but from his interview with him, he could honestly say that More was not a man who would ever have pronounced such an opinion to Richard Rich.

More was quick to make a response, which confirmed Thomas' own opinion. "In good faith, Master Rich, I am sorrier for your perjury than for my own peril." He proceeded to make an oath, denying the accusation, then cuttingly began to give his opinion of Rich. "Master Rich, I have long been acquainted with you, ever since your youth, and I am sorry to say that you were always light of tongue and not of good reputation. I appeal to the good sense of my honourable lordships, my judges. Does it truly seem likely that I would, in this trial, overshoot myself so far as to trust Master Rich, a man whom I have always reputed to be of little truth? Does it seem likely that I would utter to him the very secrets of my conscience regarding the king's supremacy?"

As More was speaking, Thomas glanced towards Rich, whose face had frozen. His entire posture was rigid, as if turned to stone. As a ripple of voices stirred around the hall, Rich suddenly flushed a deep red. At last, he moved, opening his mouth to protest, but was given no opportunity, for More, a skilled lawyer, proceeded to continue rallying to his own defence.

Thomas was impressed with More's vigour, for he knew, as did More, that the judgment was a foregone conclusion. The judges included the Duke of Norfolk, Sir Thomas Boleyn, George Boleyn, and others from the Boleyn camp; such a panel would not listen to More's argument, for the Boleyn camp wished him dead, to ensure that he could no longer cast doubt upon the validity of Anne's marriage to the king. More would be pronounced guilty, regardless of his defence.

Once the trial was over, More was marched from the hall, the blades of the axes held by the halberdiers turned towards him, signalling to the bystanders that he was guilty and condemned to die. Leaving the hall sometime later, Thomas learned that More's eldest daughter, Margaret, had forced her way through the crowds and flung herself at her father's feet, begging for his blessing. In a surprising display of sympathy, the guards had waited for this touching ceremony to be performed, whilst many in the crowd watched and wept. As Margaret was about to leave, she had turned back to her father and flung her arms about his neck, embracing him. More had uttered what words of comfort he could, holding his daughter until they were firmly parted, and he was marched back to the Tower.

The following Tuesday, More was executed on Tower Hill. The watching crowd was either silent or weeping. No one mocked or jeered. Like Fisher, he died bravely, and the crowd mourned his passing. The day after, Thomas learned that More's head had been removed from the spike upon which it had been placed on London Bridge, beside the head of Bishop Fisher. The rumours suggested that More's daughter and son-in-law were responsible – his family had no intention of this beloved man's head being pecked at by ravens – but it was impossible to say. To Thomas' surprise, the king gave no objection or indication of displeasure upon hearing of this crime; unbeknownst to his courtiers, his regard for More had been greater than any of them had realised, making the man's death all the more tragic.

A third person of importance died shortly after Bishop Fisher and Sir Thomas More, and that person was Catherine, the Princess Dowager. She was not executed, but her many supporters muttered that she might as well have been; her place of lodging had been damp and uncomfortable, and she had been separated from her beloved daughter, Lady Mary, whom she had frequently begged to be permitted to see. Had she been treated more sympathetically, her followers argued, she might well have lived longer.

"Right to the end, she insisted upon being referred to as the Queen of England." Cromwell's tone was belligerent. "She was a stubborn woman. In her last letter to His Majesty, she wrote: 'Lastly, I make this vow, that mine eyes desire you above all things. Farewell. Catherine, Queen of England'."

"Poor woman," Thomas murmured. "She was stubborn, certainly; misguided also. But she is to be pitied."

"Pitied!" Cromwell almost shouted. "Had she accepted that she was no longer queen, she could have seen her daughter whenever she wished, and lived according to her status."

"I agree." Thomas inclined his head. "But I see no reason not to pity her."

The two men had been requested to attend a masque, arranged by the queen in celebration of Catherine's death. Thomas felt that this in itself was in poor taste, and when they arrived Court, he was even more astonished to find both the king and queen dressed in yellow: a symbol of celebration. He said nothing, but internally, he could not help but feel let down by His Majesty's choice. Cromwell was, typically, more forthright in his opinions, but only to his friend, whom he knew would repeat nothing.

"Her Majesty's position is tenuous now," Cromwell whispered. "While the Dowager Princess lived, the king could not cast her aside. After all, he could hardly have two former wives; it would have been a political disaster. But now Catherine is gone, the queen is not safe until she bears a son."

"She is pregnant again," Thomas reminded his friend.

"Her security rests entirely upon the success of this pregnancy." Cromwell's tone was speculative.

"Her position is permanently secure," Thomas whispered sharply. "Lady Jane Seymour has now left Court and the queen herself is, as you well know, lawfully wed." Lady Jane Seymour had returned to her family home on the day Anne's pregnancy had been announced.

"Mistress Seymour left Court to avoid any scandal regarding her good self. I suspect she intends to use her departure to inflame the passion of the king, for she has two ambitious brothers to advise her, and they recommended that she should depart. She is following the tactics the queen herself once used, refusing to be a mistress, then keeping her distance. Trust me, my friend, she is well advised. As for the queen, she has offended every powerful nobleman at Court, including her uncle, the Duke of Norfolk. Catherine had powerful people to protect her, but Queen Anne is totally dependent upon her husband."

"The queen's position *is* secure," Thomas repeated, his tone agitated. A tingle of dread ran down his spine. Why was Cromwell implying otherwise? "What do you know?" he hissed.

"Nothing... yet," came the quick response. "We need to wait and see whether Her Majesty gives birth to a boy or a girl." Cromwell's tone was indifferent. "After that, we shall see what transpires. I can tell you this: she needs a son more than her predecessor ever did."

*****

A few weeks later, the king was knocked from his horse during a jousting tournament, and to the horror of the crowd of watching courtiers, he lay unconscious for several minutes. A messenger was immediately sent to the palace to inform the queen, and upon hearing the news, Anne waxed hysterical. By the time a second messenger arrived to inform her that the king was conscious again, she was doubled over with abdominal cramps, and tragically miscarried her baby. To add to the catastrophe, the midwife declared - once again - the child would have been a boy.

Thomas was summoned a few days later, to soothe the queen with spiritual counsel. He spent over an hour with her, listening to her anxious fears; praying with her; urging her to be gentle and submissive to her husband. King Henry, he knew, would not tolerate anything else. Since his previous effort to give her spiritual counsel had enabled her to become pregnant again, Anne respected his advice, and would have likely taken it, had the king not visited her immediately following the miscarriage to berate her for losing another male child. She had not seen him since; he was totally avoiding her company.

Two weeks passed and, upon hearing that Anne was fully recovered, Thomas visited her again. He found her almost feverishly merry. According to her ladies, her moods swayed between laughter and deep melancholy. The king, who was never subtle, had been heard several times shouting to anyone who cared to listen: 'I see clearly. God does not wish to give me male children!' Anne, who was likewise indiscrete, informed

184

Thomas, in front of her ladies, that she was afraid she would be treated the same way as the Princess Dowager had been.

"You are the queen, Your Majesty," he earnestly reminded her.

"So was she... at least, she thought she was," Anne retorted. They were both silent for a moment, then, taking a deep breath, Anne demanded abruptly, "why should I be to blame for the loss of the child? Both the midwife and Dr Butts informed me that the shock caused the loss of the babe."

"This may be true. His Majesty is shocked by both the accident and the loss of his son. When people are shocked, whether they are king or a commoner, their reactions are often bizarre." This was true enough, he decided. "As for the king, his leg is badly injured after the accident; he is in a great deal of pain."

"I know that." The queen gestured to her ladies to withdraw and seat themselves some distance away. "I wish to pray with my lord Archbishop," she stated, her tone haughty. Once they had left, her voice sank to a whisper. "Surely the loss of our children should draw us closer together. Why has he rejected me like this?"

Queen Catherine had lost a number of children, but it had certainly not helped her relationship with King Henry. Quite the reverse. It would not be of any help to Queen Anne to mention this, however, so Thomas kept his knowledge to himself. Instead, as before, he spent an hour with her, praying and trying to ease her distress, all the while knowing that he was failing miserably. The only thing that would soothe Anne was the return of King Henry's passion, and even he could see that the king's affection for Anne was totally spent.

Leaving the queen outwardly less hysterical, he sought out Cromwell, and found him looking gleeful.

"I am now Vicegerent," his friend announced proudly. "What a blow to Gardiner. He desired for the position to go to one of the Catholic Seymours, if he could not have the position himself."

Thomas congratulated him, thankful that this promotion had been given to someone whom he considered a friend, even if his and Cromwell's principles sometimes differed. A vicegerent could assume some of the sovereign's power when required to do so; this meant that, in Church matters – due to the break with Rome - Cromwell was now even senior to himself, the Archbishop of Canterbury. Thankfully, they both desired the same goal: the reformation of the Church.

"Now…" Cromwell's tone was brisk, and he rubbed his hands together, poised for action. "The king is weary of his wife. He wishes to be rid of her and says he will no longer share a bed with the woman. We, as his servants, need to find a means of granting him a divorce, even though he almost certainly intends to marry the Catholic Jane Seymour."

"How many times have I told you, he cannot," Thomas expostulated, frustrated by his friend's cool attitude.

"Ah, but he can," Cromwell pronounced darkly. "If she is unfaithful to him, she will be accused of treason."

"She is no fool, she would never—"

"She might," Cromwell interrupted smoothly. "You never know with these women. She is said to favour her musician, Mark Smeaton, and I learned from one of the Duke of Norfolk's staff that she used to be close to Harry Percy, son of the Duke of Northumberland. Perchance they were betrothed? In which case…" His voice, gleeful in tone, trailed away as he considered the use he could make of such knowledge, if it were true.

"I am sure that, if the queen was once betrothed to Harry Percy, it would be common knowledge. The son of the Duke of Northumberland has great status," Thomas reasoned logically.

"Perhaps Wolsey intervened?" Cromwell speculated. "The two might not have been formally betrothed; they may have made a private agreement to wed. Such an agreement is as binding as a formal contract."

Thomas was silent. Surely Queen Anne would not marry King Henry knowing she was legally bound to another man? As for Harry Percy, he had married a noble woman with a huge fortune… his marriage would be invalid too. "I am certain that the queen is not betrothed – or was not betrothed – before she married the king. She spoke with me on the eve before her marriage, in great confidence. She did not mention any engagement or pre-contract," he firmly assured his companion.

*****

That night, Thomas received a message informing him that his wife had gone into labour. Taking only a couple of trusted servants, one of them being Ralph Morice, he rode hastily to Canterbury, and arrived to find that Margaret had been delivered of a baby daughter. To his great relief, mother and baby were both well.

Weak with emotion, he sat on his wife's bed, clutching her hand whilst gazing upon the small bundle in her arms – his child! – and marvelling at the surge of love he felt for this tiny being. Looking pale and tired, Margaret was nonetheless eager to learn about events at Court.

"I heard about Sir Thomas More." She gazed adoringly at their child, having now placed her nearby in a rocking cot. "So

187

sad. As you said, he would have been a huge help to the Protestant cause if only he had not been so corrupted by the Catholic faith."

"I think you need to rest," Thomas informed her gently. "Do not overtire yourself."

"I have rested enough. The midwife says I had an easy labour, considering it was my first," Margaret proudly informed him, before swiftly asking how the queen was faring following the loss of her child. As Thomas described the queen's situation, Margaret promptly fell asleep. As he had suspected, she needed rest.

Some hours later, with the baby fed and settled – unfashionably, Margaret insisted upon nursing the baby herself, and would have nothing to do with a wet nurse – she asked, once more, about the queen's circumstances.

"You might fall asleep again," he teased. "But I will explain anyway. Cromwell is trying to obtain a divorce for the king, and to find grounds for this, he must find out whether Anne has ever been unfaithful to His Majesty. If she has been unfaithful, she will be accused of treason."

"These English laws seem odd to me. Why is being unfaithful to the king an act of treason?" Lying back on her pillows, Margaret held out her hand for him to hold.

Clasping her hand between both of his and chaffing it gently, he explained. "It is treason because any child she has borne during that marriage might not belong to the king."

"Ach, of course. It is obvious when explained." Unconsciously, her gaze drifted towards the sleeping baby.

"Most things are obvious once explained." He smiled briefly, then continued with his tale. "She was also once allegedly close to someone some years ago, and Cromwell is trying to prove that she was once betrothed to this man. His name is Harry Percy; at the time he was the son and heir of the powerful Duke of Northumberland. Now he is the Duke. "

"In Germany, a promise of marriage is the same as actual marriage." Margaret sighed. "If it is to be ended, it must be done so legally. I have never met the lady, but I have never heard anything good of her. She is not loved by the people. No one will mind if she is divorced. Do you think she was betrothed?"

"I have never heard it spoken of before." He too sighed. "I did hear that she was once in love with young Percy, but not that they were promised. As you have said, it is the same here as in Germany: a betrothal; a promise; a pre-contract… they all amount to the same thing. Marriage." There was no shame in a betrothed woman being pregnant when taking her actual wedding vows. In fact, especially for simple country folk, a pregnant bride was something to rejoice over. "If there is evidence of her committing adultery, or being promised to Percy, and if that promise was not legally made null and void, then I can pronounce the king to be a single man, and thus free to remarry."

"But what will happen to the queen?" Margaret leaned towards the cradle and touched the sleeping face of her baby, smiling in delight as she gazed upon the tightly closed eyes and the small, puckered mouth of her daughter.

In spite of the seriousness of their conversation, he too gave a besotted glance at his daughter. "Well, at one time, I could have predicted that the queen would be sent to a nunnery. However, everything is now in hand to have these institutions closed, so I very much suspect that she and her daughter will both have to retire to some house in the country. But if there are no grounds for divorce, well, His Majesty will have to find a means of cohabiting with Queen Anne. I admit, I am fond of

189

the woman, unpredictable though her temper is." He ran a gentle finger down her daughter's cheek. "Ah, why must I return to Court tomorrow? I find it so difficult to leave both of you, my two beautiful ladies."

"She looks just like her father," Margaret declared.

He looked startled. "I hope not, I have never regarded myself as handsome."

"But, my Thomas, I like your face," Margaret protested. "What shall we call her?"

"Margaret," came her husband's prompt response.

Margaret was thoughtful. "Only if I have a son and can call him Thomas. But two Margaret's will be confusing… could we refer to her as Marjorie? I do like that name."

"Anything you wish," he beamed indulgently. He hesitated for a moment, taking a deep breath. "I think I should like hold her, but she is so tiny."

"She will grow, my husband. Do not be afraid. Lift her from her cradle and hold your daughter." She watched, smiling, as he tentatively lifted the child. "Marjorie, your father holds you. You will always be safe with him."

His voice was hoarse with emotion. "I pray that she shall always be safe. May God bless you and keep you, my daughter."

*****

Upon returning to Court, Thomas received a letter from Philip Melanchthon, which was full of news describing how dangerous it was now to be a reformist in Germany. The emperor might be still engaged with fighting the Turks, but he was also managing to find time to begin purging Germany of Protestants. 'I suggest you make contact with a man named Jean Calvin', Melanchthon wrote. 'He is from France, where it is

190

even more violent and dangerous to be Protestant than it is here. He trained as a lawyer, and has been staying here for several months, but he will soon depart for Geneva. I consider him exceedingly learned and strongly recommend you begin corresponding with him'.

Communicating with Protestants from other countries was a source of both knowledge and support, so he was eager to make contact with this Jean Calvin. However, there was currently so much going on at Court that a letter would have to wait for another time. Cromwell's programme to close the monasteries had begun. Making use of the ruthless ambition of Richard Rich, Cromwell had sent him all over the country to plunder the wealth of religious houses and evict the monks and nuns.

His friend Cromwell's capacity for coldness often rendered him   uneasy, and on several occasions, it had caused a disagreement between them, though neither of them were of a temperament to bear grudges. Furthermore, Cromwell did not actually expect constant agreement and approval from the Archbishop of Canterbury; he had sufficient confidence to act upon his own instincts and opinions.

"What about those who are evicted, what will happen to them?" Thomas demanded, when Cromwell visited him in his library at Lambeth.

"They are to be given a sum of money, all of them, the nuns too. They are expected to use it wisely, maybe to establish themselves in some sort of employment," Cromwell responded smoothly. "After all, had they not entered into a religious house, they would have had to do so anyway. Many of them have lived in lazy luxury for years. Let them find out what it is like to live in the real world."

"But what about the elderly?" Thomas persisted. "Some of them are too old to work."

"They must seek out their families; throw themselves on their mercy," was Cromwell's cool response.

"I fear they might end up as beggars... what about those who refuse to leave?" Thomas found himself growing more and more uneasy about the programme of dissolution. Especially since Richard Rich was heavily involved. "And what about those who refused to sign the Acts of Supremacy and Succession?"

"They have no choice but to leave; their monasteries are being torn down and ripped apart. And if they do not sign the Acts, they shall be tried for treason," Cromwell shrugged indifferently. "They are no different to anyone else in this matter, Cranmer."

"I had hoped the old buildings might be retained and used as schools." Thomas gave a grimace of disappointment. It seemed such a tragedy to pull those lovely buildings down; they could surely be put to good use. He turned his attention back to the queen. "What have you managed to unearth regarding the queen and Percy?" he enquired anxiously.

"I believe that the queen should have been investigated prior to her marriage." Cromwell's face was a mask of sincerity. "Certainly, since her marriage, I believe she has been unfaithful. But I am also becoming more and more confident that she was betrothed, or promised, to young Percy, and is therefore not the king's true wife." Seeing his companion taking a breath to interrupt, he quickly added, "She would be wise to admit to her betrothal, for she has been indiscreet. Tom Wyatt, the poet, treats her with too much familiarity, as does Francis Bryan, and there are others. Her relationship with her musician, Mark Smeaton, will not stand up to close scrutiny. Her sister-in-law is certain that George Boleyn, the queen's own brother, is committing incest with her."

"That is ridiculous!" Thomas exclaimed. Lady Jane Rochford was a jealous woman, and a bitter enemy to Queen Anne; it was no wonder that she was spreading such salacious rumours. Certainly, the queen was close to her brother... but incest? It was impossible. Queen Anne had often spoken to him, confidentially, about her sister-in-law's deep hatred for her, and she had often asked God's forgiveness for deliberately tormenting and mocking the woman. "The queen has never conducted any sort of indiscretion with her brother," he stated firmly. "And I am certain that she has not done so with anyone else. If she was once betrothed to Percy, that is a valid enough reason for me to grant the king a divorce, so there is no need for you to investigate these other ridiculous rumours. Once *if* divorce is granted, Anne can go and live peacefully somewhere, perhaps at her old home, Hever Castle." Thomas began picking anxiously at his sleeve. "She will not take easily to a life of peace, but there is no alternative."

"Unfortunately, my friend, there is an alternative," Cromwell contradicted. "An alternative that she may well be forced to endure." As his companion shot a questioning glance in his direction, Cromwell dropped his voice to a whisper. "There is a significant possibility that she will die."

"What?" Thomas stood so quickly that he knocked over a side table in the process, launching a mug of ale and a prayer book across the floor. Agitated, he demanded that Cromwell explain himself.

"The king does not want another divorce; it would be too messy politically, especially since it is a relatively short time since you declared him free to marry Lady Anne. I have questioned the queen, and she vehemently denies having any form of pre-contract with Percy. The king knows that the only solution is to find her guilty of treason, for consorting with other men, and you and I both know the punishment for treason..." Cromwell's tone was cold and uncompromising.

Thomas seated himself again, corrected the overturned table, and stared silently at the wall as the shock of Cromwell's words slowly sank in. Desperately, he attempted to clarify the situation. "But if she admits to pre-contract, then she was never married in the first place, and therefore cannot be executed for treason."

"This is true." There was a sinister twist to Cromwell's smile. "But she denies that she was ever pre-contracted."

Thomas fell silent again. Automatically, he reached for his cup to take a sip of ale, but soon discovered that only a few dregs had survived the overturning of the table. Most of the ale was soaking into the rushes on the floor. He stared blindly into his empty mug, his mind elsewhere. Henry, he was certain, would not consider executing a woman whom he had once loved so deeply. He would surely banish Anne instead, permitting her to live out her life in comfortable seclusion. After all, she was the mother of his child. Certainly, Anne may have been foolish, but no one could deny that Elizabeth was Henry's own daughter; her very appearance was testament to her paternity. Cromwell had misunderstood the king's wishes.

"I am entertaining Master Mark Smeaton later tonight." Cromwell broke the silence.

Cromwell... entertaining a musician? There must be an ulterior motive. "You intend to question him, don't you?" he guessed.

"Of course," Cromwell shrugged. "The Duke of Norfolk has agreed to assist me."

"Norfolk?" Thomas was incredulous. Norfolk hated Cromwell.

"He is the queen's uncle as well you know, and the queen has now fallen from grace. Since Norfolk has no reason to like the woman, even though she is his niece, he has agreed to assist the king in getting rid of her, to avoid himself also falling from grace. It all works out very well for him, you know." Cromwell's tone was confiding. "He is Catholic, as is Mistress Seymour, whom the king intends to marry. By ensuring that this marriage goes ahead, Norfolk believes he will secure himself a position of power at Court."

The eagerness with which men such as Cromwell, Norfolk and Rich tried to obtain positions at Court constantly amazed him. Court was a place of political mind games and treachery; no one was safe, not even the king, who had to constantly monitor the mood of his subjects, to avoid giving them cause for revolt.

The following morning, he received a brief but damning note from Cromwell, stating that the musician Mark Smeaton had last night admitted to receiving sexual favours from the queen, who was now accused of treason and was on her way to the Tower. The other men who frequently waited on her, including her brother, Lord Rochford, were to be interrogated later that day. There was no way back now. The brief but tumultuous reign of Queen Anne had come to an end.

Chapter Nine

The queen's fall was swift and terrible. She was arrested; taken by barge to be imprisoned in the Tower, and within a week, was on trial in the great hall of the Tower of London. There, she was found guilty of witchcraft and adultery, and was sentenced to die by burning or beheading, in accordance with the king's mercy. As with Sir Thomas More's trial, the outcome was a foregone conclusion; several men had already been found guilty of committing adultery with her. Francis Bryan, and the poet, Tom Wyatt, were found innocent, owing to lack of evidence, but Henry Norris, William Brereton, Francis Weston and the musician, Mark Smeaton, had already been sentenced. Smeaton, being of humble birth, was to be hung at Tyburn, whist the others were to be beheaded on Tower Hill. Most shockingly, George Boleyn, Anne's own brother, was also found guilty of committing adultery with his sister; he too was to be beheaded.

At the trial, he noted that Smeaton's eyes were heavily bruised, and various visible parts of his body appeared discoloured; when he asked Cromwell whether Smeaton had been tortured to obtain his confession, Cromwell's answer was evasive, all but confirming Thomas' suspicions. The entire situation was deeply unsettling; he could accept that the king would permit his once beloved wife to be found guilty of treason, but to deliver the death penalty? The very thought of it made him recoil in horror. It was impossible for him to accept that the king would condemn her to death unless he was absolutely certain of her treachery. But whilst he frantically desired to believe that the trial had been just, he could not shake off his doubts. Having spent a great deal of time with Anne, he had never observed her being anything more than flirtatious with her admirers... but to have sentenced her to death, the king must certainly think her guilty.

His thoughts in turmoil, he decided to write to the king, in an attempt to ease his troubled mind. 'Your Majesty, I am most perplexed,' he wrote. 'My mind is clean amazed, for I never had a better opinion of a woman than I had of her, which makes me think that she should not be culpable. Then again, I know Your Highness would not have gone so far as to sentence her to death had she not been culpable. I loved her not a little for the love which I judged her to bear towards God and His gospel...'. The letter rambled on for several pages, but Thomas knew that it would make no difference. The queen would die regardless. Feeling pessimistic, he despatched Ralph Morice to Court to deliver the missive to the king.

Soon after Anne's trial, Thomas was informed that the king had chosen mercy when it came to Anne's execution. There would be no flames, nor would she have to endure the axe. Instead, a swordsman had been sent for from Calais, to strike off her head with the sharp, swift, blade of a sword. It was a relief to know that Anne would be spared a slow, painful death. Then came a summons from the king, who wished to see him immediately at Hampton Court. Concerned that this summons might have something to do with his confused letter, he travelled swiftly to Court, before his anxiety got the better of him.

He found the king standing alone in an anteroom, subdued in manner, as was to be expected. Bowing, Thomas waited anxiously for him to speak.

"We are sorely saddened by this, my lord Archbishop," the king said solemnly, his tone heavy as he began pacing around the chamber, still limping as a result of his jousting wound. "She bewitched me, you know. She bewitched everyone, even you."

Thomas did not believe he had been bewitched by Anne. Certainly, although she had occasionally caused him discomfort by reminding him of Joan; he had admired her for her intelligence, style and wit, but he could not believe that she had bewitched him, or indeed anyone else. It was her personality that had drawn people to her; women had been less fond of her because she had chosen to focus her attention on men. The ladies who had once surrounded her had simply been tolerated. by her. At least, that was his opinion, though he knew it was too late to try and explain his reasoning to the king.

They spoke for a while, shifting between various topics, until the king finally decided to reveal the reason for this visit.

"My lord Archbishop, we wish for you to travel to the Tower tomorrow to visit the queen. We are troubled regarding her relationship with Thomas Percy. You see, if she was promised to him, then she could not have been lawfully married to anyone... let alone her monarch." The king eyed his companion soulfully, his expression pained and sincere.

Thomas felt his heart give a leap of hope. "I will go gladly, Your Majesty," he declared. "I wish to see her in any case, to spend some time in prayer with her."

"Rightly so." The king pursed his lips. "We have spent much time in prayer these past few weeks."

The following morning, Thomas travelled from Lambeth Palace to the Tower. For centuries, the Tower of London had been a royal residence, but after various individuals of importance had been imprisoned there and subsequently executed, it had become regarded as a sinister, unsavoury place. Brushing these thoughts aside, he concentrated on his mission, which was to counsel Queen Anne and seek to save her from execution. He was optimistic. How could a mother desire execution, instead of watching her child grow up? Given the circumstances, Anne would now surely admit to pre-contract if she had agreed to marry Harry Percy; and possibly even if she had *not* agreed to any such betrothal. Such a false admittance was against the word of God; but Thomas reasoned that, since the guilt would lay with her soul and not his, it was not his problem whether she told the truth or not.

His barge docked at the Watergate, and he was greeted by Sir William Kingston, Lieutenant of the Tower, who escorted him to the queen's rooms.

"My lord Archbishop, you are welcome."

The lieutenant was a humane man, who was always respectful and polite, and having met him several times, Thomas had found himself warming to him.

Lowering his voice so only the visitor could hear, Kingston whispered, "my lord, I pray you, I don't know exactly why you are here, perhaps it is merely to soothe Queen Anne's soul. But if it is possible for you to entreat the king to spare her, I beg you to do so."

Thomas regarded the man's earnest face and replied truthfully. "That is the purpose of my visit. Tell me, has the queen said anything to you which might bring about her pardon?" Kingston seemed the kind of man whom Anne – or indeed any prisoner – might confide in.

"She has said nothing." Kingston was apologetic.

"Then I charge you to pray for me as I speak with her," he requested, pressing Kingston's arm gently. "Much depends upon this time I spend with her."

"I assure you of my prayers," Kingston replied quietly. "God bless your mission, my lord Archbishop."

Thomas was promptly shown into the queen's quarters and found her exactly as he had expected: bright, brittle, full of restless gaiety, and, as was typical of Anne, exuding elegance. She was wearing a gable head dress instead of her usual French hood, and the severity of the style suited her angular features.

"My lord Archbishop," she greeted him warmly, extending her hand for him to kiss. "I am glad to see you; I am sorely in need of diversion."

"May I speak with you privately?" he enquired, having bowed and kissed her hand.

"Of course. These ladies watch me constantly, but they can trust me with my husband's archbishop." She dismissed the women who hovered around her with an almost contemptuous flick of her hand, and as they retreated, she whispered, "some of them are spies. They report everything I say and do to my lord Cromwell, and, of course, my husband. I can honestly say that, thus far, they have found nothing of interest to report."

He observed Anne's attendants, most of whom were clearly reluctant to move out of earshot. They were eyeing him with open curiosity. "I wish to hear the queen's confession," he gently informed them. "I beg you to respect the confidentiality of this."

The women bowed their heads politely and reluctantly retreated further into the background, where they could no longer hear what was being said.

He held back a smile of relief; much though he disagreed with the Catholic ritual of confessing to a priest, on this occasion, it had its uses. "My lady Anne, I am here to save your life." Seating himself opposite her, he kept his voice low. "It is well reported that, some years ago, you were close to my lord Percy, and it is also said that you entertained a desire to marry him. If you admit to being promised to him, my lady, it will invalidate your marriage to the king, and thus save you from execution. You cannot be accused of adultery against the king if you were already promised to my lord Percy."

Anne was silent, twisting her hands together anxiously. For a while, he thought she was not going to reply. Eventually, her voice came out in an anguished whisper. "But I am a mother, my lord Cranmer. As a mother, can I permit my child to be a bastard? She shall be considered as such if I admit to being promised to Percy."

He wondered how to respond to this. To be a bastard child invariably meant a life of ignominy; but when the father was King of England, well, matters were different. "The bastard Duke of Richmond, the king's son, was well thought of, my lady," he eventually managed to whisper. "He had his own household and lived in fine style, right up until his untimely death."

"But he was male. Look at the fallen state of Lady Mary." Anne's tone was sharp.

Thomas nodded slowly. Yes, Lady Mary's lot was hard. But that was chiefly due to Anne's influence. Fond though he had become of the queen, he had to admit that Anne's treatment of Mary had not been kind. "Richmond was well looked after by the king, as would Mary have been, had she agreed to sign the Acts of Supremacy and Succession," he stated tactfully. "Elizabeth will be equally cared for. If you admit you were pre-contracted, not only shall she be well cared for, but she shall also have her mother by her side, to ensure she is looked after according to her status."

Anne's gaze was sad and inscrutable. Rising abruptly from her chair, she began to restlessly pace around the room.

Thomas wondered what was going on inside her head, and decided once again to stress the benefits of admitting to being pre-contracted. "My lady, you must realise that it will be impossible to execute you for adultery if you admit to pre-contract. If you have these past years not been lawfully married to the king, you will simply be guilty of the sin of lying with a man who is not your husband."

There was a glimmer of acknowledgment and hope written upon Anne's countenance. She seated herself again. "I have not committed adultery; I am innocent of that." She said this loudly enough for her ladies to hear. "Not with my brother or any of the others who have been condemned to die."

"And pre-contract?" he whispered hopefully. "I have a document within my sleeve; if you sign it, it will mean you are not lawfully married to the king and have committed no error other than to deceive him. Indeed, you will have actually committed adultery with him, since Lord Percy is, in effect, your rightful husband. You will be sent to a place of safety, of that I am sure," he urged.

"I would like to retire to a nunnery… with Elizabeth…" A loud, bitter laugh exploded from her lips. "Except that Master Cromwell is going to rip them all down."

Having already considered this, Thomas gave a slow nod of agreement. "There are other places for you though. Perhaps Hever Castle?"

"No, a convent in France. I shall settle there in obscurity, if Henry permits it," she declared decisively.

"Does this mean you will sign to say you were pre-contracted to Percy?"

"Yes." Tears rolled down her cheeks. "A while back, when he was asked, he declared that we were never betrothed. But we were in love. Deeply in love. He wanted to marry me, though we never dared to declare it publicly. As a Boleyn, I was not good enough for his family." Her voice was bitter. "His father and Wolsey forbade it, but I agreed to marry him. We were truly married." She gave him a meaningful look.

"Your union was consummated?" he clarified.

"Yes," she sighed, wiping her eyes with her fingers. "We were told never to speak of it. Wolsey and the late Lord Percy said that if we did, it would surely injure Harry's future career. Wolsey insisted that I should swear to keep silent. So I did, and have, until now. Harry went on to marry an heiress, who brought him more money and lands than I ever could. Bring out your document, my lord Archbishop; I shall sign it. Then, if you will, I request that you give me and my ladies the sacrament."

"Of course, I shall be most glad to do so." Smiling broadly, he produced the document for her to sign, and Anne signalled for one of her women to bring a pen and some ink. During that moment of delay, Thomas found himself trembling, lest she should abruptly change her mind. He shielded the document as one of her ladies, avid with curiosity and clearly straining to see what was written, placed both pen and ink on the table.

"My lord Archbishop, as well as saving my life, shall this save the life of my brother?" Anne asked, her face alight with hope. "Of course, you know how vilely his wife has testified against him. She could never bear that he was fond of me and not of her."

"I cannot say," he answered apologetically, realising that he had yet to consider the outcome for the men involved in this sorry business. "Though it is logical to assume that they shall be spared," he surmised hopefully.

Anne heaved a deep sigh. "It is strange to think that it is all over now; that I am no longer Queen of England." She regarded him with a wry smile. "I was not good enough for my lord Percy's family, yet the king was wild to marry me... and now this. It makes one wonder how things might have been different, had Harry's family been more obliging. Ladies..." Anne stood gracefully and clapped her hands. "Please come and receive the sacrament with me."

As Thomas delivered both the bread and wine, Anne clearly uttered the words 'I am innocent', prompting him to smile faintly in approval.

Once his task was completed, and with the precious document hidden within his sleeve, he bowed to Anne and departed, making his way back to the river and the barge, which would take him back to Hampton Court. Leaning back in his seat, he felt a surge of relief. She had signed the document; her life would be spared.

As the barge slowly made its way back to Court, he reflected on the time he had spent praying with Anne. It was not so very long ago that she had requested his counsel on the eve of her wedding; clearly her soul had been troubled, and now he knew the reason. Her conscience had been uneasy. She had been engaged to marry Harry Percy; the verbal contract between them had never been formally annulled. As for today, Anne had sworn innocence whilst taking the sacrament, which meant a gross miscarriage of justice had occurred. Cromwell had definitely applied torture to obtain Smeaton's confession, especially since none of the other men had admitted having carnal knowledge of the queen. He could only assume that the witnesses who had been brought forward to testify against these men, had been bribed to do so by Cromwell. But it did not matter now. The document was signed; Anne would live, and if justice prevailed, so would all the men who had been wrongly accused.

Later that day, after first of all meeting with several of his bishops to discuss the queen's admission of pre-contract, he formally declared the marriage between King Henry VIII and Lady Anne Boleyn null and void. Having carried out this duty, he attended an audience with the king and Cromwell.

The king was doleful, still playing the part of the cuckolded husband. When Thomas presented him with Anne's signed document, he perused it briefly, before promptly placing the paper upon a table. There followed a moment of unbearable silence, as Thomas awaited the king's verdict. Would he spare the woman whom he had once loved so dearly? His gaze flickered anxiously between the king and Cromwell.

Finally, the king spoke. "Well done, my lord Archbishop." In recent months, Henry had gained a considerable amount of weight, his injury preventing him from taking vigorous exercise. When seated, this caused his spreading abdomen to become unflatteringly accentuated. "We require you to announce that we have never been lawfully married to Lady Anne Boleyn. This must be publicly acknowledged."

"Of course, Your Majesty. I have already declared your marriage invalid; when I return to Lambeth, I shall prepare a public announcement. It shall be read aloud in all of the cathedrals in the country, and notices shall be placed in churches, market crosses, and other significant places."

"I am glad to hear it. The queen shall die in the privacy of Tower Green. The carpenters shall begin erecting the scaffold," the king announced with finality.

Thomas stared mutely at his monarch, desperately hoping he had misheard. Surely the king would not ignore the opportunity to save the life of a woman who had borne him a child?

Casting a sympathetic glance towards his friend, Cromwell murmured, "Your Majesty has been kind, she shall not suffer. The headsman is marvellously skilled."

Thomas fought the urge to shout, 'how would you know? You have never been beheaded!'

It was some hours before he finally returned to Lambeth Palace, and the time seemed to drag as he awaited Anne's execution the following morning. The men had been beheaded that very afternoon, and Anne's brother, George, had turned his execution into something of a social event, shaking hands with some of the crowd and even preaching a pro-Reformation sermon. It had taken the headsman several strikes to sever his head, but George had remained stoically silent throughout.

Thomas passed most of the night in his library, pacing the floor, his mind too distressed to read. He dismissed the attentive Ralph Morice, insisting that he needed to spend some time alone. Finally, he wandered outside, breathing in the sweet morning air. The coolness of the dew on the grass calmed his mind, and with rising optimism, he clung to the knowledge that the king loved dramatic gestures; perchance he might deliver a last-minute reprieve? Then, suddenly, he heard it: the sound of cannons firing. It was over. The queen was dead.

At that moment, Ralph Morice anxiously approached him. "My lord Archbishop, may I get anything for you? Some warm mulled ale perhaps?"

Thomas found himself looking into his secretary's round, kindly face, and promptly burst into tears. "No, Master Secretary. She who has been Queen of England upon Earth will today become Queen in Heaven," he sobbed, his words barely distinct.

"Indeed so, my lord," Morice acknowledged gently. "Her soul rests with God, and in His good time, we shall be reunited with her, and all others who have died belonging to the Lord."

Thomas nodded mutely. She had never been married to the king; she ought to have been spared. She had been beheaded for committing adultery against someone who was not even her husband. It was as Cromwell had so astutely observed: the king had not wanted two divorces within such a short period of time. Yet although he grieved for the queen and the injustice of her execution, he could not bring himself to point a finger of blame towards Henry. He was the king. He ruled according to God's will.

*****

Soon after Anne's execution, an Act of Suppression and Dissolution was passed, decreeing that all religious establishments with an income of two hundred pounds or less per annum, were to be suppressed; any with a greater income were to be dealt with later. Not for the first time, Thomas wondered at Cromwell's brilliance when it came to organisation. For the most part, he approved of the dissolution, though he regretted none of the wealth would be used for education. The king adored pomp and display, but this was expensive, and despite receiving the wealth which had once been sent to Rome, he still had insufficient funds for his needs.

Consequently, His Majesty had decided that all money acquired from the dissolution belonged exclusively to the monarch.

Cromwell had promised to provide His Majesty with wealth, and he knew that the sale of monastic lands would provide a hefty boost to the royal coffers. Lead from the rooves was melted down and sold, whilst jewels and plates were placed directly into the waiting royal coffers. The king, who had married Lady Jane Seymour within ten days of Anne's death, was jubilant; not only was he madly in love, but he was also rich again.

During the immediate weeks following Anne's death, Thomas found an excuse to take time away from Court. Despite the new queen being Roman Catholic, Catholic bishops were currently unpopular, and some of the Protestant clergy had managed to ensure that the Catholic Bishop of Norwich, Richard Nix, was placed under praemunire, thus prohibiting him from maintaining his papal jurisdiction. It seemed a good idea for him to visit Norwich, to see just what was happening there. Although he was heartened that Protestant clergy were gaining in popularity and numbers, it was wrong for them to misuse their advantage by exaggerating complaints against a Catholic bishop. He preached to them on this subject, but it would take time to know whether or not they had taken note of his words.

From Norwich, Thomas travelled to Canterbury, there to preach to his own clergy, reinforcing the fact that the king was now Head of the Church of England, something many of the clergy still refused to accept. Whilst there, he was also able to confide in the person whom he trusted most: his wife.

"I still consider Cromwell a friend," he informed her, as they sat in the garden one mild, fragrant summer evening. "But this business with the queen makes me…" He searched for an appropriate word.

Margaret took his hand and rubbed his palm soothingly. "It makes you regard him less favourably than you once did?"

He pondered over this for a while. "Yes, I suppose so," he finally agreed. "Now that I have seen just how ruthless and manipulative he can be, he has gone down in my estimation. It is frightening how coolly he engineered the downfall of the queen. It makes me uneasy; I find myself wondering whether Cromwell would calmly organise my own downfall, if the king wished for his Archbishop of Canterbury to be arrested."

"But you have to keep working with him?"

"I have little choice. Besides, I still find myself admiring his energy, his astute mind, and his quick thinking. I cannot keep pace with him."

"And for that, I praise God," Margaret retorted sincerely. "I too find myself liking him when we meet. But I would not wish to be his wife."

"Well, for that, my dear, I too praise God." He was thoughtful for a moment. "When I return to Lambeth, will you and Marjorie come with me?"

"Our bags are already packed," she announced, giving him a smug smile.

An hour later, while Thomas was busily going through papers in his library, a servant knocked on the door to inform him that the Prior of the Black Friars was waiting outside, firmly demanding to see the Archbishop of Canterbury. Assuming this was something to do with the dissolution of the monasteries, he bade the servant to permit the man to enter.

The prior was an austere looking man, who soon proceeded to make it clear that he disapproved of the archbishop's sermons on the subject of the break with Rome, especially

209

when they touched upon the low morals of monastic establishments. Refusing the offer of a seat, he pointed a long bony finger towards his superior. "You have preached uncharitably, I fear," he accused. "The Pope is the spiritual descendant of Saint Peter. How dare you defile the Roman Church!"

Gently, Thomas began to dispute the prior's statement. "Does not the Bible show us that the kings of the Old Testament held religious authority?" Observing that the prior was about to interrupt, he hastily added, "Saint Paul himself wrote, in his letter to the Romans, that there is no power but of God, and that the powers that be are ordained of God."

He had been quick to ask the prior if he was educated, to which the reply had been a haughty 'yes, I can both read and write'. It was soon evident, however, that the prior was unable to match the knowledge of the archbishop. He was also garrulous, and Thomas knew that he would not leave quickly or quietly. Eventually, he was persuaded to depart, still stubbornly refusing to accept the archbishop's rationale.

"I fear you have not seen the last of him," Morice remarked, as the departing figure of the prior was escorted from the room. "You have given him words of truth, my lord Archbishop, but I doubt if they have entered his heart."

"I pray he accepts them, for the sake of his soul," Thomas replied fervently.

*****

Less than a week after Thomas had returned to Court, Cromwell took him aside to inform him that a rumour had been spreading, regarding his good self, the Archbishop of Canterbury.

210

Watching his friend's cheeks flush crimson with embarrassment, Cromwell smiled slyly. "No, archbishop, the scandal does not concern a certain lady who is currently residing at Lambeth Palace," he reassured him. "The culprit is from Black Friars. A prior, in fact. He has been speaking against you, saying that you do not know what you are talking about, and he appears to be rapidly gaining support. This cannot be allowed to continue; the king himself knows of it and is furious. I have had the man imprisoned."

"I saw him at Canterbury not very long ago," Thomas admitted. "I interviewed him, and he disagreed with my views, refusing to accept any of them. But he is simply misguided, you should not have had him imprisoned."

"Certes, you mean to say that you just let him go?" Cromwell was incredulous.

"I excused him... I did not think that he would cause any trouble. It is an established fact that the friars do not like me very much. At Cambridge, they were the most badly educated of all the clergy, and I used to insist that they should learn to read, write, and learn the scriptures."

"Well, he cannot go around discrediting the Archbishop of Canterbury. Are you aware that he is declaring that you are nothing more than an ostler?"

"An ostler? How strange..."

"Is there a reason why he should think you are an ostler?" Cromwell enquired.

"When I was married to my first wife, she worked at an inn... perhaps that is where the rumour stems from?" he mused. "I was never an ostler; I have never even worked at an inn."

"Regardless, he cannot go on doing this. He must be tried and found guilty, quickly." Cromwell was brisk. "Tomorrow morning will suffice. I shall have him delivered to Lambeth Palace."

Thomas frowned. "Delivered to Lambeth… what have you done to him, Cromwell?" For a wild moment, he wondered whether the friar had received similar treatment to Smeaton, the former queen's unfortunate musician.

"As I have told you, I had him put in prison – the Fleet Prison, to be precise – several days ago. I think that experience will be enough to teach him not to meddle with the Archbishop of Canterbury." Cromwell's reply was disarmingly smooth. "Let him cool his heels in that vile place. Meanwhile, I suggest you ask a couple of your bishops to assist you with your examination of him tomorrow, to ensure you are not too lenient with him."

Thomas reluctantly agreed to Cromwell's suggestion, deliberately choosing two bishops whom he knew were sympathetic to the Protestant cause: the bishops of Ely and Rochester. The following morning, Cromwell was the first of the interrogators to arrive, entering the archbishop's Lambeth library to find the prior already seated, looking filthy; his hair and beard matted and greasy. Thomas noticed Cromwell kept a fair distance between himself and the prior, probably because the latter was likely to be verminous. The bishops soon arrived, and at last they were ready to commence. As was usual, Ralph Morice was seated at a table, ready to record the morning's proceedings.

Having already thought about how to begin this examination, Thomas addressed the prisoner respectfully. Mankind was God's creation; behaving disrespectfully towards others was an offense against God Himself. "I hear you have been speaking unfavourably of me; that you have been discrediting my knowledge to all and sundry? Perhaps you wish to discuss philosophy, sciences, or else divinity with me, so that we may understand one another better? You may address all of us here in Latin or Greek if you should prefer."

The prior's eyes widened with alarm. It sounded mightily impressive to speak against the archbishop in alehouses and such places, but it was another matter to be face to face with him, in the company of other august persons, to boot. "I beseech Your Grace to pardon me. I have no knowledge of Latin or Greek, only English," he admitted sheepishly. Perhaps it was due to his days and nights in the Fleet, but he was infinitely less belligerent than he had been at Canterbury.

Thomas nodded, having suspected as much. "Well then, if you shall not argue against me, I shall debate with you. Do you read the Bible?"

"Oh yes," the prior's expression as one of relief. "Every day."

Thomas offered a simple question. "Answer me this, then. Who was David's father?"

"I am not knowledgeable in these genealogies," the prior confessed, beginning to look distinctly uneasy again.

Thomas, seated at his desk, leaned forward. "Then I can now bear witness to the fact that you, prior – despite slandering my good name with claims that my knowledge is not sufficient to be an archbishop – know nothing. You are simply one of the many in this realm who sit upon their benches, slandering honest men. If you had any common sense in your head, you would have realised that the king, wishing to be divorced from his first wife, would not have summoned an ostler to solve the situation. He would not send an ostler to the Bishop of Rome, the emperor's council, and other princes, to discuss this matter. I was even sent to the College of Cardinals."

213

The prior, still looking sheepish, was wishing he had not been so loose with his tongue. It was unlikely he would be dismissed from this room without receiving some dire punishment.

"I can but apologise, Your Grace. I spoke wrongly. I shall never utter such things again." Immediately, the prior regretted his words. He had recognised Thomas Cromwell, the king's vicegerent, a man rumoured to be unafraid of delivering torture when he so wished. He might just have reminded Cromwell that the best way to ensure silence *was* to cut out his tongue.

Leaning back against his chair, Thomas glanced around at his companions, all of whom were muttering and shaking their heads at the folly of the accused man. He decided not to confer with them, having reached his own conclusion. This man was now terrified and, for that reason, would never again raise his voice against the Archbishop of Canterbury. "God amend you." Thomas waved a hand in a dismissive gesture. "Get out of here, and from henceforth, learn to be an honest man, or at least a reasonable man."

Almost gibbering with gratitude and relief, the prior bowed and scurried from the room, lest anyone should pronounce otherwise.

"Now you see why I insist that all clergy should have some education," he remarked to his companions, adding, "and this man informed me at Canterbury that he was educated!"

Cromwell shook his head, bemused. "This is the shortest hearing I have ever attended. I would they were all so. I have to say, if he is a typical example of a prior, then I am thankful we are dissolving the monasteries and priories." Not a man to undertake only one project at a time, Cromwell was currently also reorganising the royal household, extending his organisational skills to the Privy Council, much to the disgust

214

of its aristocratic members. Just a short while ago, there had been eighty members of that council, not that all eighty of them attended every meeting. Now, the number had been reduced to twenty, and the sixty who had been removed were furious at their loss of power. Cromwell could not be anything other than aware of how much he was hated, but he wielded so much authority that it was worth the hatred. He was Vicegerent, Lord Chancellor, and he held the Privy Seal. Like Wolsey, he was a commoner, but unlike Wolsey, he obeyed the king, and carried out his wishes. Taking a piece of fruit from a bowl, he munched steadily for a moment, swallowed, then commented, "I would have had that knave of a priest recanting his slander at St. Paul's cross."

"If he did that, the whole world might believe I was an ostler," Thomas protested.

"Only a blockhead would think that." Cromwell looked to the bishops for confirmation, but they were shaking their heads in disagreement.

"Too many papists would believe it," Thomas argued astutely.

The bishops were now nodding agreement.

Thomas continued. "Buying enough food to sustain him during his time in prison probably cost that poor man all the money he has. Would you now put him to open shame? I believe that he is truly sorry. He is not the first man to insult me, and he will certainly not be the last." Thomas spoke with finality, closing their debate.

Shortly after the bishops and Cromwell had returned to Court, Thomas stood on the landing stage, taking a moment to reflect on their conversation. As he gazed out over the water, he heard footsteps approaching, and turned to see his wife walking across the lawn, which sloped steeply downwards towards the river. He gave an amused smile. She was no doubt eager to discover what had happened during the examination.

"I saw him leave," she remarked once she had reached her husband. "He looked… erbärmlich." Though her English was now decidedly excellent, she would still occasionally stumble when trying to find an appropriate word.

Thomas tucked her arm through his own, hoping no one would see, as they began to amble back to the house. After a moment's thought, he finally identified what she was trying to say. "Ah, erbärmlich is pathetic, if I recall correctly. That would certainly be fitting; there was something rather pathetic about him."

"Pathetic," she repeated slowly. "Yes, that is the word."

As they walked, he recounted the events of the morning, then informed her of some news Cromwell had whispered to him prior to leaving. "I have no idea where Cromwell gets his energy from, but he has just received the king's permission to reorganise the Star Chamber." He shook his head in wonderment.

"The Star Chamber? What is that?"

He wracked his brain for a simple explanation. "The Star Chamber oversees the operations of the lower law courts – the courts of the common men and women – and takes on any cases that are referred to it. I often suggest to people that they might appeal directly to the Star Chamber, rather than going to the lower courts first. It saves a great deal of time."

Margaret was clearly baffled. "Why is it called the Star Chamber?"

"Because it was set up by the previous king, Henry VII, who had the ceiling of the chamber covered in stars. It has an advantage over the lower courts as it is less rigid and does not depend upon juries. However, it does sometimes lack the safeguards of the lower courts. Currently, the Star Chamber is used for prosecuting perjury, slander, crimes of violence, breach of peace... the list goes on. Punishments invariably include whipping, mutilation, fines, pillories and branding, but I have never heard of the death penalty being administered. Anyway, Cromwell is going to give it an overhaul." He observed her perplexed expression with indulgent amusement.

"I am thinking it needs one," Margaret frowned. "It sounds not very legal to me."

Thomas gave a roar of laughter. "It probably isn't, my love."

As they were nearing the entrance to their home, Margaret slipped her arm away from his. "I must see to Marjorie; she will be hungry by now. She is always hungry," she beamed proudly. Their daughter was constantly growing and gaining weight, and Margaret's most fervent prayer was that she would continue to thrive. So many infants died within their first year. One of the housemaids helped care for the child, a discreet girl with plenty of common sense, plus the decency not to ask questions about the paternity of the infant; though Margaret was sure that most people knew her Thomas was the father. Marjorie was the very image of him, in her fond opinion. "I will go into the house by the rear entrance," she told him, referring to the servants' door.

He nodded, frowning. One day, when the reformation of the Church was complete, he would be the first Archbishop of Canterbury to publicly acknowledge a wife. In the meantime, they would have to keep up this ridiculous pretence, and the respectable woman he had married would have to remain, in the eyes of the public, his mistress. The sooner he could publicly present her as his wife, the better.

*****

As the weeks passed, he felt there was very little progress made as far as religious dogma was concerned. He could never have imagined what a slow process it would turn out to be; he had envisaged a quick reformation of the Church once King Henry was no longer subject to the Pope in Rome, but alas, it was not to be. He frequently received letters from Hugh Latimer, such as the one he was reading now, reproaching him for not being more vigorous in achieving a new Protestant Church. It was easy for Latimer to say... he was not working with King Henry.

He had been working late in his library, and was about to retire to bed, when a messenger from the king arrived, summoning him to Court. At the present time, Hampton Court was being sweetened, so the king was staying at Bridewell, a palace which stood on the banks of the Fleet River. It had been King Henry's main residence in his youth, but he seldom used it these days, for compared with the sumptuous Hampton Court, it was rather drab and outdated. A barge was waiting for him, so hastily wrapping a warm cloak about his person, he hurried down to the river. Stepping into the barge, he found Cromwell already seated there, having also been summoned from his house in Stepney.

"What is this about?" It was reassuring to see that Cromwell appeared no less anxious than himself.

"I have no idea," came Cromwell's response. "But it must be serious for the king to call us at this late hour." He scratched at his chin contemplatively. "We can but wait, though I admit, I am somewhat concerned."

They talked in a desultory fashion, discussing a commission Cromwell had set up to assess and examine parish clergy, but their discussion was half-hearted; they were both uneasy. Once they had disembarked, they were escorted to a small antechamber. There they found the king pacing back and forth, his face a mask of fury. Nearby stood the new queen, Jane, her hands clasped anxiously together, clearly unable to find the words to soothe her husband.

Thomas had observed how much of a contrast she was to her predecessor, and not just regarding her temperament. Her entire persona was different. Jane lacked her predecessor's sophistication, wit and lively intelligence. Whilst Anne had flaunted the precious gems Henry had bestowed upon her, the lady who now anxiously stood beside the king wore only a few. Anne had called the king by his name, Henry, whereas Jane always referred to him as 'Your Grace' or 'Your Majesty', unless in a small informal group, such as tonight, when she would call him 'sir'. Most noticeably, Queen Jane never contradicted her husband, unlike Anne, who had never been fearful of voicing her point of view, both prior to their marriage and during it.

Cromwell bowed low. "How may we be of assistance to you, Your Majesty. You are clearly troubled."

"Read this." The king unceremoniously thrust a document into the archbishop's hand.

Thomas unrolled the scroll, trying to decipher it in the dim light. There were a few candles in the sconces, and a huge fire roaring in the grate, but it was still very indistinct.

Ever resourceful, Cromwell took hold of a long since snuffed out candle, re-lit it, and brought it over to where his friend was trying to decipher the writing.

Together, the two men read of a parish priest in Lincolnshire, who had given an inflammatory sermon concerning the commissioners who were, at Cromwell's request, pulling down Louth Abbey and removing what few valuables the small establishment possessed. His sermon had been taken onboard by a monk and shoemaker, named Nicholas Melton, and thanks to Melton's energetic preaching

219

and vigorous manner, people were flocking to him in droves. Consequently, more than three thousand Lincolnshire men had gathered together and driven out the commissioners. Such a rebellion could not be tolerated.

"What is the solution?" The king's voice was almost a growl.

Thomas found himself floundering. What was the solution? No wise suggestion sprang to his mind.

Fortunately, Cromwell was quick to produce an idea. "Summon the Duke of Norfolk," he suggested.

The king's eyes narrowed slightly. Norfolk's star had waned since the execution of his niece, Anne Boleyn. However, he was a useful man, and an excellent soldier; vigorous and unsentimental. "Go on, my lord Cromwell. What else have you to say?"

"Send him with a troop of soldiers; put down this uprising, so that the commissioners may proceed with their work. Then, send my lord of Canterbury, or another senior member of the clergy, to preach in some of the Lincolnshire churches. This will ensure that the common folk understand that what is happening is for the greater good."

"Excellent." Looking suddenly relieved, the king gave a faint smile of approval. "Let it be so. Send for Norfolk. Tell him I want the leaders to be punished, to set an example to others. Those who do not love and honour their king shall be hung, drawn and quartered."

"Sir…" The queen's voice trembled.

"Do not plead for them, madam." The king's voice was clipped. "Everyone in the country will begin telling us how to rule this realm if these men are not made an example of. We cannot tolerate such behaviour."

"Quite so, Your Majesty," Cromwell purred.

The queen looked tearful but was effectively silenced.

"Cranmer, prepare yourself to travel to Lincolnshire. We trust you more than any other clergyman to preach in the cathedral. We need the rebellion to be quashed, and the people appeased," the king briskly instructed.

"As you wish, Your Majesty," Thomas bowed. He noticed that the queen had turned away so the king could not see her surreptitiously wiping tears from her eyes. It was not in her temperament to argue or contradict her husband, and he suspected that she had also taken note of what had befallen her spirited and opinionated predecessor. It seemed Queen Jane had sufficient common sense to keep her opinions to herself. The Protestant faction had been worried about the influence of a Catholic queen, but it was becoming increasingly evident that the king would not accept any advice from his new wife, allaying Thomas' own private fears. Certainly, the king seemed besotted with Queen Jane, but if King Henry refused to reform the Church, it would not be due to her influence.

With the Duke of Norfolk at the helm, the Lincolnshire uprising was soon quashed, and the leaders were subjected to the dreaded traitor's death. As was common following such executions, the grizzly remains of their bodies were subsequently displayed in various towns, as a message to other potential rebels. Thomas gave a sigh of relief upon hearing the news. It was sad that people had to die, but at least all was calm again. As for the king, once the uprising was quashed, he was able to happily resume his honeymoon with his new queen.

Chapter Ten

Later that same year, there was another uprising, one that affected Thomas more personally. Apparently, the mob desired to be rid of both himself and Cromwell, in response to their involvement in both the dismantling of religious houses and the aftermath of the Lincolnshire uprising. Such was their rage that nine thousand insurgents had marched on York, demanding justice.

"Why has this happened, does anyone know?" the king demanded of Cromwell, Edward Seymour, the Archbishop of Canterbury, and the Duke of Norfolk, all of whom he had summoned.

"The leader is a man called Robert Aske." Naturally, Cromwell was fully aware of the facts. "He is a lawyer, from a wealthy family. People from as far afield as Northumberland and Durham are among those marching, not just Yorkshire folk," he explained smoothly.

"I have heard that people from Cumberland are also amongst the rebels," Norfolk added, eager to show that Cromwell was not the only person in possession of information.

Cromwell, as usual, was unperturbed. "They are calling this the Pilgrimage of Grace, and they march under a banner showing the five wounds of Christ."

"I understand monks, nuns, and friars, are being told to return to their religious houses," Thomas revealed, having received information on the subject that same morning. However, since many religious houses were now lacking both rooves and windows, it would be impossible for the monks and nuns to actually live there. "Also, taxes in the north are high, and this year promises a poor harvest, which will have made the people uneasy."

"But what is the purpose of the uprising?" Henry bellowed.

"It would appear that they are happy for you to remain Head of the Church of England, Your Majesty," Cromwell explained, managing not to flinch as the king hurled an empty drinking vessel at the wall. "But they want to keep to the old faith, and keep the monastic establishments, so that they may look after the sick and distribute alms to the poor as they have always done. The people want saints to be worshipped and images to be venerated again, and they wish for you to get rid of certain minsters and advisors, namely myself, my lord of Canterbury, and the bishops of Ely, Rochester and Worcester."

Thomas experienced a spasm of nausea upon hearing his name included. A century and a half ago, the then Archbishop of Canterbury, Simon of Sudbury, had been brutally beheaded by an angry mob during the Peasant's Revolt. What if this were to happen to him? Furthermore, if the requests of the mob were granted, the small amount of progress he had managed to make regarding the Reformation, would be totally lost.

"We will not be dictated to by a mob," growled the king. "Cromwell, what of the larger northern monastic houses? Are they destroyed yet?" he demanded.

"Not totally dismantled, but in the process," Cromwell assured him. "The wealth – as in the plate and jewels – has been removed and brought to London." This, he knew, was the king's chief concern. "Many of these religious houses no longer own a roof because the lead has been taken to be melted down. The statues and images likewise have been taken away. I am informed," he continued, "that people wish to be reassured that their village churches are not to be pulled down. Apparently, wild rumours state that this is to happen."

"Cranmer, you must preach otherwise; tell them the village churches are not to be closed; send word to your clergy to do the same. We desire for our people to serve and worship God, as we do. We would never tear down their churches," he announced piously. "Norfolk, get yourself to York with an army. The people must be appeased, and Aske must be executed. But placate him first, if you understand our meaning." The king's eyes narrowed as he looked sharply at his most senior duke.

"I understand, Your Majesty." Norfolk managed what could only be described as a grim smile. "They shall be dealt with."

"What about the southern monasteries?" the king demanded of Cromwell. "Hailes and Glastonbury... are they destroyed yet?"

"They are next on the list, Your Majesty," Cromwell assured him. "The monks have been expelled, and as for the lead rooves, they are due to be removed shortly."

"Norfolk!" the king roared, as the duke began to leave his presence. "Be sure to bring this man, Aske, to our presence. We wish to speak with him; to converse with him before he is punished."

"As you wish, Your Majesty." Norfolk bowed.

224

As the king had anticipated, Norfolk did his work well. He rode north with his troops, promised Aske an audience with the king, plus safe passage to and from London, and delivered the traitor to His Majesty, where he proceeded to celebrate the Christmas season. The rebel leader clearly felt that the king was in agreement with him, speaking to him at length about Cromwell's excessive authority, and about his belief that that the Archbishop of Canterbury, along with some of his clergy, were heretics. The king listened intently, revealing nothing. When Aske was departing from Court in the company of the Duke of Norfolk, Henry compounded his feeling of satisfaction by presenting him with a crimson silk coat, as a mark of favour.

There was much tension in the Court over the following days, as everyone wondered what was going to happen next. Thomas constantly felt a twinge of anxiety gnawing in his stomach. Might the king agree to Aske's demands? If he did, what would befall himself and Cromwell, as well as the other reformists? The objectionable vision of Simon of Sudbury being mutilated was never far from his mind.

As the duke headed north again with Aske, fighting broke out as the rebels rose against the king's troops. They were no match for Norfolk's seasoned men and were easily cut down. Those who were not killed during the battle we captured and promptly hung, drawn and quartered. Unlike his followers, Aske was offered a free pardon, on the condition that he return to London with Norfolk. Naturally, he agreed, riding back to London with his head held high, thinking he had escaped an untimely death. As the king had intended all along, Aske was imprisoned in the Tower upon his arrival in London, then was formally tried at Westminster shortly afterwards. Unsurprisingly, he was found guilty of treason, and sentenced to be hung, drawn and quartered, just like his followers. As a warning to other would-be rebel leaders in the north, Aske was executed at Clifford's Tower in York, on a specially erected scaffold. The protest was well and truly over; all that remained were a selection of mutilated body parts, rotting in towns and villages throughout the realm: an example of what would happen to those who angered King Henry VIII.

"This has been a terrible time," Thomas admitted to Latimer one evening. Now the Bishop of Worcester, Hugh Latimer was often seen at the archbishop's side, and Thomas could not have been more grateful for it. Latimer was outspoken and fearless; even where the Archbishop of Canterbury was concerned, he said nothing in public that he would not say in private. He was entirely honest, extremely hardworking, and a reliable friend.

"The New Learning will not happen without offending those who adhere to orthodoxy," Latimer reminded him. "I expected some sort of protest."

"Protest?" Thomas almost shouted the word. "It was more than a mere protest, my friend. Even His Majesty was fearful, such was the size of the mob. We could all have been ripped apart." His friend's blasé attitude astounded him, and he could not help but envy Latimer's cool courage.

"At least it shows they fear the spread of the Protestant faith. We must be making some impression, otherwise they would not demand to return to the old ways," Latimer retorted in his standard, logical manner.

Thomas was about to mention that he had hardly slept for the duration of the uprising, then thought better of it. There was no point; Latimer would only look surprised, then confess to sleeping like an infant throughout the whole episode. Instead, he clasped his friend's hand. "I am glad that you are now one of my bishops."

226

"May you always feel that way," Latimer grinned, his eyes sparkling fiendishly.

*****

"You are exhausted," Margaret chided, placing a plate of food and some warmed ale in front of her husband, who had just returned home from another intense day at Court.

That morning, Thomas had travelled to Hampton Court, fully determined to obtain an audience with the king and speak out boldly regarding a matter which was dear to his heart. A dangerous matter. But though Margaret was eager to hear what had transpired, she was currently more concerned for her husband's wellbeing.

He sank into his chair, the peace of Lambeth Palace soothing his weary soul. Just a couple of yards away, little Marjorie lay sleeping in her new cradle - they had already had to replace her original one, in order to accommodate her growing limbs. She was thriving, he noted fondly. Opposite him, Margaret sat, busying her hands with some embroidery. Seeing the anxiety written on her face, he leaned forward and grasped her hand, almost stabbing himself on her industrious needle in the process. "The king has agreed to see Lady Mary," he informed her, his tone one of satisfaction.

Margaret gave a sigh of relief, the burden of fear she had carried all day suddenly evaporating. There were two reasons for her relief. First of all, she believed a father should agree to see his daughter, even if the father was the King of England. Secondly, her husband had placed himself in a dangerous situation. The king had once threatened Lady Mary with death, such was his determination that his daughter should sign the Acts of Succession and Supremacy. Given that refusing to sign the Acts constituted treason, a crime punishable by death, Henry had reasoned that his daughter should be dealt with no differently to anyone else.

"I reminded him of the love he bore for her when she was a little girl, and of the love she has for him. He listened, then called her disobedient, but I kept telling him that she still loved him, and that she had simply been ill-advised regarding her faith. The king has agreed to send someone, probably Cromwell, to visit her tomorrow and ask her to sign the Acts. Thanks to our meeting, if she refuses, her life shall at least be spared. If she agrees to sign, she shall be brought to Court at last, thanks to the new queen also importuning on her behalf." Despite her religious leanings, Thomas had developed a healthy esteem for the new queen over the past few months. Though she wisely remained silent regarding matters of state, she was willing to speak up about the fate of a motherless young woman. He respected her for that.

"I shall pray for her to be brought to Court no matter what her decision. After all, she is the king's daughter," Margaret declared stoutly. "She should be with her father."

"But if she doesn't agree to sign the Acts, she will be a focus for Catholics, hence Henry's decision to ban her from Court," Thomas explained, glancing at his own daughter. How could any father ban his daughter from his presence? "But her life will be spared. I am thankful that the queen has a kind heart; she has herself been begging for Mary's presence at Court."

"Pity she is Catholic," Margaret murmured, echoing his own thoughts.

"Her brother, Lord Hertford, is secretly Protestant. Perhaps he can direct her away from her misguided views?" Thomas was optimistic; if Hertford could move away from Catholicism, his sister could do likewise.

"Perhaps Lady Mary will realise that you have been instrumental in helping her, and think kindly of you?" Margaret was thoughtful. Her husband had been kind to Lady Mary; he had permitted her to keep her Catholic confessor at her home in Hertfordshire, and he had also reluctantly permitted her to hear Mass, after she explained to him that it gave her much needed comfort.

"I doubt it." His smile was apologetic. He was the man who had announced that her parent's marriage was invalid, and that she, once a royal princess, was in fact a bastard. He doubted very much that Mary would ever feel anything but dislike towards him. "I believe that she has been hurt too deeply to see me as anything other than the man who ruined her life."

"I don't like to think that the king's daughter dislikes you. After all, she is in a position to… I don't know… perhaps cause harm." Margaret frowned anxiously.

"Do not worry, my love." He patted her hand reassuringly, only just avoiding her embroidery needle. "She is the king's bastard daughter. She will never have any real power."

The following day, Cromwell rode to Hertfordshire and obtained Lady's Mary's signature on both the Act of Succession and the Act of Supremacy. On his return journey home, he visited Lambeth Palace to triumphantly tell his friend the news.

"I hope you treated her gently." Thomas' tone was one of rebuke. "I have heard you can be somewhat bullying in manner when speaking with her."

"She needs a bullying manner," Cromwell protested. "She is so stubborn; she needs to be dealt with firmly. The Duke of Norfolk agrees," he added truculently. "He believes that her head should be beaten against the wall until it resembles a baked apple, so be thankful that it was I who visited her, not Norfolk. I finally persuaded her to sign the Acts, and to agree to be

229

referred to as Lady Mary. As you know, she has always insisted upon being addressed as Princess Mary. I can understand why, of course. It is a huge difference in status." He shrugged. "She shall just have to make the best of it. Plenty of young women throughout the land would love be in her position."

"Princess Elizabeth is now Lady Elizabeth, so both sisters are the same." As soon as Thomas had declared that the king had not been married to Anne Boleyn, Elizabeth had been declared a bastard too. "I have some good news to share with you also, which I am finally at liberty to speak of openly. The queen is with child, although no doubt you are already aware of this." His companion's smirk revealed that this was indeed the case. "His Majesty is thrilled and keeps lavishing jewels upon her. As always, he insists she is carrying a male heir." He was silent for a moment, reflecting upon this. The queen must surely feel under considerable pressure, being required to not only bear a healthy living child, but also a male.

Less than a week later, Lady Mary was presented at Court to the new queen, an event which the king insisted his Archbishop of Canterbury must attend. He arrived to find the audience chamber packed with senior members of the Court; as ever, he gravitated towards Cromwell, who was standing beside the queen's brother, the Earl of Hertford. Barely had he greeted them when the doors opened, and a herald announced the arrival of Lady Mary.

Turning to watch her entrance, Thomas felt a twinge of pity. The poor girl looked as if she had been weeping, and she had clearly not slept for some time. Her face was pale, and her thin body trembled as she approached her royal father. Dipping three perfect curtseys as she approached the thrones at the far end of the chamber, she finally knelt in front of King Henry and his latest queen.

The king, feeling a sudden rush of paternal affection, placed his forefinger underneath her chin, raised her from her position, then bellowed, "some of you suggested we should put this jewel to death!" He glared accusingly at the persons assembled. No one dared state that it was the king himself who had most desired this act to be performed.

Queen Jane, not yet visibly pregnant, rushed to take the girl's hands. "That would have been a great pity, Your Grace, to have lost your greatest jewel," she declared, beaming goodwill upon the new arrival. "You are so very welcome, my dear."

Suddenly realising the enormous danger of her situation, Mary promptly fainted.

Later that afternoon, Thomas was surprised when the queen requested to speak with him in private. Gardiner, being Catholic, was the person whom she had always been most likely to seek out when she desired spiritual counsel. However, he was not one to shirk his responsibilities, and duly went to her.

"Please sit with me for a while, my lord Archbishop." Jane looked strained and anxious, quite unlike the radiant woman who had welcomed Lady Mary to Court just a short while ago.

"Of course." Obediently he seated himself. "Is there something amiss, Your Majesty?" Thus far, he had rarely been aware of, or involved in, the queen's affairs. They had always been polite to one another, but owing to their theological differences, they had never gravitated towards each other. As he waited for her to speak, he was yet again forcibly reminded of the differences between Jane and her predecessor. Even their mottos were utterly different. Anne's had been 'The Most Happy' – the motto of someone who was always at the centre of her own world. In contrast, Jane's was 'Bound to Obey and Serve'. Again, this was appropriate. She would always place her husband's interests above her own.

231

Eventually, the queen murmured, "My lord, I shall speak plainly. I have been informed that you were well acquainted with my predecessor." Her voice cracked with anxiety.

"Indeed, I was," he confirmed. "I was her chaplain."

"Do you think she was innocent?"

Momentarily, he was taken aback by the forthrightness of the question. Then it hit him. Of course. She had realised that, had Anne given birth to a son, she would still be alive. If the king could rid himself of two queens for not bearing sons, he could easily rid himself of a third. Thomas managed to gather his thoughts together. "Queen Anne was found guilty by a jury of her peers and was sentenced accordingly." He had no intention of admitting that he had absolutely no doubt whatsoever that she had been innocent. "The king was kind and sent for a swordsman to take off her head cleanly."

"I find no solace in that, my lord." Jane looked queasy. "I am so fearful that I might give birth to a girl and find myself cast aside also. The monasteries are fast disappearing; even the bigger establishments are being dissolved. Where shall I go if I fail in my duty?" She was fighting to keep her composure, and her eyes were rapidly filling with tears. "His Majesty has even chosen a name for my baby."

"Your Highness, the king loves you. You are his wife; he has no grounds to cast you aside. Leave your fears at the foot of the cross. Give them to the Lord, your Heavenly Lord, whom even the King of England shall one day face in judgement," he replied gently.

At that moment, the door was flung open, and the king himself entered the room, looking hearty and cheerful. Walking over to his queen, he lay a huge hand upon her shoulder. "Please, please, remain seated, both of you. I see you are seeking prayer and counsel with my lord Archbishop, my love.

232

But why the tears?" With a gallant, sweeping gesture, Henry pulled a kerchief from his sleeve and handed it to his wife.

"Her Highness feels moved by God's goodness, and desires His help to fulfil her responsibilities," Thomas explained. It was partially true, in a way. "Perhaps Your Majesty will join us for a while?"

"Certainly, certainly," the king agreed wholeheartedly. "You have no idea of how blessed we feel, being wed to such a devout and obedient woman."

Thomas nodded solemnly. "It pleases me to see Your Majesty so content," he stated truthfully. It seemed the king was set to enjoy a peaceful and contented phase in his life, and it was clear that he could always depend upon this lady for kindness and support.

*****

Early one October evening, a messenger wearing the king's livery arrived at Lambeth Palace. The queen's labour had begun, and Thomas was summoned to Court, to be with the king.

The queen had been confined to her chamber since early September, in preparation for the birth, as was customary for wellborn ladies. She had not seen the sunlight for weeks, the windows having been covered and sealed to prevent noxious air from entering the room, and only the queen's ladies had been permitted to enter the chamber. Such confinement would surely have driven his own wife to insanity, Thomas brooded, as the barge took him to Hampton Court.

The cool, damp air had formed into a thick fog, sitting just above the surface of the river, and he was glad of his fur-lined cloak, hugging it tightly about himself. When the barge finally reached the landing stage at Hampton Court, he followed a torch-bearing lackey up the steps and into the palace, where he found the king pacing back and forth in agitation and anticipation. The queen's cries of suffering could be heard echoing through the corridors, despite the thick oak doors separating them from her lying in chamber, and he could not help but wince every time he heard her scream, his memory of Joan's labour was reignited.

Periodically, the midwife would send a message to the king, and after several hours had passed, she asked for Dr William Butts, the king's senior physician. Butts, who had been waiting in an anteroom since the queen's pains began, hastened to give advice. But still the labour continued. Finally, after nearly thirty hours of labour, at two o'clock in the morning, the queen was delivered of a son. Not only that, but he was a healthy, lusty babe, and thus considered likely to survive long into adulthood. The queen, according to Dr Butts, was exhausted and much in need of rest, as was to be expected, but she was in good spirits and was doing very well indeed.

Thomas, himself exhausted, felt a huge surge of relief on behalf of the queen. Her position was secure; she had given her husband a son to rule after him. The king, understandably, was ecstatic, and despite not having slept for over twenty-four hours, had practically danced with joy at the news of his son's birth. Once Dr Butts had confirmed that all was well, Thomas was dismissed by the king, who thanked him sincerely for his company and counsel. Having made his way down to the river, he collapsed onto a barge seat and promptly fell asleep.

The following day he began to make plans for the babe's royal baptism, which was to take place in a few days' time. Unlike Elizabeth's baptism, this was to be a large, lavish evening celebration, requiring a great deal of organisation. The queen, being only recently delivered of her infant, would be unable to sit for long periods in a chair, so her doting husband had demanded that a litter be brought into the chapel for her to lie on. Further requests, regarding the decoration and other features of the ceremony, were also made by the king over the coming days, but eventually, everything was set.

Watched by ambassadors and the aristocracy, Thomas entered the chapel of Hampton Court as part of a long, torch-lit procession. The babe himself was accompanied by a nurse, a midwife, and six gentlemen attendants, who held a decorative canopy over him. As Thomas performed the ceremony of baptism, he felt a surge of optimism. The prince's male attendants were mostly Protestant, and his tutor, who had already been selected, was also Protestant. Now that the king was settled in his private life, he was certain that the country would soon be guided into a new age of religious reform.

Devastatingly, his sanguine optimism was soon shattered. A few evenings later, on the twenty-third of October, Thomas was summoned once again to Hampton Court. The queen was believed to be suffering from childbirth fever, and Dr Butts had warned the king to prepare for the worst. Hastening to the king's side, Thomas sat with him, offering silent comfort and companionship as the king wept. Some hours later, the queen died. Twelve days ago, the king had been overjoyed; now, he was wracked with grief, his marital bliss tragically terminated.

The queen's funeral was to be held at St. George's Chapel, Windsor, and Thomas led the procession from Hampton Court, which slowly made its way through the streets of London, eventually arriving in Windsor a few days later. During the journey, crowds came out to bow their heads in respect, calling out prayers, blessings, and condolences, to their king and his infant son. As for Jane herself, she had been queen for less

235

than two years; the people had not had time to develop any deep fondness for her. Whilst there was sympathy for the king, no one gave much thought to the dead queen, for she had been nothing more than a pale, shadowy figure as far as they were concerned. She had not even had a coronation. The only good thing to come of her death was a rekindled affection for the king. After Anne's execution, there had been a certain degree of animosity towards the king from his subjects, but now, he was grieving, and they now loved him for his humanity.

*****

To divert his attention from his grief, Henry had turned to examining *The Institution of the Christian Man*, the book written by Thomas and his bishops to accompany the Act of Ten Articles. The book was designed to outline the reformed faith in a simple manner, understandable to the common man, and the king had spent the past few weeks eagerly discussing its contents with Thomas and Cromwell. It was during one such meeting that Cromwell, to the horror of Thomas, suggested to the king that he ought to consider taking another wife. The king, who was undeniably furious, looked ready to throttle his minister, but resisted. Instead, Henry verbally berated Cromwell, informing him, in no uncertain terms, that he was never to suggest such a thing again.

Cromwell, fearless as ever, continued, as if unaware of the king's flushed, angry face. "For the sake of your realm, Your Majesty."

"We are grieving, and you suggest we should replace our dearest Queen Jane!" The king swept from the room.

"How could you say such a thing?" Thomas gasped, as the door slammed. He had not seen that suggestion coming, and clearly, neither had the king. They had been cosily discussing what the king described as 'an end to the diversity of opinion and disunion within the Church', when Cromwell had suddenly made his outrageous suggestion.

Having anticipated the king's explosion of wrath, Cromwell closed his eyes and took a deep breath. "He wants to remarry," he replied softly. "He just wants it to seem as if he is sacrificing himself for the sake of his realm." His expression became mischievous. "He will remarry... he will just do so with a long-suffering countenance, and he will tell us all that he is simply doing it for the wellbeing of the realm."

"Let us keep our minds focused upon reform for the time being," Thomas muttered quickly, desperate to change the subject. After all, there was a great deal to do. The king had asked himself and his clerics to produce an official statement, designed to reconcile people to the dissolution of the monasteries, and also to end the confusion caused by the Act of Ten Articles and *The Institution of the Christian Man*. However, try though he might, the clerics could not be persuaded to agree. Their first official meeting at Lambeth had been reduced to little less than a brawl. Stokesley, the Catholic Bishop of London, was particularly vociferous that the Act of Ten Articles missed out four of the sacraments, whilst Latimer, equally vocal, fiercely opposed him. Eventually, Thomas had been given no choice but to intervene, accusing them of babbling and brawling about bare words.

At another meeting, Cromwell brought with him the Scottish theologian Alexander Allesius, whom Thomas knew, but only vaguely. Allesius was even more extreme than Zwingli, the Swiss reformist, whom he regarded as being excessively radical. Allesius was such an enthusiastic speaker that it was difficult to silence him - he spent the meeting arguing violently

237

with Stokesley. At one point, it seemed that the two were about to come to blows. Naturally, Allesius was not invited to any further meetings, whilst Cromwell, who was seldom embarrassed, was uncharacteristically apologetic about bringing him in the first place.

It was a relief to Thomas when the king decided to take over, but his relief at no longer being in charge of such argumentative clerics was short lived. The king soon declared that six topics, selected by himself, should be placed before Parliament, to be debated and voted upon. Still fearful of invasion from France and Spain, His Majesty's aim was to produce a document which would prove that, at heart, he was still orthodox. So, to prove his orthodoxy, Henry publicly sanctioned the reintroduction of the ceremony of Creeping to the Cross on Easter Sunday, much to Thomas' dismay, for this was one of the top items on the reformists' list of 'ceremonies to be permanently dismissed'.

Eventually, the Act of Ten Articles was replaced by an Act of Six Articles, nicknamed by reformists as 'The Whip with Six Strings'. It was a step backwards for the reformists, and Thomas was vocal in his opposition, much to the surprise of his Catholic peers, who believed him too meek to protest so vehemently. His outrage was matched by his Protestant bishops, and both Hugh Latimer and Nicholas Shaxton resigned from their positions in protest. Initially, Thomas considered doing likewise, but was persuaded to remain archbishop by Nicholas Ridley, who reminded him that a Catholic bishop – probably Gardiner – would be his successor.

The Act, designed to end diversity in religion, clearly stated that transubstantiation would remain, and that the bread and wine would truly become the body and blood of the Lord. Priests could not marry; vows of chastity or widowhood were

238

to be observed and respected; private Masses were to continue, along with auricular confession. Any person who did not adhere to these rules would be judged a felon; his property would be forfeited, and he would be executed.

Hugh Latimer reported to Thomas that the Act was causing more confusion, not less. Some churches, he wrote, were continuing to worship the saints, whilst others were not; it all depended upon the priest's degree of orthodoxy. It was a total shambles. Optimistically, Thomas responded with the news that the king was now concentrating upon *The Institution of the Christian Man*, stressing that this might have a more favourable outcome for the reformists. Whilst the Act was a bow to the Holy Roman Emperor and the King of France, the review of *The Institution of Christian Man* was expected to meet the needs of the English clergy.

In total, the king offered two hundred and forty-six alterations to the book, of which Thomas nervously objected to eighty-six.

Visiting Lambeth Palace, a smirking Cromwell declared, "I observe you are well capable of putting your foot down when necessary."

"The king says I will only permit him to make grammatical suggestions, but that is not strictly true. I cannot prevent the amendments His Majesty chooses to make," he murmured. "To be honest, I know not whether the king inclines towards Protestantism or Catholicism; it is hard to read his mind." The king, who took much comfort from talking with his archbishop, would often produce some of Queen Jane's theories, all of them orthodox and none of which Henry had ever accepted during her lifetime. It seemed to Thomas that the king had placed a posthumous halo over his late wife.

Disappointed by the Act of Six Articles, Thomas turned his attention to the possibility of producing an English Bible. Over the years, he had attempted to make his own translation of the Bible into English, but it was incomplete, and he did not have sufficient time these days to work on it. Recently, he had considered giving portions of the scriptures to the bishops and asking them to each translate their section into English. He had informed Cromwell of this idea and was gratified when he agreed.

Some weeks later, curious as to how the new Bible was taking shape, Cromwell enquired hopefully, "How are the bishop's translations coming along?"

"It was not a good idea to give a portion of *The Book of Acts* to Stokesley." Thomas shook his head in wry amusement. "He sent it back to me with a note saying he refused to translate it, as he did not wish to be blamed for taking simple people into error by giving them an English translation."

Cromwell smirked. "Well, the apostles were simple men; it is hardly surprising that Stokesley refuses to have anything to do with them. He thinks he is far too grand for such things." Suddenly becoming solemn, Cromwell suggested, "Have you never thought of using Will Tyndale's translation?"

"Yes, I have," Thomas admitted. "But the king dislikes Tyndale's work. I have also looked at Miles Coverdale's translation, but it is inaccurate in parts."

"Inaccuracies can be remedied. The man was once Bishop of Exeter; he is a person of learning, and Protestant to boot. Perhaps he can be prevailed upon to adjust his work," Cromwell mused.

"Much of Coverdale's work originates from Tyndale's anyway," Thomas reflected.

"Well, let us look at the possibilities. There is the translation by Thomas Matthews…" Cromwell scratched his chin thoughtfully. After the death of Tyndale, his great friend, John Rogers, had completed the pieces missing from his translation, and had published it under the name of Thomas Matthews, despite nearly all of it being Tynedale's work. This version was already available and circulating in Germany, and although it was forbidden, it was also sold in England to those who could afford it. Cromwell and Cranmer both secretly owned copies.

"Tyndale's is an excellent work, pure and accurate," Thomas stated. "But since the king is opposed to Tyndale, His Majesty is more likely to look favourably upon the work of Coverdale… providing the inaccuracies are expunged."

"Then we must work to expunge them then convince the king to permit the publication of the English Bible, and we must have copies placed in the churches. Speaking of the king, I am quite certain that he will soon declare himself ready to marry again, purely for the sake of the realm, of course." Cromwell's tone was ironic.

"Have a care, Cromwell. He dearly loved Queen Jane," Thomas warned.

Some days later, whilst at Court, Thomas was summoned by the king to confer with the Duke of Norfolk, Cromwell – who had recently been made Earl of Essex, much to the disgust of the aristocratic lords – and Sir Edward Seymour, the Earl of Hertford.

Cromwell had been correct; the king was indeed looking for another wife.

"We must do what is best for our people," Henry sighed. "We can never replace our late wife, your dear sister." He patted

Hertford's arm. "But we cannot simply do what our heart desires; we must seek an alliance for the sake of our realm. Cromwell here, my lord of Essex..." The king's expression was suddenly mischievous, knowing full well how deeply Norfolk hated the ennobling of a blacksmith's son. "He recommends a treaty with the league of Protestant princes." Henry was further amused by the fact that this was something else the Catholic Duke of Norfolk would be opposed to.

Cromwell gave a brief bow. "Indeed yes, Your Majesty, a treaty will be beneficial to England. A marriage... well, it is the most binding of treaties."

"My lord of Norfolk," Henry enquired. "What do you think?"

Predictably, Norfolk proposed a Catholic marriage. "Marie de Guise of Milan is marriageable. She is said to be tall, attractive and well built."

"We are a big man, in need of a big wife," Henry mused aloud. "Let us send a proposal immediately to this Marie de Guise of Milan." Seeming to have forgotten about the German princes, his tone became brisk and eager. "If she is unsuitable, there are several French princesses who are marriageable, perhaps they may be brought to Calais, so we may travel there and inspect them."

Thomas tried not to look shocked – for two reasons. Firstly, it seemed as if the king was selecting a horse, not a wife. He could feel Cromwell's amused gaze resting upon him, but he refused to meet his eye. Secondly, Henry seemed happy to consider a Catholic bride.

Norfolk, who regarded marriage purely as a means of gaining wealth, status and noble sons, saw nothing wrong with this at all. "I am willing to accompany an envoy to visit the King of France immediately," he informed the king. A Catholic

242

marriage would be a blow to that upstart Cromwell. "I shall negotiate the marriage personally."

"Do so, my lord of Norfolk." The king turned to Cromwell. "My lord of Essex, you must write a letter to this Marie de Guise."

In due course, a reply arrived from Marie de Guise. She tartly declared that she would have been willing to marry the King of England, had she possessed two heads; however, since she had only been blessed with one, she would have to decline his generous offer. Outraged, the king tore up her letter. Shortly afterwards, he learned that she had agreed to marry his nephew, James V of Scotland, which further fuelled his fury. King Henry's marital record was not good; it was evident that the only person who did not realise this was the king himself.

To make matters worse, Henry was no longer the handsome man who had married Anne Boleyn. Since the death of Jane, he had become corpulent, and his still injured leg had begun to ulcerate, making him incapable of partaking in any strenuous exercise. It was some months since he had last gone out hunting. His eyes were rimmed with pouches of flesh, and his small mouth was almost invisible, lodged between his sagging cheeks. Furthermore, his hair was thinning, and it was no longer the striking shade of red it had once been. Seemingly unaware of this, Henry still considered himself to be the handsome king who had once wooed the sophisticated Lady Anne.

As for the king's suggestion that some princesses should be brought to Calais for him to look at, King Francis, outraged at the crudeness of the idea, refused to permit any of the French princesses to be made available for inspection. This left Cromwell free to pursue an alliance with a princess linked to the Schmalkaldic League. During the past few years, Henry had blown hot and cold towards the league, balancing his desire for an allegiance with them, against his fear of overly antagonising King Francis and the Emperor Charles. However, since both Marie de Guise and the King of France had rejected him as a potential suitor, Henry was willing to cast aside his fears and embrace an allegiance with Germany and Holland.

Cromwell had discovered that the Duke of Cleves, one of the Schmalkaldic princes, had three daughters. The eldest was already married, but the two younger girls were both available, and said to be fair of face and figure.

"All princesses are fair of face and figure," Henry astutely reminded him. "Especially when they are looking for a husband."

"They are called Anne and Amelia," Cromwell continued.

"We do not desire another wife named Anne," Henry barked.

"She is most virtuous," Cromwell offered. "But Amelia is also well spoken of," he hastily added, seeing the king's expression darken.

"If my sweet Jane had lived, we would be spared this dilemma," the king plaintively addressed his archbishop, knowing sympathy would come from his direction.

"She rests with the King of Heaven and Earth now," Thomas intoned gently. "Doing your duty for the sake of your realm must be your consolation at this time."

The king, enjoying the concept that he was sacrificing himself for his kingdom, graciously inclined his head. "Care of our realm is always uppermost in our thoughts," he declared primly. "Summon the painter, Hans Holbein. He is not as good – in our opinion – as his father was, but he is very good. We wish to see portraits of the sisters. Once we have seen them, we shall decide which shall be our queen."

"I have heard the Duke of Cleves is very stern in how his household is governed; it is likely that the sisters will be very regal and well-educated young ladies," Thomas commented, relieved that the two young women would be spared the journey to Calais to be inspected. Being judged from one's portrait was far more humane – although the princess who was rejected might think otherwise.

"Quite so," Cromwell agreed amiably. Coming from such a household, whichever sister was chosen by the king would be gracious, gentle, and demure. "Do you wish to personally negotiate marriage terms with the Duke of Cleves?" Cromwell eagerly asked the king.

"When we have seen the portraits, my lord Earl," the king declared. "We shall make no decision until we have seen their portraits."

Cromwell exchanged a brief, delighted smile with the archbishop.

"And Cromwell," the king barked authoritatively. "I hear that Cardinal Reginald Pole, who has been stirring matters with the Emperor Charles on behalf of the Pope, has two brothers. I want them both imprisoned in the Tower. And his mother too." Pole was a troublemaker, and one who could not be silenced because he lived abroad. However, his family all lived conveniently close to London; if Pole himself could not be imprisoned, then, the king reasoned, his family should be.

"As you wish, Your Majesty." Cromwell bowed, smooth and urbane as always. Then, with Thomas following behind him, Cromwell departed from the king's presence.

"It seems a pity to imprison Pole's mother," Thomas whispered, once they were well out of earshot of the king. He had been at Court long enough to know that the Poles were of the Plantagenet line; they were as royal as the Tudors, if not more so. Indeed, Margaret Pole, Countess of Salisbury, was the niece of King Richard III. The king had always covertly watched this family, lest they should rise up against him.

"If the king wishes for the old lady to be imprisoned, then imprisoned she shall be. Believe me, she is just as capable of plotting to overthrow King Henry as her son, the cardinal," Cromwell declared breezily, as his friend continued to worry over the old lady being inconvenienced. "Don't fret, my friend. I shall ensure she is given comfortable rooms." Cromwell sensed she would not be there for very long. The king had been looking for an excuse to get rid of the Plantagenet's for years.

Cromwell's senses proved accurate. Cardinal Pole's brothers were beheaded on Tower Hill a few months later; as for Lady Margaret, she was beheaded on Tower Green, with a private execution being deemed necessary in case her age caused a public outcry. The old lady protested against her sentence, stating loudly that she had committed no crime. In front of a select but shocked crowd, she ran around the scaffold, pursued by the executioner. Eventually, she was pinned down, and the shaken executioner totally missed her neck, cutting her shoulder instead. Managing to jump up and escape her captors again, she ran around the scaffold as the executioner hacked at her with the axe. It took ten blows to sever her head.

*****

Some three months later, the king found himself gazing upon the faces of the two Protestant princesses, Anne and Amelia. One struck him immediately, her gentle beauty radiating sweetly from the miniature Holbein had painted. She was a vision of modesty and loveliness, so much so that King Henry was ready to forgive her for being called Anne. To Cromwell's satisfaction, he was given permission to send an envoy to negotiate marriage with Anne, and a treaty with the Duke of Cleves. This union would end the isolation of England, and the country would at last have an ally to stand against France and Spain.

Chapter Eleven

"A Lutheran delegation is enroute to England as I speak," Thomas eagerly informed his companion. He was sitting in the library at Lambeth Palace, enjoying some time with his old friend, Hugh Latimer. Unfortunately, they rarely had a chance to speak these days – they were both busy people – but despite the rarity of being able to meet,   there was no one Thomas trusted as deeply as he trusted Latimer, except of course Nicholas Ridley, the current Bishop of Rochester. Even Cromwell, whom he held in high regard, was less trustworthy than his old Cambridge companions. But, he supposed, this was because Latimer and Ridley were both of the same mindset as himself; unlike Cromwell, they did not seek wealth and power, merely truth and righteousness.

"About time. I long to see England become a Protestant country." Latimer's eyes glowed with excitement. "Change is in the air; I can feel it." Having resigned from his bishopric, he now occupied himself with preaching sermons anywhere he could find an audience, often at St. Paul's Cross. His friends feared for him, expecting to hear of his arrest at any given time, but thus far no one had laid a hand upon him.

"You are too optimistic. The Act of Six Articles is a step in the wrong direction." There was a note of bitterness in Thomas' voice. "Besides, it is only a small delegation."

Fond though Thomas was of Latimer, his forceful and impatient temperament was exhausting. Ever since he had been consecrated archbishop, he had received a steady stream of letters from Latimer, nearly all demanding to know why the Protestant faith had not been established in England yet. He had tried to explain that the political situation was incredibly delicate and complex, but his words had fallen on deaf ears. Latimer would have nothing to do with political situations. If turning England into a Protestant country caused the French and the Spanish to invade, so be it, was Latimer's forthright opinion.

"The Vice Chancellor of Saxony, Francis Burckhardt, leads the delegation," Thomas continued. "I had hoped for a Danish representative to travel here, but King Christian of Denmark is currently refusing to send ambassadors to England. Apparently, he has no wish to ally with us because we are not sufficiently Protestant. But there are a couple of ambassadors coming from the Bremen and the Low Countries."

Latimer was thoughtful. "The king's new marriage is being negotiated; it will bring more eminent reformists into the country to support us. But until King Henry accepts the Augsburg Confession, no one will consider England to be a truly Protestant Country."

"What exactly is the Augsburg Confession?" a new voice enquired. It came from Ralph Morice, who was sitting quietly at his desk.

Latimer tried to prepare a quick and succinct reply. He had huge respect for Morice; the man had studied at Cambridge, so was on a similar intellectual level to himself and Cranmer, not to mention that he was Protestant, and clearly devoted to the archbishop, who, in Latimer's opinion, needed all the friends he could get. "In short, Master Secretary, the Augsburg Confession is a series of twenty-eight articles, prepared by Philip Melanchthon, Martin Luther, the Lutheran German Princes, and others. It was introduced at the Diet of Augsburg, then presented to the Emperor Charles. The articles were drawn up in an attempt to defend Lutherans against misinterpretation of the Protestant faith. Catholics are twisting it and… well… misinterpreting it, unfortunately. The Augsburg Confession is designed as a bid to make the Protestant faith acceptable to Catholics, but I doubt it shall be successful. Catholics and Protestants will, I fear, never mix together."

"It was rejected by the emperor," Thomas interjected. "But the articles are the basis of our faith. As of yet, I have no copies of it, but once the delegation arrives, I shall be able to read them, as will you. I know the contents of the bulk of the articles though; they were signed by Denmark, Sweden and all the German Protestant princes."

"But until England also signs, the Protestant princes will not consider England as being Protestant," Latimer added.

Morice nodded slowly. "Because we are not seriously Protestant," he sighed. "Not yet." He rubbed the side of his nose thoughtfully, then asked, "What is this Diet of Augsburg you speak of?"

"Diet is a German term for a meeting," Thomas enlightened, adding solemnly, "until the king signs the Augsburg document, no Protestant country will trust him. But maybe the Lutheran delegation will impress His Majesty. After all, he is negotiating a marriage with the House of Cleves, so he may be inclined to listen to them."

Unfortunately, Thomas' optimism proved to be misplaced. When the delegates arrived and stood before the king, the monarch was in some discomfort, due to his ulcerated leg, and apart from his physical state, he was disinclined to spend time with the delegation, as relations between himself and the Emperor Charles were at present relatively peaceful. Consequently, he was unnecessarily rude to the delegates, brusquely dismissing Burckhardt and his colleagues.

Much to the dismay of Thomas, Gardiner was growing increasingly close to the king, and whenever His Majesty felt in a mood to grumble, Gardiner's smooth, flattering, tongue, acted as a balm, soothing his irritation. Gardiner felt that the spread of heresy had gone too far, thanks to the king's good-natured clemency, and that it needed checking before it spiralled out of control. The king was inclined to agree with him, especially since it coincided with his own wish, which was to keep Charles and Francis appeased. He might be negotiating to marry a Protestant bride, but he saw no reason to upset the Catholic monarchs. Politically, he needed balance. The Act of Six Articles, Henry decided, must be firmly adhered to; anyone not doing so would be punished severely. Gardiner was just the man to ensure the king's wishes were carried out.

This was a huge blow to Thomas. Since the recent passing of the Act, he had known it was possible Margaret would need to return to the protection of Osiander in Germany for a while, if it could even be called protection, given Charles' determination to persecute the German Protestants. It was a matter of weighing up which country would be safest for her: England or Germany. At present, she had returned to the Manor of Ford, and was living there quietly. But now, with Gardiner watching his every move, there could be no delay in her departure, painful though it was.

Most people regarded Margaret as a concubine, which, as always, grieved him, for she was a virtuous woman, and his lawful wife. But the passing of the Act forcefully announced that clergy must live virtuously, which meant no mistresses, no concubines, and certainly no wives. Riding to Canterbury to bid farewell to his wife, he wondered, as he often did, if the rumours of Gardiner keeping mistresses at Winchester Palace were to be believed? On his occasional visits to Winchester Palace, he had seen no evidence of a female presence there. But then if there was a mistress, Gardiner was cunning enough to ensure she was be kept hidden.

As soon as he reached the Manor of Ford, he flung his arms around his wife, his heart aching in the knowledge that this would be his last chance to hold her for who knew how long. Attempting to keep her voice steady, Margaret predicted that she and little Marjorie would return to England within the next six months, but Thomas realised this was too much to hope for. Had this occurred prior to the birth of their daughter, he knew that Margaret would have insisted upon remaining in England, but Marjorie had totally changed the situation. Neither Thomas nor Margaret would endanger their daughter.

When the time finally came for Margaret and Marjorie to leave, Thomas watched their departure with anguished eyes; the agony of not knowing when, or if, he would see them again was acutely painful. However, as was often the way with these things, he quickly had to set aside his personal problems, for shortly after his return to Lambeth Palace, he was informed that some visitors had arrived from Court to see him. His immediate thought was that he was to be arrested; heart pounding, he instructed they should be shown into his library.

Charles Brandon, the Duke of Suffolk, husband to the king's sister, was first to enter the library, followed by Cromwell and the Duke of Norfolk. Knowing Cromwell as well as he did, he saw only compassion on his friends' face, all but confirming his suspicions that he was about to be arrested. Suffolk, however, placed a beefy hand upon his shoulder, and spoke reassuringly.

"My lord Archbishop, the king has sent us to you to offer comfort. He has declared you to be learned, discrete and wise, and he knows you have endured much travail lately." Suffolk was eyeing the archbishop with wonderment. It had astonished him to hear the quiet little man speaking out so loudly against the Act of Six Articles. In fact, Suffolk had been heard to utter that Cranmer had, on occasion, nearly swayed him towards the Protestant faith. "He says we must tell you not to be discouraged." The duke had been the king's boon companion since they were youths together, and he was curious to know why the king valued this studious little man so highly.

Inviting his companions to be seated, Thomas realised that he must say something. Cromwell, with the familiarity of a frequent visitor, had summoned a servant, and was pouring ale. Ralph Morice peered curiously through the doorway, and Thomas quickly invited him to join them.

"My lords..." His voice was husky, so he tried again. "My lords..." This time his voice was stronger. "I heartily thank His Majesty for his singularly good affection towards me, and I thank you all for your pains in visiting me. I hope, hereafter, that all of my actions shall be undertaken for the good of this realm, and for the glory of God."

Cromwell replied with wry humour. "Do or say what you will, the king will always take it well from you. If any charge is laid against you, he will never believe it. If anyone else from the Privy Council is complained of, His Grace will seriously chide that person. But he will never believe anything amiss from you.

Therefore…" A warning note crept into his voice. "Therefore, you shall be most happy if you can keep yourself in this state."

Still marvelling at the king's kindness in sending these men to sit with him and offer comfort, he suddenly wondered how the king had known that he had just bade farewell to his wife? But, of course, the answer was simple. Spies. Either Cromwell's spies, or those employed by the king.

The Duke of Norfolk spoke up. "Marry, what solemn dullards we are. Is only ale served in this establishment? What about Malmsey wine?"

Hastily, Ralph Morice departed to attend to the wishes of the duke and the other visitors.

While waiting for Morice to return, Norfolk, who had never visited Lambeth before, gazed around in wonderment. "My lord Archbishop, have you read any of these books?" he enquired.

"All of them," Thomas replied, surprised by the question, but not by the brusque manner in which it had been asked; he was all too familiar with the duke's bluntness. His stomach suddenly sank as he realised how many of his books were forbidden. He simply had to hope that Norfolk would not wish to peer too closely at the contents of his bookshelves.

Fortunately for him, the duke was disinclined to waste time reading; he remained slouched in his chair until Morice returned with one of the servants, the two of them carrying a flagon of Malmsey wine, a jug of ale and a platter of food between them. Cromwell kept the conversation rolling, introducing the topic of the king's proposed wedding to Anne of Cleves, his mischievous intention being to antagonise Norfolk, whom he knew was strongly opposed to the union.

Eventually, the three visitors departed, without any altercation taking place between Cromwell and Norfolk, leaving the archbishop and Ralph Morice shaking their heads in astonishment. Thomas found it remarkable that the king had behaved so considerately towards one of his servants; if Morice had not been there to witness it, he would have believed it had been a figment of his imagination.

*****

The king was now eager to wed the beauteous Princess Anne. To his satisfaction, he had heard a report that she was far superior to the lovely Duchess of Milan, who had refused to marry him. However, the following day, a letter arrived from Cleves, informing the king that there had been a complication, for it transpired that Anne had been previously pre-contracted to the Duke of Loraine.

The king was, understandably, outraged by this sudden discovery, as was Cromwell. It had taken the latter a great deal of time to persuade the Duke of Cleves, who was not overly interested in forming an alliance with England, to agree to the marriage in the first place, and he was not about to allow his hard work to go to waste. Immediately, Cromwell suggested that perhaps the king should consider marrying the younger sister, Amelia. However, Anne's portrait was the more beauteous of the two, and King Henry was not a man who would settle for second best, not even to achieve an alliance with Cleves. Weeks of negotiation followed, which also included a proposal for Lady Mary to perhaps marry Anne's brother. The duke declined the proposition, on the premise that Mary's royal status was uncertain. Unfortunately, Henry, who had been considering this proposition with interest, was powerless to do anything about Mary's status.

"The king is in a quandary," Thomas informed Ralph Morice, as the latter was busy preparing a series of letters to be despatched. "The duke will only permit his son to marry Lady Mary if she is legitimised and becomes Protestant too. But if the king legitimises her, that will mean that he was lawfully married to Princess Catherine of Spain."

"It seems to me the king himself has become an eager bridegroom," Morice quietly observed. "Has my lord Cromwell made any progress with the Duke of Cleves?"

"I believe so." Thomas gave a wry smile. "The lawyers have announced that Anne's previous betrothal to the Duke of Loraine has been legally dealt with. So, if the Duke of Cleves is satisfied, and His Majesty likewise, then I suspect the marriage will go ahead."

Morice's eyes gleamed with mischief. "The duke's dedication to his daughter's future security is quite remarkable. It is clear that he desires for her to be securely crowned Queen of England, and for there to be no impediment which might be used to usurp her in the future."

Thomas longed to add that he could not blame him, but out of respect to the king, he remained discretely silent. Instead, he changed the subject to one which filled him with pleasure. Nicholas Ridley had just been appointed the king's chaplain, which meant they would be able to meet with each other often.

"He is so well learned," Morice enthused.

"Yes," Thomas happily concurred. "I have spent many enjoyable hours conversing with him. I have learned much from his store of knowledge."

"I look forward to learning from him also, just as I continue to learn from you, my lord," Morice declared sincerely.

At last, as the end of the year drew near, the Duke of Cleves was satisfied that Anne would not be returned in disgrace to

Cleves if she failed to impress King Henry. Cromwell gleefully hastened to Lambeth, to tell his friend the joyful news. All was legally signed, and the lady was soon to set sail for England, to become their new queen.

Thomas, however, having spent a couple of weeks at Canterbury, was more inclined to voice his own problems. "I caught them being fully disobedient to my wishes," he declared, outraged. "I arrived there, unannounced, to find them worshipping idols, and do you know what else I discovered? My own brother, Edmund, whom I recently made Archdeacon of Canterbury, was the one responsible for countenancing this behaviour. They were worshipping statues of saints!" His voice rang with indignation.

Thomas and Edmund did share brotherly affection, but Edmund had a far more boisterous disposition, and the two had not been especially close during their youth; even when they had both been studying at Cambridge, they had moved in different circles. Thomas had made his brother Archdeacon of Canterbury on the grounds that Edmund's credentials were good. He was well-educated, though not as academic as himself, and had studied the scriptures.

"As soon as I turn my back, they do exactly as they please," Thomas grumbled. "I expected more from my brother."

"No doubt your brother now understands that you expect him to carry out your wishes," Cromwell grinned, knowing how conscientious his friend could be. "I thought your brother was Protestant?"

"He is!" Thomas exclaimed indignantly. "But he is lazy. No doubt he permitted the worship of statues because it was easier than arguing with the clergy. But I forget my manners. You seem like a man who has news to impart. Could it be that the royal marriage has finally been finalised?" he speculated.

"Yes, indeed. The bride will soon be on her way to England. Such a relief," Cromwell sighed, seating himself heavily in the nearest chair. "You know, I have found it a cause for concern that England is such an isolated country. I know the king is troubled by it also, but now, thanks to this marriage, we have a genuine link to the Schmalkaldic League. Whether they like it or not, the German princes have to accept us." He gave a hearty laugh. "Without the marriage, that Act of Six Articles would have totally turned them against us."

"The Act has certainly not helped to clarify anything as far as the ordinary people are concerned," Thomas mused.

"No, but the king mistakenly thinks it has. What is all this?" Cromwell indicated to a sheaf of papers lying on what was usually Morice's desk.

"Oh, it is a treatise by Joachim Vadianus, from Switzerland. Currently, he is working in conjunction with Zwingli. They are both extremists; they sent me this, called *Aphorisms on the Consideration of the Eucharist*, to obtain my opinion.

"Which is...?" Cromwell prompted.

"I wish he could have employed his study to better advantage," Thomas admitted. "Some reformists desire to be extreme, and these two are very much in that camp. I am preparing to write to them, because it seems to me that the Protestant faith is going to end up being divided in all directions, with moderates on one side and extremists on the other. How can the Protestant faith be strong if it is divided?" This deeply worried him, and he knew Ridley and Latimer felt very much the same. The Protestant faith should be one, strong, doctrine. Instead, the fledging faith was already being argued over and divided by people producing varying doctrines.

"You are too much of an idealist sometimes, my friend," Cromwell mused. "Men will always think their view is correct, and desire that others should bow to it. Just like some believe there should be an alliance for England with the Protestant princes, others think otherwise." His eyes gleamed with sly humour. "Oh, incidentally, the king wishes you to visit him at Greenwich Palace later this afternoon. He desires that you should examine a man called John Lambert in the near future. He is outspoken and Protestant."

"I know him, although only vaguely, from Cambridge," Thomas quickly interposed. "He has publicly denied the Sacrament of the Altar. He is not an Anabaptist, but he is an extreme Protestant. I hope he is not to burn like the Anabaptists last week."

There were many negative aspects of being Archbishop of Canterbury, and this was one of them. The king had instructed him to set up a commission to seek out Anabaptists, who were people who believed that baptism was only valid when a candidate verbally stated a commitment to Christ. Although he favoured infant baptism, he was able to see their point of view as far as this was concerned. However, they also believed in polygamy, that all property should be shared, and that Christ would come to Earth again, and reign for one thousand years. Their theology was not according to the New Testament and the teachings of Christ, so he felt they were worthy of imprisonment and needed some education regarding their dogma.

Unfortunately, in the case of the Anabaptists, the king had demanded that the leaders should be burned at the stake at Smithfield, as a warning to other would-be Anabaptists. This was not the only burning Thomas had recently been involved with. A certain Friar Forrest, whose views were heretical, had been examined by himself at Lambeth. In spite of his suggestion that the man should be imprisoned, the king had once again insisted upon the death penalty being applied. Being Archbishop of Canterbury left a bitter taste in his mouth, and often disturbed his sleep, especially now that Margaret was not there to offer words of comfort.

When he arrived at Greenwich, he found the king in good spirits. His new bride, whom Holbein had portrayed as a vision of loveliness, was expected to land at Deal within the next two weeks, weather permitting. Delighted by the king's obvious happiness, he was optimistic that the examination of John Lambert would be quick, and result in the man being dismissed with nothing more than a warning to observe his faith according to the instructions of the king, who was, after all, Head of the Church in England.

Once greetings were dispensed with however, the king's good humour dissipated. Frowning, his expression solemn, he commented, "those Anabaptists who were burned last week... are you aware they are now being regarded as martyrs?"

"I am, Your Majesty," he replied. It had been inevitable, in his view. When people died for their faith, whatever that faith might be, there was always someone who regarded them as a martyr; indeed, such people were often more powerful dead than alive, which was a subtle argument to be used against killing them.

"We do not like it," the king declared. "But your commission must continue; no doubt more people will feel the heat of the flames around their ankles."

Thomas was silent for a moment, noticing that the king was rubbing his injured leg. Changing the subject, he commented kindly, "your leg pains you. Shall I send for Doctor Butts to tend to it? Perhaps the dressing needs changing." There was certainly an unpleasant odour coming from the wound.

"No, no," the king shook his head. "The ulcer had to be cauterised yesterday. There is nothing Butts can do today. He placed a poultice of goose fat on it to draw out the humours." Dismissing the subject, the king returned to the task at hand. "Tomorrow, John Lambert is to be examined; we wish to speak with him personally, accompanied by yourself and Gardiner."

Thomas' heart sank. There was little chance of Lambert being spared execution if Gardiner had anything to do with it.

His prognostication proved accurate. Although he carefully explained the Act of Six Articles to Lambert, the man refused to change his views. It was sickening to see the excitement on Gardiner's face as Lambert, again and again, refuted the arguments explained to him by the king, archbishop, and bishop. Lambert was a zealous   Protestant, who had recently lived in Switzerland, and Thomas had no doubt that he had been much swayed influenced by Zwingli. However, Lambert was not in Switzerland now, and it was not long before both the king and Gardiner agreed that Lambert should be condemned to death by burning.

Thomas had expected this sentence, but it still came as a blow. Lambert did not deserve to die. He was fanatical, certainly, and his views were extreme, but it was such a waste of a life. He was about to suggest to the king that burning Lambert would only highlight the Protestant faith, when Gardiner jumped in ahead of him, insisting that Lambert's death would show the people that the king must be obeyed. Unsurprisingly, the king agreed with Gardiner, and Lambeth was sentenced to be burned the following day.

*****

261

Perhaps his infatuation with his soon-to-be bride had softened King Henry's judgement, but as they awaited news of the arrival of the Princess of Cleves, Thomas was delighted when the king finally acknowledged his archbishop's pleas for an English Bible to be chained to the pulpit of every church in the country. The version selected was the Miles Coverdale translation; any mistakes had been corrected, and Thomas was satisfied with the revised translation. Yes, it was not perfect, but no one would be misguided by it. The most important thing was for the English Bible to be widely accessible, so that the uneducated masses could hear and understand God's word in their own language. After the tribulation of recent months, it gave him a huge surge of joy to have finally succeeded in this.

Triumphant, he wrote an uncharacteristically positive letter to his wife. Her letters to him were always full of affection, and tales of how little Marjorie was progressing; Margaret even sent him a drawing she had made of the child, which had brought tears to his eyes. In contrast, his letters were often cheerless and depressing – he was less skilled than his wife at hiding his misery – so he was pleased to finally have something joyous to write about.

In the January of 1540, the Princess of Cleves arrived at last at Deal, her journey having been delayed by inclement weather. Thomas, who had spent Christmas at Lambeth, was appointed to meet her on the outskirts of Canterbury, along with Cromwell and several bishops, and then to escort her to her lodgings, where she would spend the night. They would then accompany the princess and her entourage to London.

Cromwell was jubilant. "This is surely the highlight of my career, to have arranged such a marriage."

Thomas could not help but smile, despite the bitterly cold, biting wind, making him feel chilled to the bone. Cromwell had achieved so many things; it was difficult to gauge which of them was the greatest. "If you say so. Certainly, you have put much time and energy into convincing the Duke of Cleves to agree to the marriage. However, in my somewhat biased opinion, I think your greatest achievement has been assisting me in persuading the king to licence the English Bible."

"Come, Cranmer, you did most of the work for that." Cromwell grinned. "You were like a dog with its favourite bone."

"Translating the Bible into English has always been one of my dreams; it is certainly my greatest achievement - and yours! I am grateful for your support. " His face split into a broad smile at the very thought of the joy this new Bible would bring to so many people. The word of God would be freely available; no longer would the people depend upon the often inaccurate translation of a priest. The truth was now written on the page, for all to see.

Frowning, Cromwell looked into the distance, then announced, with some excitement, "my eyes are watering with the cold and the wind, but I do believe I see signs of an entourage approaching!" At last, he would meet the beauty who was to be the next Queen of England.

"Your eyesight is far superior to mine." Thomas squinted. "Although I do believe you are right. We shall soon see our new queen."

Clutching their cloaks about themselves, the entire entourage eagerly observed the approaching procession. In spite of the wind and sleet, a large crowd of people had gathered to greet her, though much to their disappointment, no one could see her face, for her entire body was swathed in protective furs. Nevertheless, she waved amiably to the crowd, receiving plenty of loud cheers in return. Men were doffing their hats, women were waving kerchiefs, and children were jumping up and down in excitement. It was a merry crowd who braved the cold weather to welcome the bride from Cleves.

Arriving at the inn, Thomas finally saw the princess divested of her furs. He had to force himself not to rudely stare. She was not at all like the woman Holbein had painted, and to make matters worse, she also spoke no English. Having spent some time in foreign Courts as King Henry's envoy, he had discovered that many of the aristocratic ladies were fluent in several languages. Princess Anne, however, needed an interpreter, who explained to him that the Duke of Cleves disapproved of educated women. He had therefore refused to have his daughters tutored in music, art, languages and literacy. The interpreter assured Thomas that Anne's embroidery was exquisite, she was capable of running a large household, plus she could also cook. But Thomas knew that such skills were unlikely to impress King Henry.

Conversing with her via the interpreter, he found Anne to be very agreeable woman, but with a sinking heart, he wondered what the king would think of her appearance? His Majesty was fastidious where women were concerned; he expected them to be beautiful and able to entertain him. Catherine of Aragon, apparently, had been quite lovely in her younger days, and she had been well-equipped to entertain him with her knowledge and appreciation of music. Anne Boleyn had been attractive and sophisticated – her intelligence and wit comparable with the king's own – and even Jane Seymour had possessed a pale, gentle beauty and sweet temperament. How could this lady expect to follow suit?

As he conversed with her, he tried to find good qualities in her countenance. Her nose was unattractively globular, her mouth was far too wide when she smiled, but her eyes were

264

undeniably lovely. Indeed, the more time Thomas spent with her, the more pleasing her appearance became. Certainly, she was no great beauty, but there was a kindness about her, and since King Henry was ageing, and often in pain with his ulcerated leg, he reasoned that he would find a kindly wife of more use than a vivacious beauty.

"What do you think of her?" Crowell asked anxiously.

"She does not look like the portrait, but I think she looks well enough. She is... dignified. She has a regal countenance."

"What about her figure?"

"I can see nothing of that, her gown obscures all." The princess was wearing a curious, high-necked garment, unfeminine, but extremely modest. It revealed nothing of her body shape, but he could tell that unlike Anne and Jane, she was not slightly built.

The next day, the princess was escorted to Sittingbourne, and by the following evening, the party had reached Rochester, where they were to spend the night before progressing the next day to Blackheath, there to meet with the king. From there, the princess would proceed to Greenwich by barge, where a huge banquet would be held in her honour, and on the morning that followed, she would be formally married in the chapel.

Having now spent much time with her, Thomas found he liked her enormously. She was eager to please, and keen to learn English; if the king would only take the time to get to know her, he was certain Henry would soon become fond of her. He said as much to Cromwell, who had been visibly uneasy throughout the journey.

"But what if he doesn't take the time to get to know her?" Cromwell countered.

"He has no choice. She is his wife," Thomas swiftly retorted.

Cromwell sighed. It was early evening, and they were relaxing in their quarters at the Rochester hostelry. Their rooms were simple, but at least they were warm. A roaring fire gave their room an air of cheer. "I think I shall summon the interpreter; tell him to suggest she takes a bath before meeting the king tomorrow. His Majesty likes his women to smell sweet… she does have an odour about her." In truth, he was dreading the meeting between bride and bridegroom. The last thing he had expected was for the Princess of Cleves to look nothing like her portrait.

As Cromwell opened the door to summon the interpreter, a commotion came from the courtyard outside, and the two men rushed to the window to see what was going on. A loud clatter of hooves heralded the arrival of ten men on horseback, all of whom were talking loudly. Wiping the condensation from the window, Thomas saw one of the horses was loaded with what looked like bundles of fur, and all the men were warmly and expensively clad. A huge man was being assisted from his horse, and a familiar voice boomed, 'we will woo her with gifts of furs and jewels!' Thomas and Cromwell turned to each other in horror. The king had arrived. One of the other men was also instantly recognisable: the king's friend, the Duke of Suffolk.

Sweeping through the inn, Henry demanded see his soon-to-be bride, and Thomas quickly called for the interpreter to inform the princess that her husband was eager to meet her. The word 'interpreter' confused the king, who like Cranmer and Cromwell, had never anticipated that his bride might be unable to speak English. Nonplussed, he looked at Thomas with a quizzical expression.

The princess had already retired to her bed, but she eventually appeared, having dressed herself hastily to meet her bridegroom. Smiling nervously, she entered the room, then gave an ungainly courtesy. The king's jaw dropped in astonishment, as did the Duke of Suffolk's. One of the king's favourite pages, a handsome youth whom Thomas knew to be called Thomas Culpepper, looked as if he was struggling not to laugh aloud. Finally regaining sufficient composure to speak, the king spoke a few clipped words of welcome via the interpreter, and offered his hand for Anne to kiss, before promptly turning on his heel and exiting the room. The romantic visit was very brief.

"We like her not," the king snarled. He was standing outside of the room, nearly nose to nose with a cringing Cromwell.

"I think she has a regal countenance," Cromwell protested, quoting the remark made by his friend earlier.

"We came here to nourish love, and what do we find? A Flanders mare!" the king bellowed dramatically, turning and sweeping from the inn, quickly followed by Suffolk. and his companions. With a clatter of hooves, they exited the courtyard, taking the bride's gifts with them, unseen and unopened.

The following morning, Anne, whom Thomas now deeply pitied, looked anxious and miserable. It had not taken him long to discern that she was an intelligent woman, so she could hardly have failed to realise that the king was unimpressed with her. Shortly before they set out for Blackheath, he noticed her eyes were red with weeping, which, since they were her best feature, did her no favours. He instructed the interpreter to tell her ladies to bathe her eyes to alleviate the redness, but this did little to ease her swollen eyelids.

At Blackheath, the king's behaviour was more gracious than it had been the previous evening. He could always be relied upon to behave in a circumspect manner when crowds of people were watching. On this occasion, the crowd included peers, courtiers, ambassadors, aldermen, merchants from the Hanseatic shipyards and a mass of commoners.

Later that evening, shortly before the banquet commenced, Cromwell and Thomas were unsurprised to be summoned privately into the king's presence. When they arrived, his fury was ice cold, a stark contrast to his usual, flaming rage. Somehow, it made them more fearful.

"What remedy?" he hissed, as soon as the two men entered the room.

It was the first time Thomas had ever beheld Cromwell looking fearful. "There is no remedy, Your Majesty." Cromwell's voice was a whisper.

"She was pre-contracted," the king retorted.

"All has been legally dealt with." Cromwell's tone was one of utter weariness. He had been awake all night, trying to find a means of releasing the king from his marriage. There was none.

"The marriage is supposed to take place tomorrow, Sunday. Defer it until Tuesday. By then, you shall have found a means of releasing us." The king's voice was louder now. "We will not marry her."

Sweating profusely, Cromwell remained silent.

Thomas felt chilled by the king's wrath, and simultaneously relieved that he had not been involved in the marriage negotiations.

"We have been dealt a pig in a poke," The king's voice suddenly rose to its usual volume. "We like it not. Foxnose Francis will cry with laughter if I marry that woman."

"I do believe she has a regal manner; she shall look especially so when her ladies attire her in the English style of clothing." Cromwell's tone was desperately persuasive.

"It is not you who must wed and bed her!" the king snapped. "She should be shipped back to Cleves immediately. If she is a beauty by their standards, it is painful to consider the plight of their plain women."

"It will offend the League of German and Protestant princes if she is returned unwed." Cromwell's voice sank to a whisper.

The king's rage grew cold again. "Examine the contract between the Duke of Loraine and the Princess of Cleves. Find a legality which makes this marriage impossible. Go!"

The two friends swiftly quit the king's chamber, with Cromwell shaking uncontrollably as they made their way back to their chambers.

Thomas laid a sympathetic hand on his friend's shoulder. "Can anything be done," he asked gently.

"No." Cromwell's voice was hoarse. "I spoke truthfully when I said that everything has been legally dealt with. It will only be a matter of time before I am banished from Court."

Thomas could not see that happening. Cromwell was too valuable a servant. "If you are banished, you will soon be recalled," he soothingly predicted.

The king's behaviour at the banquet was exemplary, though those who knew him best soon detected that his behaviour towards his bride was far from that of an admiring lover. As for Anne, she smiled so much that her face was aching by the end of the night. The only person who endeavoured to speak with her, via the interpreter of course, was the kindly Archbishop of Canterbury.

Despite the king's request to be released from his contract, there was nothing that could be done, and the following Tuesday, the king and Princess Anne stood before the Archbishop of Canterbury, taking their vows. Thomas noticed that the king did not so much as glance at his bride during the ceremony, and when the time came for him to place a ring on her plump finger, he did so with unnecessary venom. He desperately hoped His Majesty would come to see Anne for the person she really was: a sweet woman who would be a cheerful, kindly wife... providing he gave her the opportunity.

As they left the chapel, Gardiner sidled up to Thomas and pressed a sheaf of papers into his hand. "Here is a list of words from the Vulgate Bible. I find they are superior to the new English version, so perhaps you should have the relevant English words expunged and use these instead."

Glancing briefly at the list, which covered several sheets of paper, Thomas stared at Gardiner in amazement. "But these words are in Latin. How do you expect Latin and English to be mingled? No one will understand it at all."

Gardiner was unruffled. "My lord Archbishop, educated people will know what it means."

"But what about the uneducated?" he demanded sharply.

Gardiner did not deign to supply him with an answer; he simply shrugged and walked away. Tucking the sheaf of paper into his sleeve, Thomas resolved to burn it at the earliest opportunity.

The wedding ceremony dispensed with, he set out for Canterbury, to ensure that his clergy – including his brother – were acting and worshipping according to the king's instructions, instead of their own preferences. Though he did not enjoy berating his fellow clergymen, it was a relief to leave Court and return to his beautiful country manor. Having the opportunity to worship in Canterbury Cathedral was an added bonus, for it was a spectacular structure. Sometimes it troubled him that he enjoyed gazing at the stonework and carvings, and he often had to reassure himself that he was truly worshipping God, and not the artistry of man. After all, he could hardly remonstrate with his priests for worshipping false idols if he was doing likewise.

Chapter Twelve

Much as he loved the king, he kept away from Court as much as possible following His Majesty's marriage to Anne of Cleves. Richard Rich was gaining more and more influence, and Thomas Wriothesley had recently returned from an embassy to Brussels, so it seemed likely that he was destined to receive a higher office in the not-too-distant future. Thomas trusted neither of these men. The former would ally himself to anyone who could further his career and would think nothing of deserting them when fortune failed them. Wriothesley had a similar attitude, and though he had arrived at Court a Catholic, he had quickly switched sides to support the faction he considered closest to the king. Thomas very much suspected that neither man had any deep commitment to anyone or anything; their allegiance was to wealth and power, nothing else. At least Cromwell, though desirous of wealth and power, was deeply committed to the Protestant faith, and structured all his endeavours around that commitment.

When he did return to Court, he was warmly welcomed by the king, but was quick to note that both Wriothesley and Rich had the royal ear, as did Gardiner. Cromwell was nowhere to be seen, and Thomas had been several days returned to

Lambeth before Cromwell finally visited him in the library at Lambeth.

"I have decided to spend more time at my own home now, and to only attend Court when I am required to meet with the Privy Council, or if I am requested by the king," Cromwell explained. "The fact is, I know my authority is not what it was, so I feel it is wise to remain out of sight as much as is possible."

"The king needs you," Thomas reassured him. "Give him time."

"But this marriage has been a disaster." Cromwell began striding around the room. "Have you not heard? On the morning after the wedding, the king declared to his gentlemen that he had felt her breasts, decided she was no maid, and had neither the heart nor the courage to do the rest. He turned over and went to sleep! The queen's ladies tell me they have asked her if she thinks she shall be soon with child. She replies that, every morning, the king kisses her and says, 'good morning', and every night he kisses her and says, 'goodnight'. They say that, judging by this, she expects very soon to be pregnant. It is laughable!"

"She is no fool," Thomas mused. "I believe she is deliberately keeping her own counsel."

"I agree," Cromwell nodded. "She is playing the innocent, which is wise in itself. She is also learning English remarkably well. The king has despatched all of her Dutch ladies back to where they came from, so she is completely isolated."

"Poor woman."

"And she is very frightened too. The king now has grounds for divorce, as well you know."

With a sinking heart, Thomas had to agree. If it was unconsummated, then it was no marriage. "But he will offend the Duke of Cleves if he divorces her."

273

"The King of France and the Emperor Charles are currently at loggerheads, so for the time being, the king no longer fears them. If they are arguing with one another, they will not invade England,' Cromwell paused. "And he has found a new romantic interest."

"Yes, so I heard from Wriothesley," Thomas admitted. "I hoped it might be an exaggeration."

"No exaggeration," Cromwell assured him. "She is Lady Catherine Howard, another niece of the Duke of Norfolk. She is no more than a giggling teenager, but she is very beautiful. Nearly every night, the king travels by barge to the duke's residence to dine with her." After a moment of contemplative silence, he changed the subject. "How fares the treatise you were writing? The one against the Act of Six Articles?"

Thomas' expression brightened. "Completed. It has kept me occupied whilst at Canterbury, alongside my other, ongoing occupation – that of ensuring my clergy are well-versed in the scriptures."

"You need to choose your moment carefully if you are to present it to the king, though I know I need not warn you on that score." Cromwell noted that the fur on the unworldly archbishop's tippet looked well-worn. Had his wife been here, she would never have allowed him to wear such a shabby garment. "Tell me, how does your wife fare?" His expression was one of sympathetic concern.

"She is well." Thomas always felt uneasy discussing his wife, despite knowing that he could be open with Cromwell. "She is frustrated that she cannot return to England. Our daughter, however, is thriving. Osiander assures me that Marjorie is becoming a good Protestant." He managed a faint, wry smile. It saddened him that he was not able to educate his own daughter in the ways of the Protestant faith, but at least he knew she was in good hands with Osiander.

The two men sat in comfortable silence for a while, before returning to Court matters.

"Sir Edward Seymour is becoming increasingly influential," Cromwell observed. "He is a cold sort of person, yet fiercely ambitious - as is his younger brother Thomas. Though it has to be said that the latter cannot be accused of being cold, especially where ladies are concerned."

"So I have noticed. I met Sir Thomas Seymour yesterday, and he was all but surrounded by ladies." Jane's younger brother looked to be a bold, bluff man; witty and energetic. He was just the sort of person whose company appealed to the king. "Wriothesley informed me that Thomas Seymour is looking for a rich wife. But then, I suppose the same can be said of most men who come to Court," Thomas reflected. Returning to the matter of the queen, he wondered aloud what would become of her.

"The king can hardly execute her." Cromwell knew exactly what his friend was thinking. "There are no grounds for that. She is a good woman. Sadly, because she is illiterate and does not speak fluent English, people take her for a fool, but it is hardly her fault that she has not received an education. Indeed, had she been educated, I sense she would have been an excellent student, for she appears to be making good progress. Conversation with her is slow and difficult, her vocabulary is limited, but she improves by the day."

Thomas was about to remark that his own wife had been extremely diligent about learning the English language, and had very quickly become proficient. Thinking better of it, he simply replied, "I think I shall visit her in the very near future."

275

"Good idea," Cromwell approved. "You are probably the only courtier who can be bothered to seek her out. They are all far too busy visiting Catherine Howard."

*****

Two days after Cromwell's visit, the king and Court had moved to Westminster. Nervous as to what the king's reaction might be, Thomas gave his decidedly Protestant critique of the Act of Six Articles to Ralph Morice and despatched him to deliver it into the hands of King Henry.

"Let us pray that His Majesty does not imprison me for this," he muttered through clenched teeth. "Or worse." The critique would, he hoped, spur the king to retract the Act of Six Articles. It might also cause his own downfall.

Not knowing what to say to reassure his master, Morice simply tucked the treatise into his sleeve and summoned a passing barge.

No more than ten minutes later, after they had drawn away from Lambeth Palace, Morice noticed a commotion occurring on the opposite riverbank. "What is happening there?"

The oarsman pulled on the oars to steer the barge towards the opposite bank. "Looks like a bear baiting gone wrong, sir," the oarsman informed him, as they drew closer. "The bear appears to have fallen into the water. No need to worry yourself. All manner of strange events unfold on the river. A few days ago, I recovered the bodies of two drowned women, and the body of a man; they had obviously been robbed and stabbed, then thrown into the river. The fellow was still alive, mind you, but only just. Then, yesterday, I rescued a dog which had jumped overboard from the Duke of Norfolk's barge. It was the duke's favourite hound, so he gave me a tidy reward. Guess I got lucky."

A veritable flotilla of crafts was eagerly rowing towards the scene of the accident, hoping to rescue the bear and perhaps gain a generous remuneration. Bears were valuable animals. Quite suddenly, their barge was rammed with such force that Morice, who had been leaning over the side to see what was happening, tumbled into the river.

Within minutes, the terrified secretary was pulled out of the water, then promptly escorted back to Lambeth. He immediately hastened into the palace to shed his heavy and sodden garb, encountering several startled servants as he walked through the halls, water dripping from his garments. As he removed his clothing, he realised something was missing. The thesis was no longer tucked into his sleeve.

In due course, he joined the archbishop in the library, apologetically explaining that he had managed to lose the thesis. "It must have fallen from my sleeve into the water."

Thomas regarded his obviously shaken secretary with concern. "I am simply thankful that you did not drown. Go and take a hot posset to warm yourself, then, once you are recovered, we shall begin rewriting this thesis. I have the notes, and I can remember much of it anyway." It was a nuisance, certainly, but at least his secretary had not drowned.

Thinking nothing more of it, the two men soon began rewriting the thesis, imagining this was the end of the matter.

The bearward, whose animal had unfortunately drowned as a result of the accident, was a relatively poor man, whose sole asset had been his bear. He could neither read nor write, but it was he who chanced to find the thesis which had fallen into the water with Ralph Morice. Fishing it out, he realised it was smudged but still legible, so he took it to a priest to be interpreted. After all, it might be a valuable document, he reasoned. As a result of his consultation with the priest, he journeyed to Lambeth Palace the following day, and was escorted by a servant to see Ralph Morice.

"Are you the Archbishop of Canterbury?" The bearward demanded briskly, finding himself standing before a scholarly looking man wearing sombre attire.

"No, I am not. My lord Archbishop is at Court today. How may I help you? I am his secretary, Master Morice," he replied, with great civility.

"Do you recognise this?" The bearward thrust the now dry sheaf of papers towards the scholarly looking man, who was alone in the library.

"Yes." Morice was delighted to see the thesis again. "I thank you for your honesty." He reached out to take the papers, wondering how much money he should give by means of a reward.

To Morice's surprise, the bearward held the papers close to his chest and smiled unpleasantly, showing his stained and broken teeth. "I took this to a priest to read, and he said the person what wrote this should burn. I'm guessing the person what wrote it must be your master?"

"How much do you wish the archbishop to give to you for these papers?" Morice sighed inwardly. This was blackmail. Having lost his bear, which was his livelihood, obviously he would wish to purchase another.

The bearward, however, backed away. "I don't want money. I just want to see the archbishop burn. He's a heretic, and this…" He waved the thesis at Morice. "Will prove it."

"The work is not heretical," Morice explained, trying to sound convincing. "The king himself instructed the archbishop to write it."

The bearward hesitated, and for a brief moment, Morice thought he was going to hand the thesis to him. But it was not to be so.

"I think I'll show this to the Bishop of Winchester. Then he can decide if it's heretical or not." The bearward, clinging tightly to the thesis, began walking backwards from the room.

"The king and my master will be displeased to hear of your conduct." Morice hoped his voice was authoritative.

The bearward was unconvinced, and with another unpleasant grin, promptly departed.

Shocked and sickened by the man's open hatred of the Archbishop of Canterbury, whom he considered to be a dear friend as well as a master, Morice hastened to the home of the one person who could extricate Cranmer from this situation: Thomas Cromwell.

Cromwell acted with his usual speed. Several of his servants intercepted the bearward before he reached Gardiner's London residence, Winchester Palace. Fortuitously, he had not gone directly to Winchester Palace, but had seen fit to visit a tavern first. It was at the tavern where they forcibly extracted the thesis from his clutches and returned it to Morice, who was anxiously awaiting the outcome with Cromwell at the latter's home.

"It is incredible that a mere bearward can cause such grievous harm to someone as eminent as an archbishop," Cromwell pronounced ruefully, before firmly removing the papers from Morice's hands and thrusting them into the fire.

The secretary's eyes widened in surprise, but he made no protest. "And to try and cause harm to someone who is himself so kind. The archbishop would never hurt anyone," he remarked loyally.

"His faith is enough of an offence to some, as you saw," Cromwell shrugged. "But you acted well." He placed a hand on the secretary's shoulder. "Your loyalty is commendable."

Morice found himself blushing. "I wish you well, my lord Cromwell. Maybe one day, I can return the favour."

Cromwell smiled, but it did not reach his eyes. "I trust I shall never be in such a position," he pronounced bleakly.

*****

When he returned to Lambeth, Thomas was shaken to hear the story of the bearward, but grateful to Morice for his quick thinking, and to Cromwell for his prompt intervention. What would have happened if Gardiner had seen the treatise? It was meant for the king's eyes alone, but Gardiner was high in the king's favour. He might have succeeded in convincing the king that his Archbishop of Canterbury was a heretic, and ought, therefore, to be punished.

"Did His Majesty say anything about the treatise?" Morice queried, feeing responsible for the loss of the papers, even though it was hardly his fault that the barge had been rammed.

"I spent very little time with the king," Thomas replied. "His Majesty was busy, so I sought out the queen and spoke with her instead. Actually, my purpose in visiting Court was to speak with her and give encouragement. She has made tremendous progress; she does not use an interpreter at all now. Admittedly, her English is not perfect, but she can manage. She is an apt scholar; after only a few months in this country she can converse sufficiently to get by, though I must confess, we used a lot of sign language too." He smiled. Speaking with Anne had reminded him of the early days of his marriage, when Margaret had been determined to learn English quickly, and had refused to speak in her own tongue. Anne was similarly diligent.

The queen was astute enough to know that the king was regularly travelling to dine with the Duke of Norfolk and his beauteous niece. She had spoken frankly of the matter, though it had been a difficult conversation, not only because of her lack of vocabulary, but also because of her modesty. Eventually, however, he had discovered that her marriage to the king had most definitely not been consummated.

"I am acting like the innocent little girl," Anne had explained in her strong, guttural accent. "I pretend I do not know there is something missing." She was lonely, often bored, and very much aware that few wished to be in her company. She had a very small band of ladies-in-waiting, for the majority had left, not wanting to be part of her Court. Those who remained pitied her and continued to keep her company for that reason. But she did not want pity. She understood that there was nothing to be gained from serving a queen who was totally without influence. This she had explained as well as she could to the kindly archbishop, whom she had grown incredibly fond of. He was always so willing to talk with her, and he was patient too, never placing her under any pressure to speak better English than she was capable of. "I am so glad you are here. I have the frightened," she had informed him.

"Madam, what have you to be fearful of?" he had asked, quickly realising it was a foolish question. King Henry might not have actively killed Catherine of Aragon, but he had not treated her kindly; it was well accepted that if she had been well cared for, she might be alive now. His second wife had been beheaded, and his third had died in childbirth. Looking at the fates of Catherine and Anne, how could the new queen not be fearful of what might happen to her? She knew that the entire

Court deferred to little Catherine Howard now, yet Thomas could not seriously believe that the ageing king would marry such a flighty young girl.

"I fear I shall be..." She had mimed an execution, swinging an imaginary axe.

"He has no reason to have you executed," Thomas had reassured her. Then again, there had been no reason to execute Anne Boleyn either.

"The queen is in low spirits," Thomas informed Morice. "And His Majesty is the opposite. He acts the way he did when he was first in love with Anne Boleyn."

Morice shook his head sadly. "Poor dear lady... the queen, I mean. She seems such a kindly person and is clearly a devout Protestant."

"Unfortunately, as things stand, the king no longer needs a Protestant alliance," Thomas sighed.

For the next few weeks, Cromwell continued to keep to his house as much as possible, only leaving when required to attend formal meetings. It was on one such occasion, during a meeting at Lambeth Palace, that a furious row broke out between him and the Duke of Norfolk. This, in itself, was unsurprising, for the two had never seen eye to eye, and often opposed one another. But this particular row was something different, more menacing, and the fact that the duke made his dislike of Cromwell so apparent boded ill for the latter. Until now, outwardly at least, Norfolk had shown at least a degree of respect for Cromwell, but this had disappeared.

Thomas remained positive that the king would soon need Cromwell's energetic mind; he refused to listen to the insinuations of Richard Rich and Thomas Wriothesley, who regularly seemed to seek him out when he was at Court, asking leading questions such as: 'has the Earl of Essex uttered

282

anything heretical during your private meetings?' The answer Thomas gave to these men was always the same: 'no, the Earl of Essex is nothing but discrete and loyal to His Majesty', which was entirely true.

In early June, the king summoned his archbishop to Court, and the king's favourite page, young Tom Culpepper – a youth clearly destined for high office – ushered Thomas into an anteroom, where, for the first time in over a month, he found himself closeted alone with His Majesty. In the hot, airless room, the stench from the king's injured leg was pungent.

"Ah, my lord Archbishop." The king's tone was jovial, his face beaming. "We have missed your company recently. We suspect you are offended because we have not accepted your treatise against the Act of Six Articles," he boomed.

A couple of weeks ago, Thomas had sent the rewritten treatise to the king, who had promptly returned it to him, with a note saying that he agreed with none of it. He was disappointed, but at least he had not been arrested. "Your Majesty." Bowing, Thomas kissed the king's extended hand, noticing how fat and swollen his fingers were. His rings appeared to have become entirely embedded into his skin; they were certainly no longer removable without being cut from his fingers. "I have been kept well occupied. As for the Act... under God, I am guided by my king," he stated sincerely.

"Well then, let us forget the Act, for we have a task for you that none other can carry out." The king's expression was indulgent; he was regarding his companion with the air of a parent surveying his favourite child. "We desire a divorce from our queen, my lord Archbishop. The marriage has not been consummated, and is therefore no true union, as you are fully aware. We request that you speak with the lady and persuade her to admit that it is indeed so."

There was a lengthy moment of silence as Thomas took this in. "But what shall happen to the lady?" His voice was little more than a hoarse whisper.

"She shall be…" The king thought about it carefully. "She shall be well kept and shall be… our much beloved sister. That's it!" He slapped his sound leg. "She shall be our sister." He tapped his teeth thoughtfully with a fat index finder. "We must keep the Duke of Cleves sweet… just in case."

"Perhaps Cromwell would be the best person to deal with this," Thomas suggested hopefully.

"No." The king's tone was sharp, making it clear Cromwell was still not in favour.

"Her Majesty is a woman of modesty and discretion, but I shall endeavour to achieve the response you desire." Thomas felt a surge of relief. At least the lady was going to be treated with dignity.

The king was beaming again. "We shall send word to the queen, to inform her that you will be with her shortly. Culpepper," he bellowed. Seconds later, the youth appeared; obviously he had not been very far away. "Bring us wine; we would speak with the archbishop for a while. Then, inform the queen that he shall be visiting her within the hour."

Culpepper was quick to bring a flagon of wine, then, bowing, he disappeared.

"A fine and loyal youth," the king said approvingly. "One day, we shall find him a more significant role. We think he shall go far."

"He is certainly obliging and devoted." Thomas had not missed the expression of admiration the youth had cast in the king's direction. King Henry was quick to differentiate between those who were sincere and those who were not.

After half an hour of stimulating talk with the king, who remained an excellent theologian, Thomas left to visit the queen.

"Deliver to us her reply before you return to Lambeth," the king called after him, as Thomas quit the stuffy anteroom.

He found the queen almost hysterical; she knew something significant was about to happen. Her eyes were wide with fear as he entered her audience chamber. Two ladies-in-waiting had brought wine to restore her – he had never before seen a queen with so few ladies attending her – and once she was settled, he asked permission to speak with her privately.

Soothed by his calm gentleness, and knowing she could trust him, the queen listened to him intently, and his task turned out to be one of the simplest he had ever undertaken. Yes, she would admit that the marriage was not consummated; yes, she would happily be His Majesty's sister, as long as she did not have to return to Cleves, unmarried and rejected. After all, who would want to marry her now?

"His Majesty is anxious for you to remain in England," Thomas informed her in his kindly, reassuring manner.

"He want for to imprison me?" Her eyes once again became wide with fear.

"No, no." He took the liberty of patting her hand. "He wants to give you houses. Several of them, in fact. They shall all belong solely to you, for you to live in as you please."

"With the garden? I am wish of mine own garden… and I am wondering if this is dreaming." Bemused, the queen took a sip of wine.

"With gardens." He smiled. She had once told him how much she loved gardens. It was a relief to know that the king was not going to humiliate this sweet woman, and even more of a relief to know that he did not intend to execute her, though

285

given that her father was Duke of Cleves, it would have been a most unwise decision.

"So, king will wed little Miss Howard next," she nodded sagely.

"Of that I am not informed." His smiled broadened as she looked at him with an arch expression. "It is the truth, Your Majesty. The king has said nothing to me about Lady Catherine Howard." He produced a document the king had given to him just a short while ago. "Would you please sign this, Your Majesty? It says that you admit to the marriage being unconsummated, but that you desire to remain in England. In this realm, you shall be known as Princess Anne, the king's beloved sister, and shall be treated as such. At Christmas, Easter and all other festivals, the king will invite you to join him at Court, where you will be honoured above all women, except the queen herself."

Anne took a deep breath, then gave one of her wide, beaming smiles, as she finally accepted the reality of her new situation. "I have learned to sign mine name," she informed him proudly. "When I live in mine own house, I will ask that you come and dine with me. I will be able to do mine own cooking in mine own home, no one shall stop me. You see, mine father would not have his daughters learning readings and writing, but we all cook very well."

"Your Majesty, I shall be honoured," he replied sincerely.

Anne readily signed the document, and he returned to the king. For his part, the king looked undecided as to whether he should be relieved or offended by her readiness to accept a divorce. He settled for relieved; he would soon be a free man, able to marry the beautiful Lady Catherine Howard.

Bidding farewell to the king, Thomas returned to Lambeth, looking forward to seeing Cromwell in few days' time, when the Privy Council was due to meet. For once, he would be the person delivering information to Cromwell. He grinned. His heart felt lighter than it had done for some weeks. With a clear conscience, he could pronounce the king to be divorced, and free to remarry. The queen's situation had weighed heavily upon him, for he liked her enormously, and her future had looked bleak. But she was safe now and would be treated with kindness and honour. Had the situation had been different, and he had been able to openly declare his marriage to Margaret, he firmly believed that the two women would have become close friends, for they were very similar in temperament and personality. Perhaps, in the future, when the king fully accepted the Protestant faith, he would be able to introduce them.

On the tenth of June, the Privy Council met, and Thomas hurried to Cromwell's side as the two of them walked towards the Council Chamber, to whisper the details of the forthcoming divorce in his ear. As they were about to walk into the chamber, side by side, Richard Rich tugged at Cromwell's sleeve, begging to speak with him. As Thomas entered the room alone and seated himself, he realised that the only member missing was Cromwell – Rich was not yet a member of the Privy Council – and he began to wonder whether Rich's little stunt outside had been a deliberate ploy.

On this occasion, the king was not expected to make an appearance, making the Duke of Norfolk the most senior person present. Norfolk was sitting with a grim smile on his face, looking expectantly towards the doorway. There had always been an austere grimness about Norfolk's countenance. When Thomas had first become a member of the Privy Council, it was Norfolk who had terrified him most. There was something so very imposing about him, and it had come as a great consolation when several other members of the council admitted to feeling likewise.

When Cromwell finally walked into the Council Chamber, Norfolk stood up from his chair, which meant everyone else must do likewise. Walking over to Cromwell, the Duke promptly tore off Cromwell's Order of the Garter.

"A traitor may not wear these, Master Cromwell." His voice rang with satisfaction, as he proceeded to swiftly remove, one by one, the clearly stunned Cromwell's badges of office, including the Great Seal. "You are to proceed to the Tower, sir, where you shall be imprisoned, on charges of treason and heresy."

Quickly regaining his wits, the outraged Cromwell flung his cap to the floor. "Is this my reward for the service I have done?" He glared at Norfolk, and then at the clearly delighted Stephen Gardiner. "On your consciences, I ask you, am I a traitor?"

The Catholic faction of the Privy Council had already started thumping their fists on the table, shouting, 'traitor! Traitor!'.

"Such faults as I have committed deserve grace and pardon, but if the king, my master, believes so ill of me, let him make quick work and not leave me to languish in prison." Cromwell's gaze swept around the room, easily identifying those who were opposed to him and those who were not. For his part, Cranmer looked white and shaken, as if it was he who had been accused of being a traitor, whilst Edward Seymour's mouth hung open in shock.

The Catholic faction continued to rhythmically beat their fists and shout obscenities in his direction as Cromwell was hustled out of the chamber. Blinking in astonishment, Thomas glanced around the room, and found the Catholic faction eyeing him gleefully. There was no doubt about it: his downfall would be next.

Cromwell had been arrested under an Act of Attainder, a method of sentencing someone to death, usually for treason, without first going through a trial. Thomas knew that, unless the king pardoned him, Cromwell stood no chance of getting out of the Tower alive. In desperation, as soon as he returned to Lambeth Palace, he wrote to the king.

'Your Majesty, he whose surety was only by Your Majesty; he who served Your Majesty no less than God; he who studied always to set forward whatsoever was Your Majesty's will and pleasure; he that cared for no man's displeasure to serve Your Majesty; he that was such a servant in wisdom, diligence, faithfulness and experience, as no prince in this realm ever had, can surely not be deemed a traitor. I loved him as my friend, for I so took him to be, but I chiefly loved him for the love which I saw him bear ever towards Your Grace, singularly above all others. Whom shall Your Grace trust hereafter if you might not trust him? Alas, I bewail and lament Your Grace's chance herein; I know him to be whom Your Grace may trust'.

It was impossible to imagine the king not sparing this servant. No one else possessed such energy and cunning intelligence as Cromwell; he was a great asset to the king's Court. But whilst the king read the letter, and announced himself to be as shocked as his archbishop by Cromwell's sudden fall, he did nothing about it.

In response to this, Thomas asked Ralph Morice to visit the Tower, to request a list of the charges that had been laid against Cromwell.

Morice returned with a long list of accusations.

"He has never done any of these things!" Thomas exclaimed, his gaze rapidly skimming down the list of crimes as he restlessly strode around his spacious library. "This is ludicrous, all of it. He has not given heretics licence to preach, and he is certainly not an Anabaptist..." His hands were shaking as he tried to make sense of it. "It says he has failed to enforce the Act of Six Articles..." his voice trailed away. That could well be true. Cromwell was, after all, Protestant. "And it says he has been plotting to marry Princess Mary."

"Ridiculous," Morice exclaimed, his face a mask of shock. No one had served the king as diligently as Cromwell. That this man should now be placed in the Tower... it was too much to take in.

"Princess Mary and Cromwell have never been on civil terms. She has always disliked him as much as she dislikes me," Thomas declared.

Slowly, he read the list afresh. Cromwell was accused of corruption; of giving heretics licence to preach; spreading heretical literature; and of being an Anabaptist. The latter accusation meant he could be burned at the stake. "I don't know what I can do to have him spared," he informed Morice forlornly. "I have written to the king, but it has done nothing to aid his release."

Collapsing into a chair, he regarded the list yet again. Norfolk currently had King Henry's ear, thanks to his pretty niece being a royal favourite these days. Since Gregory, Cromwell's only surviving son, had married Queen Jane's youngest sister, Elizabeth, a few years ago, the aristocratic Norfolk had found it impossible to hide his displeasure. In Norfolk's opinion, the Cromwells were marrying too close to the crown, and Thomas knew that Norfolk had been waiting for any opportunity to get rid of the person whom he considered to be an upstart statesman. The disastrous marriage between King Henry and Anne of Cleves had left Cromwell in a vulnerable position, so Norfolk and his Catholic supporters had seized an opportunity to strike.

There had been times when Thomas' own relationship with Cromwell had been strained, but it was a fact that the two of them needed one another; despite their differences and disagreements, they held each other in high regard, and respected one another's opinions. Witnessing his friend's sudden arrest had shaken him to the core.

From his room in the Tower, Cromwell also wrote to the king, asking for mercy. He knew only too well that he was destined to die, and his enemies would desire for him to endure the traitor's death. They wanted him to be hung, drawn and quartered, or else burned. Whilst it was evident that the king did not feel inclined to save his life, Cromwell hoped that he would at least agree to a beheading instead. His letter sent, he soon received a reply, not written by the king, but by a secretary, which stated that he was to be beheaded. Being of lowly stock, he was unfit to be executed on Tower Hill, but was informed that he would be beheaded at Tyburn. Ironically, the date set aside for this was the twenty-eighth of July, the same day on which the king intended to marry Catherine Howard.

As Archbishop of Canterbury, Thomas had been informed that he must perform the marriage ceremony, so he travelled to the Tower the evening before the wedding, to visit his friend. Cromwell had been denied visitors, but the Governor of the Tower, Master Kingston, sympathetically turned a blind eye to the arrival of the Archbishop of Canterbury. After all, he reasoned, a man who was about to die could not be denied the attendance of a member of the clergy.

It was a painful meeting, for both men. It had all happened so suddenly. At Christmas, Cromwell's execution would have seemed impossible. He had been high in royal favour; no one had been more so. Thomas hardly knew what to say to him now, other than to suggest they should pray together, which Cromwell was eager to do. He sat with Cromwell for over an hour: sometimes they were silent, sometimes they prayed. His friend was no longer buzzing with suppressed energy; there was a stillness about him, as if he had accepted his fate and already belonged to another, higher realm.

"We had a good partnership, you and I," Cromwell quietly remarked as his friend prepared to depart. "You were my conscience you know. What ever I planned, I always took your conscience into consideration."

Thomas managed a weak smile. "I have to say I never noticed my conscience hindering you in anything!"

When they parted, his eyes were brimming with tears that he was trying not to shed. Cromwell's were dry, and the hand which he extended to grasp that of his friend was firm. It was some time before he released his grip.

Ralph Morice had agreed to the grizzly task of attending Cromwell's execution in place of his master. Cromwell's unpopularity meant the crowd would be gleeful and disrespectful, and Thomas had wanted to ensure that at least one well-meaning and supportive presence was there. He prayed that Cromwell would spot Morice's kindly face.

"He died bravely," Morice later reported. "The executioner was clumsy; it took three strikes of the axe, but he didn't make a sound. As for the crowd, they were mostly gleeful. He was jeered at on the journey from the Tower to Tyburn, but there were a few kind people. He saw me, and I beheld a glance of glad recognition."

"I am grateful to you for attending, Morice," Thomas responded. His own position would be a lonely one now. Since coming to Court, he had worked side by side with the stocky, clever, energetic statesman. Just a few weeks ago, he could have been brought down by a bearward, but he had been saved by the quick thinking of Morice and Cromwell. The Court, always a viper's nest, would be even more dangerous without Cromwell by his side.

*****

During the following weeks, Thomas spent most of his time at the Manor of Ford in Canterbury. Gardiner, Rich and Wriothesley were in high favour at Court; it was thanks to their influence that there had recently been a spate of executions. More Anabaptists had been burned at Smithfield, all of whom had allegedly been closely associated with Cromwell. In addition to this, three men, including Thomas' old friend, Robert Barnes, had been accused of heresy, and promptly burned alive. It had come as a great blow to to learn of his friend's untimely death.

Considering the volatility of the situation at Court, Thomas felt it was prudent to keep out of the way. In addition to the burnings, the plague was making another unwelcome appearance, so he had a legitimate excuse to leave the city. He soon discovered that the citizens of Canterbury were pleased to hear Cromwell had been beheaded, for they blamed him for the dissolution of the monasteries and for the high taxes they were forced to pay. No one seemed to understand that all of this had been enthusiastically sanctioned by the king. Cromwell was a scapegoat, and the king's popularity soared in response. Slowly, Thomas had realised this was probably the reason why the king had signed Cromwell's death warrant.

As was ever the case at Canterbury, his clergy were obdurate, resenting the recent demolition of Becket's shrine, for they detested any form of change. Clutching a sheaf of notes, Thomas stepped into the pulpit, yet again, to explain the true meaning of reformation in England.

"The clergy are minsters of the Crown," he began, not failing to detect the disinterest of his audience. "Instead of receiving Papal Bulls, we receive Letters Patent from the king." Out of the corner of his eye, he could see his brother, Edmund, already stifling a yawn on account of having heard this several times already. "Parishes, dioceses, cathedrals and so forth, are all under the control of the king, and he may visit, repress, reform and restrain them as he wishes, or may appoint anyone under the Great Seal to do so for him. However, it remains for the clergy to command, reward and punish their congregation. The legal system of the clergy in no longer a separate court; we are tied to His Majesty's Court of Chancery. I stand in place of Papal authority, to receive supplications for dispensations and licenses, being empowered to do so by the Dispensations Act." He sensed a ripple of disapproval from those who were most deeply entrenched in Catholicism.

For a short while, he talked of the Act of Six Articles, then finally closed his lecture with the subject of the king's divorce and remarriage, news of which was gradually filtering through the realm. "His Majesty's recent divorce from the Princess of Cleves has been passed by Parliament, therefore His Majesty has been deemed free to marry the rightly virtuous Lady Catherine Howard, who was wedded to the king a few weeks ago." Given the age of the bride, Thomas reasoned this would be the last marriage ceremony he would perform for the king. Catherine was young and lovely; her cheerfulness and vitality would strongly appeal to the king's love of beauty.

Once Edmund was alone with his brother, he demanded, "Did the king instruct you to speak of his latest marriage?"

"Yes, he did."

Edmund, helping Thomas to remove his chasuble and dalmatic before they left the cathedral, was irate. "The poor lady of Cleves was cast aside because of her plainness, so that Henry, who is no vision of beauty himself, may hastily marry a girl young enough to be his daughter. In fact, she is younger than his daughter, his eldest one at least." His tone was outraged.

"Hush, you speak treason," Thomas gently warned. His brother could be fiery sometimes.

"I speak the truth," Edmund protested.

"Even so, you must be careful with your speech." Uneasily, he wondered what his brother said when he was not nearby to urge caution.

Edmund had seen the king six months ago, when he had cause to briefly visit London; he had beheld the king riding in a procession through the streets and had been shocked by the sight of the monarch, a man whom he had heard was tall, magnificent and handsome. He knew he and the king were more or less the same age, yet the man he had seen appeared haggard and old. Like Thomas, Edmund was still agile, and they could both walk for miles or spend a day in the saddle without discomfort. By contrast, the king looked uncomfortable, sick, and grossly fat. His eyes were pouched, and his cheeks red and bloated. King Henry was not ageing gracefully at all, and it was Edmund's opinion that the king did not need a young wife, he needed a nurse. Unfortunately, it was treason to utter this aloud, even if it was true.

During the first two months of the king's new marriage, the weather was the hottest it had been in living memory, and the king promptly sent a letter to Canterbury, instructing his archbishop to pray for rain. Meanwhile, he and his young wife, to escape from the plague, were staying at the Palace of

295

Oatlands, in Weybridge. Edmund Cranmer would have been surprised to see the king now displaying a suddenly renewed vigour, which everyone, himself included, attributed to his lively bride. He began hunting again, and plunged himself into frantic celebrations, to honour his marriage to his 'Rose Without a Thorn', as he called her. He even took to jousting again, though not with the speed and aggression of his younger days.

As the weeks passed and the weather cooled, the cases of plague diminished, and king and Court returned to London, as did Thomas. Christmas drew near, and to his dismay, he found himself expected to join the festivities at Court. He had hoped to spend his time at Canterbury, but the king had taken to sending for him regularly; his society appeared to be more sought after than anyone else's, with the exception of the queen, much to the chagrin of Gardiner, Rich and Wriothesley.

"My lord Archbishop, you do not seem delighted by our invitation," the king observed, his eyes alight with mischief.

"On the contrary, I am overcome with such honour," Thomas murmured. This was at least partly true. It *was* an honour to be invited to spend the festive season at Court.

"The queen is planning a selection of games, and there shall be mummers and much music and dancing." The king's expression remained amused. He had summoned his archbishop to attend him at Hampton Court for no other reason than to enjoy his company. At Christmas, he would be surrounded by courtiers, and his wife would no doubt be dancing with the younger men at Court, so amid the noise of the music, laughter and raised voices, to sit and talk with this learned man would be an oasis of calm.

"I request to be excused, as usual, from dancing and games," Thomas begged. "I have never danced... at least, I do not recall dancing. Maybe I attempted it as a child." He shrugged. "But I enjoy watching others dancing, whilst listening to music is one of my pleasures."

There was a slyness to Henry's smile. He knew exactly why his archbishop was dismayed at being required to attend the queen's Christmas celebrations: the archbishop's wife and daughter, who had fled to Germany, had recently returned to Canterbury.

"Our sister, the Princess Anne, is to join us for Christmas. The queen invited her; they are close friends, you know," Henry confided. "I never would have thought it possible that a current wife and a previous wife could be such good friends."

"I am glad, for the queen's sake, that they are friends, Your Majesty. The Princess of Cleves is a sensible woman, and a kind one. If she remains at Court, she will provide a worthy example for the queen to follow, and will provide her with wise feminine advice. I see the Lady Rochford is also at Court now." Thomas had never been fond of Jane Rochford, but since her damning testimony against her late husband, George Boleyn, he felt a considerable distaste towards the disagreeable woman. Most people felt likewise.

"The queen feels sorry for her, widowed and alone. She has such a soft heart." The king's voice rang with indulgence. "It pleased her to be able bring her back to Court." Like Thomas, the king felt there was something unsavoury about a woman who would willingly testify against her husband, but he was glad to please his little queen.

As they were speaking, the Duke of Norfolk, in higher royal favour than ever before, thanks to his niece being so beloved of the king, drew near, wishing to speak with His Majesty. Standing aside to permit Norfolk some privacy, Thomas wondered how quickly he could take his leave of the king and return to Canterbury, without causing offence. Three weeks ago, he had been totally taken aback to discover that his wife had returned to England. Not daring to journey to London, she had wisely travelled directly to Canterbury, and upon learning that her husband was at Court, she had sent a message informing him of her presence.

Eager to be reunited, he had hastened to pay a brief visit to the Manor of Ford, yet his delight had been combined with fear. When he had enquired why she had not written to him first, to be advised whether it was safe to return, her reply had been simple. She had not asked because she had known that his response would be 'no.' She had discerned from the tone of his his letters that he was feeling low, so she was, she insisted, here to stay. If Thomas was honest with himself, he did not think she was any safer in Germany than she was here, and besides, the king was all too aware of his marriage. Some years ago, His Majesty had consistently mentioned packing cases when they were together, and several times during the past few days, he had taken to mentioning them again. It seemed the king, who missed very little, was fully aware of Margaret's return.

Chapter Thirteen

At the beginning of January, Thomas was able to spend a couple of weeks at Canterbury with his wife, and though her sudden return had been a shock at first, it turned out to be just the balm he needed. The death of Cromwell had been a bitter blow, and although he had tried to sound cheerful in his letters to her, she had been astute enough to know otherwise. There was no hiding anything from Margaret; as far as she was concerned, he was totally transparent. The death of his old friend, Robert Barnes, had also dampened his spirits, and it sickened him to behold the glee in the faces of Gardiner and his companions every time they successfully condemned a 'heretic'.

As always, there was work to do at Canterbury, and in the peaceful setting of the Manor of Ford, he began to devise a litany in the English language, which he hoped to present to the king, hoping that His Majesty might agree to it being used in the churches. Thanks to the late Cromwell's influence, the Lord's Prayer, the Creed, and the Ten Commandments, were now taught to the laity in the English language, so they were at last able to understand them. However, though he had anticipated that the clergy would translate additional Latin into

English, many were still unable to do so, despite his efforts to educate them, hence his decision to write a new English litany.

"I am disturbing you?" Margaret, clutching a basket of clothing, came into the library, intending to sit quietly and keep him company whilst she attended to some mending.

"No, I enjoy it when you are here." He gave a contented smile.

"Poor Master Morice is still coughing in his room," she informed him. "I sent the hot posset to him; he will be better soon." She had great faith in her hot, herbal possets.

"He works too hard, and before you say anything..." He waggled a finger at his wife. "I am well aware that I do too. But the clergy totally exasperate me. The Lord's Prayer, the Creed, the Ten Commandments... they should be taught to the common people in English! The clergy should teach them, except many of them still cannot translate these texts into English. Even here, in Canterbury, where I harangue them to educate themselves, there is a stubborn number who refuse to learn Latin. The entire litany needs to be printed in English; it will make everything so much simpler." He rolled his eyes expressively. "As long as the officiating priest can read English. Some can't even do that!"

"The Latin sounds beautiful," Margaret reflected. "But you are right. What use is beauty if the meaning is not understood?"

"Exactly. I intend to spend the next week completing a litany in English, to show the king when I return to London. Then, all I can do is pray to God that he will authorise it to be printed and circulated to churches throughout the realm."

"Will that be dangerous? I mean..." Margaret looked frightened. "Will it get you arrested?"

He hesitated for a long while before replying. "At present, the king favours me. Admittedly, when he hears the litany, he might not. But I must try. I have to make God's word understandable to everyone."

"I know." Margaret looked down at her sewing, adding in a low voice, "I was blessed to be told of God's word in my own language. Everyone in England should be likewise blessed."

*****

Latimer and Ridley, the former having recently been released from prison, visited Canterbury upon Thomas' arrival, and both enthusiastically offered help with the new English litany. He was grateful for their help, but decided that, despite their assistance, he would claim the project as purely his own work, and therefore his own responsibility. He did not wish for Latimer and Ridley to suffer the backlash should the king be unhappy with it.

Upon returning to London, he immediately received a summons to wait upon the king, and found him alone with the queen, who was seated cosily upon his sound knee. This boded well for the interview. Her girlish laughter, which he had heard as soon as he opened the door to the room where they were seated, always put His Majesty in an excellent mood.

Seeing the archbishop, Catherine jumped from the king's lap, snapping her fingers at a small greyhound which lay beside the fire. "Come. I shall summon Master Culpepper. He and I shall take you outside for your exercise. You are growing fat." She gave a joyous giggle, patting the greyhound's head fondly. "Greyhounds cannot be fat." Kissing Henry soundly, she gaily departed.

"Good morrow, archbishop." The king radiated good humour. "We understand you have something you wish for us to read."

"Yes, Your Majesty." Thomas was suddenly struck by uncertainty. This English litany could certainly be viewed as heretical. Before his courage disintegrated completely, he pulled the papers from his sleeve.

"Before we read this…" The king waved the sheaf of papers aloft. "We must make you aware that, in the coming months, we are to embark upon a Progress with our beloved queen, and we are thinking of perhaps journeying as far as the northern parts. We shall need plenty of packing cases." His eyes gleamed with mischief.

Thomas managed a faint but embarrassed smile.

"We are not taking our son, Edward, with us. He is too young, but we shall be taking a large retinue. As such, you shall be required to remain here, in the city, with the Duke of Norfolk and Lord Seymour." Whilst his archbishop digested this, Henry turned his attention to the English litany, read it slowly, then sat with his eyes closed, deep in thought.

Watching the king, he felt such a surge of anxiety that it rendered him queasy. His stomach felt as if it were tying itself in knots. He wished the king would say something.

At last, the king spoke. "We have had it in mind to have an English version," Henry remarked reflectively. His expression again became mischievous. "If nothing else, it will certainly irritate the Pope."

Uncertain whether he was supposed to reply, Thomas remained silent.

The king was also silent, once again perusing the sheets of paper. Finally, sitting back in his chair, he proclaimed, "We desire for this to be amended and made public. There are changes we would suggest, especially where the sacrament is concerned, but on the whole, we like it."

Feeling a thrill of exhilaration and relief, Thomas gave a beaming smile. "Your Majesty…"

The king waved a hand in a silencing gesture. He was too busy enjoying his prolonged honeymoon to concentrate deeply upon an English litany. His mind was fixed upon travelling throughout the realm in the company of his beautiful little wife and showing himself to the people. Not for the first time, he demonstrated the caprice that so exasperated his courtiers. "The Progress needs planning, and we have much to consider during the coming months. The Venetian Ambassador is due to visit, and an envoy from Naples," he explained to his archbishop. "Make the taking of the sacrament more traditional – but still in English – and bring this litany back to us later in the year."

The delay was an irritation, but Thomas quickly thrust this aside. The changes were hard to swallow, but at least the king had agreed to an English litany. He could hardly wait to write to Latimer. Ridley was at Court, so he would be the first to hear the good news. In fact, he knew for certain that, as this meeting was taking place, Ridley was sitting quietly in his chamber, praying for a favourable outcome. His prayers had been granted.

"Your Majesty looks so well," he could not resist remarking. Henry seemed to have lost some weight; his face was less bloated, and his injured leg, which often emitted a foul odour, was currently not offensive at all. Even the rings on his hands seemed to be less sunken in fat.

"Archbishop, our queen is a gift from God. We wish she would provide us with an heir, but she is very young, still a teenager. Her lively chatter and good nature are like a tonic to an old man." He eyed his companion, waiting for him to comment favourably.

Thomas obliged but would not deliver false compliments. "Your Majesty, your mind is an example to us all; your speed of thought is equal to that of a teenage youth. I find myself slower at recollecting facts; I often have to pause to remember, whilst I hear Your Grace speaking without hesitation. The facts simply jump into your mind. As for a new royal baby, God will bless you with this in good time," he sincerely assured him.

The next few months sped past, and the king embarked upon his Progress with the queen. They would be absent from Court for two months, probably returning in late October. Thomas, by nature of his position, had to spend the bulk of his time London, but it was possible to insert brief visits to Canterbury into his busy schedule. However, since most of the courtiers were travelling with the king and queen, Margaret was able to discretely spend some time at Lambeth.

A couple of weeks before the king and queen were due to return, Margaret peered anxiously around the door of their Lambeth library.

"You are alone?" she asked.

"For the time being," he replied. There was an excited expression on her face. Obviously, she was about to report something amusing that Marjorie had done or said. He sat back in his chair, waiting to be entertained.

She perched herself on the edge of his desk, smiling broadly. "I was going to tell you last night, but you were working late. So, I will tell you now. Marjorie will be having a baby brother or sister in early spring." She was beaming with delight. "I am certain this baby shall be a boy."

Though he knew he should be overjoyed by the news, he felt anxious. Yet again, memories of Joan's pale, broken body flitted through his mind.

304

"You look exactly as you did when I told you I was expecting Marjorie," Margaret protested, edging closer to him, and clasping his hand.

Kissing her hand, he gave a deep sigh. "I am delighted, my dear. But also fearful. You must have the best of care..."

"I had the best of care last time," she stubbornly informed him. "I had the prayers of the Archbishop of Canterbury." Heedless of the fact that Ralph Morice might enter the room at any moment, she boldly slid across the desk and seated herself on his lap.

"You always have the prayers of the Archbishop of Canterbury," he assured her, laughing at her expression. "You look so pleased with yourself, like a cat with a bowl of cream."

"I *am* a cat with a bowl of cream," she smiled, kissing her husband tenderly on the mouth, before standing up again.

Her timing was most fortunate, for at that moment, Ralph Morice walked into the room, looking ruffled. After giving a polite bow of acknowledgement to Margaret, he announced, "John Lascelles desires to speak with you, my lord Archbishop. He says it is something he can tell only to you, and it cannot wait." His tone was apologetic. John Lascelles was a minor courtier, devoutly Protestant, but self-important, and with a tendency to elaborate unnecessarily.

"I wonder what he wants?" Thomas frowned.

"As I said, he will not tell me the reason for his visit," Morice replied, aware that his master was likely reluctant to see the man. Lascelles was usually difficult to get rid of. "But he desires to be seen immediately. I declare, he is so excited he looks ready to dance!"

Thomas sighed. "Send him in."

"I will leave you to deal with him," Margaret murmured, still looking like a cat with a bowl of cream as she discretely left the room.

Lascelles entered the library, his face flushed and wearing what could only be described as an expression of triumph. Gazing pointedly in Morice's direction, he promptly declared he wished to be alone with the archbishop. Already irritated by his visitor, Thomas protested that Morice was very discrete, and that he required him to be present to take notes. Lascelles reluctantly agreed, accepting a seat without preamble. Grandly, he announced, "My lord Archbishop, I have the means of bringing down the Catholic queen."

This was the last thing he expected to hear. "Bring down the queen?" he repeated incredulously.

Morice's mouth hung open with surprise.

"Don't tell me you of all people are happy to accept a Catholic consort for our king?" Lascelles could hardly contain his glee. A fervent reformist, he was often to be found listening to a certain Dr Crome, who regularly preached at St. Paul's Cross. Crome was said to rival Hugh Latimer with his fiery, bombastic preaching and outspoken opinions.

Thomas' voice was quiet. "What is it you wish to tell me?"

"The queen," Lascelles paused for effect. "The queen is not chaste. She never has been," he announced airily. "Before her union with the king, she was betrothed to a man named Francis Dereham, and prior to this, she had a carnal relationship with a musician named Henry Manox, when she was living in the household of the Dowager Duchess of Norfolk."

"Where have you received this information from?" Thomas frowned. Such accusations could not possibly be true; the queen was but a teenager. Surely, she could not have been unchaste prior to her marriage to the king? She was simply not

306

old enough to have been anything but pure. Furthermore, she was the niece of the Duke of Norfolk; she would have been strictly chaperoned every hour of her existence. Of a surety, the information was false, and, as such, the rumours must be crushed immediately.

"The Dowager Duchess, the Duke's mother, ran a very lax household," Lascelles explained. "My sister, Mary, was one of her ladies."

Glancing at Morice's aghast expression, Thomas realised it mirrored his own socked visage. "So, Master Lascelles, where is your sister now? If she knows the queen, surely she would have been given a position as one of her ladies at Court?"

"When I asked her why she had not applied for a position in the queen's household, she told me she felt sorry for the queen, being trapped in a royal marriage, but that she would not apply for a position because she did not wish to be involved in any immoral trysts the queen might partake in. Then, she proceeded to tell me about the queen's former lovers."

"You are referring to these men, Dereham and Manox," Thomas clarified.

"Yes." Lascelles had now graduated from looking gleeful to being intensely serious. "I asked Mary how she could speak so of the queen, and that was when she informed me that the queen had lain in bed, with Francis Dereham, many times at night in the maids' dormitory, when others were present. Dereham used to speak of her as his wife, and he is now attached to the queen's household. As for Manox, the musician, he knows of certain private marks upon the queen's body, so he too must certainly have lain with her. Upon hearing this, I knew that even had I been a staunch Catholic, I should report this matter." A good-looking man, with a lean physique and a broad smile, Lascelles regarded the archbishop with an air of satisfaction. "You must realise what this means. The king can put aside his Catholic wife and you can recommend a Protestant lady."

Thomas closed his eyes, propped his chin on his hands, and thought deeply. Lascelles made it sound so simple, when in truth, it was an extremely complex matter. The Privy Council needed to be informed, whilst the accusations required thorough investigation, so that the queen's name could be cleared. Queen Catherine was still very young; these tales could not be true. But something about Lascelles story was undermining his certainty. "I need to speak with your sister. Please bring her to me," he instructed the visitor, who eagerly agreed.

"She will tell you exactly the same as she has told me." His manner had become almost exuberant, his ready smile had broadened to a grin. He simply could not subdue his glee at the prospect of the fall of a Catholic queen.

"If these claims are proven to be true, it will be a great tragedy. It is not something to delight in," Thomas warned the courtier. "They must be honestly investigated, according to law. Proof will be needed. Have your sister sent to me this very evening," he ordered gravely.

Thomas then proceeded directly to the Privy Council. Though most of its members were with the king and queen on their Progress, there were some who had, out of necessity, remained. These included Thomas Wriothesley, Edward Seymour and the Duke of Norfolk. The latter was looking visibly shaken by the accusations.

"They are but rubbish!" the duke shouted, his ruddy cheeks nearly purple with indignation.

"But they must be proved to be so," Wriothesley echoed Thomas' words to Lascelles. "It must be investigated thoroughly, so the queen's name can be cleared."

Edward Seymour was nodding agreement. "You are the person to do this, my lord Archbishop."

His heart sank. The reality was, no one wanted to be in charge of the investigation, because if the queen was found guilty, then that person would have to inform the king. No one would willingly undertake that task. Thinking rapidly, he glanced towards Sir Thomas Wriothesley. He was a man who knew no serious religious bias; currently, he was leaning towards the Duke of Norfolk and the Catholic faction, next week, he might claim to be Protestant, depending upon what favours or promotions he desired. "Sir Thomas, will you work with me on this? You are linked to my lord of Norfolk. If we work collaboratively, we can sincerely state that the investigation is balanced and without prejudice."

Wriothesley was only too pleased to assist, as long as he would not be required to deliver any bad news to the king.

"Tomorrow, we are to examine Manox and Dereham at Lambeth, and we shall be interviewing Lascelles' sister this evening," Thomas solemnly informed him.

Wriothesley nodded grimly. "We shall have this sorted before the king and queen return from their Progress, my lord Archbishop."

That evening, they examined Mary Lascelles, who verified everything her brother had said, and suggested they speak to another maid called Joan Bulmer. Joan, now a member of the queen's household, had once been in the employ of the Dowager Duchess of Norfolk. Thomas and Wriothesley made a note to act upon this information. This maid, Joan Bulmer, would not only be privy to what had happened in the Dowager

Duchess' service, but would also most likely know of any rumours being whispered in the queen's circle.

The following morning, Thomas and Wriothesley were seated in the library at Lambeth, opposite the musician, Henry Manox, a most unsavoury looking character. Manox admitted to being over familiar with the queen's person when she had been Lady Catherine Howard, but denied any further intimacy. His task had been to teach music to her, but he claimed she was very eager for him to educate her in a more pleasurable pastime. The Dowager Duchess of Norfolk had once caught the two of them embracing, and had promptly blamed Catherine, slapping her soundly for being a forward minx. He, Manox, had not even been rebuked.

"The queen was very agreeable to my intimacy," Manox informed his interrogators.

There was something about this man that made Thomas' flesh creep. The queen had been no more than twelve or thirteen when Manox had been behaving in this way with her. How could anyone be so vile?

"I would place my hands beneath her skirts and stroke her private parts," Manox confessed readily enough. "And I would unlace her bodice and kiss her breasts. But nothing else, even though she seemed willing enough to proceed further," he added, with an air of virtue.

Sickened, Thomas glanced towards Ralph Morice, who was quickly taking notes, his lips pursed in an expression of disapproval.

"Torture would get more out of him. We need to send him to the Tower," Wriothesley suggested, once Manox had been dismissed.

"No torture." Thomas was firm. "The information must be freely given."

Wriothesley gave a snort of disgust. Under torture, people were quick to admit their faults and follies.

Dereham was next to enter the library. Not as unsavoury as Manox, he was a good-looking man, well dressed, and with an air of confidence about him. However, he looked to be a man who harboured a grievance.

"You are recently attached to the queen's household?" Wriothesley clarified.

"Yes." Dereham gave a brief inclination of his head.

"A rumour is circulating that you have previous carnal knowledge of the queen, from when she resided with her aunt, the Duchess of Norfolk," Wriothesley continued.

Dereham's gaze flickered from the elaborately clad Wriothesley, to the solemn, sombre looking Archbishop of Canterbury. "Is that so?" His voice was almost a whisper.

'Well, is there any truth in this?' Wriothesley prompted.

Dereham turned his gaze towards the gentle looking archbishop. "It is true," he candidly admitted.

"What?" Thomas could not believe what he was freely hearing.

"Yes," Dereham repeated. "I used to creep into the ladies dormitory at the Dowager Duchess' home. I would lie with her night after night. I considered her to be my wife – we were betrothed, you know. The Dowager Duchess found out, and Catherine was sent to London. I was despatched to Ireland for a while, until someone informed me that she was Queen of England."

"You cannot have been betrothed to the Lady Catherine Howard, as she then was. You are beneath her, a mere servant! Who are you to propose marriage to such as she?" Wriothesley was sitting bolt upright, his tone one of outrage.

311

"Maybe not, my lord, but I tell you, I was her betrothed husband, and I lay with her many times. There are witnesses to this. But suddenly, my betrothed wife was removed from the Duchess' household and sent to Court." Dereham's expression was one of infinite sadness. "As I have said, I was sent to Ireland; I returned just over two months ago."

"And does the queen... does she still have feelings for you?" Thomas queried.

"No." Miserably, Dereham shook his head. "Her Majesty's women will inform you better than I, but I would say her relationship with Thomas Culpepper lacks innocence. You need to speak with them, particularly Lady Jane Rochford."

Thomas gasped. How many times had he seen the queen with King Henry's favourite page, walking the king's dogs; dancing; singing; laughing... all with the besotted king indulgently looking on.

Wriothesley, the first to recover his wits, demanded, "then you believe the queen has been indiscrete?"

Dereham gave a bitter half smile. "I have not personally witnessed anything. But I do hear rumours."

Looking at Dereham, Thomas was reminded of the Admiral Thomas Seymour, who was handsome in a swashbuckling way, energetic and charming. He could imagine how the queen, as a young maid, might have found this man attractive. But it was objectionable the way Dereham had taken advantage of that. Dereham was dismissed, to be confined in prison along with Manox, until the inquiry was concluded.

Joan Bulmer, when summoned to Lambeth, proved to be a born gossip. She had expected to accompany the queen on Progress, but had not been selected, and did not know why she had been missed. She was clearly offended at being passed over and was only too eager to talk. Yes, the queen had been

312

considered betrothed, if not actually married, to Dereham. Yes, before Dereham came on the scene, Manox had been sweet on her; she had often walked into a chamber to find him placing his hands where a gentleman should never place his hands on a young woman. But Manox had never visited Catherine in the dormitory. Dereham had though. In fact, all the maids had heard the unmistakeable sounds of lovemaking coming from the Lady Catherine's bed. Bulmer was also frank about rumours regarding Tom Culpepper.

"What have you observed between the queen and Culpepper?" Thomas asked.

"They are close. They talk together and laugh a lot," Bulmer stated. "They exchange letters. I have several times seen Lady Jane Rochford take letters to the queen and whisper to her that they are from Master Culpepper."

"What about letters from the queen to Master Culpepper?" Wriothesley demanded.

"I have never witnessed Lady Jane taking any letters from the queen," Bulmer replied. "Although I assume, since he writes to her, she must provide a reply."

"Is the queen always chaperoned when she is with Master Culpepper?" Surely even flighty little Queen Catherine must realise that her position required a constant chaperone?

"The queen and Master Culpepper spend a lot of time together; they often closet themselves somewhere without a chaperone," Bulmer admitted. "The best person to speak to is Lady Rochford." She uttered the name with distaste, clearly implying that the lady was not popular amongst the maids. "She has the queen's confidence, and she always arranges the times when Master Culpepper comes calling."

"Culpepper and the queen meet unchaperoned? Marry, I never expected any of this," Wriothesley uttered once Joan Bulmer had departed.

"Me neither," Thomas concurred. The young queen, poor child, had been woefully neglected during her early years. Clearly, she had been so lonely that she had readily fallen into the clutches of Manox and Dereham.

Thomas and Wriothesley were neither friends nor enemies. Neither cared much for the other – they were too dissimilar – but somehow, during this investigation, they managed to work together amiably enough, and gathered as much information as they possibly could. The king and queen were due to return to London at any time, and, unsurprisingly, not a single member of the Privy Council was about to volunteer to deliver the results of their investigation to the king. At an emergency meeting of the council, Thomas found all eyes fixed upon himself. Having already assumed that whoever headed the investigation would also inherit the task of delivering the report to the king, he consented to act as messenger. He supposed it was his duty. After all, he was Archbishop of Canterbury.

That evening, Nicholas Ridley arrived at Lambeth Palace. He was not a member of the Privy Council, but it was rumoured that something momentous was afoot, and he had noticed the pensive, anxious expression on his friend's face as he had departed from Hampton Court that day. "I have not come to pry. I am merely here to offer support in whatever troubles you. I can pray with you, if you so wish?" he clarified, in his sweet, kindly manner.

Thomas gave Ridley a grateful smile. "You are most welcome, my friend. Come, sit with me, and I will tell you what has occurred." After revealing the entire, tragic tale, he explained, "here are the complexities of the situation. The

314

queen appears to be guilty of being pre-contracted to Francis Dereham. If that is all, she has made a fool of the king, but I am optimistic that she shall not be charged with treason, after all, if she is married to Dereham, she cannot be married to His Majesty. She may be imprisoned for a while, but that will be the end of it. However, it seems she has also possibly cuckolded the king with Culpepper, though we have yet to examine him, as he is travelling with the royal retinue. If she has had a relationship with him, but is not the king's lawful wife, she has not committed treason. But…" He waved a finger expressively. "If she states that she was never married to Master Dereham, but has enjoyed a relationship with Master Culpepper, then she *has* committed treason, for she is lawfully wedded to the king. If this is the case, she will no doubt be executed."

"I am sure it will not come to that. It sounds very much like she has been promised to Francis Dereham. Poor child, it is not her fault. She has not been properly protected, why, she must have been only twelve when that Manox was over familiar with her, and only fourteen when Dereham took advantage." Ridley's expression was one of infinite sadness.

Thomas nodded agreement. "Poor little maid. She was left to follow the poor example of immoral women; no one taught her otherwise. She will not take it well to be imprisoned; she loves laughter and dancing too much. As for the king, I dread telling him. It may well be that I shall be the one who ends up in prison."

Ridley was reflective. "She would do well to immediately admit to being pre-contracted to this man, Dereham. It will cause a scandal, certainly, but all scandals disappear eventually."

"I agree. In the meantime, I must inform the king, though the very thought of doing so terrifies me."

"I shall be praying for you," Ridley solemnly promised.

*****

The following Sunday, early in the morning, Thomas was transported to Hampton Court, where the newly returned king and queen were due to hear Mass in the chapel. There was a cold, chill wind, but, as ever, the river was busy. The quantity of traffic on the water, regardless of the time always fascinated him. Prior to living in London, it had never occurred to him that people might use the Thames in the same way that people elsewhere used roads.

Arriving at Hampton Court, he was relieved to hear that the Mass had not started yet. The previous evening, a letter had been delivered to Lambeth Palace from King Henry, requesting that he conduct a service of blessing and thanksgiving on All Souls Day, in celebration of the queen: Henry's 'Rose Without a Thorn'. Reading the letter had caused a cold sensation of horror to trickle down his spine. Such a service would make the king a laughingstock once the accusations against the queen circulated, so he had promptly written a note, describing Queen Catherine's liaisons with Manox and Dereham, which he intended to give to the king as soon as possible. It would not be appropriate to hand the note to His Majesty prior to Mass, so he anxiously waited until the service was finished.

As the king left the chapel, he spotted his archbishop and flung an arm about his shoulders, exclaiming heartily, "Lord Archbishop! We intend to go hunting later this day; you must join us."

"Your Majesty." His knees nearly buckled under the weight of the king's meaty arm. Somehow, he managed to extricate himself from the embrace and produce his carefully written letter. "I am honoured, but respectfully request that you read

this first, somewhere private. I shall wait here, in the chapel."
He could see Ridley eyeing him sympathetically, whilst other
members of the Privy Council observed his exchange with the
king eagerly, guessing at what had just transpired.

Less than a half hour later, a pageboy – not Culpepper –
came to summon Thomas into the king's presence and directed
him into an anteroom. Not knowing what to expect, he walked
into the room to find King Henry standing in front of a blazing
fire, alone, his expression one of infinite sorrow.

"You have written this, by your own hand, none other?" the
king demanded.

Bowing, Thomas affirmed that this was so. "I have tried to
keep this as discrete as possible."

"And these people… they spoke freely? No torture?"

"They spoke freely, sire." His voice was a hoarse whisper.

"And this man, Lascelles. He came to you freely?" Henry
demanded, his voice also husky.

"Indeed, he did," Thomas confirmed.

"Was he asking for money?"

"No, Your Majesty, he did not wish for money. He had
heard something from his sister which he felt to be amiss,
therefore he came to me, at Lambeth." Obviously, he avoided
mentioning Lascelles' delight at having news which might cause
the downfall of a Catholic queen. "The Privy Council and I
gathered as much information as we could, to try and clear the
queen's good name. We have yet to speak with Master
Culpepper, since he was on the Progress at the time of our
investigation. We also need to speak with the queen and her
household, with Your Majesty's permission, of course."

Tears were now pouring down the king's face. "Why do we
always marry such ill conditioned wives?" he groaned. Then,
drawing himself to his full height so that he towered over his

archbishop, he managed to announce regally, "let the examination continue. Examine the queen's ladies first; leave the queen for the time being. See to it personally, archbishop. That way we shall know it has been dealt with fairly."

Feeling choked with emotion, Thomas nodded briefly. The king's grief was one thousand times worse than his rage.

The following day, he and Wriothesley interviewed the queen's ladies. It was discovered from these interviews that Culpepper had been heard to say he would marry the queen if the king were dead, which in itself was treason, regardless of his relationship with the queen.

The last of the ladies to be examined was Lady Jane Rochford. By merit of age, she ought to have been wise, but she soon revealed herself to be quite the opposite, admitting to Thomas and Wriothesley that she had encouraged the relationship between the queen and Culpepper. She even confessed to having stood guard at the door, lest the king came whilst Culpepper was in a chamber with the queen.

"Would you say that the queen and Master Culpepper were sexually intimate?" Wriothesley demanded crisply.

"Considering all the things I have heard and seen between them, I would say they were," Rochford replied, her thin, austere face, was cold and expressionless.

When they questioned Thomas Culpepper, he denied having any carnal knowledge of the queen, insisting that they had done nothing more than exchange love letters. Even when Wriothesley, to Thomas' indignation, threatened him with the rack, Culpepper's statement was ambiguous. Given that he continued to dodge their questioning, Thomas decided that continuing the interview was futile, and he promptly sent Culpepper to the Tower, hoping that some time in prison might loosen his tongue.

That evening, after an exhausting day of interviews, he sat with his secretary, Ralph Morice, and tried to make sense of what he had learned. "I hear the queen is distraught," he informed his secretary. "She has been confined to her rooms and is served by only four women. She had been told that she cannot dance any more, not until this matter is resolved. I doubt the poor child ever stopped to consider what she was doing. She has lacked guidance throughout her young life."

"Will you examine her?" Morice enquired.

"When the king gives permission I shall." Frowning, he picked meditatively at his sleeve. "I would prefer to speak with her alone, without Wriothesley. He will intimidate her."

"He intimidates me," Morice remarked, without irony.

The following Sunday morning, Thomas and the king were attending a service at Hampton Court chapel, when they were suddenly interrupted by the sound of fists battering on the closed wooden doors, and the shrill voice of the queen screaming 'Henry! Henry!', over and over again; somehow, she had managed to escape from her confinement. It seemed to go on for a long time, though, in reality, it was only a few minutes before some guards captured her and forcibly pulled her away. Throughout the incident, the king's face remained stoically expressionless.

Later, they discovered that Catherine had been begging for an opportunity to see the king, after one of her ladies had informed her that her life might be spared if she were able to convince the king of her innocence. In the hope of being forgiven, and knowing that the king would be in the chapel at this hour, she had managed to elude her guards. Thomas pitied her optimism; he knew that even if she had been granted an audience with His Majesty, he would not forgive her for humiliating him.

319

A few days after the chapel incident, having not yet been examined, the queen was despatched to Syon House, for the king wished her to be removed from Court. In her absence, King Henry took to spending much of his time hunting, sometimes accompanied by his Archbishop of Canterbury.

By early December, Culpepper was charged with treason, and was promptly beheaded at Tyburn for committing adultery with the queen. Francis Dereham was condemned to die on the same day, also at Tyburn, his charge being principally of piracy. Being of lower birth than Culpepper, he received the traitor's death, enduring the agony of being hung until unconscious, then, once revived, being castrated, disembowelled, then finally beheaded.

The Dowager Duchess of Norfolk was imprisoned in the Tower, charged with withholding information regarding the queen's impurity prior to her marriage. A rich woman, she had cunningly hidden her gold coins and jewels before entering the Tower, so that the king could not confiscate them, which he was entitled to do. Manox remained in the Tower, but was expected to be released, as there was no evidence of him being anything other than over familiar with Lady Catherine Howard.

It was the middle of January before the king, finally, gave his Archbishop of Canterbury permission to examine the queen. Two men had been executed, yet the queen had not even been examined, Thomas reflected, as he was transported to the Tower where Catherine recently been transferred. Thankfully, he had been able to persuade the king to allow him to speak to the queen alone, without Wriothesley.

It was a shock to him that, despite there being no concrete evidence that any treason had been committed, Culpepper had been beheaded and Dereham had endured a traitor's death. Given their fate, he had little hope for the queen, though lawfully it was possible that the queen was in fact the wife of the late Francis Dereham, and in which case, she had done no wrong. Her life entirely depended upon whether or not she would admit to being pre-contracted… and the whim of King Henry.

Upon his arrival at the Tower, he was met by the departing Chapuys, the Emperor Charles' Ambassador, who had just been visiting Catherine.

"How is the queen?" Thomas enquired.

"She is in good spirits," Chapuys replied. "At least, she seemed so to me. She dislikes the Tower, she said she preferred Syon House, which is not surprising. Perhaps she is merely showing a brave face. I am told that viper of a woman, Lady Rochford, weeps and wails. She knows that if the queen dies, she too will die, and no one will try to save her."

He nodded slowly. Lady Rochford was one of the most disliked people at Court. He had always privately wished the queen had not placed permitted this woman within her inner circle. It was an ill-judged act, but probably the result of Catherine's sweet, compassionate nature: she was undoubtedly foolish and flighty, but her heart was kind.

Bidding farewell to Chapuys, Thomas followed the Lord Lieutenant of the Tower to the queen's quarters. There, he found Catherine, prettily attired, and genuinely pleased to see him.

"You have brought a message from the king?" she demanded eagerly, extending a hand to receive whatever it was he had brought.

"I have brought nothing, madam, except my prayer book and a document for you to sign." He felt his heart melt with sympathy. The poor girl seemed to anticipate that he had brought a sign of forgiveness from the king. "His Majesty has also asked me to speak with you, in order to spare your life, if possible," he explained gently, signalling to the four ladies who attended her to withdraw for a while.

Catherine looked ready to weep with despair, unable to understand why the king, who had once so dearly loved her, refused to send her a token of clemency.

"I strongly advise you, madam, to read this and sign it," he urged, laying the document on the table in front of her.

"I do not read very well," she admitted.

"But you wrote love letters to Culpepper," he reasoned.

"Poorly written letters. Lady Rochford helped me," she explained.

Again, he wondered at the queen's folly. To ensure that she understood the contents of the document, he carefully read it aloud to her. It stated that she had agreed to be married to Francis Dereham, therefore she had unlawfully consented to marry the king whilst being pre-contracted to Dereham. Casting a glance at her, he realised she was vigorously shaking her head.

"No, I was never pre-contracted to Francis Dereham. I was foolish, yes, but I am a Howard. I would not have agreed to marry a common man like Francis Dereham." Her entire posture had become one of regal hauteur.

"It could save your life, madam. Think again. I do not wish to see you die, and neither does the king."

"I do not wish to die… but the king loves me, surely he will not let that happen?" Her regal hauteur swiftly evaporated as she pouted childishly.

"He is king, and cannot be cuckolded," Thomas spoke sternly.

"I was not pre-contracted." She paused, then asked innocently, "is Tom Culpepper in the Tower too? No one will tell me anything."

"No, madam, he died some weeks ago. Before Christmas. He was beheaded." There was no gentle way he could inform her of this.

Catherine's face was white with shock and grief.

"Madam, I cannot save you." His voice was almost a whisper. "If you were not pre-contracted, then you have committed adultery with Master Culpepper—"

"I was not pre-contracted."

"Then you are guilty of committing adultery with Master Culpepper." His heart felt heavy. He had travelled to the Tower in a spirit of optimism, anticipating Catherine's life could be spared. Surely the girl could see there was a chance that she could be allowed to live?

"I loved him." She dashed tears from her eyes, summoning one of her ladies to bring her a kerchief with which to dry them.

He regarded her forlornly. Love meant nothing in the world of politics. She was insisting she was married to King Henry, which meant she was guilty of treason. The king would not spare her, even though he loved her.

At trial, Catherine was found guilty of committing adultery with Thomas Culpepper, and Lady Rochford was found guilty of assisting her. AS was expected, the judges condemned them both to death.

"It is pitiful that the queen was not guided and guarded during her young life," Thomas muttered to Morice, once the trial was over. "She will die, whilst those who were responsible for her wellbeing continue to live."

On the day of Catherine's execution, Thomas was informed that she had asked for a block to be brought to her room in the Tower, so she might practice kneeling before it.

"Poor child," he remarked to Morice. "She is so tragically young. I wish the king had arranged for the swordsman from France to strike off her head. She should not have to suffer the fall of an axe." *And possibly a clumsy axeman,* he added inwardly.

It had initially puzzled him that the king had granted Anne Boleyn the swift sword, yet Catherine was to endure the axe. Then, the night before Catherine's execution, whilst he had been sitting peacefully in his library, the answer had come to him. Anne had been innocent; the king had known that, so to assuage his conscience, he had dealt with her as painlessly as possible. Catherine, on the other hand, was guilty, so King Henry felt it was necessary for her to suffer the indignity of the axe.

"God have mercy on her," Morice replied solemnly.

"And God take her to Himself and grant her peace," Thomas added.

At that moment, they heard the sound of the guns firing. Another queen had perished on Tower Green.

Chapter Fourteen

Less than an hour after the queen had been executed, Thomas was preparing to travel to Oxford, with his chaplain, Dr Barber.

"You need not go to Oxford in person," Barber reasoned, as they mounted their horses.

"I need to go," he replied grimly. "I need to get away from London; visiting Oxford is the perfect excuse." He laid heavy stress upon the word need. Unable to see his own face, he was unaware of how grey and weary he looked, hence Barber's caution. "I hear there is much scandalous behaviour going on amongst the clergy there. From Oxford, I shall travel to Canterbury, to complete my final draft of the new English litany, so that I may present it – once again – to the king."

It was February, and the watery morning sun was giving forth very little light, and no heat at all. Vapour flew from the mouths of riders and horses as they galloped across the countryside. As they journeyed, Thomas could not stop thinking about the young Catherine Howard. The poor girl had been led astray by the promise of jewels, fine clothes and power. It was a mercy she had not given birth to a child; if she had, his or her parentage would have been severely in doubt, and the situation would have been even more tragic than it was already.

During the past few months, there had been no progress with regards to a Protestant Reformation, mostly because, since Cromwell's death, Thomas had carefully avoided calling attention to himself. Many Protestants – his good friend Latimer included – thought him wrong for holding back and being cautious, but Thomas knew that this reformation could not be rushed.

Oxford, unlike Cambridge, had always leaned towards Catholicism, and was consequently not a city wherein he felt comfortable. He expected to achieve very little, unpopular as he was in the staunchly Catholic city, but after spending over a week there, debating, teaching, advising and arguing with the clergy, he departed with an optimistic feeling. There was something about academia that made people more willing to accept alternative points of view. *Perhaps I have planted a few seeds of change*, he mused.

From Oxford, he travelled to Canterbury, where he found his wife fit and well, but very obviously pregnant.

"I am very much bigger with this child." She patted her abdomen fondly. "I am almost certain that this babe is a boy, but God works in mysterious ways; if it is a girl, she will be equally treasured."

"We shall just have to wait and see what God has created." Thomas eyed her anxiously. Whenever he bade her to be careful, she would simply shrug and remind him of a woman she had known in Germany, who had given birth fifteen times and lived to a ripe old age.

"I cannot go through this fifteen times," he had informed her on one of these occasions.

"You cannot?" She had burst out laughing. "My husband, you are not the one who must carry each babe for nine months and push them out at the end!" She smiled tenderly. "But I would not have it any other way. Children are a blessing from God, and I shall gladly accept the good things He gives, and trust in His goodness."

Fortunately for Thomas, he had a vast quantity of work to distract him from his wife's pregnancy. Not only was the English litany to be presented to the king, but so was a revision of *The Institution of the Christian Man*, to be renamed *The Erudition of the Christian Man*. When this book had initially been presented to the king, Henry had been deeply in love with Jane Seymour and had not wished for his mind to be diverted by theology. But now, the grieving Henry wanted a diversion, and had provided Thomas with an annotated version of the original book, within which he had personally written detailed comments and suggestions. To the wonderment and delight of Thomas, the corrections showed a steady drift towards reform.

'Confirmation', the king had written, 'should be relegated to the form of sacrament, in effect restoring the sacraments which the recipient has already received, such as Baptism and Penance. It is a restoration and new illumination of the graces, given by other sacraments, and a new restitution and restoration for graces granted by Christ to the sacraments instituted by Him'. However, later in the book, regarding the anointing of the sick or dying, the king had stressed his belief in the Extreme Unction: the anointing of a dying person with oil. He had written that it ought to be a sacrament. The Protestant view was that this was not a sacrament, although if it was requested and gave comfort to a dying person, it should certainly be administered.

Carefully, Thomas read through the book, reading the annotations made by the king and making his own notes regarding those comments. The king was an able theologian; whilst some of His Majesty's remarks were undeniably

327

orthodox, a number of them inclined towards Protestantism, whilst others came straight from the mind of King Henry VIII. After weeks of study, Thomas had at last completed his own corrections, and was ready to take them to the king at Hampton Court.

When he arrived, he found the king in severe pain. His leg had been, His Majesty explained, cauterised again that very morning, by Dr Butts. The very thought of such a procedure made Thomas feel nauseated. Some months ago, he had entered a room sometime after Butts had performed a cauterisation, and the smell of burned flesh had still lingered in the air. It must be an agonising procedure, yet the king endured it time and again without complaint.

It took several stimulating meetings between king and archbishop for the two men to reach a compromise on the contents of the new book, but they finally reached an agreement, and the book was sent to be printed and circulated amongst the people. Thomas suspected that the orthodox faction would say it was too Protestant, and that the Protestants would say it was too orthodox; it was exasperating, but he had long since learned that he could not please everyone.

"It shall be known as *The King's Book*," Thomas assured Henry.

The king looked pleased. His features were still marked by the grief of Catherine's perfidy, but he was now beginning to move on. "No, archbishop. It is, and always has been, *The Bishop's Book*," he responded graciously.

"Your Majesty has put much of himself into this, therefore I predict that, whilst it may be printed as *The Bishop's Book*, everyone shall refer to it as *The King's Book*."

Henry's lips twitched. "We see your own hand in much of this." He ran a fat forefinger down one of the book's pages, then read aloud, "the principle means whereby all sinners shall attain their justification is only by Jesus Christ, by whom our access is to the Father." The king grinned at Thomas, revealing yellow stained teeth. "I read this and heard your voice saying those words."

Several hours later, Thomas returned to Lambeth, having enjoyed his time in the king's company. Due to his wealth of learning, Henry could be very entertaining when he felt so inclined, and they had engaged in various rousing theological debates. Unfortunately for him, though he did not know it, this peaceful evening was to be the last peace he would know for some months.

*****

When he had been consecrated Archbishop of Canterbury, he had reorganised the Canterbury Cathedral staff, and had abolished the granting of a prebendary: an honorary position which merited a stipend, usually drawn from the income of the cathedral's estates. Naturally, this had caused much muttering and unrest amongst the cathedral staff. In spite of this, he now intended to extend this abolition, and apply it to all other cathedrals throughout the realm.

Since the execution of Catherine Howard, Stephen Gardiner, the Bishop of Winchester, had felt that he was being pushed aside by the king, who seemed to prefer the society of the Protestant Archbishop of Canterbury. Consequently, Gardiner had been searching for a means to discredit his rival, and so it was with great pleasure that he learned of the archbishop's unpopularity amongst the Catholic clergy of Canterbury.

The archbishop's unpopularity was first brought to Gardiner's attention when two former Canterbury prebendaries, both Catholic, named Serles and Shether, were committed to prison for attacking the English translation of the Bible. Whilst in prison, they managed to contact Gardiner, informing him that they did not wish to be subjected to the judgment of Archbishop Cranmer, but would rather Gardiner himself tried them. However, Thomas had been commanded by the king to conduct the trial personally, which he duly did, resulting in an outcry of discontent from prebendaries throughout the realm. Many squires also objected to the archbishop, suspecting him of spreading Lutheran teaching – which, of course, was true – and fearing that the introduction of the new English litany was a sign that he had all manner of modernising changes up his sleeve.

Serles, once released from prison, was determined to lodge a formal complaint against the archbishop. To assist him with this, a notorious heretic hunter, Dr London, was employed to collect signatures of complaint against The Archbishop of Canterbury. These accusations were duly given to Gardiner, who looked down the long list of complainants gleefully. A commission of enquiry would surely be made against the archbishop, and once Cranmer had been removed, and most likely burned at the stake, who else but Stephen Gardiner would be consecrated as Archbishop of Canterbury?

Naturally, news of the complaints soon reached Thomas, who was deeply perturbed by such evidence of unpopularity. Late in the evening, having seen for himself a copy of the lists, he dolefully walked through the gardens of Lambeth Palace alone. It was discomforting to be so deeply unpopular. Margaret had been delivered safely of a baby boy by this time, named Thomas. This burden of unpopularity forced him to contemplate sending her and the children back to Germany again. So engrossed was he in his own thoughts, he failed to hear the noise of a barge docking at the water step, until a familiar voice boomed out across the gardens.

"Archbishop! Are you ignoring us?"

Startled, he wondered if he was dreaming. The king himself was waving at him, gesturing for him to join him on his barge. The royal barge, no less. Amazed, he did as instructed. Was this a bad omen? Was the king coming in person to tell him he was a heretic and must be imprisoned? No, he could answer this irrational query himself. He had been at Court long enough to know that the king never dealt with heretics personally. But this did little to quell his feeing of panic.

Once he was seated, the king jovially declared, "well, my chaplain, I have news for you. I now know who is the greatest heretic in all of Kent."

Trying to hide the sudden shaking of his hands, he stared at the face of the king, who looked as if he was enjoying a good jest. "Sire…" he stammered. "Sire… I… I would request a commission of enquiry into these accusations."

Henry thumped his sound leg. "Marry, we will do so."

Feeling queasy, Thomas mutely nodded agreement.

"We have such confidence in your honesty and fidelity that we will commit the examination wholly to you, and those whom you choose to appoint." The king eyed his companion keenly, assessing his reaction.

"But I shall not be an impartial judge," he protested, as it slowly dawned on him that none other than the King of England was saving his life. If Stephen Gardiner was placed in charge of the enquiry, there was no doubt he would uncover enough evidence to prove that the Archbishop of Canterbury was a heretic. King Henry, he noted, was smiling benignly.

"It shall be conducted in no way otherwise. We believe that you will tell us the truth, even of yourself, if you have offended. Now, make no further ado. Let a commission be made out of yourself and any other you shall name, so that we can understand how this confederacy came about."

As it sank in that he was saved, he began, almost incoherently, to thank the king.

His thanks were regally brushed aside. "Enough of that. Now, tell us, whom do you have in mind to assist your good self?"

His thoughts muddled, he hastily attempted to draw up a list of suitable persons, but to little avail. Eventually he murmured, "Dr Simon Haynes, the Dean of Exeter, he shall be one of them. The others... I shall decide by tomorrow." Haynes, he knew, was one of his staunch supporters.

Signalling to the oarsman to turn around and return to Lambeth, the king abruptly asked, "And what of your lady wife's health? We trust she is well?" The king laughed heartily at his companion's terrified expression. He looked like a frightened rabbit. "Come man, we know you are married."

"I... she... she is well, Your Majesty," he managed to mutter, too shocked to form a coherent response. But though he was surprised, it was a relief to speak of his wife to the king.

There was a moment of silence, broken only by the rhythmic sound of the oars dipping into the water. "A wife is a comfort," Henry remarked at last. "You are blessed to have such a good and loyal woman."

Thomas longed for some wise words to come into his mind. None came. "A wife is, indeed, a blessing," he murmured ineffectually.

"A blessing we expect to enjoy again... in time." The king gave a sentimental sigh, his small mouth becoming characteristically pious. "We must remarry for the good of the realm. A king needs more than one son, and we are young enough yet provide another heir. A king's first duty is always to his people."

Thomas agreed. A king could not think only of himself; he had to consider the wellbeing of his realm. "Your Majesty has always put the realm first. Your life has never been your own to do as you please," he sympathised. "Power brings responsibility."

"We wish more people would realise this," the king sighed. "A ploughman has more freedom than a king."

Thomas nodded. That was very true... though no doubt many a ploughman would gladly change places with a king.

*****

Soon after his unexpected meeting with the king, Thomas travelled to Faversham, where the commission of inquiry was to be held. Travelling with him was Nicholas Ridley, who, naturally, was a member of the commission. For the first few miles, Ridley kept chuckling and shaking his head.

"It is a merry jest," Ridley kept repeating. "The Catholics wanted a commission to be set up against you, the king gave permission, but then placed you at the head of it. You must now see what I have been telling you all along. His Majesty thinks very highly of you, and he values your goodness and sincerity."

"Whatever his reason, I am glad of it," he uttered with feeling. "My life was in danger."

Standing face to face with those who wished him dead was less difficult than he had imagined, for when he stood amongst them, it was easier to remember that they were merely men;

333

they were no different to anyone else. He proceeded to examine and to deal out punishment to those who had complained against him, but later was censured by the king for the lightness with which he had punished them. Most of the offenders, Dr London included, were easily dealt with, and were promptly despatched to a pillory. Stephen Gardiner, on the other hand, whom he knew had been directly involved in this plot, was impossible to prosecute, for he had acted with such subtle cunning that there was no evidence to use against him. According to Gardiner, a string of complaints had been handed to him regarding the Archbishop of Canterbury, implying that the man was a heretic. His face a mask of piety, he declared that, as a good servant of the king, he had deemed such accusations worthy of investigating.

Thomas knew full well that Gardiner would strike again as soon as possible, but all he could pray for was that King Henry would continue to favour and support him.

His plot having failed miserably, Gardiner consoled himself by identifying inaccuracies in the English translation of the Bible. He then successfully managed to persuade the king to have it withdrawn until a better translation was available. Copies of the Great Bible were immediately removed from the churches; they were to be revised by the universities, an action which distressed Thomas greatly, for he knew this could take years. At least, he reasoned, the new *Bishop's Book* was in place, so people could still access the word of God, albeit in less detail.

The year was passing swiftly, and it seemed to Thomas that, as he grew older, the years flew by more quickly. As another season of Christmas festivities approached, a rumour began to circulate that the king was considering remarrying Anne of Cleves. Certainly, the two of them seemed to get along very well, and over Christmas, when they were together, there was much laughter and hilarity. They shared a similar sense of humour, and both roared with laughter over the antics of the king's jester, Will Somers, whose tricks had not always endeared him to the king's wives. Thomas found himself respecting Somers, for the man was a good and loyal servant, and utterly devoted to the king. But as far as humour was concerned, personally he found his jests foolish, and failed to appreciate them. After the festive season had passed, Anne returned to one of her houses, without an announcement of marriage being made.

Early in the New Year, a lady of mature years, named Catherine Latimer, formerly Catherine Parr, came to Court. She was a tall, very attractive woman, and had already been twice widowed, despite only being in her early thirties. Her first husband, Lord Edward Burgh, had died when Catherine was only sixteen, and her family had quickly arranged for her to marry Lord Latimer, who possessed daughters older than she. Lord Latimer had been one of the leaders of the Pilgrimage of Grace, but had escaped the retribution that followed, and had even managed to keep his wealth and estates intact. Upon Lord Latimer's death, Catherine had become a very rich woman, which made her more attractive still. Inevitably, she very quickly accumulated her fair share of admirers at Court, chief among them being Admiral Thomas Seymour. However, her modesty and discrete behaviour soon attracted another admirer: King Henry himself.

When the king informed his Archbishop of Canterbury that he was to marry Lady Latimer, Thomas was warmly sincere in his congratulations. Lady Latimer was not only a sensible woman, she was also a secret Protestant, and he was certain that proposing to this lady was the wisest choice the king had ever made. She was both intelligent and compassionate, and she was certainly capable of acting as Henry's nurse as well as his wife. No one could have imagined little Catherine Howard changing the king's bandages, but everyone could see that Lady Latimer would be perfectly comfortable with such a task. The marriage took place in the chapel at Hampton Court, but this time, Thomas did not officiate, having already made plans to return to Canterbury to enjoy some semblance of peace.

As ever, it was a relief to be away from Court, and to have the freedom to lower guard a little. Despite having been saved by the king, other plots had since been hatched against him. A few months ago, a man named John Gostwick, the Member of Parliament for Bedfordshire, had lodged a complaint against him in the House of Commons. It was generally thought that Gostwick had been acting on the behalf of others, in exchange for bribes. Certainly, he was judged to be inclined towards Protestantism, probably because he had eagerly benefitted from the dissolution of the monasteries. Whether Protestant or not, Gostwick had clearly not seriously listened to any of the archbishop's sermons. When invited to repeat any preaching which had specifically offended him, he could not think of a single sentence.

Once again, the king had stepped in, shouting, "Tell that varlet Gostwick, that if he does not acknowledge his fault to my lord of Canterbury, we will make him a poor Gostwick, and punish him as an example to others."

Perhaps it was due to the influence of the secretly Protestant new queen, but as soon as Thomas returned to Court, the king requested that he form a committee, to devise a Rationale of Rites and Ceremonies.

He duly did so, but unfortunately, the committee recommended that existing rites should continue to be used. He energetically argued against this, but it made no difference.

As for the litany, although now in English, it was still very Catholic in its text. He dreamed of producing a new Protestant litany, but he knew that was not going to happen any time soon. However, he persistently continued to try and sway the committee to put aside the old rites, until he eventually achieved a minor success. With the king's permission, he was able to decree that all books should be expunged of any mention of the Pope, or the Vicar of Rome as he was now known. Oddly enough, until this moment, orders of service had still deferred to him and not the king. It was only a minor victory, but even a minor victory gave him a sense of achievement.

Gardiner continued to strike at heretics, and having realised that, for the time being, it was unwise to attack the Archbishop of Canterbury personally, he began to seek out courtiers who had Protestant leanings. Sir Philip and Lady Hoby were questioned, as was Lord Herbert, the queen's own brother, along with his wife, Lady Anne, but they were all released due to lack of evidence. As for the queen, she was in high favour, so Gardiner merely observed her from a distance, biding his time. The king was still in a honeymoon mood; his queen could do no wrong.

"I dislike it intensely whenever I find my lord of Winchester looking at me," Ridley confided in Thomas one evening. "I find myself wondering if he is seeking to strike."

Thomas hardly knew what to say. It had always been dangerous to be inclined towards Protestantism, and with Gardiner currently watching everyone who was rumoured to have an interest, it was all the more dangerous. It would ever be this way, until the king openly declared that he himself was Protestant. He realised that His Majesty's fear of causing a revolt prevented him from making an outward declaration; little Prince Edward was being raised a Protestant, and his tutors were certainly committed to the cause of Reformation. Lady Elizabeth, likewise, was inclined that way. Only Lady Mary stubbornly clung to her Catholic beliefs.

With the assistance of Wriothesley, who was now Lord Chancellor, the persistent Gardiner turned his attention to Sir George Blage, arresting him on charges of heresy. This was an unwise choice, for Blage happened to be a great favourite of the king; indeed, the king affectionately referred to him as his 'pig'.

As he had done for Thomas, the king energetically intervened; using a series of oaths, he publicly berated Gardiner and Wriothesley, 'for coming so near to us, even to our Pricy Chamber'. Consequently, Blage was immediately pardoned and released.

A couple of days later, when Blage was in the king's audience chamber, Henry asked, "My pig, are you well?"

"Why yes, sire," Blage cheerfully replied. "If Your Majesty had not been better than your bishops, your pig might have been roasted by now."

After the incident with Blage, Thomas hoped that Gardiner and his followers might cease threatening the Protestant members of Court, but alas, he was gravely mistaken. Gardiner was unrelenting and had no sense of gauging when he was going too far. His desire to dispose of the Archbishop of Canterbury, and his ambition to step into that same position, clouded his judgement. Late one evening, Thomas received a visit from one of the king's messengers, Sir Anthony Denny, who informed him that the king wished to see him immediately.

"Do you know why?" he enquired anxiously, wondering if the king might be ill. It was the first time since the king's latest marriage that he had been summoned to Court so late at night.

"No," Denny shook his head. "His Majesty sent for me and told me to bring you to him as soon as possible. Perhaps it is another instance of him requiring your opinion regarding some treatise or other?"

"Possibly." Thomas nodded, though he was inwardly dubious. "Well, I shall find out soon enough what he wishes to ask of me." Pausing to pick up a mantle – the river was invariably chilly at night – he followed Denny to the waiting barge.

Having been escorted to the king's presence, he found Henry seething with suppressed anger. He was soon made aware that certain members of the Privy Council had, that very day, approached His Majesty, requesting permission to arrest the Archbishop of Canterbury and examine him on a charge of heresy. Feeling the familiar chill of fear travelling down his spine, he unconsciously hugged his mantle closer to his body.

"Some members of our Privy Council have requested to arrest you tomorrow, during the meeting of the council." The king's low, outraged growl was always more alarming than his usual angry roar.

Common sense told him that the king had some remedy in mind, hence the fact he had taken the trouble to send Denny to collect him and bring him to Westminster. The feeling of cold fear was difficult to suppress though.

"We have begrudgingly granted their request," Henry admitted, regarding his companion with pouched, watchful eyes.

"I thank Your Grace for this forewarning, and gladly subject myself to royal justice," Thomas managed to murmur, as the fear crept more deeply into his bones. His mouth was dry; his pulse quickened, and his palms were damp.

339

"Oh Lord God!" The king was seated on a chair, with his ulcerated leg placed, as usual, on a stool. In one hand, he held a goblet of wine, which he vehemently brought down onto a nearby table. "What fond simplicity you have," he exclaimed. "To let yourself be imprisoned so that every enemy you have may take advantage against you."

Blinking in surprise, Thomas began to pick at the fur of his mantle, wondering how to respond to this. He immediately realised he was not required to say anything.

"Are you aware that, once they have you in prison, three or four false knaves will soon be procured to witness against you? Persons who, if you were at liberty, would never dare open their lips to say anything against you?"

Thomas opened his mouth to speak, but his companion required no response.

"It shall not be so, my lord Archbishop. We have better regard for you than to permit your enemies to overthrow you."

Still blinking, Thomas again opened his mouth to speak, but the king was not yet finished.

"We will have you come to the council tomorrow," the king continued, his eyes lighting up with an impish gleam. "And when they break this matter to you, ask them to have your accusers brought before you. If they will, under no circumstances, consent to your request, and are determined to send you to the Tower, then appeal from them to our person, and give them this, our ring, by which they will understand that we have taken your cause into our hands and away from them." With some difficultly, and much manoeuvring, the king managed to remove a large ring from a plump forefinger, passing it to his archbishop.

Thomas had seen this ring many times before, mostly upon the king's finger, for he wore it frequently. He was, however, aware that Henry, who was fond of such grand gestures, had been known to temporarily offer the ring as a mark of preference to a favoured courtier.

Following his archbishop's thoughts, the king added, "As we have said, they will know this ring, and that we use it for no other purpose but to take matters from the council into our own hands."

Clutching the ring tightly in his hand, he remained with the king for a while longer, truthfully complimenting the king upon his current good health, among other things. As he had suspected, the new queen was not averse to attending to His Majesty's dressings.

"She changes our bandages regularly," the king beamed amiably. "No matter what the hour of night, she insists upon attending to our needs personally, without calling for a page. She tells us she is glad to do so, for she cannot bear to see our discomfort."

"She combines beauty with kindness. The two do not always come together." He was overjoyed to see his beloved master looking content again. Admittedly, he still ate far too much, but somehow, the queen had coaxed him into moderating the size of his meals. As a result, he had lost a little of the weight he had gained following the execution of Catherine Howard. His features looked less bloated, and his once purple cheeks were a healthy pink.

"She knows how to use herbs to soothe inflammation. Even Dr Butts has confidence in her potions." The king gave a contented smile. "Before long, we might even be able to dismiss Butts."

Nearly an hour later, the bemused archbishop followed a torchbearer to the darkened quayside and was rowed back to

Lambeth. Not surprisingly, for the remainder of the night, sleep eluded him.

The following day, he travelled to the Council Chamber at Westminster, and was provoked to find the door locked against him. This was a slight indeed, especially since he was kept waiting for an hour in an anteroom, in the company of tradesmen and commoners, who had petitions to place before the council members. Finally, Stephen Gardner, looking undeniably self-satisfied, opened the door and permitted him to enter; even then, he was required to remain standing, as there was no seat available for him. It had gleefully occurred to Gardiner to arrest him under the Act of Attainder, meaning the archbishop would not even be required to be present when his case was tried, as had happened to Cromwell.

Thomas quietly listened as Gardiner, his voice clipped and business-like, read aloud the mandate for his arrest. Glancing around, he could see a large number of people were uncomfortable, including Edward Seymour and Sir John Russell. At last, Gardiner finished speaking, and in accordance with king's instructions, he requested to be allowed to speak face to face with his accusers, so he could reply to their charges.

Smirking, Gardiner shook his head.

"Then I am sorry, my lord, that you drive me to this exigency. I now appeal to you from His Majesty the King, who has taken this matter into his own hands." Carefully, his hand shaking, he laid the ring upon the council table.

Sir John Russell stood up sharply, pushing his chair back with such force it fell over. He then proceeded to deliver a voluble series of oaths, which could easily have come from the king himself, before shouting, "did I not tell you, my lord Bishop, what would come of this matter? I knew the king would never permit my lord of Canterbury to be imprisoned unless it

342

was for high treason." He struck his fist upon the table, then rushed from the room, vowing to appeal to the clemency of the king. He was soon joined by Edward Seymour; suddenly, a steady stream of council members jostled to get out of the room, each wanting to be first to stand before the king. Soon, there was only himself and Stephen Gardiner left in the Council Chamber.

It was disquieting to be face to face with a man who was capable of such hatred. Uneasily, he wondered what to say. Finally, he suggested, "maybe you should seek the king? His Majesty values you and will not censure you unduly for this."

Gardiner stood motionless for a few seconds. Then, his breast heaving with outrage, he abruptly strode from the room, having not uttered a single syllable since the Archbishop of Canterbury had displayed the king's ring to him.

Long before he reached the doorway of the king's Audience Chamber, Thomas could hear the king's voice bellowing down the corridor.

"Ah, my lords, we thought that we had a discrete and wise Council. But now we perceive we were deceived. How have you handled my lord of Canterbury? What do you make of him? A slave? Shutting him out of the Council Chamber amongst serving men."

He arrived at the doorway of the Audience Chamber, in time to see the king glare accusingly at Gardiner. His Majesty then proceeded to shout at some length, before ordering all the Council members to shake the archbishop's hand, then proclaiming that each should individually invite him to dinner, to cement a good relationship. This latter gesture was a mixed blessing as far as Thomas was concerned. There were members of the council whom he had always been glad to dine with; some were Catholic, but this had been no hindrance to friendship. It was the minority who caused trouble, but since the king had commanded it, he would have to endure dining with the likes of Gardiner, Bonner, Rich, and Wriothesley. No doubt it would be as irksome for them as it would be for him.

During his recent troubles, Thomas had found out exactly who his friends were. Morice, Ridley and Latimer had been unfailingly supportive for as long as he had known them, and he had always been aware he could count on them. But there were many others, including the king's physician, Dr Butts, who had openly befriended him during this difficult time. Whilst it made him uneasy to consider those who were vigorously opposed to him, it was a comfort to know there were also many people were supportive.

Gardiner was, of course, his most powerful enemy, but unfortunately, the king found him useful, and had no intention of dismissing him. He suspected the king was only forgiving towards Gardiner because he had lost Cromwell, and was aware that the king privately regretted sentencing one of his most able and energetic servants to death. As a result, he was consequently reluctant to dismiss another long-serving courtier without good reason.

During the weeks and months following the incident with the council, the Protestant faction gained ascendancy at Court. Gardiner was lying low, whilst Latimer and Shaxton, both of whom had been absent from London for some time, returned, and were once more to be found preaching at St. Paul's Cross. The pair of them were also invited to dine with members of the queen's circle, making it apparent to everyone that the queen leaned towards the Protestant faith.

Urged on by Gardiner – who was trying to maintain a low profile – Bishop Bonner ordered a burning of heretical literature, but this only served to publicise The New Learning.

From his pulpit at St. Mary's, Dr Edward Crome was attracting gatherings of fashionable listeners, who listened to him preaching with much the same vigour and energy as Hugh Latimer. Groups of people met privately to discuss the Bible, whilst those who could read – a few people had managed to keep forbidden copies of the English Bible – taught the scriptures to those who could not. The gentry were teaching the word of God to their servants. Lawyers, merchants, and nobles began to discuss the word of God as zealously as any theologian. John Lascelles, reporter of the infidelity of Catherine Howard, was now the leader of a prominent Bible reading group.

This was an exciting time for the Protestants, but Thomas constantly reminded them to be cautious. Yes, they all had a responsibility to spread the word of God, but they needed to be watchful too.

Frequently, he would visit the queen's chambers, where he would inevitably find her surrounded by her ladies. Queen Catherine loved fine clothes and jewels, but this was the only similarity between herself and her predecessor. The circle surrounding the queen would spend hours embroidering clothes, not for themselves, but to be distributed among the poor, and were more likely to be found listening to an erudite reading – or else engaging in a serious discussion related to an erudite reading – than they were to be found dancing.

His relationship with the queen had quickly become one of mutual admiration and respect, and he was often invited to speak, his task being to lead her and her ladies towards a deeper understanding of God's word. The king was often also present, and he too was invited to preach. Catherine was no light, frivolous queen; she was an intelligent woman, whom Thomas was confident would be able to keep the king's mind diverted on those occasions when he required a distraction from the pain of his leg.

One day, he arrived at the queen's chambers to find a young woman talking to the queen and her ladies. He had never seen her before, but he recognised her name. Anne Askew had once been married, but her husband, terrified of the trouble her ferociously Protestant beliefs were likely to cause, had ultimately ordered her to leave their marital home. Listening to her speak, Thomas realised her knowledge of the Bible was impressively extensive.

Once Anne Askew had departed, the king himself arrived, his face beaming with pleasure as the queen's ladies, after curtseying, eagerly begged him to read to them, or play one of his musical compositions. Radiating good humour, the king picked up a lute and began to play.

Quietly listening, Thomas felt a brief moment of peace. If only the Catholic faction would leave the queen and her Protestant friends alone, the king could be left to continue enjoying the company of this gentle, devout queen, and her retinue of wise and intelligent ladies.

*****

It was only a matter of time before the Catholic faction began to reassert themselves, and unsurprisingly, Gardiner – who was not inclined to lurk in the background for very long – was the first to make a move, deciding to try and push an Anti-Heresy Bill through Parliament. It was accepted by the Lords but rejected by the Commons. Unfortunately, this did not prevent action from being taken. Dr Edward Crome was promptly arrested at St. Paul's Cross, and made to publicly recant, whilst the notorious Dr London turned his attention to three musicians from the Chapel Royal at Windsor: Robert Testwood, John Marbeck and Henry Filmer. Testwood and Filmer were burned at Smithfield, but Marbeck was pardoned, and Thomas soon learned that it was the queen herself who had saved him. Apparently, she had asked the king to pardon all three of them, but she had only been successful with Marbeck.

When alone with Thomas, the queen had wept over this terrible tragedy, heartbroken that she had not been able to save them all. He had solemnly reminded her that she had saved one man, and that Marbeck would no doubt go on to save numerous souls during his lifetime. She must be content and give thanks to God for that. But whilst he supported and honoured her commitment, he also feared for her. She, as much as he, was a target for the Catholics.

In the midst of this, the king was considering war on two fronts. The north of England had succumbed to Henry's charm during his Progress of the northern parts with his late queen. The Scots had not. During the course of the Progress, Henry had arranged to meet with James V of Scotland at York, but James had failed to arrive. His excuse had been the tragic death of his infant son, but it had been no more than that: an excuse. In reality, he had feared that the English would kidnap him should he set foot on English soil. After this failed meeting came a series of violent border raids by the Scots, so King Henry decided to send the disgraced Duke of Norfolk, who had memorably been victorious at Flodden, to bring them to heel. Eager to return to favour, and equally eager to repeat his former victory, Norfolk was ready and willing to lead an army into battle.

The Scots had no desire for war, but faced with the prospect of doing battle with Norfolk King , James appealed to Rome for aid. Unfortunately for him, he did not live to see the result, suffering a crushing defeat at the hands of the Duke of Norfolk at Solway Moss. He subsequently died of what was rumoured to be a broken heart. His only living heir was a one-week-old baby girl, named Mary, and King Henry immediately angled for Princess Mary to be brought to England, to be betrothed to his son, Prince Edward. The child's mother, Marie de Guise – who had notably once refused to marry Henry – was a force to be reckoned with, and staunchly refused, sending the infant to France instead.

At the same time, the king was preparing to lead an army into France. He had been negotiating an alliance with Francis, whilst simultaneously trying to ally himself with Charles. The French negotiations had failed to bear fruit, despite the king offering his daughter, Mary, as a bride for Francis' son. Consequently, Chapuys, the Spanish Ambassador, was instructed to suggest to his master, the Emperor Charles, that the English and Spanish armies should join forces and march on France together.

As the king entertained himself with the prospect of battle, Thomas returned to Canterbury, also bent on warfare, but of a different nature. As ever, his clergy were troublesome, and were preaching according to whatever they believed. Supporters of Zwingli were very much in evidence now at Canterbury, and clashed violently with the Catholic faction, sometimes even coming to blows. The pro-papists also concocted inflammatory literature about pro-reformists, and vice versa; even Edmund Cranmer joined in with the violence. He deliberately broke off the arms and legs of a statue in Canterbury Cathedral, as a statement against statues in churches.

The irritated archbishop gathered all his clergy together and delivered a lengthy lecture, informing them that they were to worship according to the king's instructions, since His Majesty was Head of the English Church. No one was given any favouritism, not even Edmund, who later complained bitterly of this to an unsympathetic Margaret. For once, Thomas was glad when the king summoned him to return to Court.

His Majesty demanded that he should reason with some of the aristocratic prisoners whom Norfolk had taken at the Battle of Solway Moss. They were being kept under mild restraint at the residences of various courtiers, including Thomas' own residence, Lambeth Palace. He was currently hosting the Earl of Cassilis, who was known to be a devout Catholic. The archbishop's task, the king informed him, was to convince the Earl of Cassilis of his erroneous orthodoxy, and persuade him that his deference to the Pope as the Head of the Church was erroneous.

Thomas patiently spent many hours talking with Cassilis, and in due course, Cassilis developed a grudging respect for the archbishop. Persuading him to change his ways was a slow task, but an enjoyable one, for Thomas delighted in talking and reasoning with educated men, and the earl was certainly well educated. Eventually, Cassilis *was* converted, and agreed to accept the Protestant faith as truth. His task completed, Thomas was granted the deep satisfaction of seeing the earl returned to his native Scotland, now determined to ensure that a reformation would soon take place there.

Chapter Fifteen

The preparation for the English campaign in France took far longer than Henry would have liked, but eventually, all was ready. Against all advice, the king insisted upon accompanying his troops to France, despite being too heavy, and in too much pain, to travel on horseback. Furthermore, as he would be absent for some time, he appointed his wife Regent, to govern in his place, causing considerable muttering amongst the Catholic members of the Privy Council.

In the north, border raids were escalating, and the Scots were becoming increasingly unruly. Also, to King Henry's anger, the Scots had signed a new treaty, allying Scotland with France. A second army was promptly assembled, to march north and teach the Scots a lesson. This time, Sir Edward Seymour was to lead the campaign, instead of Norfolk, who was to travel to France with the king. As the armies departed, heading in two different directions, Thomas observed the behaviour of the queen. She understandably wept as Henry mounted his horse and bade her farewell, but otherwise, she was poised and calm.

"I am glad she wept. If she had not, His Majesty would have been offended." Ridley, who was standing next to Thomas, looked mischievous. More seriously, he added, "Could you imagine him leaving the previous queen as Regent?"

"Certainly not," he replied, watching the queen dab a kerchief to her eyes as the king rode away. He had been standing for over an hour, blessing the king, the armies, and anyone and everything else he could think of to bless, as well as praying for a successful outcome. He was exhausted.

The previous evening, the king had spoken sternly to his Council, warning then to respect the queen and heed the advice of the Archbishop of Canterbury, whom he believed to be wise and cautious. Wryly, Thomas suspected that few people would pay heed to the king's demands.

"I know I have told you this before, but His Majesty thinks highly of you," Ridley murmured, as if reading his friend's mind. "You are simply too modest to believe it."

"Cromwell fell. No one is secure," he replied, his voice barely audible over the noise of departing troops.

"That is true; no one is safe. As for our friend, Latimer, I understand that he was arrested again yesterday, though I gather he was released a short while later. I pray to God that he will stay quiet for a while, but somehow, I doubt he will. I fear for him," Ridley sighed. "Why can he not preach quietly?"

"It defeats the object of his preaching." Thomas gave a faint smile. "Our friend Latimer does nothing quietly. He gives himself totally to the service of God."

"As do we all but… some less noisily than others," Ridley reflected. "If we are too quiet, we fail to spread the word. If we are too loud, we are arrested, and sometimes executed… perhaps people will take more notice if we are executed."

"I have no desire to be executed," Thomas protested.

"Me neither," Ridley agreed calmly. "But we have all observed that, sometimes, the dead speak more loudly than the living."

*****

Barely had the king set sail for France, when Thomas received news from Canterbury. There had been a fire at the Manor of Ford. Mercifully, no one had been killed or injured – his wife and children were safe – but the house would be uninhabitable for some weeks, if not months. He had no recourse but to bring his family to Lambeth, fervently hoping that they could lodge there discretely without causing undue gossip. Since the king and many of his courtiers were currently absent, the fire had at least happened at a time when he could bring his family to Lambeth. Keeping his two young children from prying eyes would be challenging, he knew that, but if he was honest with himself, he was delighted to have his family with him.

In her capacity as Regent, the queen had decided to improve the circumstances of the king's daughters, Mary and Elizabeth. She brought both young women to Court, encouraging them to undertake some serious study. Elizabeth, the queen soon discovered, needed no encouragement, but Mary was more stuck in her ways, having only ever read religious books written by Catholic authors. However, over time, under the queen's gentle influence, Mary began to slowly further her interests, happily discussing her reading with the queen and her ladies, although she still avoided anything that so much as hinted of The New Learning. Catherine herself had embarked upon her own project, a solemn work called *The Lamentation of a Sinner*, and after reading her first draft, Thomas sincerely informed her that it could have been written by Erasmus himself, much to the delight of the queen.

As the weeks swiftly passed, an uneasy peace between England and France was announced, marking the end of Catherine's regency and the return of the king. The French campaign had been totally pointless; nothing had been achieved, and His Majesty had been left exhausted. A few days later, once the king had recovered, Thomas placed before him a request that, by Royal Injunction, churches must use the new English litany. A significant number of clergymen had reverted back to the Latin version, much to the exasperation of the archbishop, on the premise that their parishioners enjoyed the familiarity of it. Thomas doubted that this was the case, believing instead that the priests were simply being stubborn, and purposefully rebelling against his changes. After all, why would someone wish to listen to something they did not understand?

The king agreed to his request regarding the litany, but he was less obliging when Thomas suggested that His Majesty should also consider closing the remainder of the chantries, many of which had already been shut down by Cromwell. These were a considerable link with Rome, and people were willing to pay large sums of money for priests to pray for the souls of their departed loved ones. Such prayers were unnecessary, and he had been requesting that they be closed for some time. But though the king had entertained the idea of agreeing to his archbishop's demands, he ultimately decided that, at present, they were more useful to him open, as they were a valuable means of extracting much needed funding.

The royal coffers were emptier than they had ever been. Henry's divorce from Anne of Cleves had been costly, for he had given valuable palaces and huge sums of money to her, as well as gold plate, gems, tapestries and furnishings. The wars with France and Scotland, even though the latter had been a huge victory, had further depleted the coffers, once so richly filled with the wealth of the monasteries and religious houses. In response to this crisis, the king decided to pass an Act, enabling him to confiscate funds from the chantries. To Thomas' surprise, there was little opposition from the Church. He had expected the Catholic bishops to protest. As for Thomas' suggestion that the money – or at least, a portion of it – should be used to fund educational establishments, the king once again ignored him. As had been the way with the monasteries, Henry fully intended to purloin all the money for his own needs.

At around this time, the Protestant movement began to suffer various setbacks. After months spent encouraging the reading of Protestant literature throughout the realm, Thomas was shocked when the king abruptly declared that writings by Coverdale, Tyndale, Luther, Barnes and all leading reformists were to be m once again banned. The king's mind seemed to move enigmatically these days; his policies, both foreign and religious, were confusing. One moment, he veered towards orthodoxy, the next, towards reform. In fact, since Henry's return from France, Thomas had become seriously concerned for His Majesty's health.

Somehow or other, the king had gained yet more weight during the French campaign, leaving him barely able to walk. As a result, he was now pushed around the palace corridors on a specially made chair, with wheels attached to its legs, or else carried through the streets on a litter. Thomas could vividly remember the splendid man he had met some thirteen years ago; the man who had so expertly wooed Anne Boleyn and charmed the people of England with his majesty and wit. King

Henry was no longer that handsome, magnificent man, and were she able to return from beyond the grave, he had no doubt Anne Boleyn would fail to recognise him.

Whilst he once again wrestled with his plans to try and direct the king's mind towards religious reform, he received criticism from an unexpected quarter: the late Queen Jane's brother, Admiral Thomas Seymour. Seymour had apparently complained to the king that the Archbishop of Canterbury was a niggardly man, which had amused His Majesty greatly, and he had promptly informed his archbishop to expect a visit from Admiral Seymour, so that he might inspect the splendour of the archbishop's household, or lack thereof.

Naturally, Thomas was less than pleased by this turn of events. In his opinion, his role did not demand that he should live in splendour. "There is truth in his accusations, Your Majesty. I prefer to live as simply as possible, and I see no reason why I should not," he admitted, trying to suppress his exasperation.

"All you must do is emulate the Bishop of Winchester for a short ;wile," the king's eyes gleamed roguishly. Gardiner lived in fine style.

"No one departs hungry from my table," Thomas stated defensively. It was a waste of money to live like Gardiner. Besides, unlike himself, Gardiner loved to impress; he was also still receiving large sums of money from the brothels in the vicinity of his London residence. The fact was, the Bishop of Winchester was a far wealthier man than the Archbishop of Canterbury.

"Then ensure the Admiral does not depart hungry," the king chuckled. The Admiral was one of his favourites; a man of presence and energy, much like he himself had been in his youth. "He will certainly call upon you without prior warning,

355

so we suggest you increase the splendour of your table, archbishop."

Thomas begrudgingly acted upon this advice, borrowing plate from the Duchess of Suffolk and the Earl of Hertford. Fortuitously, shortly after the plate arrived, so did the Admiral Thomas Seymour. Unfortunately, the day which the latter had inadvertently chosen, coincided with the arrival of a group of seriously minded theologians, all clad in their dark academic gowns. Seated amongst them, Seymour looked like a gorgeous peacock surrounded by drab starlings.

"You dine in good state," the Admiral observed, impressed with the food and the quality of the plate, but not the conversation. It was earnest and studious, and the company was distinctly lacking in women to flirt with. He had heard a rumour that there was a Mistress Cranmer residing at Lambeth, but to his infinite disappointment, she was nowhere to be seen.

"I try to maintain a certain standard," Thomas replied. "But I need to have a care, lest people accuse me of being extravagant and a wastrel." He looked small and dowdy next to his tall, magnificent guest. According to rumour, the Admiral had once hoped to marry the queen, following the death of her second husband, Lord Latimer. However, the king had made his intentions known where Lady Latimer was concerned, and the Admiral had made himself scarce.

Seymour, lacking the perception of his older brother, Edward, failed to realise that the archbishop was staging this display for his benefit. "I must admit, I have eaten well. In fact, it has been some time since I last enjoyed such a meal." The food had been excellent, far beyond his expectations.

"I am so glad you have enjoyed it." Thomas managed what he hoped was a sincere smile.

Later, when their guests had all departed, Margaret appeared, wishing to know whether or not the Admiral had been favourably impressed. When informed that he had been well-pleased, she remarked, "well, my husband, let us hope he does not return tomorrow, expecting more of the same."

"I am informed that the ladies at Court adore him," he remarked playfully.

Margaret gave what sounded like a snort of disgust. "I don't. I saw him getting out of his barge and walking across the garden... he adores himself too much!"

*****

A couple of days after the Admiral had dined at Lambeth Palace, Thomas was saddened to hear of the arrest of Mistress Anne Askew. Her imprisonment was hardly surprising; she was so outspoken that her arrest had been inevitable. After all, the equally outspoken Hugh Latimer was regularly imprisoned for his vociferous preaching. But, unlike Hugh Latimer, Anne Askew regularly mixed with the queen's inner circle, and Thomas knew that the Catholics who had accused her were using her arrest to strike at the queen. Catherine, and many of her ladies, were suspected to have forbidden books in their possession, and Gardiner and Bonner were obviously hoping Anne would implicate Her Majesty during her trial.

The queen, understandably, was uncharacteristically anxious, but there was nothing Thomas could say to ease her mind, other than to remind her that she was never alone; God was always present to support and sustain her, just as He was supporting and sustaining Mistress Askew. There were days when this knowledge was the only thing that kept him going. Every reformist at Court was unable to sleep easily, knowing that, at any time, Anne Askew might reveal their names to her accusers. As for Queen Catherine, she knew she could expect no support from the king should she be implicated. She would be executed; the only mercy she could expect was the axe instead of the flames.

Anne was promptly put through an initial examination, conducted by Bishop Bonner, whose obtuse questioning was no match for Anne's intelligence and quick-witted nature. She remained calm and composed throughout, revealing nothing to Bonner. Indeed, she made him out to be a dull-witted fool, commenting that his questions were not worthy of an answer. She even earned an outburst laughter from the assembled Londoners, by responding to Bonner's vocal frustration at her silence with the words, 'my lord, Solomon says that a woman of few words is a gift from God'. Naturally, the trial was swiftly concluded, and a second trial was arranged for a later date.

Gardiner, meanwhile, was revelling in a veritable heretic hunt, arresting numerous courtiers on charges of heresy, including Ralph Morice's own father, William. Thomas, naturally, was deeply sympathetic, and was determined to deliver the old man from Gardiner's clutches.

"Do you know why Gardiner might have chosen him?" he asked Morice, trying to figure out how easy it would be to secure William's release.

"My lord, I sincerely believe he was only arrested because he owns lands at Chipping Ongar, near to Sir Richard Rich's estate in Essex," Morice explained, his frustration and distress evident in his voice. "He has never openly expressed Protestant tendencies."

Thomas now understood full well the implication of this. Rich, who was working for Gardiner, was eager to extend his estate, and William Morice stood in his path. With this in mind, he requested for Morice to be released, on the grounds that there was insufficient evidence to convict him. After a brief trial, his accusers agreed with his opinion. As for Anne, her trial was forthcoming, and was to be conducted by the quick-witted Gardiner, whom Thomas knew would use every trick in his arsenal to try and fool Anne into revealing more than she intended.

During her time in prison, Anne had become something of a celebrity, so naturally, Londoners flocked eagerly to observe her trial. Thanks to her supporters, she had been gifted a clean dress for the day of the trial, but no item of clothing could hide her physical fragility. Yet though imprisonment had shrivelled her body, it had not broken her spirit, and despite her trial lasting for many hours, she remained assertive throughout, standing proudly upright, determined to fight for her life but unafraid to die. Thomas, who was observing, sincerely hoped his own spirit would remain as strong, should he be placed in the same situation.

When Gardiner asked for her opinion on the sacrament of the altar, she cleverly replied, "I believe that, so often as I, in a Christian congregation, do receive the bread in remembrance of Christ's death, and with thanksgiving according to His holy instruction, I receive, therewith, also the fruits of His most glorious passion."

"This is a prevarication," Gardiner snapped. "Tell me your opinion of transubstantiation. Do you, or do you not, accept it?"

Anne continued to thwart his questions, and time after time, she was accused of prevarication, until Gardiner, exasperated, finally declared, "You are nothing but a parrot!".

Even Gardiner's threats proved ineffective against her, and by the end of the hearing, he had failed to extract anything of use. For the remainder of the week, Anne was taken daily before the council, but still nothing could be proved against her. Gardiner even tried to cosily gain her confidence, but she merely informed him that his was the same attitude taken by Judas, when he betrayed Christ.

In the end, it was Anne's own writing that condemned her.

"What think you of this, archbishop?" Gardiner gloatingly thrust a sheet of papers under the Archbishop of Canterbury's nose. "Written by Mistress Askew, at Newgate."

Thomas found himself looking at Anne's writing, smudged, but legible:

'They said to me there that I was a heretic, and would be condemned by the law if I were to stand in my opinion. I answered that I was neither a heretic, nor deserved any death by the law of God. But as concerning the faith which I uttered and wrote to the council, I would not, I said, deny it, because I knew it was true. They then asked if I would deny the sacrament to be Christ's body and blood. I said yes, for the same Son of God, who was born of the Virgin Mary, is now glorious in Heaven, and will come again from there at the latter day, just as He went up. As for that you call your God, it is a piece of bread. For more proof thereof, mark it as you wish, for if it but lies in the box three months, it will become mouldy, whereupon I am persuaded that it cannot be God.'

Thomas longed to tear up the paper and throw it into a fire. But it was Anne who would burn, for this letter, originally destined to be sent to a friend, was all the evidence her enemies needed.

Once the letter had been made public, her final trial was a foregone conclusion. Having been found guilty, Anne refused to recant, and was condemned to death. Her fate decided, Anne was returned to her cell, whilst Thomas made his way to Court to inform the queen that, whilst Anne was now condemned to die, she had boldly protected her Protestant associates. As the queen and her ladies wept with sorrow at the sentence, the sense of relief in the room was palpable. Their names had not been revealed; they were safe. Or so they thought.

Unbeknownst to anyone, other than those working closely with Gardiner, the bishop was not finished with Anne just yet. Gardiner wanted more information from her, and that night, she was smuggled to the Tower, to be further questioned by Richard Rich, Thomas Wriothesley and the king's professional torturers.

That same evening, Thomas was at Court, discussing the trial with the king and Edward Seymour. The queen was also present, sitting quietly nearby, busying herself with some embroidery. Suddenly, there came a commotion outside, and a dishevelled Sir Anthony Knevett, the latest Lord Lieutenant of the Tower, came rushing in. Without making the usual obeisance's, he hurried directly to the king and flung himself at his feet. His eyes were streaming with tears.

"My lord King." Knevett unconsciously drew the cuff of his coat over his streaming nose. "Mistress Anne Askew has been delivered to the Tower; to the chambers below."

Everyone knew which chambers he was referring to. The king nodded slowly, and Thomas sensed the queen stiffen with tension as she gave a sharp intake of breath.

"The courtiers who accompanied her told me they had your permission for Mistresses Askew to be placed upon the rack, to obtain information. They want the names of people who attended her talks, and those who are interested in The New Learning. I initially believed they would merely place her on the rack, to frighten her. But they instructed my professional torturers to attach her wrists and ankles to the ropes, and to begin pulling on the paddles. I knew this would not be according to your instructions, sire." Glancing anxiously at the king's face, he was relieved to see an expression of horrified disgust.

"They're racking a woman?" Henry's voice was an outraged whisper.

"Indeed, sire. I trust I acted correctly. I instructed my torturers to cease until I came to you." Knevett was becoming less breathless and flustered, but he was still almost incoherent.

"Who were the courtiers." Henry's eyes narrowed.

"My lords Rich and Wriothesley," came the prompt reply.

"Rich and Wriothesley!" The king gave one of his famous bellows. "Send for my lord Gardiner," he shouted to one of his pages. "We care not where he is, just bring him." Turning again to Knevett, he asked, "did the lady say anything?"

"No," Knevett shook his head vehemently. "When I departed, my lords Wriothesley and Rich had shed their coats and were themselves vigorously applying the paddles. The lady knew nothing other than her own pain. She had passed out and was being revived in readiness for more racking when I left."

Thomas heard the queen exhale in relief. This examination of Anne had been aimed at bringing her down. Why could these men not just leave this good lady alone, and allow the king to enjoy her society?

"A woman... racked!" The king bellowed again, incredulously. "Get back to the Tower and send those men here. We wish to speak with them. You have acted well," he conceded.

"Thank you, Your Majesty. I have to say, she is a very brave lady." Bowing, this time in the prescribed manner, Knevett quit the chamber.

"A frail woman! We must speak with these men!" The outraged King shouted.

Some hours later, the king, from an anteroom some distance away, could be heard bellowing at Gardiner – whom he had correctly assumed was responsible for the ghastly episode – along with Wriothesley and Rich. The three of them quit the king's presence sweating visibly, whilst looking utterly discomfited. To be face to face with an angry Henry VIII was never a confrontation for the faint hearted. Even seasoned statesmen, such as the Duke of Norfolk, were pale with fear when leaving the presence of an enraged King Henry.

Two days later, Anne, along with three men, who included John Lascelles, were burned at Smithfield. Anne's limbs were so broken by the racking that she had to be carried in a chair. Out of sympathy, a bag of gunpowder had been hung around her neck, to speed her death. It was a dry day, and the kindling ignited quickly, but until she was able to speak no more, Anne screamed only prayers and encouragement to the three men dying beside her.

At the time of the execution, Thomas and the queen were praying together, asking God to speed the deaths of the four martyrs.

Catherine looked around anxiously. "My lord Archbishop, I wish for you to see this." She produced a slip of paper from her sleeve. "John Lascelles wrote to Anne from his prison cell; he feared she needed strength and support. This was her response to him, and he asked that it be sent to me, as a keepsake."

Taking the letter, Thomas was saddened to see that Mistress Askew's usually neat writing had been replaced by a barely legible scrawl, such was the terrible effect of the rack. 'Oh friend', the letter read, 'most dearly beloved in God. I marvel not a little what should move you to judge me in so slender a

363

faith as to fear death, which is the end of all misery. As for my tormentors, regarding their cruelty, God forgive them'. Thomas looked up at the queen, the glint of a tears in his eyes.

The queen sighed deeply. "Such courage," she murmured, as Thomas handed the paper back to her. She now faced a dilemma. The letter was her only keepsake from Anne, whom she had loved dearly, and whose dedication to the Protestant cause had never failed to inspire her. But she was afraid to keep it, lest it be used as evidence against her.

Thomas, sensing her quandary, shook his head. "Your Majesty, there is nothing incriminating written there. It is a supremely Christian note. I see nothing heretical in those words."

"I am fearful of being next to die." The queen took another deep breath to calm her anxiety.

"Dear lady, God forbid. You have many who love and support you, and you are constantly in my prayers. May God preserve and uphold you."

"My thanks, my lord Archbishop." She smiled tremulously. "Today, I received another letter, this time from one of my predecessors, Princess Anne. She too offers prayers for me. She is Protestant; she knows what it is like to be fearful."

She does indeed, thought Thomas. More than the queen would ever realise.

"I often wish she could be permanently at Court," Catherine admitted.

"A wife and an ex-wife together would potentially complicate matters for the king." Thomas smiled, and was rewarded by a tremulous smile in return, brightening the queen's strained face.

"You speak truly, my lord Archbishop, but I do enjoy the times when she joins us for celebrations."

Suddenly, they heard the sound of the king approaching. Thanks to his chair on wheels, he could never achieve a quiet entrance, not that he had ever made a habit of quiet entrances. The queen smiled broadly as she rose to curtsey; only Thomas, standing close to her, could sense the tension behind it.

"And what are we discussing now? Where are your ladies?" the king boomed amiably.

"My ladies are dismissed, sire, for the time being." The queen rose from her curtsey. "I felt a need for some serious spiritual conversation. Since you, my lord, were not available, I asked my lord Archbishop to provide counsel."

Thomas inwardly applauded the queen's common sense. The king despised flatterers yet loved flattery; and she had learned to deliver it so subtly, that even the astute monarch accepted it at face value.

"Well, what counsel can we give?" Interested, the king eagerly leaned forward.

Trying to think quickly, and introduce something not too topical or inflammatory, Thomas hastily stated, "John the Baptist, Your Majesty. We were appreciating afresh his role in preparing the world for the Messiah."

"Ah yes," the king beamed happily, enjoying being given an opportunity to display his own learning. "A man who did everything that was asked of him, yet paid the ultimate sacrifice."

"Exactly, sir," the queen replied. Her smile was still brittle, but it escaped her husband's notice. "I believe I am taking a woman's view, but I think his fate was unfair."

The king continued to smile, patting her hand benignly. "Ah, it is not as simple as that. Come, let us instruct you."

Later that evening, as he made his way back to Lambeth, Thomas decided that it was time to send Margaret and the children back to Canterbury. Life at Court was becoming increasingly perilous, and he needed to know that the three people he loved most in the world were safe in the countryside. The Manor of Ford was now totally repaired following the blaze, so there was no excuse for them not to return.

A few weeks later, he was grateful for his forward thinking, as things at Court were once again thrown into turmoil. It was openly reported that the king and queen had argued, and the king had been heard complaining that his wife was getting above herself.

"I heard him myself," Edward Seymour soberly informed the archbishop. "His very words were, 'it is not much to my comfort in my old age to be lectured at by my wife!'. He was most irate."

"But, why…?" Thomas was lost for words. Seymour was a cold, serious man; his reports were never exaggerated. His word was to be trusted.

"The king and queen were talking together yesterday when the queen began to oppose accepted doctrines. As chance would have it, Gardiner was nearby at the time, and heard the king becoming increasingly irritated with his wife. Naturally, Gardiner fanned the flames, stating loudly that he thought opposing such doctrines 'set a bad example, not only in the Court, but also amongst the lower people'. I sincerely wish the king would send that man from Court; his meddling has caused enough grief." Seymour scratched his beard fretfully. "Since their argument, the king has refused to see the queen, and has been most glacial in his tone whenever she is mentioned."

"We must pray that nothing more comes of the incident," Thomas murmured. "We have received nothing but threats recently; I cannot say when I last slept easily. But I believe the

366

king loves his wife, so by God's grace, we shall hear no more of it."

"I hope it is so," Seymour fervently agreed.

The following day, Gardiner presented the king with a warrant for the queen to be arrested and examined by the council, which Henry promptly signed.

Edward Seymour hastily despatched a messenger to Lambeth Palace to inform the Archbishop of Canterbury about what was happening. Having read the brief letter, Thomas hurried to Court, determined to reason with the king, and there found him looking grey and ill. His leg was clearly causing him agony, having not been freshly dressed by the queen for a number of days; the vile smell coming from his person testified to this. His cheeks were heavily threaded with purple veins, and his lips also had a purple tinge. Furthermore, the king, and his courtiers too for that matter, were disturbed by frantic wails and sobs that could be heard coming from Catherine's chambers. As far as the king and most of the council were concerned, the queen had not been informed of the warrant, so the king reasoned that her distress must be due to some other predicament.

"Perhaps the only person who can determine what ails the queen is your good self," Thomas ventured, his courage bolstered by the fact that Edward Seymour was standing beside him, nodding agreement.

Magnanimously, the king decided to visit his wife and discover the cause of her anguish, calling for some pages to carry him to her apartment. Whatever happened between the royal couple, the queen used the time alone with her husband wisely, and over an hour later, the king reappeared, looking much more comfortable and smelling considerably sweeter,

367

with his leg newly bathed and dressed by his wife. He promptly took his archbishop aside.

"The queen was distraught; she thought she had offended us," Henry whispered.

"Ah, she loves you too well to be a deliberate cause of distress," Thomas earnestly stated.

"She said she opposed us in conversation to divert us from this painful leg." The king indicated to the offending member. "She thought that if she agreed with us, the discussion would have ended, and we would not have been distracted. She was most distressed by our rage, and by Bishop Gardiner's interruption. She had expected to gain knowledge from our learned discourse, not to cause offence." The king gave a satisfied sigh. "She truly is a perfect wife, my lord Archbishop."

"I perceive she used her womanly wiles to divert her lord and husband from his pain, and to gain knowledge in so doing." Thomas beamed with relief. "A pleasing situation for both parties concerned. She is a wise and loving wife."

The king contentedly nodded agreement.

The following day, as the king and queen were walking through the gardens together – the king using his wife's shoulder and a walking stick for support – Gardiner, Wriothesley, and a group of guards appeared. Gardiner was clutching the warrant in his hand, bent upon arresting the queen. In a fury, the king ripped the document to shreds, berating the astonished courtiers for their temerity, and even hitting Wriothesley on the head with his stick. As one, the courtiers and guards made a hasty retreat.

Nothing more was said of the warrant; sensibly, the queen accepted Henry's brief explanation that the warrant was 'a mistake', despite knowing full well it was not. Unbeknownst to the king and his courtiers, she had been secretly informed of the warrant on the day it was issued, and had exaggerated her cries of distress in the hope of attracting the king's attention. Fortunately for her, it had worked, else Catherine might have ended up as yet another discarded wife. It would never be known whether the king had really intended to permit her to be examined, or whether he had planned to save her, as he had saved his archbishop. Thomas suspected it might be Edward Seymour who had warned her; Ridley suspected it was the Archbishop of Canterbury. Whoever her saviour had been, the queen kept his, or her, identity to herself.

*****

As the year passed, Thomas heard unwelcome news from Germany. The Emperor Charles had begun his purge, seeking out the German reformists and arresting them, or worse. Anxiously, he awaited news from Andreas Osiander, Martin Bucer, and his other German associates, who were now in grave danger. Margaret, as she always was when times were tense, was philosophical.

"We pray for them constantly; we pray for ourselves constantly. We are in God's hands, my husband. Stop worrying."

At least there was the new peace treaty with France to celebrate. The king had finally reconciled with King Francis and was to greet his official representative soon. Much to Henry's gleeful satisfaction, Francis was currently suffering, as he periodically did, from the pox, and so was unable to attend in person. A grand ceremony was held at Hampton Court, and as was often the case these days, the king had chosen his archbishop to lean on during the welcoming ceremony. Prior to the ceremony, he confided to Thomas that it was his plan to unite with France against the Emperor Charles… if Francis agreed, of course.

During the ceremony, Henry displayed the caprice which so often confused his courtiers. Greeting the French representative with his customary bluff charm, the king suggested that not only should France and England combine their efforts to banish the power of the Pope from France, but that they should also, in both realms, replace Mass with a Protestant Communion Service. The French king's representative, looking nonplussed, diplomatically replied that he would, of course, take this matter to his master as soon as he returned to France.

Unfortunately, the opportunity to discuss this further never arrived, for less than six months later, King Francis died unexpectedly. The death of the man who for decades had been his sometimes enemy, sometimes friend, plus a constant rival, shocked Henry to the core. His death had been sudden, believed to be the result of poison entering his bloodstream from a lanced abscess. The French Ambassador informed Henry that when they had opened up the body of the late king, his internal organs had been very much diseased. It was a wonder he had lived so long. He was succeeded by his son, Henry II, but without King Francis to compete against, life for King Henry VIII of England would never be the same again. Old friends – and enemies – were irreplaceable.

Chapter Sixteen

Shortly before Christmas, the king made a visit to Lambeth Palace, and Thomas found himself flattered by His Majesty's unexpected interest in the Cranmer ancestral coat of arms.

"It has been the same for some generations," he explained. "Three cranes."

The king rubbed his chin thoughtfully. "Have you considered changing it?"

It had never occurred to Thomas to change his coat of arms. It was three cranes, and always had been. His family was well contented with it.

"We have given the matter some thought and have concluded that it is definitely time it was changed." With an air of triumph, the king produced a sheet of paper from his sleeve. It was a sketch of a new Cranmer coat of arms, designed by himself. "What do you think?"

Even had he not liked the new badge he would never have dared to openly disagree; but it was suitable and pleasing. "I like it, sire," he pronounced, after closely studying the drawing.

"Three pelicans. A pelican will give its own blood to save its chicks, symbolising your willingness to shed your blood for your young ones, brought up in the faith of Christ." The king studied his handiwork with satisfaction.

Thomas, meanwhile, felt a spasm of apprehension tricking down his spine. The king's statement had sounded uncomfortably prophetic. "I thank Your Majesty for undertaking this. I am overwhelmed by your kindness." He rolled up the piece of paper. "I did not know Your Majesty was such an artist."

"We do not have much time to draw or paint, my lord Archbishop. To rule a realm is a task requiring constant self-sacrifice." The king looked regretful. "Maybe we could have been an artist, if given the opportunity."

Thomas permitted himself to smile, hoping he looked sympathetic rather than amused. The king loved being the king; he just sometimes felt inclined to appear regretful about his lot in life. "Or else a musician and composer?" he suggested.

"Indeed," the king concurred.

"Or a theologian..."

The king gave a guffaw of laughter.

"You see, sire..." Thomas spoke sincerely. "God placed you on the throne and gave you gifts as blessings, some for you to enjoy personally, others to help you guide your people."

The king nodded slowly. "We all must accept what God gives us, and use His gifts to serve Him, my lord Archbishop. A king even more so that his subjects."

He nodded agreement, enjoying this short time alone with the king. There was richness in his company. Occasionally he could be frightening, of course; but, when they were alone together, their conversations were informative and varied. Though he knew the king loved being a ruler, had he not been so, Thomas was confident that he would have been splendid at whatever career he chose. His knowledge was varied, his skills equally so. Few people were blessed with such a wide variety of gifts.

372

On Christmas Eve, the king surprised Parliament by insisting upon making the closing speech – a task usually undertaken by the Chancellor – and despite his ailing health, it was one of the most eloquent speeches he had ever delivered. He spoke for some time, reprimanding the clergy for speaking out against one another, scowling at Gardiner as he did so. He also accused the clergy of being morally unclean, of acting without charity and, also, of sowing doubt and discord amongst the common folk, who looked to their clergy for enlightenment.

His closing words concerned the English translation of the Bible. "It was intended to inform your own consciences, and to aid you in the instruction of your children and families. Preaching your own fantastical opinions, and vain expositions, is to usurp the duty of judging what is truth and what is error, which is a duty to be committed only by God. It pains me to know and hear how irreverently the most precious jewel, the word of God, is disputed, rhymed, sung, and jangled, in every ale house and tavern. Of this I am sure: charity was never so faint amongst you, and virtuous and godly living was never less used, nor was God Himself amongst Christians ever less reverenced, honoured or served."

When the king had finished speaking, many of those present were emotional. It had been a remarkable oration; such had been the sincerity of his voice that it had touched the hearts of even the most self-seeking courtiers. They would have been even more emotional had they known it would be his last public speech.

Thomas spent Christmas Day at Court, in the delightful company of the now hugely respected Anne of Cleves. He remained in London for two weeks before travelling to Canterbury, but within a week, he received a letter from Edward Seymour, asking him to hold himself in readiness to return to London. A few days later, another communication arrived, this time informing him that the king was putting his affairs in order for his young son, who at only nine years old, would require a regent to guide him. It had been decided by the king that Edward Seymour would fulfil that role. Henry had also drawn up a list, detailing the members of the new Privy Council. Seymour recommended that, as Archbishop of Canterbury, Thomas should return to London immediately, to be with the king.

Mounting a horse, he duly did so, hurrying in a snowstorm to Whitehall Palace. Leaving his now steaming horse with a groom, he hurried directly to the king's quarters.

Seymour met him at the door. "You have arrived just in time, I believe," he stated calmly. His voice, always dry and cold, was totally without emotion. "His Majesty has been asked if he would like to see Gardiner or Stokesley, or anyone else available, but he will see only you."

"I... I did not realise he was so desperately ill," Thomas stammered, deeply shocked by the finality of Seymour's tone.

"He has arranged everything in readiness for Prince Edward." Seymour permitted himself a grim smile. "Someone mentioned to him that he had forgotten to place Bishop Gardiner on the Privy Council. The king replied 'marry, I remembered him well enough, and left him out. I myself could use him and rule him, but you shall never do so'. It appears Gardiner's authority has been severely lessened, thankfully."

They hurried along the corridors, but as they neared the king's bedchamber, the queen and Lady Mary stumbled out, weeping, supported by the queen's sister, Lady Herbert.

Trying to dust off the snow that was caked to his cloak, Thomas entered the dying king's chamber. He had seen death many times before, and knew immediately that this king, whom he had loved and feared, would not last much longer. Dr Butts was nearby, as were the Admiral Thomas Seymour and Sir Anthony Denny. They stood back, allowing Thomas to approach the royal bed. The king himself was unable to speak, but the expression in his eyes showed relief that his trusted friend was near.

"Sire." The voice that came out of his mouth was so strangled by grief he barely recognised it as his own. "Your Grace, do you call upon the Lord, Jesus Christ, to forgive your sins?"

The king could not answer but squeezed his friend's hand.

"Do you die in the faith of Christ?" Thomas choked on a sob. This was even more difficult to utter. King Henry had been a monumental force in his life; everything he knew was about to change forever.

Again came that pressure from the king's hand. Then, a few moments later, King Henry VIII peacefully passed away.

"His Majesty has died in the true faith of Christ," Thomas intoned, and all those attending the king bowed their heads. Feeling emotionally drained, the peace of his Lambeth library beckoned, and he turned to Edward Seymour. "I shall return to Lambeth, if—"

"That would be unwise." Seymour looked him squarely in the eye, taking his arm and pulling him into the deserted corridor, followed by Sir Anthony Denny.

Thomas stared at the two men in shock.

"We are now in the early hours of Friday the twenty-eighth of January," Seymour hissed.

375

Wedged between the two men, Thomas had too many emotions racing through his mind to comprehend what they were saying. The date clearly meant something, but he could not recall its significance.

"My lord of Norfolk should have been executed this day. The warrant is not signed," Seymour continued with exaggerated patience.

"But now the king is dead, surely the execution will not continue," Thomas reasoned.

"I am appointed Regent." Seymour radiated satisfaction. "I have the power to sign the warrant."

"I pray you, do not begin this new reign with bloodshed," Thomas pleaded, shocked to the core.

Seymour's voice was tinged with impatience. "This matter must be discussed by the Privy Council, but my lord Archbishop, you, more than anyone, are aware that Norfolk is determinedly Catholic. It would be to the advantage of the reformist party if he were eliminated."

Thomas vehemently shook his head. "I shall not vote for that."

Seymour gave another exaggerated sigh. "It shall be considered at the next council meeting. As for the king's death, it must not be announced."

"I do not see why an announcement should not be ma—"

"We need to secure the prince," Edward Seymour coldly interrupted. "He and his nurse are now being brought here, to Whitehall. We need to ensure he is safely guarded before the Catholic faction get hold of him."

"Also, the king is a minor," Denny added darkly. "There is always a danger of someone declaring they have a better claim when a minor succeeds to the throne."

"A person such as the Duke of Norfolk," Seymour voiced meaningfully.

Thomas could understand the situation, but still could not accept the signing of Norfolk's death warrant. As for securing the king, this he could concur with. Whichever faction had the young king in their possession, also had the government. Edward was a child, and Thomas had, thus far, had very little to do with him. He knew the boy was clever and devoutly Protestant, partially due to his Protestant tutors. However, the Catholic faction, if they managed to seize him, might attempt to change his opinion. Children could be easily manipulated.

"I understand the king must be brought here. That I agree with," he stated.

"My lord, with all due respect, in spite of your great learning, you are no statesman." Denny's gaze was warmer than Seymour's. "The fact is, the death of Norfolk will be a political action, not one of spite or vengeance."

"That does not make it necessary," Thomas stated firmly.

Denny and Seymour exchanged exasperated glances.

"We shall see what transpires during the first meeting of the council," Seymour declared coldly.

It was decided that both the boy-king and Lady Elizabeth should be brought to the palace, for their own safety, and by the time the king's death was announced, both King Edward VI, as he was to be known, and Lady Elizabeth, were in the hands of Edward Seymour.

At his first appearance in the Council Chamber, the young king, standing on a stool so as not to be hidden by the table, presented a tearful but dignified face to 'his' Privy Council. The council members, though all respectful of his status as king, knew that it was not young Edward whom they were accountable to; the real power lay in the hands of his uncle,

Edward Seymour, Earl of Hertford. Not only had this man been chosen to be Lord Protector, but according to King Henry VIII's instructions, he was also to be Governor of the king during his minority. Already, there was acrimony between the Seymour brothers, Edward and Thomas. They had never been close, for their temperaments were totally opposite; the only thing they had in common was ambition and greed.

"It is preposterous that you should be both Protector and Governor," Admiral Thomas Seymour protested once the Privy Council was seated. "I also am the prince's uncle… the king's uncle,'" he quickly amended. "I have the right to be his Governor." He jabbed a finger towards his own chest. "I should have the care of his person, not Hertford." He jabbed a finger towards his brother. "The honours should be equally distributed."

The young king shot a glance of admiration at his younger, more glamorous uncle, and looked to be in favour of the Admiral becoming his Governor. The new king was a pink cheeked, healthy-looking child, Thomas noted. Fair, small, and slight, like his mother had been. It was doubtful that he would grow to his father's impressive height and width, but his mouth was prim looking, a feature he had most certainly inherited from King Henry.

John Dudley, another ambitious courtier, was nodding in agreement. The more ill-feeling there was between the Seymour brothers, the easier it might be for courtiers such as himself to progress up the ladder towards power and wealth. However, the remainder of the council proved to be in favour of the older, more respected Seymour brother, and the majority voted that he should hold the dual role.

As he carefully scrutinised John Dudley, Admiral Seymour, and his brother, the newly appointed Lord Protector, Thomas suspected there would be trouble between the three of them. Both Dudley and the Admiral were already in favour with the boy; their outwardly merry personalities appealed to a child far more than Edward's cold, aloof presence.

Having finished discussing who would assist the king, the topic of the meeting shifted to the fate of the Duke of Norfolk. Despite much deliberation, it was decided – thanks mostly to Thomas' own fervent suggestion that the new reign should not begin with the shedding of blood – that the Duke of Norfolk's death warrant should remain unsigned, to be dealt with at a later date.

*****

During the next few days, though Thomas was hardly away from Court, it dawned on him that now would be the perfect time to bring Margaret and his children back to Lambeth. Edward, child though he was, had already stated that he wished for England to fully embrace Protestantism, so it was likely that Thomas and his family were now safe from the charge of heresy.

In the meantime, there was the late king's funeral to be taken care of. His massive corpse had been embalmed; Requiem Masses were to be held throughout the country at Henry's instruction, and prayers offered for the repose of his soul. Henry had abolished purgatory, but he had clearly decided not to take any chances where his own soul was concerned.

"It is difficult to persuade anyone to keep watch over the late king's body at night," Seymour informed Thomas one morning, as they were discussing Henry's funeral arrangements. Currently, the former king's body was lying in state at Whitehall, in a massive lead coffin, draped in black velvet. The funeral would take place at Windsor, where he was to be interred next to Jane Seymour, the only wife to bear him a son. The simple truth was that there was no other queen he could rest beside. Two had been executed, and now lay in the Chapel of St. Peter ad Vincula in the Tower of London; his first wife had been repudiated, and lay in Peterborough Cathedral. The Princess of Cleves still lived, as did his final wife, Queen Catherine.

"Why?" Thomas was surprised. After all, usually several people were employed to watch the body; it was deemed an honour to do so.

"It has been reported that a headless woman has been seen hovering near to the coffin." Seymour rolled his eyes expressively. "It is foolish talk, but we must find someone who is willing to undertake the task. I take it you will be officiating at the ceremony?"

Thomas had given this a great deal of thought; indeed, he had lain awake all night thinking it over. "I do not wish to officiate," he finally replied. "I intend to ask Gardiner to do so. I know I cannot be anything other than emotional, whereas Gardner, well, he shall be able to carry the whole event through without shedding a single tear."

"You genuinely loved the old king, then?" Seymour's eyebrows rose in surprise.

"Of course. He was a remarkable individual. Frightening at times, I will admit, but he always gave me much to think about. He was a true intellectual."

Seymour looked at him curiously. "Hmm… perhaps so."

On its journey from Whitehall to Windsor, the king's body was taken to Syon House, and despite being kept in a lead coffin, grizzly reports revealed that the coffin had burst open, and proceeded to emit a vile odour, leaking blood and bodily fluids all over its velvet coverings. The people of England, who loved a thrilling story, recalled that Syon House was the very place where Catherine Howard had resided prior to her execution, and thus suspected that this incident had been caused by the vengeful queen.

When he heard this, Thomas admitted that it was a far more exciting story than the truth. He was hardly surprised that many people had chosen to believe that the ghost of Catherine Howard was to blame. In reality, owing to the delay in announcing the late king's demise, the embalmers were several days late in carrying out their grim task of preserving the royal corpse, and could not prevent the progress of decomposition. Henry's body, now having been dead for eight days, had begun to expand in the coffin, as was natural. Being already very large in size, the pressure had built up so much that the body had burst, forcing the lid of the coffin open. It was not something he cared to dwell on.

As was to be expected, the funeral was a magnificent affair. The lead coffin, having been repaired, had been covered with a clean black velvet covering, and positioned atop a grand carriage, which was then pulled through the streets by eight horses, each of them mounted by a child. On top of the coffin was an effigy of the king, wonderfully crafted and dressed in clothes bedecked with jewels. The face, being a death mask, was particularly lifelike.

Gardiner, smarting over not being a member of the new Privy Council, performed his role very well. Outraged though he might be, he adored being the centre of attention, and at the funeral of such a magnificent and popular monarch, he was certain to be noticed. Thomas, meanwhile, had the coronation of King Edward VI to occupy his thoughts, for only the

Archbishop of Canterbury could place the crown upon the head of the new king.

Because of the inclement weather, Margaret was, as yet, unable to travel to London, eager though she was to do so. The roads were entirely frozen, making it difficult to travel by carriage, and a woman with two young children could not possibly travel by horse. There was nothing else she could do but patiently wait for the weather to improve.

On the twentieth of February, the young king, attired all in white and riding upon a white palfrey, set out from the Tower of London to attend his coronation at Westminster Abbey. There was no disguising the fact he was pathetically young. The sight of him prompted the women in the watching crowd to dab at their eyes and call out blessings, whilst the men lifted their caps and cheered. Free wine flowed in the conduits, adding to the sense of merriment and good cheer.

In the abbey, the dais on which the throne stood was draped in red and gold, as were the tombs on either side of the altar. Once seated upon the throne, Edward looked smaller than ever, though to his credit, he conducted himself with a precocious dignity. In due course, after all the peers of the realm – in order of seniority – had vowed allegiance and fealty to their king, Thomas took the boy to present him to the four corners of the abbey, where his subjects were seated, crammed together, to witness the occasion.

"Sirs, I present to you King Edward, the rightful heir to the throne of this realm." Gently, he held the boy's shoulders, turning him in each direction to receive the roars, cheers and shouts of 'God save the king!'. After the huge bulk of his father, Edward felt frail and delicate. Silently, he prayed the boy would live a long and happy life. He was a healthy child, but child mortality was high, even where royalty was concerned.

Finally, it was time for Thomas to deliver an oration. He had prepared much of this speech weeks before the king's death, when it became clear that Henry's health was failing, and he was glad that he had done so, for he had still spent many hours during the past weeks reading paragraphs from it to the patient Ralph Morice, and promptly rewriting them. Now, the time had come to deliver it.

He began by commending the king to God's guidance, asking that he would obey God and be a wise ruler of the realm. "Your Majesty is God's Vicegerent and Christ's Vicar within your own dominions. You must see God truly worshipped, idolatry destroyed, the tyranny of the bishops of Rome banished from your subjects, and images removed. These acts are the signs of a second Josias, who reformed the Church of God in his days. You are to reward virtue, revenge sin, justify the innocent, relieve the poor, procure peace, repress violence and execute justice throughout your realm."

As he was speaking, he noticed that the boy-king's earnest face was fixed upon his own, taking in every word that he said as though it were the word of God Himself. As Thomas turned to the congregation, he saw that the Princess Elizabeth – who, like her sister Mary, had been given royal status once again, according to the late king's Will – was also listening intently. Princess Mary looked pale and ill, but she suffered much from abscesses in her mouth, so it could be she was focused on her own pain. Certainly, she was not listening.

Thomas took a steady breath, as he prepared to conclude his speech. "Being bound by my function to lay these things before your Royal Highness, may the almighty God, in His great mercy, grant you a prosperous reign, defend you and save you, and let your subjects say amen. God save the king!"

"God save the king!" The cry was repeated again and again by the peoples assembled. It was done; Edward VI was the crowned and anointed King of England.

Later, during the celebratory banquet at Westminster Hall, the king summoned his Archbishop of Canterbury to his side, and Thomas found himself suddenly wishing to laugh aloud. There was definitely something of King Henry's pomposity in the young king.

"Your Majesty." Thomas bowed, noticing that the child had spilled marchpane down his white doublet. He had heard tell that Edward had a sweet tooth, but then, most children liked sweet things.

"We applaud your speech, my Lord Archbishop," Edward declared formally.

"Thank you, Your Majesty." He bowed again. Edward was obviously following his father's example of referring to himself in the plural. The boy was known to be very serious indeed regarding his faith, and his tutors had often written to King Henry, telling him how precocious he was with his reading and learning; how capable he was of forming his own opinions. Since the death of the old king, Thomas had spoken several times with Edward, to his infinite satisfaction. The rumours of how earnestly the boy was inclined towards The New Learning had not been exaggerated. He optimistically suspected rapid changes would soon be made within the realm.

Edward was beaming with delight. "We especially applaud your reference to the Bishop of Rome. Such is what he must always be."

Thomas too beamed with delight. "Assuredly so, sire."

Seconds later, Edward was a little boy again. "Look, my Lord Archbishop, a juggler! I have seen him before and he is very clever indeed. He used to come to Eltham Palace to entertain me. Come, let us watch him!"

*****

It was mid-March before Margaret arrived at Lambeth with the children, and Thomas was startled by how much Marjorie and little Thomas had grown. Margaret also received a shock, for Thomas, who had been clean shaven his whole life, had begun growing a beard, as a sign of mourning for King Henry. Since his once dark hair was now grey, Margaret's reaction, when she first saw him, was to clap a hand to her mouth and cry, 'my husband, you look like a grey goat!'. He had also allowing his hair to grow over his priestly tonsure, but since this change was mostly obscured by his cap, it received no comment from his wife.

Her exclamation only served to remind him that he was getting olde; indeed, they were all getting older. A couple of weeks previously, Hugh Latimer had visited, looking thinner and more haggard than Thomas had ever seen him. But his spirit remained feisty, and his eyes still held that same fiery brightness. His friend's former position at Worcester had become vacant again, and he had tried to persuade him to return to it.

Latimer, however, had been adamantly against it. "I find it too restricting," he had explained.

"But a bishopric will not stop you from preaching!"

Latimer had been silent for a moment, before replying with finality, "no, my friend. I feel God's will is for me to continue as I am. I know our friend Ridley has been persuaded to take up his old position at Rochester, whilst you naturally wish to have a Protestant majority in your clergy. But the land is now

385

in the hands of a Protestant-majority council, so be content with that. Shake hands and leave me to go the way God sends me." He had extended a bony hand, and Thomas had gladly shaken it.

"If you feel it is God's will, then I cannot suggest otherwise. I am meeting with the king tomorrow at Hampton Court. I shall inform him of your decision."

Upon arriving at Hampton Court, he found the boy-king translating his stepmother's book into Greek, purely for his own amusement. Uncertain of how to approach a child with the news of someone refusing a bishopric, he decided to speak openly, as if to an adult, proceeding to explain Hugh Latimer's reasons for so doing.

Putting his work aside, Edward stated reflectively, "we like Master Latimer, but that is from hearsay, for we have never actually heard him preach."

"That can be arranged very easily, sire," Thomas replied eagerly. "Dr Latimer will be very pleased to speak the word of God to you, and to anyone else whom you might choose to invite." It was wonderful to be able to openly make such a suggestion. Finally, Protestants could be candid about their faith.

"My cousin, Lady Jane Grey, would also love to hear him." Edward was now an eager boy. "I love my cousin, and it is a pleasure to please those whom we love, is it not, my lord Archbishop?"

"Indeed," Thomas heartily agreed.

"I would like to send presents to her, but I have no pocket money left. My lord Seymour keeps me short of money." The boy's mouth pursed with displeasure.

He had heard about Seymour's miserly behaviour, and had been informed that the Admiral was making good use of his

386

older brother's niggardly nature, undermining the Protector's authority by secretly sending money to the boy. Inch by inch, Admiral Thomas Seymour was turning the boy against the Lord Protector. However, he was not the only person bent upon this project. John Dudley was doing pretty much the same.

"I shall speak with the Lord Protector about this," Thomas assured him.

"Please do. As for my uncle, the Admiral, he is to be made Lord Sudley."

Thomas nodded; he had already been made aware of the Admiral's promotion. The Protector was not keen on elevating his brother, but it would reflect badly on him if he did not seem to be looking after his own family. "Now, sire." He looked serious. "I need to speak with you regarding the Act of Six Articles. You do understand what this Act involves?"

Edward did indeed understand the document; his intelligent little face, eyes wide and full of knowledge, clearly displayed this.

"The council plans to repeal this. Are you in favour?" The king might be a child, but if this boy announced publicly that he wished the Act to remain, it would make matters difficult for the Protestant faction. The Catholics would instantly side with the king, and the Act might well remain in place.

"Oh yes," Edward nodded eagerly. "We think the principles of the Church and the country should be in accordance with the Bible. My tutors agree with me. Everything that is true is written on those pages. I... we believe the Act of Six Articles is not according to the truth of God's word. Do you agree with that, my lord Archbishop?" Looking pathetically young and uncertain, he regarded his companion earnestly.

"You are correct, Your Majesty. The word of God is the only guide we need. If I ever need something to refer to, the first place I visit is the Bible." The boy had been well tutored. "There are also hopes that clergy shall be permitted to marry," Thomas continued, gently and hopefully.

"Oh yes." The boy became lofty. "All men should marry. We intend to marry wisely when the time comes, and we shall marry whom we desire to marry, not according to the Lord Protector!" His mouth pursed, transforming into a small, petulant 'o'. Already, the Protector had arranged a betrothal between Edward and the young Queen Mary of Scotland, who was now living in France under the protection of the French king, Henry II. Edward objected, because Mary was Catholic. "And I intend to marry more wisely than the Protector, for I dislike his wife. I know she tells her husband he is acting rightly by keeping me short of money." He had quickly switched from stately king to aggrieved child.

Thomas wondered what to say. The Protector's wife could be an unpleasant woman, and he was well aware that even the kindly Queen Catherine was not fond of her. The Duchess was every bit as niggardly as her husband when it came to money, and equally as glacial in manner.

Diplomatically ignoring the latter part of the king's statement, Thomas focussed on the earlier comment. "Your Majesty is wise to choose carefully. A king must marry a woman who can stand beside him and help him rule."

"Like Queen Catherine." Edward was boyish now. "My sister Elizabeth is now in her household, as is Lady Jane. I do wish I could be there with them."

"Sire, you are king." Thomas shook his head sympathetically. "But I am sure we can arrange for you to see all of them more regularly. In the meantime, I shall bring Dr

388

Latimer to you, so you may listen to him personally," he promised, by way of compensation. The boy's genuine delight was touching to behold.

Leaving the king, he ventured to speak with Edward Seymour, immediately giving his opinion that there was nothing to be gained by keeping the child short of money, for it would only foster resentment. Seymour merely gave the excuse that King Henry had left the royal coffers empty; the sooner Edward realised this, the better. But Thomas well knew that this was not the real reason Seymour kept the boy short of money; it was in Seymour's nature to be miserly.

"Look at this." Irritably, Seymour thrust a document into the archbishop's face.

Taking it, Thomas discovered it was a letter from Henry, the eldest of the Seymour brothers, who never bothered to visit Court, much preferring to live simply at Wolf Hall, the family seat.

"He has refused a dukedom and a place at Court!" Edward Seymour, who had recently given himself the title of Duke of Somerset, was indignant. "The uncle of a king cannot be merely Sir Henry Seymour; he must have a title, yet he refuses it!" Irately he snatched the paper from Cranmer's hands.

"So I have read," Thomas mused. "But I think he must be an honourable man. I dare say he is far happier than any person at Court."

"He's a bumpkin," Seymour snapped. Trust Cranmer to take the side of Henry Seymour. They were two of a kind, he supposed. "He is the uncle of the King of England. He needs to act like the uncle of the King of England."

"Not everyone desires to live at Court, where there is wealth and power for those who seek it. The country needs people who are content to rear sheep and cattle, and provide crops to fill our stomachs," Thomas reasoned.

Seymour looked aghast. "A king's uncle should have dignity; he should be above such peasant duties as rearing sheep and cattle."

"If he is happy, leave him alone," Thomas advised, pulling his cloak about himself in readiness to return to the relative peace of Lambeth Palace.

At Lambeth, he found his wife eager to reveal the latest scandal to him. Astonishingly, it involved that soul of discretion, Queen Catherine.

"She has a lover," Margaret announced.

"Where have you heard this?" He could not believe this of the Dowager Queen. Catherine was no flighty girl. She was a devout, sober matron. And besides, her husband had been dead only a few brief months.

"There is a tradesman who has been delivering supplies to Hatfield House, where the Dowager Queen is currently living with Princess Elizabeth," Margaret gleefully revealed. "He told one of our housemaids, who has told me, that the Admiral Seymour visits Queen Catherine at night, and he has been seen riding away early in the morning."

He could believe it of the Admiral, but not of Catherine. It was well known that Thomas Seymour had been her suitor before Catherine married King Henry. However, if the pair still had feelings for each other, then it was more seemly, more dignified, to wait at least a year before engaging in any form of courtship.

Astonishingly, the rumour proved true; only a couple of weeks later, the Admiral, Lord Sudley, requested permission to marry the Dowager Queen. He was cunning enough to first place the matter before his nephew, the king, and since the

Admiral and Queen Catherine were young Edward's two favourite people, the lad was naturally inclined to agree to their marriage. When it was brought before the council – a necessity, given Catherine's proximity to the late king – the young king loudly gave his opinion, before his Lord Protector could utter a word. Once the king had made his position clear, no one saw any reason why the marriage should not take place, except, of course, Edward Seymour. By marrying the Dowager Queen, his brother, the Admiral, would become infinitely wealthier than himself, and indeed any other member of the Seymour family. After years spent vying for the better position, Thomas Seymour had finally found himself a prize that Edward could not compete with.

Chapter Seventeen

During the first year of Edward's reign, Thomas was occupied every minute of every day, and Margaret began to worry he might die of exhaustion. At the age of sixty, he was far too old to be working such lengthy hours. But he felt utterly fulfilled. The king seemed fond of him, and Edward Seymour frequently sought his opinion, appearing to regard him with great respect. Whilst he could never feel as comfortable and relaxed with Seymour as he had with Cromwell, he nonetheless felt that they worked well together. It was a stimulating time for those of the Protestant faith, yet also a challenging one.

Only a minority of the English population favoured reform, but despite this, change was happening quickly. The Act of Six Articles and anti-heresy laws were repealed, meaning preachers were able to preach without being imprisoned. Men such as Hugh Latimer, who had spent the past few years of their lives either imprisoned, under house arrest, or else expecting to be imprisoned, were now able to speak out and make converts. Wherever preachers could find someone to listen, there they would preach, be it from pulpits, market stalls, town squares, or street corners.

English Protestants who had moved abroad out of fear of punishment now returned to England. The Schmalkaldic

League of German princes had been destroyed by the Emperor Charles, and German reformists who feared the emperor's wrath now fled to England. Under Thomas' leadership, the use of images began to be abolished, and to the infinite anger of Stephen Gardiner, a translation of Erasmus' much revered *Paraphrase* was, once again, rendered available for the common man, in English. It was not a Protestant work, but it did incline towards reform, and was much beloved by Nicholas Ridley, who carried his treasured copy of it everywhere he went.

In addition to this, a series of twelve sermons, written by Thomas, and dealing with subjects such as adultery, perjury, and justification by faith alone, were made widely available. The sermons were collectively known as *Homilies*, and were lauded by people such as Coverdale and Bucer. The forthright and honest Hugh Latimer also loudly praised Thomas' work, which was gratifying to the author. He had originally written *Homilies* during the late king's reign, as a guide for lay preachers, to help them understand religious dogma, but he had not dared bring it to light until now.

The most important change of all was that church services were now held in English only, regardless of the inclination of the officiating clergy, many of whom still preferred the familiarity of Latin. Mass was soon to be abolished and replaced by a Eucharist, in the English language, whilst all Bible readings and prayers were now required to be in English. As yet, clergy were not lawfully free to marry, but it was a change that would certainly happen in the not-too-distant future. To the surprise of Thomas and the Protestant clergy, protest against this principally came from the general public, who wished to see their clergy free from the duties of marriage, which they imagined would distract them from their commitment to God.

In response to this sudden surge in Protestant fervour, the government agreed to release guidelines where necessary, and Thomas immediately set to work, proposing recommendations that the Creed, the Lord's Prayer, and the Ten Commandments, should be taught to all people. He also advised against the selling of benefices; in his view, the sale of anything spiritual was surely wrong, and most of his senior clergy were in agreement with this.

He had also been working on a new litany, and with the aid of his clergy, and the young king himself, it was now completed. Nicholas Ridley wept tears of delight when Thomas showed him the Prayer of Humble Access – the writing of which had taken Thomas numerous weeks – which was to be uttered by the entire congregation when preparing to take the sacrament.

"'We do not presume to come to this, Thy table, O merciful Lord, trusting in our own righteousness, but in Thy manifold and great mercies...'. I perceive this is a wonderful prayer," Ridley announced enthusiastically. His lips then moved silently until he reached the conclusion, which he uttered aloud. "'That our sinful bodies may be made clean by His body, and our souls washed through His most precious blood, and that we may evermore dwell in Him and He in us'." Wiping tears from his eyes, he declared, "my friend, I pray you do not alter one word of this. It must remain as it is."

"I hope everyone else thinks likewise," Thomas remarked dryly.

It was anticipated that the new litany would be printed and introduced to the churches within the year, and despite Margaret's fears that he was overworking and ruining his health, it was an exhilarating time. He was free to journey throughout the country to interview and examine the clergy, usually without issuing a warning of his imminent arrival. Unfortunately, a number of bishoprics, such as Gardiner's in Winchester, still remained in the hands of the orthodox bishops, slowing the speed of the Reformation. He had hoped that some bishops might resign in outrage, but there was no evidence of this happening; they were all too eager to cling onto their lucrative positions of power.

Amid this climate of change, war broke out again between England and Scotland. Mary, the young Scottish queen, was no longer betrothed to King Edward – who still stubbornly claimed he would not have married her anyway, because she was Catholic –she was instead betrothed to the French king's son, Francis. Most members of the Court judged this to be a snub, if not a downright insult, from the Scots to the English. To add fuel to the fire, the Scots were inflicting more and more raids on the borders, some of them very violent, prompting Edward Seymour to decree that it was 'time to make a war to end all wars'.

Seymour's standing had sunk exceedingly low in the eyes of both the king's courtiers and the common people. After making himself Duke of Somerset, he had proceeded to build himself a new palatial home in London. He had not decided upon the name of it yet, but was considering calling it Somerset Place, or perhaps Somerset House. The ordinary people of London were not offended by the building of a great house; they were used to such constructions appearing in their city. They were, however, outraged that he had chosen to pull down parts of their beloved landmark, St. Paul's Cathedral, to make use of the bricks. As far as Seymour was concerned, it saved money. If it happened to outrage the Londoners, so be it.

Regarding making war upon the Scots, to everyone's surprise, Edward Seymour made it clear that he intended, once again, to lead the army in person. The English army headed to

Scotland at the beginning of September, and despite them being heavily outnumbered, their impressive firepower won the day. Unfortunately for Edward Seymour, whilst he was away from the king's side, the insidious voice of John Dudley, the Earl of Warwick, was subtly whispering in the king's ear, amusing and flattering the youth, and turning him away from his austere uncle. As for Seymour's brother, the Admiral continued to lavish money upon the young king, thus maintaining his position of favour.

It was also during the war with Scotland that Thomas tried to reason with Princess Mary. During King Henry's reign, he had felt huge pity for her, and even now that she was officially a princess again, she seemed to have few friends. According to King Henry's Will, Princess Mary was now first in line to the throne, followed by Elizabeth, at least until King Edward produced an heir, which, given his age, was not likely to happen any time soon. As such, Mary was now a person of significant importance, and after much consideration, when the council reviewed her situation, it was proposed that Princess Mary should, according to the law, be prevented from holding her private Masses, which she had obstinately continued to hold daily in her current home, Copt Hall in Essex, despite the Mass now being illegal. During Henry's reign, Thomas had been lenient with her, but this time, he was in full agreement with the council's decision. Her very status would make her a central figure for Catholics to turn to; she could not be seen to be setting a bad example to others.

Unfortunately, she refused to accept the council's terms, writing a long, laborious letter to the Archbishop of Canterbury, explaining why she would not stop hearing the Mass. It ended on a note of reproach:

'But though you have forgotten the king, my father, yet both God's commands and nature will not suffer me to do so. Wherefore, with God's help, I will remain an obedient child to his laws as he left them, till such a time as His Majesty, my brother, shall have reached years of discretion to order the people that God has sent him, and to be a judge in these matters himself. I doubt not but he shall then accept my so doing better than those who have taken some of his power upon them in his minority.'

He read the letter several times, each time hoping he might spot some indication that Mary might be softening towards Protestantism. He found nothing.

John Dudley, who read the letter aloud to the Privy Council, was gleeful. He took it as a broadside against the Protector. Laying the pages on the table, he looked directly at Thomas. "What do you say, my lord of Canterbury?"

"That it is not a slight against the Lord Protector alone. She will not abandon her private Masses, nor will she accept The New Learning," he replied simply. "As you know, I have always believed that, by treating her gently, she might warm to The New Learning. Unfortunately she remains devoutly Catholic."

"She should be in the Tower," Dudley snapped. "She should be arrested."

"Whatever you threaten her with, she will not change," Thomas warned. "I see in her the determination of her mother. If she is placed in the Tower, she will become even more of a figure head for Catholics than she is now," he reasoned logically. Mary was troublesome, yes, but he did not want to see her incarcerated in the Tower. She was a princess; a daughter of the great King Henry VIII.

"She needs a husband to control her." Dudley looked around at the council members, awaiting suggestions.

Dudley was a tall, good-looking man, very much similar to the Admiral, Thomas Seymour, and therefore also totally different to the Lord Protector. Of the three of them, Thomas much preferred Edward Seymour, who was apt to be more just and merciful, in spite of his chilly exterior and avaricious nature.

"My lord, she has been betrothed many times. They have all come to nothing," he reminded Dudley. "If you dangle a Protestant prince in front of her, she will not take him. My advice is to treat her gently. Kindness will prevail more with her than threats. And do not forget, she is not only King Edward's sister and therefore heir to the throne, she is also the daughter of King Henry VIII."

He was relieved when Edward Seymour victoriously returned from Scotland. Once again, the Lord Protector took charge of the Council, deciding to leave Mary alone for the time being, as long as she did not make her private Masses public knowledge.

As the first year of Edward's reign came to a close, the new litany was almost complete, and would soon be in circulation. Images and statues had been removed from churches, though not without a certain amount of protest, and most of the distinctly Catholic features of religious services, ceremonies, and celebrations, had been abolished.

In January, around the anniversary of the death of King Henry VIII, Hugh Latimer, by invitation of the Archbishop of Canterbury, gave an enthusiastic sermon at St. Paul's Cross, attracting vast crowds. Thomas needed someone to convince the English populace that God desired for England to follow the Protestant path, and there was no better man to do that than Hugh Latimer. People flocked to listen to him, and he was utterly fearless regarding the subjects he addressed, directing his teaching towards lewd women, brutal husbands, dishonest shop keepers, and anyone or anything he considered in need of correction. Even the pickpockets listened to him; some had been known to drop their stolen purses in shame upon hearing his oratory.

Even his very good friend, the Archbishop of Canterbury, was not exempt from Latimer's criticism. Latimer believed that the archbishop's new catechism was not nearly radical enough, and he was not afraid to say so to his friend's face. Thomas, knowing Latimer's criticism was meant constructively, and having himself criticised Latimer's own opinions many times in the past, gladly listened his views, though he did not always act upon them. Unfortunately, as archbishop, he had other, less considerate critics, the most prominent being Stephen Gardiner, who had written a scathing book, criticising Thomas Cranmer's views and actions, and arguing against reformation. The book was purely a malicious endeavour. It was an attempt to make Thomas' life more difficult than it needed to be, rather than a work of constructive critique. After years of enduring Gardiner's constant disparagement, he was growing increasingly weary of his antics.

There was good news, however, from the household of the Dowager Queen. Catherine was pregnant, and delighted to be carrying a child at last. It was the king who informed Thomas of this, in the grave, formal manner he always used when trying to appear regal.

"We are well pleased to hear that our beloved stepmother is with child," the young king declared.

"The dear lady has always longed for a child," Thomas replied. "I shall write to her and assure her of my prayers."

"We have already written to her." Edward was solemn. "We have assured her of our continuing love and prayers. We have also advised her to take care of her person, and recommend that, in due course, she employs a wise and skilled midwife."

Thomas had difficulty hiding a smile, though his now considerable beard was useful for disguising moments such as this, when his lips twitched with amusement. The boy could be very pompous at times, yet it was somehow endearing. Edward had never had the chance to be a child, and was far too young to know how to be an adult.

Back at Lambeth, Margaret, her face serious, informed Thomas that she had some new gossip to impart from the Sudley residence.

"I know, she is pregnant," Thomas stated quickly, smugly pleased to have trounced his wife for once. She always managed to acquire the latest gossip, before he had even heard the faintest of rumours.

"Not only that," Margaret revealed.

He sighed. Apparently, she had outdone him once again.

"From what I have heard, the Admiral is said to be in an improper relationship with the Princess Elizabeth." Her face was a mask of concern. "She is but fifteen years old, my husband, and he is a married man. It is wrong."

He nodded seriously, his expression equally concerned. If this was true, something needed to be done.

"Apparently, he goes into her bedroom on a morning, when she is wearing only her shift, and tickles her until she awakes." Margaret shook her head vigorously. "The Dowager Queen must surely be aware of what is happening?"

"I wonder at the princess being left alone with him... surely her ladies are present?" he speculated. Elizabeth had a governess, Mistress Ashley, who would no doubt be aware of this. "Perhaps I should speak with Mistress Ashley... but how on Earth did you find this out? It could simply be a vicious rumour."

"My lord Sudley's gamekeeper is betrothed to a buttery maid at Sudley Castle, and she informed him of this. His own sister happens to be my laundry maid," Margaret explained, with an air of triumph. "I pray it is idle gossip, but whether true or not, it is a cause for concern. Elizabeth's reputation might suffer."

"Since I am godfather to the young princess, I have a legitimate right to know exactly what is happening. I shall correspond with Mistress Ashley, her governess, and if I cannot obtain any information from her, I shall visit Sudley Castle." He could ill afford to spend precious time visiting Sudley, but as her Godfather, he had a responsibility to protect the girl.

"I knew you would know what to do." Margaret gave her bright, beaming smile, which never failed to raise his spirits.

He promptly sent a letter to Mistress Ashley, who immediately wrote back to him, saying that she too was concerned about the familiarity with which Lord Sudley treated the princess. She explained that she had remonstrated Lord Sudley, but that he had told her he was doing nothing amiss, accusing her of being an interfering old woman, seeing evil where none existed.

Relieved that Mistress Ashley was taking the situation seriously, he suggested that perhaps she should speak with the Dowager Queen and take her concerns there. After all, Elizabeth's reputation was at stake; in the not-too-distant future, it was probable that a marriage would be arranged for her. What sort of prince would want a princess with a sullied reputation?

A few days later, Mistress Ashley wrote to say she had acted upon this advice, and that the Dowager Queen was now joining Lord Sudley with the morning games. Sometimes, said Ashley,

401

the Dowager Queen was as lively as her husband; on one occasion, the princess had appeared wearing a gown which was much too old and sophisticated for such a young girl, so the Dowager Queen had held her while her husband cut the dress clean off, leaving the girl standing in her undergarments. This was startling, but at least the Dowager Queen was a well-respected figure; her presence should keep Elizabeth's reputation clean. Optimistically, he hoped the situation was now resolved.

Soon afterwards, the Dowager Queen and Lord Sudley's household moved to Chelsea, enabling the Admiral to visit Court more frequently, and also continue his seductive ploys to gain favour with the king. Edward Seymour was continuing to lose favour with both the king and his subjects, whilst John Dudley, ever the able statesman, was doing everything in his power to encourage this steady decline.

Thomas maintained his respect for Seymour. He was humane, genuinely cared about the poor, and he was tolerant of heretics. The Act of Six Articles had been repealed, which meant no heretics were being burned, and so far, the most severe action he had taken, was to insist upon some Anabaptists publicly repenting at St. Paul's Cross. As for Dudley, he was a ruthless and uncaring man, and Thomas found his excessively rapacious – even cruel - nature repulsive. He sincerely hoped that the young king would see Dudley for who he truly was. Unfortunately, given Dudley's charm and charisma, he sadly doubted that this would happen quickly.

The numbers of Protestant clergy were slowly increasing, and a steady stream of Catholic bishops and priests had begun to vacate their positions. Bishop Gardiner, his behaviour having become even more inflammatory and provocative, had been imprisoned in the Fleet Prison, and his position at

Winchester had been given to a man named Ponet. Furious with his poor treatment, Gardiner wrote to the Protector, stating that he had been 'somewhat straitly handled', and that he wished to have some creature comforts. Edward Seymour, sick and tired of Gardiner's provoking outbursts, charged the Archbishop of Canterbury with the task of speaking to him. With an utter lack of enthusiasm, Thomas agreed; after all, Gardiner was his responsibility. He promptly sent for the man who had so far been his greatest enemy. He could only hope imprisonment had mellowed him.

Gardiner arrived at Lambeth Palace accompanied by two gaolers, who waited outside whilst Thomas examined him in the library. Gardiner's garments bore the stains of his sojourn in prison; it was apparent that he had neither been permitted a launderer nor a barber. Invariably, a prisoner such as Gardiner could purchase such help, but as he had complained in his letter, he had been 'straitly handled', and permitted no luxuries. Not failing to notice the belligerent expression upon Gardiner's face, Thomas resigned himself to a difficult interview.

"Pray be seated, my lord Gardiner. Please, take some mulled ale and refreshments, if you desire them." He indicated towards a platter of meats and cheeses, which Margaret had earlier laid on the desk.

Gardiner sat down with poor grace and accepted a cup of ale.

"My lord, you know that I sent for you only because the Protector desired it. I am requested to convince you of various points of theology, such as justification by faith alone, marriage of the clergy—"

"I do not support justification by faith alone," Gardiner interposed abruptly. "As for marriage of the clergy, did not blessed Saint Paul himself explain the advantages of being an unmarried servant of Christ? A priest ought to be celibate." He helped himself to some cheese, with hands that had not seen water for some days.

Thomas bit his tongue, refraining from pointing out that Gardiner himself had probably been far from celibate. "Saint Paul stated it as an advantage, not a law," he reasoned gently. "Besides, marriage keeps a man from sin." He gave his companion a meaningful look. "As for justification by faith, it is according to the word of God. If you read the New Testament, Christ Himself did not recommend that people should do anything other than be repentant to gain forgiveness." Noting that his companion was readying himself to deliver one of his tirades, he swiftly changed the subject. "What about Erasmus' pamphlet, *Paraphrase*? The Protector desires that you should resign yourself to the free use of this. Even Sir Thomas More approved of it."

"More approved of Erasmus because he believed certain things in the Church needed improving. He did not, however, consider a complete reformation to be necessary," Gardiner stated waspishly, before taking a deep draught of ale. "I have read *Paraphrase* and found things in it which condemn the work. I agree with those who say that Erasmus laid the eggs and Luther hatched them. Every monstrous opinion that has risen, has come from evil men, who have had a wonderful time extracting passages from that book."

"They are not evil men—"

"I am not passing judgement on Luther, or anyone else. I merely believe that from this one man has arisen a whole nest of evil beliefs, which question and condemn the truth of the Roman Church." Gardiner lifted the jug of ale from the desk and proceeded to refill his cup. Clearly, he intended to enjoy the archbishop's hospitality.

"The Church of Rome is corrupt. You must see that—"

"It was founded on truth," Gardiner yet again interrupted. "The Church of England and The New Learning is nothing but hot air. The Catholic Church is best left alone and should be allowed to do what it has done for centuries, which is to bring people to God." This was uttered with an air of finality.

The meeting Progressed with Gardiner continuing to interrupt and contradict every utterance.

"Listen. If you accept The New Learning as it is, I can do much for you." Thomas leaned forward earnestly. "You are a valued man, but your obstinacy angers many. If you are reasonable, you might live in comfort again, instead of dwelling in that foul and stinking prison." His voice was low and urgent. Having leaned forward over his desk, he quickly leaned back again. Being too close to Gardiner was an offence to his nostrils. Ralph Morice was more fortunate; his desk was some distance away, allowing him to faithfully record the conversation, without being assaulted by the stench of their guest.

"I would never begrudge or complain of anything for myself." Looking pious, Gardiner, who had already eagerly eaten several pieces of bread and meat, took a slice of lean and tender looking beef. "You must do with me as you will, for I will never change my opinion."

"Then I must return you to the Fleet. However, I shall instruct for your food and conditions to be considerably improved."

"Do so. For so long, my lord Archbishop, I have opposed you. I have waited, not always with patience, for the day when I see you fallen." Suddenly, Gardiner slammed his hand upon the desk, startling both the archbishop and his secretary. He leaned forward, his posture threatening. "But that day will come," he hissed venomously. "Surely my diligence shall be rewarded; one day, you shall be in the position I am now. When that day comes, I shall surely rejoice."

Gardiner was swiftly led away, leaving Thomas to write to the Protector, and explain that the interview had been an abject failure.

*****

Later that month, more shocking news arrived from Sudely Castle. The Dowager Queen had requested that Princess Elizabeth be removed to some other household, as she had been caught kissing the Dowager Queen's husband, Lord Sudley. The weeping and disgraced princess had written many tearful letters of apology, but Catherine had made her decision; she was kind in her dealings with the princess, but adamant that, for the foreseeable future, she must lodge elsewhere. Lady Jane Grey, who shared tutors and studied with the princess, was to remain.

"The sooner she is married, the better," John Dudley gruffly declared.

Dudley and Edward Seymour were sitting with Thomas in an otherwise empty audience chamber.

"Who will marry her if her reputation is tainted?" Seymour reasoned logically.

"I cannot correct what has happened, but I should like to visit the child," Thomas advocated. "She is much in need of spiritual guidance."

"She needs a husband who will whip her soundly," Dudley snarled, his upper lip curling with contempt. "Wolsey called her mother the Great Whore; clearly the daughter – who, might I

406

add, is no child, my lord Archbishop – is heading in a similar direction!"

"Queen Anne was no whore," Thomas protested.

"Ceres, this is getting us nowhere." Seymour eyed Dudley with dislike. The man was getting far too cosy with the king, as was his own brother, Lord Sudley, who had so recently been caught kissing the princess. How typical of Tom; his wife was great with child, so he felt the need to entertain himself with a ripe young girl. Dudley was blaming the princess, clearly, but Edward knew his brother was equally culpable, if not more so; he was in a position of care. Looking at the archbishop, he could see a simmering of anger beneath the man's usually kindly exterior, and sensed he shared his own low opinion of Lord Sudley, and Dudley too, for that matter.

"If she is moved to Hatfield, she will be away from Lord Sudley. If she lives quietly and prayerfully, perhaps this episode will blow over. People have short memories when it suits them." Thomas looked at the Lord Protector. "Do I have your permission to visit her?" he requested.

"Pray do so, my lord." Seymour nodded in affirmation. "As soon as you are able."

"I shall go tomorrow." Thomas shook his head sadly. "She has no parents to guide her, and so has been led astray by a handsome man. It is a grievous episode, but one I trust she can live down."

Arriving at Hatfield, he found the princess penitent. She did not blame Lord Sudley for the situation, seeming to accept the blame personally. She looked dejected and weary, as if she had not been sleeping; she was seriously concerned about the pain she had caused the Dowager Queen.

He talked earnestly with her in the presence of Mistress Ashley, her governess, and recommended that she must live soberly, dress modestly and generally behave like a penitent. She should pray and study, avoiding all things giddy and frivolous. In due course, her reputation would be redeemed. When the princess assured him that she had done nothing more than permit Lord Sudley to kiss her, and deeply regretted her rash decision, Thomas believed she spoke sincerely. It was a great pity that one rash moment had the power to change someone's life so radically.

Not long after Elizabeth had been relocated, grave news arrived from Sudley Castle. The Dowager Queen – a woman much loved by the people – had been delivered of a baby girl but had died in childbirth. A huge outpouring of grief swept across the country, which did nothing to redeem the reputation of Princess Elizabeth. Catherine's husband pronounced himself to be stricken with grief, but perhaps inevitably, the Admiral had not been widowed very long before he began to seek out another rich wife. To his brother's frustration, he was aiming high, his attention torn between King Edward's cousin, Lady Jane Grey, and Princess Elizabeth herself. In his typically swaggering fashion, he seemed to believe both of them would welcome any overture of marriage from him. The choice was his.

Edward Seymour's anxiety concerning his brother's potential rise to power, was soon made obvious to Thomas, when the archbishop quietly commented that there was no legal reason why Sudley should not marry Princess Elizabeth. "They are not related," he reasoned. "And if he marries the princess, he will, of a surety, clear her reputation."

Edward Seymour gave a snort of disgust. He was no fool, and well aware that his hold on the government was tenuous; both Dudley and his brother persisted to shamelessly undermine his authority. "He needs to be locked away... in the Tower," Edward declared, his face flushing with annoyance.

"Do nothing hastily, my lord," Thomas advised. "Simply observe him carefully." He thought for a few moments, then added, "perhaps you could have his servant, Parry, investigated, so that you may find out for yourself exactly how much money your brother gives to the king?"

Seymour recognised this as sound advice, but before he could act, his brother played right into his hands. On the sixteenth of January 1549, under the cover of darkness, Thomas Seymour broke into the king's apartments, intent upon kidnapping his nephew and forcing the child to make him Lord Protector, in place of his brother. Mercifully, the Admiral's entrance disturbed the young king's beloved spaniel, whose barks awoke the king's guards. In panic, Thomas Seymour struck at the dog, killing the poor creature. The king's guards quickly apprehended the king's errant uncle, and promptly escorted him to the Tower.

Unfortunately, Princess Elizabeth was also implicated in her brother's kidnapping. Thomas Seymour had visited her at Hatfield, just a few hours before he had been apprehended at Hampton Court. Edward Seymour – and some of the Privy Council – believed the purpose of the visit was to ask her to agree to a betrothal. Consequently, no one could be sure whether or not the princess had been involved in the plot. This prompted the Protector to order the arrest of Elizabeth's governess, Catherine Ashley, and place the princess in the care of Lord and Lady Tyrwhitt.

"Lord Tyrwhitt is trying to obtain information from her," Seymour explained, during one of his now frequent visits to the archbishop at Lambeth Palace. "Gently, of course," he added hastily, seeing a look of horror cross his companion's face.

"And what have they learned?" Thomas demanded, more severely than he intended.

"Nothing," Seymour swiftly replied. "She has said nothing. Everything she does or says is monitored and reported. But she cannot be coaxed, or even threatened, to say anything regarding my brother or his intentions."

"Threatened?" He frowned.

"Not with violence," Seymour hastily explained. "They simply threatened to take her books away... things like that," he added lamely.

There was a lengthy silence before Thomas replied coldly, "Could it not be that she is innocent and therefore has nothing to say regarding this matter?"

"We need to be certain," Seymour replied.

"I think you should send her governess back to her; she is very much attached to Mistress Ashley. Quite frankly, I cannot envisage her, or her governess, freely plotting with your bother."

Seymour was unsure. Depriving the princess of her governess meant she must rely upon Lady Tyrwhitt; perhaps she might open up to her and admit that she and Thomas Seymour had agreed to wed. Ashley was loyal to the girl – she would reveal nothing seriously incriminating – but Lady Tyrwhitt had no fondness for her, and would certainly inform the Lord Protector if anything was said.

As if reading his mind, Thomas murmured, "I cannot foresee the princess confiding in either of the Tyrwhitt's." They were cold, humourless people, much like the Lord Protector and his wife, and were certainly not the type of people to coax confidences from a young girl.

Seymour sighed, then passed two documents to him: the signed confessions of Parry and Mistress Ashley. Both revealed

410

that there had been much flirtation between Elizabeth and Lord Sudley, but neither mentioned anything of a betrothal. Ashley admitted she had sincerely hoped to see a union between the two, whilst Parry stated he had heard Sudley speak of his desire to marry the princess, and then added that he had promised Lord Sudley never to speak of this.

"You have shown the princess these?" Thomas queried, handing the papers back to Seymour.

"Yes. It seemed a good ploy to break her resistance." Seymour was beginning to feel uncomfortable under the archbishop's disapproving gaze.

"There is nothing incriminating in either document as far as the Princess Elizabeth is concerned." He could hear the sharpness in his voice and did not regret it. Seymour was handling the girl as if she were already a condemned criminal. "What did the princess have to say?"

"She wept at the treatment of her governess; claimed she would not tolerate the presence of Lady Tyrwhitt, then said it was a great matter that Parry broke his promise to Lord Sudley." Seymour snorted in disgust. He knew that Parry was not an honest man, and he was certain that he felt no guilt in breaking any promise he might have made to his master. "She then announced that she has heard a rumour going around, saying that she is with child. She desires to be brought to Court, so that people may see her and know that she is in no such condition; she even suggests that she should be examined by a physician of my choice, to confirm this."

"What do you intend to do?" Thomas was curious. This seemed a sensible action in his opinion. So sensible, the blinkered Seymour might overlook it.

411

"Do you think it wise to bring her to Court?" Seymour questioned. "After all, a physician could be sent to Hatfield to examine the girl."

"I do," he nodded earnestly. "My lord, you must surely see that the princess is simply a girl, not yet a woman, who has had her head turned by an attractive older man. Let her come to Court and permit her see her brother. The king is fond of his sister Temperance, as he calls her. He will welcome any opportunity to see her."

Seymour sighed, bowing his head in contemplation.

In that moment, Thomas felt sorry for the man before him. Seymour had desired power, but was overwhelmed by it, and now found himself drinking from a poisoned chalice. At least Cromwell had enjoyed the power he had possessed.

Seymour looked up, deciding to change the subject. "I have heard that some of your more..." He searched for a suitable word, "... modern clergy, are wishing to get rid of clerical vestments. Do you agree with this motion?"

"No." Thomas gave a half smile. "Hugh Latimer has tried to persuade me, but I think I have convinced him that not everyone is like him... or indeed, myself. There are those who, if free from clerical robes, will strut around like peacocks."

Seymour nodded gravely in agreement, relieved at having momentarily managed to escape from the uncomfortable subject of his brother and the Princess Elizabeth. "Yes, I think that is a probability, especially with the younger clergy. They would parade around in the latest fashions and set a poor example for the laity."

"That is what I wish to avoid. There should be a certain dignity about the clergy, otherwise people will not respect their position. They expect us to be above vanity," Thomas reflected.

Edward Seymour rose from his seat, ready to leave. "I bid you farewell, archbishop. I shall take myself back to Court and arrange for the princess to be brought to see the king and a physician. As for my brother... did you know that the Duchess of Rochester is besotted with him? She has been importuning me to release him."

"She is one of many, I gather," he soberly replied. He doubted if Thomas Seymour returned the affections of any of them. He seemed the kind of man who enjoyed female admiration, but whose heart remained untouched, set upon worldly wealth rather than love. "My wife tells me that the female servants love to be in the streets when he rides past." He uttered the words 'my wife' with a sense of triumph, for finally Margaret could openly call herself the wife of the Archbishop of Canterbury – the very first woman to ever be able to do so. At last, an Act had been passed permitting clergy to marry.

Seymour noticed a fond expression pass over the archbishop's face when he mentioned his wife. Momentarily, it irritated him. It seemed as if everyone's marriage was happier than his. His own wife, Anne, was a haughty, demanding woman. He had seen the archbishop's wife; indeed, he had recently been introduced to her. She had been pleasant to look at and modestly attired; in short, there was nothing amiss with her, apart from the fact that she was not an heiress. He failed to understand why any man would wish to marry a woman who had no dowry. Gloomily, he returned to Court, there to make arrangements for Princess Elizabeth to come and show herself to members of the Court, and be examined by a physician.

Some days later, the princess was escorted to the Court at Greenwich. She looked pale, but otherwise healthy, and had ensured that she was demurely attired: her gown had a modest neckline and was plain and unembroidered. She wore no jewels, whilst her hair was obscured by the primmest of headdresses. As for the king, he was delighted to see his sweet sister, and the two chatted eagerly together for over an hour, mostly in Greek. Once she had been seen by Dr Butts, who declared that she was most certainly not pregnant, there was nothing Edward Seymour could do but take the archbishop's advice. He permitted Elizabeth's governess, Mistress Ashley, to return to her.

A few days later, Thomas Seymour was charged with High Treason, and condemned to die on Tower Hill. The king, to the surprise of his Privy Council, did not protest against the Admiral's charge, and calmly accepted his favourite uncle's fate. When the day of the beheading finally arrived, to the superstitious horror of the watching crowd, the Admiral refused any ministrations from the clergy.

Immediately after the execution, Thomas learned that Edward Seymour had sent Lord and Lady Tyrwhitt to Hatfield, to inform Princess Elizabeth of the execution. In one final attempt to extract an admission from her of being illegally betrothed to his brother, Edward Seymour had requested that the shocking news be delivered to Elizabeth without any warning or former preparation. This, he hoped, would provoke an emotional reaction. Yet again, he was disappointed.

Visiting the archbishop at Lambeth, Seymour bitterly revealed the result of the Tyrwhitt's visit to Hatfield. "She is an abnormal girl!" he exploded with suppressed anger. "Do you know what she said?"

"I have no means of knowing," he replied coldly, disapproving of what he perceived to be an unkind act. "You have not yet told me."

"When informed of my brother's death, the princess replied: 'this day died a man of much wit, but little judgement'. What sort of girl is that?" Seymour demanded waspishly.

Thomas privately suspected that the young princess was similar to her brother, who had also appeared unmoved by the death of his uncle. Both siblings were uncommonly clever, though in his opinion, Elizabeth was wise beyond her years. Her mother had been beheaded and she had subsequently been declared a bastard, unlike her brother, who had always been held in high honour. Elizabeth's life had taught her to look after herself.

Chapter Eighteen

It was now November, and Thomas had returned from Canterbury late the previous evening. His clergy there had certainly improved as far as education was concerned, but some were anything but grateful for it. He always found it difficult to imagine how anyone could not thirst for knowledge. All of the Chantries were now closed, with the money from them having been put towards funding educational establishments. He now acted as Patron of Grammar Schools and Universities, and it gave him great pleasure to discover that these institutions were flourishing more than ever before. This was openly proclaimed to be due to the combined efforts of King Edward and the Archbishop of Canterbury, for although King Henry had encouraged and welcomed artists and musicians to his Court, he had never supported learning in any decisive way. His scholarly young son was remedying that.

A newly revised litany had finally been completed, and now lay in front of Thomas on his desk in his beloved Lambeth Palace library. As he picked it up to read through it yet again, there was a gentle knock on the door, and when he called out for whoever it was to enter, Ralph Morice opened the door and peered into the room, only to be rudely thrust aside without ceremony.

A tall, respectable looking man entered, his clothing suggesting he might be a clerk, and beside him, being forcibly dragged forwards, was an unwilling man, clad in clerical robes, whose hands were bound behind his back.

"I am Master Underhill," the clerk introduced himself. "Apologies for my rude entrance, but I am here upon a grave matter. This man is the Vicar of Stepney." His tone suggested that this, in itself, was sufficient explanation for his visit, and he regarded the archbishop with an air of expectation.

"Please, Master Morice, untie the vicar," Thomas gently requested, laying aside the litany. "What reason do you have, Master Underhill, to bind him up like a criminal?"

As Morice fumbled inexpertly with the bindings, Underhill quivered with outrage. "This man has been preaching Popery! There are plenty of eyewitnesses to prove it, too. He is addicted to the old superstitions! When men of the true and Protestant faith speak of it aloud in his church, he causes bells to be rung so they cannot be heard. Sometimes, he even challenges the speaker in the pulpit! Knowing this to be vile practice, I apprehended him myself and brought him to you." There was a note of virtue in his voice.

"Tell me, vicar, how long have you been at Stepney?" Thomas enquired of the prisoner.

The vicar looked indignant, as well he might. "I was formerly the Abbot of Tower Hill." His voice was a low, sullen growl. "As recompense for the loss of my abbey, I was given this present position."

He spent some time talking to the vicar, who was clearly orthodox. Unfortunately, like so many of the clergy, he was also badly educated. Yet again, he was faced with someone who did not understand Latin, yet preferred the services to be in Latin

417

because it was familiar. The vicar frankly admitted that he 'liked things the way they have always been'.

"Can you read and write?" Thomas asked.

"Yes." This was said with pride. "That I can. In English."

"Then I suggest you discover The New Learning and put aside the old. Read the Bible in English, good vicar. If you do not accept The New Learning, you must either publicly recant, or be punished," he explained calmly. "Return now to your church. You shall be watched, and if you give no further cause for complaint, then nothing more will be said of this matter. Go now."

The Vicar of Stepney shot a triumphant glance at Underhill, who was bridling with indignation.

"My lord Archbishop, you are too gentle with so stout a papist," Underhill blurted, as the vicar scurried hastily from the library, clearly in a hurry lest the archbishop should change his mind.

Thomas gave a brief smile. What had this man expected him to do? Have the Vicar of Stepney burned to death on Lambeth Palace lawn? Clearly, he was ignorant of the fact that no heretics had been burned since Edward Seymour had become Protector. "We have no laws to punish him by," he gently explained. "The heresy laws have long since been abolished."

"Abolished!" Underhill was outraged; his cheeks flushed bright red, his eyes widened with horror. Already a tall man, he seemed to rise to an even greater height. "No laws, my lord? If I were in your position, I would make a law. I would..." He searched for the right words. "I would unvicar him, or else administer some sharp punishment upon him, and others like him. If ever it comes to your turn, they will show you no favour," he predicted belligerently.

418

"Well, if God so provide, we must abide by it," Thomas replied quietly

"Surely God will never give you thanks for this?" Underhill refused to be placated. "Rather, He will take the sword from those who will not use it upon His enemies."

"I can only repeat: he shall be watched," Thomas replied firmly. "Meanwhile, Master Underhill, I thank you for your diligence." There was nothing more to be said. As he had already stated, there were no laws under which to convict the former abbot, and for that, he was truly grateful.

The visibly disgruntled Underhill departed, his spine rigid with indignation as he quit the library. During the coming weeks, the Vicar of Stepney was observed, but there was no more cause for complaint. Thankfully, it seemed he had heeded the archbishop's advice.

*****

That same year, to the great joy and excitement of Protestant reformists, an Act of Uniformity was passed, meaning churches could only use the English litany. The Latin Mass was now illegal, but because the majority of people were inclined towards Catholicism, principally because they had known nothing else, the Act resulted in a certain degree of upheaval. Fortunately, thanks to the enthusiastic preaching of eminent Protestants – including Thomas Cramer, Hugh Latimer and Nicholas Ridley – more and more individuals were willingly converting to Protestantism.

At Court, the position of Edward Seymour, Duke of Somerset, was becoming increasingly precarious. He was not a strong leader, and the Privy Council was full of individuals who were far more assertive. The conservative, orthodox faction, hoping for a return to traditional Catholicism, was headed by Thomas Wriothesley – who was both Chancellor and newly created Earl of Southampton – and the Earl of Arundel, both of whom were feisty characters. The Protestant faction of the council was led by the Archbishop of Canterbury himself, along with Edward Seymour and John Dudley. The latter was rapidly gaining the upper hand, largely due to his involvement in suppressing a bloody rebellion on Mousehold Heath, in Norfolk, during the summer months.

Edward Seymour's authority was further threatened by another rebellion, this time in Cornwall. It was initially believed this rebellion had been sparked by an ancient wish of the Cornish to be independent from England, but those in the know were aware that it was more complex than that. Discontent had been rumbling for years, as far back as the reign of King Henry VII; many of the Cornish people were desperately poor, and the new poll tax on sheep, combined with the price of wheat increasing fourfold, only added fuel to their resentment. The recent Act of Uniformity had made it illegal to use the old Latin prayer book, but many of the Cornish people spoke only the Cornish language. Despite understanding neither the English or the Latin litany, they were well used to the Latin, and to have it taken away was a terrible blow.

Outraged, the Cornish began to form an army, and gathered at Bodmin, under the leadership of the Mayor of Bodmin, Henry Bray. Many of the gentry hid themselves in their castles, as the mob fought and looted their way across the Tamar, intending to join forces with Devon rebels near Crediton. Finally, they laid siege to Exeter, demanding that the old Catholic Mass should be reinstated, and the Act of Six Articles restored. The city was under siege for a month, and eventually, John Russell, the Earl of Bedford, was sent with an army to put down the Cornish rebellion. In a series of brutal skirmishes, he did so, killing many Cornish men in the process.

Unfortunately, in order to maintain peace, English troops had to be taken from France, where there was constant bickering over England's governance of Boulogne, a valuable trading post. Once enough English soldiers had been despatched to fight against the Cornish rebels, the French people raged war on the few remaining troops, ultimately regaining Boulogne. As the leader of the government, Edward Seymour was forced to take accountability for this disastrous series of events.

Seeing John Dudley riding high on public popularity for his success in Norfolk, Edward Seymour sensed that his role as Protector was under threat. It had been a difficult year; holding power might be something of a poisoned chalice, but nonetheless, it was a chalice he was determined to hold on to. Realising Dudley was poised to take over the government of the realm, Seymour took drastic action one night, seizing the king and taking him to Windsor Castle, hoping to strengthen his own position. It was an ill-advised move; in the absence of the Lord Protector, Dudley used this opportunity to unite the council and overthrow Seymour. The majority of the Privy Council were in favour of this, on the basis that Dudley was the stronger person to govern, and so he was swiftly proclaimed leader of the government. Meanwhile, in secret, Wriothesley and the Earl of Arundel had joined together to try and persuade Princess Mary to support them, promising her that if she did, they would make her Regent for her brother. Mary refused; having always accused Seymour of keeping power from her brother, she was not about to do so herself. Even those who disliked Princess Mary for her stubborn Catholicism, respected her unwavering loyalty to her brother.

Edward, when finally taken from Seymour's clutches, was suffering from a heavy cold, as a result of being dragged away from his bed by his uncle and into the cold night air. Resentful of this treatment, he was not about to support his relative. Meanwhile, Wriothesley had somehow managed to regain favour with John Dudley, in spite of his recent display of Catholicism. How this had happened, Thomas could not understand, He would only wonder if their ruthless personalities enabled them to understand one another.

"I know Dudley declares himself to be Protestant, but I cannot judge how sincere his faith actually is," Thomas confided to Nicholas Ridley, as they walked through the grounds of Lambeth Palace. They had both agreed that the English litany needed some adjustment and were intending to work together to produce a revised version.

"I have heard that Gardiner is hoping to regain his position in Winchester, should Dudley turn out to be only pretending to support reform," Ridley remarked.

"I truly believe Dudley's only interest is Dudley himself," Thomas reflected.

"He is a courtier; most of them are like that." Ridley shrugged.

"Yes, but... oh, you know what I mean. Some are worse than others." Thomas scratched his beard thoughtfully. "I have to say, so far, it appears that he will support reform."

Ridley cast a shrewd glance at his friend, detecting an air of tension clouding his countenance. "I perceive something else is troubling you." He kept his voice low, despite the gardens of Lambeth being otherwise deserted. "Has the soon-to-be consecrated Bishop Hooper been demanding the casting aside of clerical vestments again?" It was possible. Hooper was very belligerent regarding vestments, stating that they were symbols of Catholicism. Personally, Ridley believed the clergy should be above fussing over what manner of garments they wore.

"No, Hooper is not the problem."

"Dudley, then?" Ridley prompted.

"Yes, Dudley." Thomas knew that he could discuss anything with this dear and respected friend. Like Latimer, Ridley had chosen to remain celibate, feeling that marriage would be a distraction from serving God, although both men were supportive of the clergy being able to marry. "I spoke with him this morning. Following the recent rebellions, any grievances the commoners have are to be shelved; he is not going to address them at present. He is also going to reintroduce the heresy laws, and legalise the enclosure of lands, which is what the peasants were fighting against." Thomas was ticking items off finger by finger as he spoke. "It will be treasonable to even speak against a member of the Privy Council, and he is going to have all of the old service books burned, though at least this indicates commitment towards Protestantism. Finally, he is going to allow the Crown to appoint a commission, to reform canon law."

"Reform canon law? He cannot!" Shocked, Ridley instantly focused on the last item on his friend's list.

"He can," came the grim reply. "I have argued with him and will oppose it. But I think it will be accepted by the council. I explained that this will undermine the clergy; furthermore, the Crown is not an authority on ecclesiastical affairs." This was a raw point. The Crown should not be able to reform canon law without seeking advice and guidance from senior clergy.

For a while, the two men walked in contemplative silence, the only sound being the crunching of their feet upon the gravel path.

"Have you thought about accumulating a list of signatures from your most senior bishops, to present to the Privy Council?" Ridley suggested.

"I told Dudley I intend to do just that. He said I am free to do so, but that it shall not make any difference. In other words, he has made a decision, and if the clergy, or even the Council, oppose him, he will still proceed according to his own wishes." He gave a deep, troubled sigh. "But I know the majority of the council will not oppose him. At the moment, he is so popular that he can do no wrong."

There was another period of silence as they reflected on this. "What about the new, revised litany we are working on?" Ridley queried.

Thomas brightened. "That, at least, is to go ahead. I am bound for Cornwall in a few days' time, but will think on it as I travel, and we shall finalise matters when I return." Dudley desired that the Archbishop of Canterbury should spend some time speaking with the Cornish clergy, in an attempt to soothe ruffled feathers. Since he did not speak Cornish, and many of the Cornish people did not speak English, he would need to rely on an interpreter, though he was optimistic that perhaps a few of the clergy might speak some English, or Latin. "I hope I can convince these Cornish rebels that the litany is in accordance with Christ's own instructions."

"A Cornish litany is needed," Ridley commented.

"Indeed, all men should be able to hear the blessed word of God in their mother tongue, but for the time being, it must remain in English," Thomas replied. "We have no Cornish version to offer at present."

"My bones do not travel the way they used to," Ridley sadly remarked. "But my prayers shall go with you. Will you ride?"

"No, my bones are also unable to travel the way they used to. I cannot ride to Cornwall." He managed to smile. "I shall travel mostly by carriage, so that I may sit and work... depending upon the state of the roads. I hear they are abominable in Cornwall. No doubt I shall need to use a horse once I am there. The journey will be long, but I am looking forward to sharing the Protestant faith with these people. By God's grace, I shall deliver His word to them."

*****

As he had predicted, the long journey to Cornwall was an uncomfortable experience. The roads – especially in Cornwall – were appalling, and the Cornish landscape was blighted by the sight of hundreds of gibbets, with the rotting remains of what had once been human beings dangling from them.

From the moment of his arrival, he was swept into a whirlwind of busyness. He spent a great deal of time talking with the clergy, and also tried to communicate with the laity, relying on his translator to keep up with his oratory. After a few weeks, he felt he had made a good impression, and had successfully started to soothe the bruised and battered emotions of the Cornish people. So many had lost friends, relatives, husbands, and sons, in the recent conflict; such tragic losses would take time to heal. Religious change was difficult for everyone, he accepted that. It had taken him some time to accept the Protestant faith. However, he left Cornwall feeling positive. The people were simply suspicious of change; given time, they too would acknowledge the truth of the Protestant faith.

Regarding the rest of England, it appeared the laity were cautiously adapting to the Reformation; some clergy, to the delight of Thomas, were even enthusiastic about it. Naturally, others were less so, but he would have been suspicious if it appeared otherwise; he did not expect people to impulsively cast aside their old beliefs. However, it now seemed that the Protestant faith was finally taking root in England.

On the day Thomas had set out for Cornwall, Bishop John Hooper, one of his most vocal critics, was imprisoned in the Fleet, for both criticising the new litany and for refusing to wear religious vestments, even at his own consecration. Unsurprisingly, by the time Thomas returned, Hooper was more reasonable about his protests, and was released from prison.

Shortly after his return to Lambeth Palace, the new English litany was completed, and a second Act of Unification was passed. This clarified that Dudley was genuinely committed to reform, much to Thomas' relief, and revealed that Dudley was a far more radical reformer than the cautious Edward Seymour had been.

The new Act of Unification involved more than just a change of litany. The Mass was now the renamed, it was The Lord's Supper; private confession was totally banned, and the officiating priest was no longer required to wear vestments, only a simple cassock. Thomas had also ensured that baptism was simplified: the infant was only to be dipped into the water once, not three times, and only a single sign of the cross was to be drawn upon the child's forehead. As for offering the sacrament, the priest was only required to say 'take and eat this', followed by 'drink this'. Finally, the Agnus Dei and the prayers for the departed were declared obsolete; the ancient canon of the Mass was changed beyond belief. The Protestant clergy, even those who were more radical than Thomas, were quick to praise the Archbishop of Canterbury for this move forward.

426

He was modest about his achievements, but he had fulfilled no small task, providing the Church with both a new prayer book and an English Bible, thereby giving the common people a simplified explanation of faith, so they might understand and approve the changes, and more importantly, come to know and love God. Without his hard work, the Reformation would never have succeeded.

*****

Since the young king had come to the throne, there had been no heretics burned, but Dudley was far less squeamish than Seymour when it came to burning people. He desired to make an example of one of them: a young Anabaptist named Joan Boacher, who had been imprisoned in Newgate for over a year now. Aware of this, Thomas visited Joan at Newgate Prison, as did Latimer, Ridley, and the eminent reformist, Peter Martyr, all of them bent on correcting her skewed religious beliefs.

"The virgin birth is stated in the Bible," Ridley mused quietly, whilst seated in the gardens at Lambeth Palace with the archbishop and Ralph Morice. It was a lovely summer evening; the air was still and smelled sweetly of roses. Such an evening should not be wasted indoors. "Yet she persists in declaring that there was no virgin birth. Such a statement is heresy." His mild countenance was troubled.

"It is a concern to me that she has been spreading this belief." Morice shook his head sadly. "She can apparently be very persuasive in her teachings. I fear she will lead others into sin."

"Dudley, wishes her to burn if she does not recant." Thomas sighed. He was feeling unwell, and supposed it was probably due to overwork. Despite Margaret's constant

427

rebukes, he had failed to slow down his intense work schedule. "But she will not accept that Christ was born of the Virgin Mary, which the Bible clearly proclaims. To say otherwise is, as you rightly say, heretical."

"If she should burn, I have heard there is another who is also likely to be burned, a man named George Van Paris, who is currently in the Fleet." Morice looked anxious.

"His claims are similar to Mistress Joan's. If one dies, the other must do likewise," Thomas responded gloomily. Turning to Ridley, he suggested, "Do you think you and I should continue to visit her during the next couple of weeks, to see if we can guide her to the truth?" He looked hopefully at his friend.

Ridley's kindly face beamed. "A good idea. We must at least try and save the maid."

Over the next two weeks, the two men alternated their visits to Newgate Prison, but to their frustration, Joan refused to change her views. To make matters worse, it was a vile place to visit, even worse than the Fleet. Joan Boacher was held in a cell with eight other women; in order for them to speak with her, she had to be led out by two gaolers and taken to the prison chapel, as there was nowhere else where they could speak with her privately. She was clothed in rags, and judging by the way she energetically scratched her head, her hair was teeming with lice. She was also half-starved; her cheeks were sunken and her eyes huge, a certain sign of someone whose diet was lacking. Since those who governed the prisons were not held responsible for feeding the inmates, the latter were dependent upon the generosity of friends, relatives, or anyone else who would send food to them. Some of the food was appropriated by the gaolers, especially if it looked appetising. In cases like Joan's, where a number of prisoners shared one cell, the food would be snatched by the strongest and fittest, and Joan Boacher was neither strong, nor fit.

"If she would recant of her heresy, she would be free." Ridley looked at his friend with a concerned expression. Thomas was looking more and more unwell; there were dark circles beneath his eyes, and he had lost weight. He had always been slightly built, but at present, he looked positively frail. "As for you, my friend, are you not sleeping of a night, or taking time to eat?"

"I don't feel well," he admitted. "I sleep well... in fact, I find it hard to wake up." He suppressed a yawn. "Margaret desires that I should see a physician, but I doubt if he would help, they seldom do. You know, my wife often jests that my beard has grown so long it has taken away my strength." His beard was getting long and ragged, but he hated the thought of trimming it. It seemed disloyal to consider trimming it, even just to make it tidy. After all, it was a sign of affection for the late king.

Regarding physicians, Ridley had to agree. In his experience, they were of little help at all. "You need rest, my friend. You never stop working," he rebuked gently.

So much had happened during the past few years, he had certainly been kept busy. But he was also getting older. How much longer would he be able to work at his current pace? "I will try to take things more slowly," he assured his friend. "It is summer; the Court will probably leave London to avoid the plague, so that should at least give me a chance to rest, I hope. Meanwhile, Joan Boacher and this George Van Paris are now at the mercy of Dudley, Earl of Warwick. The outlook for both of them is not good. If she must die, I will request of Dudley that it should be done... well, you know... kindly. Perhaps a hanging?"

As Thomas had predicted, the two were sentenced to be burned at the stake together, at Smithfield, and his plea for something less painful was ignored. The king did not sign the death warrants, nor did Dudley; it was the Chancellor, Thomas Wriothesley, Earl of Southampton, who signed away the heretics' lives. Rumours circulated that the Archbishop of Canterbury had signed the warrants, rumours which Ralph Morice suspected had been circulated by Wriothesley himself. People were hardened to the sight of executions; they would gather to observe a burning, but they were not a hugely popular spectacle, unlike a hanging or beheading. There had been none for a few years, and as far as these two burnings were concerned, the mood of the people was one of anger. Boacher and Van Paris had somehow gained public sympathy, therefore Wriothesley would rather people were annoyed at the archbishop than himself. After all, some people were still privately inclined towards the Church of Rome, which meant they disliked Thomas Cranmer anyway. As far as popularity was concerned, he felt the Archbishop of Canterbury had nothing to lose.

The weather soon turned hot, and Dudley decided to take the king to Eltham Palace, to escape the plague that would surely be sweeping through the streets of London in the near future. The journey to Eltham was by road from Greenwich, so the young king was able to show himself to the people, following the example of his magnificent father. As for Thomas, who felt even more exhausted than ever, he travelled with his wife and family to the relative peace of the Manor of Ford.

Barely had they arrived in Canterbury when he began to shiver, his limbs shook so violently that Margaret, frightened, immediately summoned a physician. The physician diagnosed an ague and declared that total rest was required. This Margaret agreed with, and she took it upon herself to remove her husband's books from the bedroom where he was lying. Before departing, the physician announced that he would visit again in two days, whereupon he expected to see a significant improvement. He then left a prescription, informing her to make it up herself, if she had the ingredients, or to seek an apothecary to assist her. Once he had departed, she read the recipe aloud to Thomas' friend, Dr Barbar, who had accompanied them to Canterbury, and also to Ralph Morice.

"The blood of a newly killed pigeon?" she gasped, waving the recipe before their eyes.

"Well, if he thinks it shall work, perhaps you should try it?" Barbar suggested carefully, frowning as he read the remainder of it. "The intestines of a rabbit?" His bushy eyebrows shot upwards. "Boiled in the urine of an infant?"

"Nein!" Margaret's accent was much in evidence, as it always was when she was upset or angry. On this occasion, her English disappeared altogether. "Ich werde es nicht tun."

"I beg your pardon?" Barbar's eyebrows shot up again.

"I won't do it." Margaret threw the recipe into the fire. "Beef broth and wholesome soft food will rest his stomach, and sleep will rest his mind. He must stay in bed."

Uneasy at this flagrant flouting of the orders of a physician, Barbar, nonetheless, bowed to the instincts of his friend's suddenly fearsome wife. In his opinion, women were born with a mysterious, instinctive knowledge of these things, so, he reasoned, Mistress Cranmer should be permitted to do what she felt was best.

When the physician returned, he was delighted to see his patient very much improved, although still pale, weak, and prone to tremors of his limbs.

431

"My prescription seems to be having the desired effect, so continue with it for another week," he instructed Margaret.

"What prescription?" Thomas murmured. He was lying comfortably on top of the bed, wearing only a long, linen shirt. The windows were open, and a cooling breeze drifted into the room.

"He doesn't remember being given it," Margaret explained, her expression angelic.

"Well, keep giving it to him. I also recommend you should close the window; a good fire will sweat the ague out of him." The physician smiled at her benignly, then promptly departed.

"A fire?" Thomas was horrified. The breeze was so cooling and refreshing.

"You are not getting a fire, and the window stays open." Margaret wondered why she had bothered summoning a physician in the first place. "He wanted me to give you pigeon blood and the entrails of a rabbit, boiled with the urine of an infant."

"Why did you summon him?" It was totally against his nature to lie quietly and not actually do anything, but at this moment, he was content to do so.

"Panic," she replied truthfully. "You are so rarely ill... I feared for your life."

Once he began to feel stronger, Margaret, who was very much in charge, agreed for a small number of books and papers to be delivered to his bedchamber, on the condition that he only worked during daylight hours. He gladly conceded, using his recovery time to write a treatise against Stephen Gardiner. From his prison cell, Gardiner had been prolific in his written protests against the Archbishop of Canterbury over recent months, despite Thomas being responsible for granting him access to pen, ink, paper, and books.

"He did me a great disfavour," he complained to Margaret. He was still very much confined to the bedroom, but he could now sit at the table and write for a few hours each day. In fact, he was surprised at how feeble he felt when walking around; his legs were apt to tremble in a most disconcerting way. "I thought my work on the sacraments was a very persuasive book, until he produced a pamphlet against it."

"Whatever you write, he will find something to say against it," his wife replied grimly.

Thomas smiled, for she spoke truly. Gardiner would always oppose him; he had to accept that. The man was an implacable enemy; it was always frightening whenever he contemplated it. After all, no one wanted to be deeply and irrevocably hated. Personally, he disliked Stephen Gardiner, and always had; they had little in common. Yet he had never actively *hated* him.

"The other bishops who were deprived of their dioceses – Bonner, Heath and Day – say little against you. But the former Bishop of Winchester cannot control his tongue… or his pen," Margaret tutted, putting clean sheets onto the bed.

"Tunstall, Bishop of Durham, is to be deprived of his diocese." Thomas frowned. In his hands, he held a letter from Ridley, updating him on current events. Tunstall was orthodox, but at least he outwardly complied with the Protestant changes. For this reason, Thomas had been satisfied with him retaining his position. John Dudley, however, believed that the bishop should be replaced by someone devoutly Protestant. "I have objected to his deprivation, as you know, but Dudley now has more say in the Church than the clergy. Tunstall is to be replaced, and I shall be blamed; most people do not realise that Dudley is in charge. However, I shall propose that, if he agrees, Ridley shall be created Bishop of Durham." Edward Seymour would never have done such a thing without consulting the

Archbishop of Canterbury. "And you have been shielding me from bad news, my love."

Margaret was now standing beside him, looking over his shoulder at the letter he was holding.

Reaching for her hand, he kissed it. "According to Ridley, Paul Fagius and Martin Bucer are now dead, and have been for several weeks."

Margaret nodded. She knew them both very well. They had taken refuge in England from the Emperor Charles' persecutions in Germany, and upon their arrival in England, they had lived for some time at Lambeth Palace. Eventually, places had been found for them at Cambridge University. Bucer, especially, had been of great help during the writing of the latest Protestant litany. "I did not tell you, but I knew someone would write to you with the sorrowful tidings. I judge that you are now well enough to be given ill news. I cannot protect you from it forever." She squeezed his hand. "I too was fond of them. They were people whom I shall always be proud to have known."

Thomas kissed her hand again.

"What have you been writing?" She picked up a sheet of paper and scrutinised it. "Oh, is this the beginning of your work against Stephen Gardiner?" She read aloud, "'the taking away of beads, pilgrimages, pardons, and suchlike popery, is but the lopping off of a few branches, which should soon spring up again, unless the roots of the tree, which are transubstantiation and the Mass, are pulled up. Therefore, out of a sincere zeal to the honour of God, I would labour in His vineyard to cut down that tree of error'." Margaret paused. "You know, though I have never met him, I feel a deep hatred towards him. I often ask God to forgive me for that." Margaret returned the sheet of paper to her husband.

434

"Well... God looks at the heart. He will perceive that your hatred is not for Gardiner, but for his behaviour towards me. If you met him, you would see a flawed man. In fact, it might be beneficial for you to visit him in the Fleet when we return to London," he suggested, amused to observe the succession of emotions fighting for supremacy on his wife's face.

"You would permit me to visit him... knowing I might..." She was lost for words. "Knowing I would find it hard to be polite to him?"

"There is nothing you can say which would offend him." Thomas smiled. "I doubt if he would take notice, even if you were to grossly insult him. But, in seriousness, I would not permit that you should meet him, my dear." He felt strangely saddened that they must return to the chaos of Court. He was enjoying this quiet time with his wife and two children, both of whom were clever and eager to learn. Clearly, he had needed physical and mental rest.

Nearly two months after he had first fallen ill, Thomas decided that he must soon return to Court, despite not being entirely recovered. Rumours had reached him that John Dudley was attempting to getting rid of Edward Seymour in a very permanent way. Although Seymour was currently imprisoned in the Tower, he remained a threat to Dudley, and Dudley was a man who would not tolerate threats. Thomas had also learned that the council were abusing their newly acquired clerical authority. Members of the council had been taking plate from churches – valuable pieces that had been Church property for centuries – and had either been selling it or else blatantly using it in their own homes. He had received numerous letters from his clergy, begging him to help stop this sacrilege, but there was nothing he could do. A year ago, he could have prevented it; but now, he was powerless to intervene. All he could do was try and persuade the council to cease this selfish, greedy behaviour.

In mid-November, Thomas set out for London, accompanied by Margaret, who had decided that the children should remain at the Manor of Ford until Christmas. They had been left in the capable hands of Edmund Cranmer, his wife Alice, and their children, so she was satisfied that they would be well cared for. Although he admitted he was not yet fully returned to heath, Thomas felt fitter and stronger than he had felt in a long time. He had needed the rest, though naturally he had done a lot of writing and studying during the latter part of his sojourn at Canterbury. Indeed, he had spent his final few weeks there teaching and lecturing to his clergy, and riding with his brother, Edmund. It had been a very long time since he had ridden for the sheer pleasure of it, and he was grateful to have had the opportunity to do so. It was satisfying to know that he was still a skilled rider.

Soon after arriving at Lambeth, he presented himself at Court, and went immediately to see the king. The sight that greeted him was not a cheerful one. Edward had been complaining of a cough ever since Edward Seymour had abducted him, but whatever ailed the lad, it was not the result of a mere chill. Thomas realised, with a sinking heart, that the fourteen-year-old king was gravely ill. Yet though the boy was clearly unwell, somehow or other, his mannerisms had become even more akin to those of his father: the way he spoke, the way he sat, the way he stood... all were reminiscent of the great King Henry.

Christmas was still some weeks away, but the Princesses Mary and Elizabeth were both at Court in readiness for the celebrations, and of the two young women, Elizabeth seemed the most strikingly changed. Fashions at court, for women at least, were outlandish, and Mary, a keen follower of anything fashionable, was obviously enjoying wearing elaborate gowns and having her hair intricately frizzed. Elizabeth, meanwhile, was continuing to heed the advice the archbishop had given her; attiring herself in plain, high-necked gowns, combing her auburn locks away from her face, tucking her hair beneath a modest cap, and wearing very little jewellery. There was a maturity about her now; she was a young woman and no longer a mere girl. Looking at her, it was impossible to imagine that she was the same giddy girl who had once flirted with Thomas Seymour. A number of courtiers believed Lady Jane Grey, the king's devoutly Protestant cousin, was so keen to imitate Elizabeth, that she too was covering her hair and wearing plain, modest gowns. The fact was, Lady Jane had always dressed this way.

Prior to the commencement of any festive celebrations, John Dudley had Edward Seymour accused of treason. Twenty-three articles had been drawn up against him, but as he read through them, Thomas felt his anger mounting. The charges of greed and self-advancement were clearly applicable, but none of the others were viable; they were simply trumped-up charges, devised by a man who was determined to get rid of his rival. The most frustrating thing about the whole incident was that he could do nothing to save Seymour from execution. Dudley's decision was final.

As soon as Christmas was over with, Seymour was tried and promptly condemned to death for treason. The trial was farcical in Thomas' opinion. Unfortunately, since the day he had first come to Court, he had witnessed numerous farcical trials. On the eve of Seymour's execution, he was permitted to visit him in his cell, and, as always, when faced with such circumstances, he wondered what he could possibly say that would be of any

437

comfort. He found Seymour looking not only greyer of hair and beard, but also plumper of face and figure. Clearly, he was at least well looked after.

"I am here to pray with you, if you will permit it, and also to give you the sacrament." Opening the bag he had brought with him, he seated himself and proceeded to unpack the vessels necessary for Holy Communion.

"I will take it gladly from you," Seymour replied, implying that he would not have taken it from anyone else.

Opening his own prayer book, he showed his companion the words he had written only minutes previously: 'fear of the Lord is the beginning of wisdom. Put thy trust in the Lord with all thine heart'.

"I intend to carry it with me to my execution tomorrow. These will be the last words I shall ever read," he stated gravely.

"Would you prefer it if I were to accompany you?" Thomas asked, his voice hoarse. The profoundly touching words Seymour had written, had caused his throat to constrict.

"No, my lord Archbishop. I am glad of your presence now, but I am content to go to my death alone," Seymour replied coolly. "I am ready to go."

The former Lord Protector took Holy Communion graciously, then spent some time in prayer, speaking to the archbishop with the countenance of a man who was at peace with himself. Finally, he shook hands with his visitor, this simple gesture almost making Thomas forget that the man was to die the following day. It felt as though they were simply bidding each other good evening, and would meet again in the Council Chamber come morning.

Early the next day, Seymour, who only a short while ago had been regularly booed in the streets, died on Tower Hill, surrounded by a now silent, sympathetic crowd. The ordinary people of London always seemed able to differentiate between those who deserved the death penalty, and those who did not. Edward Seymour, they knew, had done nothing to deserve this.

Concerned that the death of his uncle might have upset the young king, Thomas made haste to visit him, and found him writing in his journal. Edward had kept a regular diary for some years, and he could not fail to glimpse the most recent entry:

'The Duke of Somerset had his head cut off upon Tower Hill, between eight and nine o'clock in the morning.'

Shocked by the cool brevity of Edward's words, he could only speculate that the boy was in shock. But then, he had shown no emotion at all when Thomas Seymour had died.

"We are planning to send ships to the New World," Edward informed him, obviously not intending to touch upon the subject of his uncle's death.

"Indeed, sire, I had heard." Thomas gave a nod of affirmation. "An exciting project." He noted the boy's flushed cheeks; perhaps they were a sign that his health was improving. He could only pray to God that it was so. If anything happened to this youth, the next person on the throne would be Mary, and, as ever, it was apparent that she considered him to be her enemy. Her demeanour towards him was cold; if anything befell Edward, his own fate looked grim, as did the fate of the Reformation. Mary was as fervently Catholic as she had ever been, and she had no intention of changing her mind.

Chapter Nineteen

By the end of January, Princess Mary had returned to her residence at Hunsdon, in Hertfordshire. Before she left Court, Thomas had requested that Nicholas Ridley should spend some time talking with her, to try and persuade her to shed her orthodox beliefs once more. If he were honest with himself, he did not think there would be a successful outcome. However, given the delicate state of the king's health, they had to keep trying to persuade the princess to recognise the truth of The New Learning. If Ridley could not convince her that the Protestant faith was pure, and in accordance with the gospels, no one could.

Unfortunately, but not unexpectedly, Ridley arrived at Lambeth Palace to report on an utter failure.

"She was very polite," he observed.

"Well, that is an improvement. She was certainly not polite towards me during the Christmas festivities," Thomas stated gloomily. "She sees me as her enemy."

"Well, you know how plain speaking she is," Ridley gave a reminiscent smile "There is no falsehood about her at all. She said to me, as soon as I entered her presence, 'my lord, for your gentleness to come and see me, I thank you, but for your offering to preach to me, I thank you never a whit'. She was clutching her rosary all the while; in fact, she constantly fingers it, as if it is some sort of talisman."

"I know," Thomas sighed. "It gives her comfort. I believe it once belonged to her mother. She has led a tragic, difficult life. She may have been born in a palace, but her life has been far from easy."

At that moment, they heard a gentle knocking upon the library door, and Margaret's head appeared. Stepping inside, she waved a letter at them. "I apologise for being of disturbing, but I have heard from Germany, and I know you will wish to read what it says. Please be to sit down, Dr Ridley." Ridley had immediately stood up as she had entered the room. "I think this letter will   of interest be to you also."

Thomas observed that not only were her hands shaking, but her grammar was all over the place. His wife was clearly distressed. Taking her hand, he gently guided her to a comfortable chair. "Bad news, my dear?" he surmised.

"My uncle has died," she informed him. "Andreas Osiander," she added, for Ridley's benefit.

"I am so sorry, Mistress Cranmer." Ridley's face was a mask of compassion. "He was a great man; so very gifted. His essays are a privilege to read."

Ridley had spoken so kindly, Margaret needed to take a few deep breaths to compose herself. Her husband, meanwhile, had pressed a cup of ale into her hand; taking a sip, she addressed Ridley. "He and my husband did not always agree. Just as my uncle did not always agree with Martin Luther." She tried to smile. "I have learned that you clever men are often splitting the hairs over details, but it does not necessarily ruin the friendship. Indeed, it can strengthen it, which is as it should be."

"God speaks to us as individuals, and He gives us free will," Thomas murmured. Scanning the letter, he decided to read some of it aloud. "It begins by announcing the death of Osiander, then delivers what appears to be promising information. There is to be a diet. An assembly." He paused, holding the letter close to his eyes as he tried to interpret the writing, which was small and compact. "It says, 'an assembly shall be summoned to deliberate about composing the differences of religion', and it goes on to say, 'dissension about religion shall be composed by placid and easy methods. None shall be molested for religious and other matters'." He sighed. "As reformists, we need to work together. We cannot be a strong Church if we argue and quarrel over trivialities and dogma." It was a source of uneasiness for him that Protestants were beginning to divide into factions. Such fragmentation would no doubt weaken, rather than strengthen, their cause.

"Let us pray to God that these men can find a means of being at peace," Ridley spoke with feeling. Like his friend, he was troubled by the knowledge that disagreements were occurring between reformist groups. Turning to Margaret, he added, "I too did not always agree with your uncle, but I agreed with most of his writing. Over the years, his work has both educated and strengthened me. I can state with honesty that I respected him, and I regret that I was never able to meet him. As you have wisely said, we must respect each other's differences, and keep our friendships strong."

Thanking him for his kindness, Margaret departed from the library, and the two men returned to the subject of Princess Mary.

"She is very fond of Lady Jane Grey," Thomas remarked. "Despite the latter being so devoted to Protestantism. I wish they could meet each other more often; Lady Jane might be able to influence the princess. Did you know that Lady Jane engages in regular correspondence with Calvin in Switzerland?"

"No!" Ridley gave an incredulous bark of laughter. "Such a young maid, corresponding with Calvin! Marry, I know she is seriously Protestant, but I did not imagine she was sending letters to him."

"He helps her with her Old Testament studies, apparently. She also corresponds with Heinrich Bullinger." Thomas gave a sigh. "It must be said, Lady Jane has endured an even worse upbringing than the Princesses Mary and Elizabeth. When I spoke with Princess Elizabeth over Christmas, and asked if she was happy, the princess said that she is content, and finds her lot far easier than that of Lady Jane, who is constantly beaten, whipped and bullied by her parents."

"She is but a maid, and dutiful too, from what I have seen." Ridley was shocked. "Why should they need to whip a maid of..." He tried to recall her age and failed. "A maid who cannot be more than fifteen years of age," he concluded sadly. Changing the subject, he enquired, "Have you heard anything from our friend Latimer lately?"

"Only that he is reading through my soon-to-be distributed forty-two Articles of Faith, and is due to comment on them." He referred to a series of articles he had compiled to teach the clergy – and anyone else who chose to read them – about Protestant doctrine. The Protestant faith was built upon the Bible; the Word of God Himself. The articles were aimed to demonstrate that the Protestant faith was grounded in this. He rolled his eyes upwards. "I anxiously await his opinion."

"He will certainly be frank." Ridley gave a throaty chuckle.

As the weeks sped past, he waited to hear from the foremost reformists abroad. He had, at the beginning of the year, written to people such as Bullinger, Luther and Calvin, suggesting they come to England to participate in what he described to them as an 'Ecumenical Council', where they would be able to air their opinions and doctrines, and perhaps form a strong, united, Protestant Church. Dishearteningly, thus far, all the meetings that had been held to resolve differences had failed to do so. Calvin sent a reply; he was keen, as was Luther, but neither had time to make the journey at present. The others did not respond, which was disappointing. By contrast, the orthodox Church had met in Trento, Northern Italy, in response to the now rapidly growing Protestant faith. The meeting was intended to strengthen the Catholic Church against what they referred to as 'Protestant heresy'. He had hoped that, by gathering leading Protestants in England, they could formulate a response to what was now referred to as the 'Catholic Council of Trent', but clearly it was destined not to happen, not yet at any rate. He wrote back to Calvin, saying that he would continue to reform the English Church to the best of his ability, and work to improve its doctrines according to the Holy Bible.

Meanwhile, at Court, rumours surrounding the king's poor health were circulating, and the boy was looking pale and weak. Unlike Edward Seymour, who had tried to keep the king in the background, John Dudley encouraged him to attend council meetings, giving every indication that, one day, he would hand over the reins of government to him. Thomas found himself often surprised by Dudley, and although he was certainly not fond of the man, he regretted his early suspicion that Dudley was not a committed Protestant. He had proved himself to be a staunch believer in The New Learning, and could even be considered a radical, having recently disclosed his friendship with the Scottish preacher and reformist John Knox, who was now one of Edward's chaplains.

444

Knox was a fiery preacher, and totally unafraid to publicly oppose even the Archbishop of Canterbury, when he felt it necessary. Thomas and Knox had disagreed many times, their most recent point of contention being the taking of Holy Communion. In the new litany, Thomas had recommended that people should kneel, if possible, when receiving the sacrament. Knox objected, saying this instruction was nothing less than idolatry! Since Protestants did not believe in transubstantiation, the bread and wine only symbolised the body and blood of Christ, so why should people kneel when receiving it? He had called upon Thomas to defend the practice, so, in the revised litany, he explained that there was no adoration intended when kneeling. He personally felt the act of kneeling displayed respect; Knox and his supporters thought otherwise. He had always envisaged that, when the Reformation finally occurred, everyone would be united in this great cause: a set of like-minded individuals, coming together to spread the true word of God. He pondered ruefully over how naïve he'd been back then, to think there could ever be unity amongst the clergy.

*****

Another year had passed swiftly. Having received considerable feedback from Latimer, Thomas had completed his forty-two Articles of Faith and presented them before the council, but much to his disappointment, they were not issued and distributed throughout the churches. Heavily influenced by Knox, Dudley had refused to have them authorised. His treatise against Stephen Gardiner, however, was printed and circulated, though no one doubted that, in the very near future, Gardiner would produce a scathing response.

As the new year began, he found himself accused of being niggardly with money yet again. This time, it was Dudley who informed him of the rumour, though Dudley declared he had no idea who was spreading it. Thomas suspected it was probably one of the more orthodox clergy, but he never succeeded in tracking down the root of the accusation. Margaret, when informed, was furious, taking it as a personal insult. She felt they provided a hospitable household, which he agreed with, but their lack of wealth could not be denied. He sent a significant amount of his income to war torn Germany, to aid impoverished reformists, plus he also supported German refugees who had fled to England. The food served at Lambeth might be simpler that the fare served in the great households, but it was wholesome and nourishing. Likewise, the clothing worn by himself, Margaret and their children, was simple and practical, but of good quality. It seemed ludicrous to him that anyone should expect the Archbishop of Canterbury to run his household any other way, therefore he duly ignored the rumours. Soon, he was certain, some other rumour of a more compelling nature would replace those concerning his management of money.

One evening, at dusk, he and Margaret were sitting in the grounds of Lambeth Palace, enjoying some well-earned peace and quiet. Until a week ago, the weather had been cold, damp and windy, but now it was possible to sit out on an evening and enjoy the open sky, albeit swaddled in a cloak or woollen shawl.

"Look, that barge seems to be heading for the landing stage." Margaret, whose eyesight was far superior to her husband's, pointed at a dark shape on the water.

Thomas saw that a vessel was indeed approaching, the sound of its oars dipping rhythmically in and out of the water breaking the cosy silence. Walking towards the barge as it reached the landing step, he recognised one of Dudley's servants.

"My lord Archbishop," the servant bowed, having disembarked. "I am come to respectfully request your presence at Greenwich Palace, immediately. My lord Dudley says it is of supreme importance." He pulled a piece of paper from his sleeve and handed it to Thomas.

"This gives no indication as to why I am summoned... something must have happened." Bidding a swift g farewell to Margaret, he followed the servant onto the barge, clambered in, and seated himself. He wondered how many times he had travelled thus to the royal residences... hundreds? Thousands? It was a pleasing way to travel, especially when the river was not heaving with traffic; plus it was certainly convenient once he had got used to judging the tides.

A nocturnal summons these days was unusual, but not unheard of, unlike during Henry VIII's reign, when it had been a fairly common occurrence. What was unusual, however, was Dudley's behaviour when he arrived, and Thomas immediately recognised that something was truly wrong. Dudley was waiting at the Greenwich landing stage to greet him, striding impatiently up and down while his torchbearer tried to keep pace with him, lest he should stumble and fall into the river.

"My lord Archbishop," Dudley greeted him. "We must speak at once, there is no time to lose. Follow me."

Wondering at the apparent urgency in Dudley's voice, he followed him into the palace, struggling to keep pace with his long-limbed companion.

At last, they reached a vacant anteroom, and Dudley threw aside his cloak, seizing his companion's wrist in a vice-like grip.

Startled and out of breath, Thomas stared at him in mild surprise.

447

"My lord." Dudley released the archbishop's wrist. "The king is dying." As Thomas opened his mouth to speak, he hastily added, "not right at this very moment, but soon. When did you last see him?"

"No more than three weeks ago, just before I left for Canterbury. Has he declined so quickly?"

Dudley nodded solemnly. "I shall take you to his bedchamber. He sleeps as present; he has been given poppy juice by his nurse to soothe him." Beckoning for Thomas to follow, Dudley led him briskly to the king's chambers.

Two halberdiers stood on guard outside, but quickly opened the door to admit Dudley and the archbishop. Entering the bedchamber, Thomas' nostrils were assaulted by the rank smell of sickness, making him regret not having a pomander to hold to his nose. He noticed Barnaby Fitzpatrick, one of the king's pages, who was standing half hidden in the corner of the room, gazing anxiously at the king's frail body. Fitzpatrick had once held the position of Edward's whipping boy.

"Master Fitzpatrick," Thomas whispered, lest he should disturb the sleeping king. "I thought you were in France?" Nearly a year ago, the page had been sent to the French Court, to learn polished social graces.

"I was." Fitzpatrick walked over to the archbishop, accompanying him as they moved towards the splendid, canopied bed where the king lay. "But I heard His Majesty was not as well as he could be." It was obvious that the page was choosing his words carefully. "So I returned, to assure myself of his good health. I arrived last week, to find him much altered." His voice cracked with emotion. "Once he recovers, pray God, I shall return to France to continue my education."

"You are loyal," Thomas approved.

"His Majesty has done much for me and my family in Ireland." They had reached the king's bedside, and Fitzpatrick gently stroked the young king's hair, brushing Edward's damp fringe away from his forehead.

Ignoring Dudley, who was hovering impatiently in the background, Thomas quietly repeated, "You are loyal, and that is something I respect." The young king needed loyal friends. Most people wanted something from him, usually money or power; he needed people around him who were honest and selfless. He looked upon the frail young monarch. If he were honest with himself, the king did not look 1 as if he would be needing Fitzpatrick for much longer. The boy's once rosy cheeks were red with sickness, and sunken too, for he had lost a significant amount of weight. His arms and hands, which lay on top of the sheets, were thin and shrivelled in appearance, and glowed an unhealthy yellow in the dim light. The boy remained sleeping, thanks to the poppy juice, but he was restless; his breath was foul, coming in wheezing gasps, and he coughed frequently.

"I shall leave, lest I disturb him," Thomas whispered sadly, turning towards Dudley. He felt choked. This poor boy was the heir King Henry had so longed for and had loved so dearly. "I hope he remains sleeping for a while longer. He needs rest."

"His nurse, Mrs Penn, sleeps just next door. She will give him more poppy juice if he needs it," Fitzpatrick reassured the visitors. Mrs. Penn had been the king's nurse ever since he was an infant, and was reputed, like King Henry, to love him dearly.

Not knowing what else to say, Thomas simply nodded, before following Dudley from the room. They returned to the anteroom, where someone had clearly pre-empted their need for refreshment; a jug of ale and some cups stood in readiness, as did a platter of meats. The smell of sickness still clung to his

449

nostrils, so food was not something he felt able to relish. The ale, however, was welcome.

Dudley immediately took hold of a knife, speared a slice of meat, cramming it into his mouth, as if he was starving. "Help yourself, my lord Archbishop," he mumbled. "What do you think of the king?" The words were indistinct.

"He is mortally sick." Thomas poured ale into a cup and gratefully took a deep drink.

"I fear he has little time." Dudley now turned his attention to the jug of ale. "Eat, my lord," he urged, spearing another slice of meat.

Thomas picked up a slice of beef, but for the time being, only held it in one hand. With the other, he held on to his cup of ale. He felt sick, and it was not solely due to the stench of the king's bedchamber. Once the king was dead, Mary would rule.

"The king produces foul, black sputum. The stench is vile, as you will not have failed to notice." Dudley viscously bit into another slice of meat, swallowed, then began speaking again. "The doctors do not know what is amiss. They say his humours are at fault; I could have told them that without even examining the boy." He almost spat the words. "I am inclined to say he has little time."

"I would concur with that." Thomas took an unwilling, dainty nibble from his slice of beef.

"So, who will rule after him?" Dudley stood, legs apart, as if challenging his companion.

"Princess Mary. She is the rightful ruler." Thomas whispered the words.

"I say no," Dudley declared. "She will return the country to orthodoxy."

"She is, according to the late king's Will, next in line." Mary had to become queen; there was no one else to take the throne... apart from the Princess Elizabeth, but she was the younger of the two daughters.

"The king can bequeath his throne to whomsoever he wishes," Dudley contradicted.

"No, my lord, he is not of age—"

"He is king." Dudley sharply interrupted. "He can leave his throne to whomever he desires to leave it to," he added with a degree of hauteur.

"Princess Elizabeth?" Thomas was shocked. Dudley could surely not be suggesting the younger sister should supersede the elder.

Dudley gave a vulpine smile. "Lady Jane Grey."

Thomas sat down heavily on the nearest chair. Lady Jane Grey was royal, no doubt about that. She was the great niece of King Henry VIII. Also, unlike both Elizabeth and Mary, there was no doubt about her legitimacy.

"Lady Jane Grey is next in line after Princess Elizabeth." The vulpine smile lingered on Dudley's lips.

Thomas remained silent.

"King Edward is anxious for a Protestant to rule after him. Lady Jane is the perfect person," Dudley explained smoothly, not making it known, as yet, that Lady Jane Grey would shortly be marrying his own youngest son, Guildford Dudley. "He has already informed me that he will gladly sign a Will, bequeathing his throne to her."

"He knows he is dying?" Thomas felt immense pity for the poor child.

"Yes, and he wishes to legally leave his throne in the care of Lady Jane. After all, there is no one else; she is the eldest granddaughter of King Henry's much-loved sister, Princess Mary Rose."

"I find it difficult to agree to this." Giving up trying to eat any meat, he swallowed more ale instead. "What will happen to the princesses? And don't you dare say something so vague as 'I will ensure their safety'. You gave your word that Edward Seymour would remain safe, and he is now buried in the Tower Chapel." His tone was bitter.

"I know, my lord. You wrote to me objecting to his execution, as I recall." Dudley was impatient. He needed the support of the Privy Council, and the Archbishop of Canterbury was one of its pivotal members.

"I believe you are hoping to keep some threads of power," Thomas accused indignantly. "Lady Jane is young; she will need advisors."

"Of course," Dudley snapped. "But if Mary rules, you and I will both find ourselves being blamed for the reformation of the English Church, and we both know her opinion on that." His tone became persuasive. "Just think, my lord, of the amount of work which shall be reversed if Mary is ever crowned queen."

Thomas sighed. "I do not condone going against the former king's wishes… but I know you are right. Catholic heresy cannot return to this land. The truth, the Reformation, must be protected at all costs."

During the next few days, Thomas reflected constantly upon that meeting with Dudley. A niggling part of his mind told him it was wrong to rob Mary of the throne. According to King Henry's Will, she should be queen. Yet, as Dudley had cunningly pointed out, a king could bequeath his throne to whomsoever he wished. Princess Elizabeth was the natural successor to Mary, and Protestant too. But if Mary was passed

452

over on account of her parents' marriage being declared invalid, then Elizabeth could not take the throne either, for her parents' marriage had likewise been deemed invalid. So, that left the avidly Protestant and legitimate Lady Jane Grey.

He longed to discuss the situation with Ridley, and that very evening, he was granted the opportunity, when a letter arrived from Dudley, inviting him to visit Greenwich, where a meeting would be held with the king, several members of the Privy Council, and a couple of legal experts. The presence of Dr Nicholas Ridley, the newly consecrated Bishop of Durham, had also been requested.

As they travelled to Greenwich together, Ridley, who had only heard of the matter a few hours previously, delivered his opinion.

"If it is legal, I would dearly prefer Lady Jane Grey to take the throne. She is a clever maid and devoted to the Protestant cause. But I do keep asking myself, *is* it lawful?"

"That is my concern," Thomas admitted, as their barge headed towards its destination.

Upon arriving at Greenwich, they were escorted by a servant to the king's rooms, and were admitted by Barnaby Fitzpatrick, who greeted them affably. Fitzpatrick proceeded to inform them that the king was dressed and sitting upright, but no matter which great people were present, Mistress Penn ruled here; if she thought the king had endured enough, she would take him to his bed, and woe betide the minister who opposed her.

The king was seated in the room adjacent to his bedchamber, and as they bowed before him, Thomas could not help but pity the boy. He looked utterly exhausted; the simple act of being dressed in his doublet and hose had clearly wearied him. As before, the room reeked of sickness; the king's body

453

stank of stale sweat, and his breath was fetid. John Dudley, who was already present, rose to greet them, looking well pleased with himself. "My lords, we await the lawyers, and some other representatives from the Privy Council."

"Whom should we expect?" Thomas wondered aloud.

"My Lord Wriothesley," Dudley replied. As Chancellor, Wriothesley's presence was required by law, even though it was recognised that his religious convictions were   flexible, and always had been. "And the Duke of Suffolk." The latter was the father of Lady Jane Grey.

Soon, everyone who had been invited to attend stood before the king, listening to the lawyers explaining his right to bequeath the throne, which was legally his, to whomsoever he wished. This would invalidate King Henry VIII's Will. Courageously facing his impending death, Edward did not shrink from making his own Will. He did not wish the country to fall into Catholic hands; by leaving his throne to his sweet cousin Jane, as he called her, he knew England would remain safely Protestant. He had drawn up a list of his wishes, which he called 'my device for the succession'. The list validated the fact that his sisters were both bastards, and unable to sit on the throne.

Dudley, unable to contain his excitement, decided it was time to deliver some news which would poleaxe everyone present. "My lord of Suffolk, here…" He nodded towards the now beaming man. "Has agreed that his daughter, Lady Jane Grey, shall very shortly marry my youngest son, Guildford Dudley."

There was silence.

"The king has approved it." Dudley's expression was one of piety. "It is an honour to link my house with that of the great house of Suffolk."

454

Thomas, shocked, could only gasp at the sheer ambition of John Dudley. He had organised a union between his son and Lady Jane, so he could rule, for as long as possible, through the two young, inexperienced people, such was his lust for power.

"Of course, at present, my daughter is stubborn, and says she desires to remain single. But never fear, my lord." Suffolk nodded cheerful assurance towards Dudley. "She shall be whipped until she performs her daughterly duty."

"Poor child," Thomas could not help muttering.

Suffolk heard him. "Oh, she shall do as I bid her, my lord Archbishop," he stated grimly. "She knows her duty towards her house and family."

Wriothesley had uttered very little throughout the meeting, but agreed to support the matter when it was laid before the entire council. Thomas remained cautious. He would not commit himself to either Jane or Mary. Ridley thought likewise and asked for time to contemplate the issue.

"I require you to make your decision in readiness for the next Privy Council meeting, which is in four days' time," Dudley snapped. "Meet again with the lawyers; talk with them."

Edward, looking stooped and frail, managed to summon enough strength to speak. "At the next council meeting, our sisters shall be declared bastards again, therefore, they cannot take the throne. Our cousin's birth is unquestionable." He began to look around the room; his regal act swiftly evaporating. "Where is my nurse?" He became fretful. "I need Mistress Penn!" The words were followed by a fit of coughing, followed by a stream of black mucus, which dribbled lethargically down his chin. At that moment, a vigorous figure of a woman rushed into the room. Effortlessly, she scooped the fragile king into her arms, and without further ado, carried him into the bedchamber next door.

455

Thomas felt choked with emotion; glancing at Ridley, he realised that he too was similarly affected. The expression of peaceful contentment upon the king's face, as that devoted motherly nurse picked him up, spoke volumes. Like Barnaby Fitzpatrick, she loved him for being Edward, not because he was king.

The lawyers were looking expectantly at the silent, austere figures of the Archbishop of Canterbury and the Bishop of Durham. One of them asked, "where do you wish to speak with us, my lords?"

"We can find an empty anteroom," Thomas replied, eager to escape the vile air of the king's chambers.

"Of course." Dudley rubbed his hands together briskly. "As you wish. Fitzpatrick will escort you to a vacant room. Meanwhile, I shall leave you learned gentlemen together."

"My lord, when you summoned me, just a few nights ago, were you aware then of this marriage between your son and Lady Jane?" Thomas found some pleasure in Dudley's look of discomfort.

"I had an inkling," he explained cautiously. "But I could say nothing because it was not a signed agreement. You must understand that."

"But the girl has said no," Ridley reminded him.

"She will do as her father wishes." Dudley's voice was curt and cruel. "They will be married by the end of this week."

"I would remind you that it shall be Jane who is monarch, not your son," Thomas remarked quietly.

Without uttering another word, Dudley stalked furiously out of the room.

Thomas and Ridley spent a number of hours closeted with lawyers, who verified that Lady Jane Grey could lawfully ascend the throne, and assured them that there was nothing irregular

456

in signing the Will of King Edward. But no lawyer could soothe Thomas' conscience. King Henry had left the throne to Edward, Mary and Elizabeth, in that order. The lawyers reiterated, time and time again, that Edward, as king, could leave the throne to whomsoever he wished, and Thomas could see the truth in this. The throne did indeed belong to Edward; he ruled by the will of God, and he should be obeyed... but King Henry had also ruled by the will of God. For some reason, it felt wrong to flout his instructions.

The following day, Ridley joined his friend at Lambeth Palace. Only Thomas, as Archbishop of Canterbury, was required to sign the king's Will, but he was grateful for Ridley's counsel. When Ridley departed, Thomas knew he would sign the document, however much it might trouble his soul. The defining fact was, if Mary ruled, the Reformation would come to a grinding halt. As for the pious but dying king, his chief concern had always been the wellbeing of the Protestant Church, and if he felt the fledgling Church was safe, he could die peacefully. For these reasons, he travelled to Court and reluctantly witnessed King Edward's Will, placing his signature on the document, next to Dudley's.

A few days later, the Privy Council met again, and it was declared that the Princesses Mary and Elizabeth were once again bastards, and thus erased from the line of succession. This was an act which was to be kept strictly secret until the king died. If it were to be made public, the princesses would have time to protest, or even lead a revolt.

As spring moved into summer, the frail king still lingered, and at the very beginning of July, he showed himself to his people for what would be the last time, waving from one of the palace windows. Unsurprisingly, the people of London were horrified by his emaciated appearance; some of those who beheld him wept.

On the sixth of July, Thomas was once again summoned to the king's bedside late at night. Edward's breathing had become shallow and quiet, and as he entered the royal bedchamber, he found the young king lying in the arms of one of his favourite Gentlemen of the Bedchamber, Sir Henry Sidney. The boy was mumbling incoherently, seeming to take peace and comfort from Sidney's calm presence. The king's page, Barnaby Fitzpatrick, and his nurse, Mistress Penn, stood nearby, occasionally patting Edward's hand, or stroking his hair. Suddenly, the king fell silent, and all those present held their breath, waiting for his breathing to return. It did not.

With tears trickling down his face, Sidney gently released the young king and laid him on his bed, whilst Mistress Penn, tears falling down her ruddy cheeks, solemnly closed Edward's eyelids

Wiping tears from his own eyes, Thomas turned away, leaving the king with his two most faithful servants, Barnaby Fitzpatrick and Mistress Penn.

Sidney, who was now sobbing, accompanied Thomas from the death chamber. "The last thing he said to me was, 'I am faint; Lord have mercy upon me, and take my spirit'," Sidney whispered hoarsely. "I tell you, my lord Archbishop, I never saw anyone die so bravely, or with such dignity."

"He trusted in God. God supported him," Thomas replied simply. At that moment, his arm was seized by the firm grasp of John Dudley.

"My lords, I must speak with you. Both of you. Please, do not mention the king's death to anyone yet. It must go no further than the death chamber, for the time being."

This was the second time he had been in this situation, and he felt just as uncomfortable now as he had when the young king's father had died. "His illness was no secret," he objected.

"But his death must be... at least for a few days," Dudley insisted. "Now is the time for me to summon his sisters to Court. I shall tell them that he is sinking fast and wishes to see them. When they arrive, they shall be placed in the Tower." Dudley smiled slyly. "Once they are in the Tower, Lady Jane will be safe from them."

"My lord, that is wrong. King Edward's Will clearly bequeaths his throne to Queen Jane, as she is now. It is not necessary to imprison the princesses," Thomas protested. It was ludicrous. They were both daughters of a king and deserved respect. Furthermore, they had done nothing to merit being imprisoned in the Tower.

Sidney, looking perplexed, nodded agreement with the archbishop.

"There is no harm in a short delay," Dudley declared. "If necessary, I shall imprison everyone who was present at his death, if they will not keep silent."

"I want your word that the princesses shall be treated well," Thomas requested urgently, uncomfortably recalling Dudley's word was rarely binding.

"I am not a man who will mistreat women," Dudley looked affronted. "They shall be treated in accordance with their status as the bastard daughters of the late King Henry. They will be lodged comfortably and will be released once Jane is established on the throne. Remember, my lord Archbishop, they are no longer princesses. They are bastards and are to be referred to as Lady Mary and Lady Elizabeth."

"I see that we do not have much choice in this matter," Sidney muttered. "But as my lord Archbishop has observed, it is wrong to imprison them. They must be released as soon as possible."

Two days later, there was no sign of either Mary or Elizabeth arriving in the city. According to the messengers, Elizabeth had declared herself ill, and had taken to her bed. As for Mary, she had been stopped enroute from her house in Hunsdon, and had been warned that King Edward was already deceased. She had immediately stopped travelling, and her current place of lodging was unknown. With both sisters unattainable, they had no recourse but to announce the death of the king.

Lady Jane Grey, now married to Dudley's son, was promptly proclaimed queen, and a couple of days later a huge banquet was held at Westminster Palace in her honour. However, to the surprise of those present, the most eminent people there, namely John Dudley, his son Guilford, and the new queen, looked most discontented. Indeed, John Dudley was furious, for not only had he failed to capture the two bastardised former princesses, but Queen Jane was refusing to pander to his demands. That day, having been shown the new crown she was to wear, she had made it clear that no similar headpiece was to be made for her husband. Guildford Dudley would not be receiving the crown matrimonial, nor would he be addressed as King Guildford. Meanwhile, a rumour was circulating that the marriage between Jane and Guilford had not been consummated, putting both Guilford and the Dudleys in an uncertain position. To his intense frustration, John Dudley had no control over these matters. The new queen herself had an air of dutiful resignation about her; she kept fidgeting with the crown she was wearing, finding the weight unfamiliar and uncomfortable, and throughout the evening, she did not smile once.

Just as the banquet was ending, a messenger arrived with a message for the queen. As Dudley extended his hand to take it, Queen Jane insisted upon receiving it personally. Snubbed, Dudley tried, with limited success, to arrange his features into a benign expression. Eventually, Jane passed it to him. It stated that the Princess Mary had been lodging at Kenninghall but was now heading to the heavily fortified Framlington Castle. He did not fail to observe that Mary had been referred to as 'Princess' Mary.

Dudley quickly beckoned for the key members of the Privy Council to follow him into an anteroom, before promptly demanding the opinions of those gathered.

"Mary has always been popular in the south-east," Thomas mused aloud, receiving an impatient glance from Dudley.

"Yes, which is why I need advice." Dudley's expression was sour, as though the contents of his wine cup had turned to vinegar.

"She could be planning to contact her uncle, the Emperor Charles?" Wriothesley suggested.

"Framlington Castle is heavily fortified. She might be planning to fight for the throne," Jane's father, the Duke of Suffolk, contributed.

"Then I must raise an army," Dudley stated crisply. He was a man who was unafraid of conflict.

The next day, Margaret reported to her husband that the mood of the Londoners had turned ugly. The general populace – whom Henry VIII had always known were responsible for keeping the crown on a monarch's head – disliked seeing Princess Mary, whom they considered to be the rightful queen, overlooked. In response, Thomas retired to his library, and began writing letters to the German Protestant scholars who were taking refuge in England, informing them that England

461

might soon be unsafe for them. He suggested they should prepare to leave for Germany, unless they deemed it too risky, in which case they should seek refuge in Switzerland. Ralph Morice, entering the library, found his master writing frantically.

"Permit me to write some of those letters." Morice was quick to realise what would happen if Mary should ascend the throne. England would no longer be a place of refuge for reformists.

The two men wrote in silence for several hours, until a messenger arrived from Greenwich, holding in his hand a letter, informing the archbishop that John Dudley had raised an army and was heading towards the south-east, his intention being to halt the Progress of Lady Mary. As for Lady Elizabeth, she was still allegedly clinging to her sick bed.

During the next few days, he rarely left Lambeth Palace, waiting anxiously for the outcome of the battle to be decided. There was an air of tension everywhere, not just at Lambeth; Margaret revealed that one of the servants had told her the atmosphere in London was equally strained, though there was also an air of excitement and expectancy. The Londoners felt Princess Mary had been badly treated by Dudley – who had rapidly fallen from his pedestal – and they now gave their support to the person whom they considered to be the rightful Queen of England.

"What news do you have, my husband?" Margaret asked one July evening, as they sat out in the gardens of Lambeth. Her husband looked preoccupied and worried, which was not unusual, but the sadness in his eyes concerned her. "It is not good news?" she prompted.

"No, the news is not good. Princess Mary's supporters are steadily increasing in number, and are nearing London. As for

Dudley's army, many men are defecting, and joining the princess. I doubt if Jane will remain queen for much longer; the people regard it as an injustice that Princess Mary has been deposed. I very much doubt that this is a battle Dudley can win."

Margaret looked at him earnestly. "If Princess Mary becomes queen, will you resign as Archbishop of Canterbury?"

"No, I cannot resign. I cannot let everything that has happened during the past six years of King Edward's reign be cast aside. But you..." His voice broke; taking her hand, he squeezed it gently.

"I will remain with you," she assured him, guessing his thoughts.

"You and the children must go to Zurich."

"I will not go, but the children shall... I will join them later," she reasoned.

"You must go. The children cannot go without you. I will join you when things settle here, when I have made it clear that I cannot apologise for the reformation of the English Church." He suspected he would probably never be permitted to leave England, let alone travel to Zurich, but earnestly he prayed that somehow, God would find a way. "We shall only be separated for a few months. For the children's safety, you must leave as soon as possible. I will write letters for you to present to Calvin and Zwingli; they will see you are cared for until we meet again." This was a good strategy, he knew that. She would only leave England to ensure the safety of the children.

"I will not leave until we are certain Mary is queen," she informed him, in a tone that meant nothing he could say would persuade her otherwise. "Mary may prove to be lenient," she optimistically suggested. "Perhaps she will be so delighted to be queen that she will leave the Protestants alone?"

He was certain that the opposite would be the case. Mary would restore the Catholic faith, and seek to punish those who had allowed her to be usurped... those who had signed King Edward's Will. He might have saved her life once, but he had also declared her mother to be unlawfully married to King Henry. He had declared Mary a bastard, twice. He knew she would never forgive him for those slights; Mary had always been one to bear a grudge. All he could do was cling to the hope that once he had spent some time in prison, she would have mercy, and cast him out of England. He would much rather be an exile than dead.

"What do you think shall befall Queen Jane?" Margaret's voice was almost a whisper. "Poor young girl."

"Even her parents have deserted her, to save themselves and their estates," he replied, also in a whisper. "Princess Mary has always been fond of her, despite her Protestant beliefs. I pray to God this affection will save the young lady."

"And I pray to God that she will spare you," Margaret exclaimed, burying her face against his shoulder to hide her tears.

Chapter Twenty

It was a time of unease and apprehension. Two weeks had passed, and Queen Mary had now victoriously seized the throne of England. From Lambeth Palace, he had heard the joyful clamour of the people as she had been ceremoniously escorted into the city. Riding in procession through the city gates, and progressing through the streets, she had cut a regal figure as crowds of ecstatic Londoners sang her praises and cheered, overjoyed to see the rightful queen taking the throne. The cheers of the people had been accompanied by the ringing of church bells, and whilst men had doffed their caps, women had hurled flowers at the radiant queen.

To his relief, he was informed that Mary had at least been merciful to Lady Jane. The girl, along with her husband, were placed in separate cells in the Tower of London. Her life, according to the information he had received, looked likely to be spared. Jane had ruled for a mere nine days.

John Dudley, on the other hand, having surrendered to Queen Mary, had been promptly accused of treason. In a vain effort to appease the new Catholic queen, he had declared himself to be Roman Catholic again. This achieved nothing, indeed, it only served to earn him contempt from both the Catholic and Protestant factions. Immediately after entering the

465

city, Mary ordered Stephen Gardiner to be released from the Fleet Prison, and Thomas Howard, Duke of Norfolk, to be released from the Tower, thus making it abundantly clear she intended to reinstate the Catholic Church in England.

Despite the disruption, as Archbishop of Canterbury, Thomas was still expected to officiate at the king's funeral in Westminster Abbey. Edward had stated his desire for a Protestant ceremony, whilst his sister desired a Catholic Requiem Mass, so there was a significant delay while it was decided how best to proceed. Having died on the sixth of July, it was not until the eighth of August that the young king was finally laid to rest; the first monarch to be buried using the English Prayer Book. As Thomas travelled to the ancient Abbey to conduct the service, he fervently prayed that King Edward VI would not be the last, and that future monarchs would also abide by the true Protestant faith.

It was the most poignant funeral service he had ever conducted, not only because of the tender age of the deceased, but also because he feared for the future of the Protestant Church which Edward had so loved. He, along with many others, had worked hard to bring the Protestant faith to England. What was going to happen under Queen Mary? He was aware that, whilst he was conducting the Protestant service at Westminster, Stephen Gardiner was holding a Catholic service for the late king at the Tower of London, in the Chapel of St. John, at the queen's behest.

After the king's burial, he returned to Lambeth and anxiously awaited the new queen's next move. Margaret had now left for Zurich with the children; their parting this time had been particularly painful, as they had no idea when, or if, they would see each other again. His dearest wish was that Queen Mary would, at some point, exile him to Switzerland; this he could accept, as it would not compromise his beliefs. Realistically, he doubted that wish would ever be granted. That wish was but a dream. John Dudley was massively despised for reverting to Catholicism; even Catholics regarded him with a mixture of contempt and suspicion. As far as Thomas was concerned, any public figure who spontaneously changed faith damaged the Protestant cause, instilling doubt amongst its followers, especially new converts. As Archbishop of Canterbury, he had to stand firm, a stance which both Hugh Latimer and Nicholas Ridley agreed with. Like him, both Latimer and Ridley were simply waiting to see what would happen next. They did not have to wait long.

Shortly after King Edward's funeral, a rumour was circulated that Edward's burial had been conducted according to Catholic rites. No one knew where it originated from, although Stephen Gardiner was an obvious culprit. Whilst it was a fact that Gardiner had conducted a private Mass in the Tower of London for the queen's benefit, this Mass had not been the king's actual funeral service. It had been a Service of Remembrance, which was a totally different event. Thomas felt duty-bound to respond, producing a counterstatement refuting the rumour, which he intended to personally read aloud at St. Paul's Cross. King Edward had been devoutly Protestant; such a Protestant figurehead could not be alleged to have been interred with anything other than Protestant funeral rites.

"This is stern stuff, my friend. It will provoke a reaction," Latimer remarked, as he sat with this Thomas in the library at Lambeth, reading over his friend's statement. Thomas Cranmer might come across as a timid man, but Latimer knew he could stoutly defend his opinions when it was necessary to do so.

"I tried to caution him against it, but he wouldn't listen," Ralph Morice admitted, looking pointedly at the archbishop.

467

Like his companions, Morice was finding this waiting period intensely stressful.

"I know," Thomas muttered. He looked strained and anxious, which was hardly surprising given the rapid changes during the past few weeks. "But what else can I do? I must defend the beliefs I hold dear."

"Quite," Latimer agreed. "I too must defend my beliefs." There had been many times during his life when he had felt himself to be in danger, mostly during the reign of King Henry. But at least he, and other Protestants, had been aware of what Henry did and did not approve of, and what the punishment was likely to be. Now, everything was uncertain. They knew Queen Mary was devoutly Catholic, but they did not know what she was capable of doing, or how far she was willing to go to ensure Catholic domination. Undeterred, Latimer continued to do what he had always done, and his public preaching continued to draw large crowds.

On the fifth of September, the Archbishop of Canterbury spoke at St. Paul's Cross, and the queen reacted with more speed than he had anticipated. Within a few hours, a servant rushed into the library at Lambeth to inform him that a barge was docking at the landing step, and men at arms, wearing the royal livery, were disembarking. Thomas had just enough time to bid an emotional farewell to his faithful secretary, before he was immediately escorted to the royal barge.

As he was removed from his London home, he knew Morice was in the library, gathering together some of his master's writings, and as many books as he could, for safe keeping. This was something they had already discussed; Morice had been adamant that, should the worst happen, he would preserve as many books and writings as he possibly could. Soon, Thomas Cranmer would no longer be Archbishop

468

of Canterbury, that was a certainty. His successor would be Stephen Gardiner, and Gardiner would joyously burn anything he considered heretical… which encompassed most of the contents of the Lambeth Palace library. It was some comfort to know that Morice would try to preserve some of his most well-used and valuable tomes.

The journey to the Tower was eerily silent; broken only by the familiar sound of oars dipping in and out of the water. The oarsmen were solemn and uncharacteristically mute. Eventually, the barge docked with a dull thud at the water steps, known to the Londoners as 'The Traitors Gate'. He was following in the footsteps of Thomas More, Catherine Howard, the Earl of Surrey, Bishop Fisher, Edward Seymour, and, of course, his friend Cromwell. None of them had lived. Anne Boleyn had been accorded the dignity of making her final entry via the Court Gate, in the Byward Tower.

Once in his cell, he immediately made a requested for writing materials, which was granted. Wasting no time, he promptly began to write a defence for himself, to be addressed to the Privy Council, in anticipation that it would be read at the next council meeting. By late evening, he had completed it.

'I have been well exercised these past twenty years to suffer and bear evil reports quietly,' he wrote. 'But when untrue reports and lies cause God's truth to be hindered, they cannot be tolerated or suffered. If Her Grace, the queen, will give me leave, I shall be ready to prove against all who say to the contrary, that the book of Holy Communion, set up by the Godly King Edward, is conformable to the order which our Saviour Christ commanded us to observe. The Mass, in many things, not only has no foundation in Christ, His Apostles, or the primitive Church, but also is manifest contrary to the same, and contains many blasphemies in it.'

469

He closed the letter by apologising for signing King Edward's Will, stating, 'my heart was penitent and sorrowful for this'.

His room in the Tower was not a cell as such, and though it lacked luxury, he could endure it. He had other things to consider other than personal comfort. The current whereabouts of his wife was unknown to him. Was she safe? Were the children safe? As for being released from imprisonment, he doubted it would happen in the near future. His assumption was, he would be accused of heresy.

In addition to his statement of defence, he also wrote a personal letter to the queen, again apologising for signing Edward's Will, and offering to instruct her in the way of the Protestant faith. He received no response to either of his letters, languishing in the Tower for some days, awaiting news of when he would be brought to trial. So far, no one had uttered the word 'heretic' to him. However, he soon realised the Tower was steadily being filled with Protestants, so it came as no surprise when he was informed that he would have to share his cell with two other people. To his joy, which was almost immediately replaced by sorrow, his two fellow prisoners were none other than his dear friends, Nicholas Ridley and Hugh Latimer.

"My mind cannot decide whether I should laugh or cry at the sight of you," he greeted them. "I dearly wish you were both safe elsewhere."

"We could say the same of you," Latimer retorted, fixing him with a piercing but compassionate stare. "You could have escaped with your wife."

"I could not. It would have indicated that I did not accept responsibility for my own beliefs," he responded quietly.

Ridley chimed in. "It is the same for me. I refused to travel to Geneva; I followed the example of my archbishop. What of you, friend Latimer?"

"I was doing what I do best," Latimer replied, looking aggrieved. "Standing at St. Paul's Cross, explaining that Catholicism is utter heresy and imperils the immortal soul, until I was dragged away by the queen's soldiers."

The three friends looked at one another gravely.

"Do you think we shall survive?" Ridley asked solemnly.

There was a long moment of silence.

Eventually, Thomas shook his head. "I wish I could say otherwise. I have, during my days here alone, tried to be optimistic. But I fear the worst."

"Likewise." Hugh Latimer shrugged his thin, bony shoulders apologetically. "I truly believe I have preached my last sermon at St. Paul's Cross."

Ridley nodded, his gentle face calm and thoughtful. "Well, my friends, I think the wisest course of action is to pray."

*****

Intellectual as they were, the three men set about examining their beliefs, but after hours of talking and questioning, they found no reason to reject anything they believed in. They drew strength from one another, their confinement together tightening the bonds of friendship that already existed between them. They knew time was running out, but Latimer, in his typical fashion, robustly tried to rally their spirits, regularly reminding them that, as brothers in Christ, they would one day be reunited, not only in a better place, but in the arms of the mighty risen Lord. Ridley and Latimer had been summoned before a committee of senior Catholic clergy and declared to be

471

heretics, but so far, they had not been condemned. As for Thomas, he remained in their shared cell. Waiting.

By this time, the country had reverted to Catholic orthodoxy, meaning the Pope was no longer referred to as the Bishop of Rome, and was once again considered Head of the Church. As a result, the city of London was in turmoil; the Tower, the Fleet, Newgate, and the Marshalsea Prisons, were almost full to overflowing with Protestant supporters. Some of the married clergy had resigned and were living on the streets, homeless, whilst others callously cast their wives aside. The most powerful man in the clergy was Stephen Gardiner, now Chancellor of England, much to the chagrin of Sir Thomas Wriothesley, whom the queen deemed unsuitable for the position. Gardiner was so close to the queen that rumours were circulating about the possibility of them having an affair. Such salacious behaviour might be believable of Gardiner, but not the queen, whose prudery was well known.

In truth, the queen had her eyes set upon a bridegroom, and he was most certainly not Stephen Gardiner. Her choice was one Prince Philip of Spain, her cousin; since she was required to provide an heir to the throne, she reasoned that she might as well marry someone who would provide her with political stability. In her uniquely blunt manner, she explained her reasoning in a letter to the Privy Council:

'It is not for my own pleasure to choose where I lust, nor am I desirously in need of a husband. For God, I thank Him, I have hitherto lived a virgin, but if it may please God that I might leave some fruit of my body behind me to be your governor, I trust you would not only rejoice, but that it would be to your comfort'.

The Catholic members of the council agreed with this. If Mary died, the Protestant Elizabeth would take the throne.

Mary had to marry; she had to provide a Catholic son and heir. Her choice of Prince Philip of Spain, son of the Holy Roman Emperor, Charles V, was a grand alliance, but it was unpopular. Mary knew her mother had been a popular queen, so she could not envisage that the great nephew of Catherine of Aragon would be anything less than popular too. However, what she failed to appreciate, was the glaring difference between the two. As a woman, and wife to King Henry VIII, her mother had worn the crown matrimonial, and had not been expected to take any part in the actual ruling of the realm. A Prince of Spain, being male, would, everyone assumed, take over the leadership of England, and the people of England did not wish to be ruled by a Spaniard.

Mary's popularity, riding high during the first weeks of her accession to the throne, suddenly began to plummet. Even Stephen Gardiner, sensing the mood of the people, took it upon himself to advise her against the Spanish marriage. Instead, he recommended she should wed the aristocratic Cardinal Reginald Pole instead, providing, of course, that he was willing to resign his clerical office. Mary was dismayed, for unbeknownst to Gardiner, she was intending to overlook him and place Reginald Pole in the office of Archbishop of Canterbury. She did not wish to marry the man she had in mind for the archbishopric.

Regarding her sister, Elizabeth, Mary knew that they could not both be legitimate, therefore she promptly wrote to her, explaining that, regretfully, Elizabeth was now a bastard again. Unfortunately for Mary, this only increased her sister's popularity; she had always been loved by the people, who now perceived her as having been unfairly snubbed and rejected by her sister, the queen. They did not care about the reason why only one sister could be legitimate, but they did care about Elizabeth being side-lined. Mary's popularity took another dip.

As the weeks and months passed, autumn turned to winter, and the Tower became so full of prisoners that it was impossible to adequately heat all the cells.

Knowing he was likely to be burnt at the stake, Latimer, who at the best of times had little padding on his bones, complained to a gaoler with his usual dry humour. "Sir, if you do not provide fuel for a fire, I am likely to defeat your expectations and freeze to death."

Their cell, however, remained cold, and although his companions tried to heap cloaks and blankets upon him, Latimer stubbornly refused to accept their largesse, lest they too should freeze.

It was during this glacial time that their gaolers informed them that the Act of Six Articles had been reinstated, which was sobering news for the three prisoners. The reintroduction of the Act meant anyone convicted of heresy would be executed. As for the queen's negotiations regarding her Spanish marriage, everything appeared to be progressing smoothly, especially since the Emperor Charles approved of the Act of Six Articles being passed. Then, to their interest, the prisoners were informed that a rebellion was brewing.

The group was headed by Thomas Wyatt, the son of the poet who had once been in love with Anne Boleyn. The rebels were not only upholding Protestantism; they were firmly against the Act of Six Articles, and the forthcoming Spanish marriage. According to the news Thomas and his friends heard from their gaolers, these people were marching through the streets of London, waving banners and shouting that they did not want to be 'under the rule of proud Spaniards or strangers!'

On the contrary, what they wanted, was for Lady Jane to become Queen.

Eager for more information, the three friends begged each gaoler who entered their cell for news of what was happening.

"Six hundred rebels have died," one amenable gaoler informed them, lingering for a cosy chat. "Including Master Wyatt. Unfortunately, I have also heard that Prince Philip of Spain... at least, I think he is a prince?" He regarded his audience questioningly.

In unison, the three prisoners nodded eagerly, desiring to hear what he was going to say next.

"Well, apparently, this prince person has told the queen that he will not marry her; not until she makes the throne secure by getting rid of Lady Jane. But I can tell you truly, that young girl had nothing to do with the rebellion. I've seen her; I've talked with her. I know she will not side with anyone, nor does she want to be queen."

"What will befall her?" Thomas wondered aloud. "It seems likely that the poor young maid will remain in the Tower for the rest of her life."

"Poor young thing. I doubt she likes her husband; he has written to her, asking to see her. It was I what gave her the letter." The gaoler was sitting contentedly on one of the few chairs, clearly happy to divulge information. "She wrote back to him, telling him she would rather wait until she sees him in heaven. It is believed he will be executed soon, on Tower Hill rather than Tower Green, because he isn't royal. The Dudleys aren't real aristocrats; his father, John Dudley, died on Tower Hill, and in my opinion, he were lucky. He ought to have been taken to Tyburn like any other commoner!'

The execution of John Dudley had come as a surprise to no one, other than Dudley himself. Thomas and his friends had learned that he had recanted of his Protestant faith, then proceeded to take the Catholic sacrament in the Chapel of Saint Peter ad Vincula, hoping to be spared. He had been executed the following day.

"They have no reason to execute Guildford Dudley though," Thomas objected. "The boy has done nothing wrong." He had simply obeyed his parents and married Lady Jane Grey... plus, if he was executed, what fate would befall his wife?

Ridley was clearly thinking the same thing. "But Lady Jane Grey... do you think she shall be spared?"

"That is a good question..." The gaoler prepared to leave. "I'll tell you good gentleman when I hears anything."

A week later, true to his word, the gaoler imparted grave news. "Sir John Bridges, the new Lieutenant of the Tower, has orders to be ready to erect a scaffold on Tower Green. There can only be one use for this: the poor little maid is to be executed." The gaoler shook his head sadly. "It's a real shame. I've seen a lot of executions in my time, but it's always sad to see a maiden perish. I hope they find a decent executioner to take her head off clean. I saw Catherine Howard die you know. She died bravely."

"She cannot die, it is not her fault that she was made queen. She had nothing to do with the rebellion," Ridley protested.

"But she is a focus for other rebels." Thomas' voice was husky with emotion. His hope that she would simply remain a prisoner in the Tower had been horrendously sanguine.

"It's tragic," Latimer murmured, having remained uncharacteristically silent. Using the sleeve of his gown, he unashamedly wiped his eyes.

"Well, I can't linger. I'd best be about my business. We have to prepare to receive even more prisoners." The gaoler opened the cell door with a sigh. "This place is overcrowded as it is."

In the end, there was no need for him to deliver news of Lady Jane Grey's execution. A few days later, the three friends heard the unmistakable noise of sawing and hammering; as the gaoler had stated, a scaffold was being constructed on Tower Green, and there was no doubt who it was for. The day after, in the early morning, they heard the equally tell-tale sound of mournful drums, signalling Lady Jane was being taken to the block. Silently, the three men stood, heads bowed in prayer, with tears unashamedly trickling down their cheeks.

"She died well," announced the gaoler, visiting their cell shortly after the execution. He was eager to describe the event. "Before her own execution, she watched out of her window as her husband was taken up to Tower Hill, then brought down again, a bloodied headless corpse. When she was taken out, she told the Lieutenant that her life had not been all that happy, so she was glad to go... well, it was something like that. She was a brave girl."

"She's at peace now." Latimer had compressed his lips together to prevent them from quivering. "What a vile act to do to such a good maiden."

"Indeed," agreed the gaoler. "She now lies between the Queens Anne Boleyn and Catherine Howard, and not far from the Dukes of Northumberland and Somerset... seems queer that those two men should lie almost together, given how much they hated each other."

*****

Apart from the lack of warmth, the three men had been treated well in the Tower, which they appreciated. Each day they anxiously awaited their fate. Would they be taken to trial? Would someone examine them for their beliefs? Nothing significant had happened so far, not since the day Latimer and Ridley had been informed that they were heretics. Then, shortly after Lady Jane Grey's execution, they were peremptorily informed that they were to be taken to the Bocardo Prison, Oxford. The implication of being taken to Oxford was not lost on any of them. Oxford was a Catholic stronghold. There would be little Protestant sympathy for them amongst their examiners and judges.

"I hope your memory is still sharp," Latimer warned Thomas, as they gathered together their meagre possessions. "We cannot guarantee that we shall be permitted books at Oxford."

"Certainly not Protestant books," Ridley concurred. "They probably won't have anything to do with Protestant books at Oxford."

"I suspect we shall not be allowed to speak up for The New Learning, but they will require us to be convinced of the old," Thomas surmised. That morning, he had finally been informed of the charges against him, namely treason and heresy. Ridley and Latimer had been charged solely with heresy. This information failed to surprise any of them.

"We have God Himself to support us." Ridley gave a gentle smile. "My friends, we shall never be alone. I implore both of you to remember this."

"I know." Thomas tried to return the smile, hoping his lips did not quiver as he did so.

"I understand you will be the first to be examined." Latimer squeezed his friend's arm. His hands were now gnarled and

478

arthritic; his weeks in the Tower had aged him considerably. Every movement was painful, yet his spirit was undaunted. The fire that had burned within him throughout his life, remained undimmed and bright. "Speak the truth according to the word of God, friend Cranmer."

He nodded slowly. "It is the only truth; I can speak no other."

*****

The journey to Oxford was slow, for the roads were thick with mud, constantly trapping the wheels of the wagon in a murky, sticky embrace.

"We might as well walk to Oxford," Latimer stated dryly. "It would be quicker for us, and easier for the horses."

Despite the rigours of the journey, the three of them relished the opportunity to be out in the open air. They had spent so much time in one room,   the simple things they had previously taken for granted – the sky, hedgerows, sheep... even the smells of cow byres and manure heaps – brought smiles of pleasure to their faces.

In due course, they arrived at the Bocardo Prison, and after spending months waiting in the Tower, it was immediately obvious that matters were about to move at a brisk pace. No sooner had the doors closed behind them, than they were informed they would all be examined very soon. Immediately, they requested books to assist them in their discussions, but their request was refused.

"As we suspected, it would seem we are not supposed to defend our Protestant faith, but rather we are to be convinced of Catholic ideology," Latimer murmured, as they were taken to their cell. At least, for now, they were still together.

The day following their arrival, the three were informed that they were to be examined; Thomas was to be taken first. Having waited so long for this moment, after spending weeks preparing his case, he now felt totally ill-equipped to tackle the task at hand. "I pray I shall find the words to say." His voice was a whisper. "Pray for me."

"We will," Latimer reassured him. "Remember, you have your vast knowledge to assist you. I was never interested in doctrines, so I must rely on my wits, but you have a wealth of information stored in your mind. I suggest you use it."

"My friend, you are as well informed as Ridley and I. Cast your modesty aside, and when your turn comes, you shall dazzle them with the truth of the gospel." After shaking hands with his two dear companions, he was escorted from their cell.

He held onto Latimer's assurances as he walked towards the interview chamber, and finally came face to face with his accusers. He had expected to be instructed to stand in the centre of the room, but he was instead offered a seat, and a cup of ale or wine, should he require it. Taken aback by their gentleness and respect, he thanked his accusers graciously and sat down.

The prolocutor was a certain Dr Weston, well known for his orthodox convictions; he opened the debate by stating clearly, the intention of the Court was to convince Thomas of Catholic truth and unity, 'of which you were once in that same unity'.

Weston fixed Thomas with a forthright stare. "But you are now separated from that unity, by teaching and setting forth erroneous doctrines. It has pleased the queen to send you, and your two companions, here, to recover your Catholic faith once more. These are the articles to be disputed." He handed some papers to a clerk, who passed them to Thomas.

"Will you sign these articles?" demanded Weston, after giving the prisoner time to read them.

"No," Thomas replied gently, laying the papers on a nearby table. They were strongly anti-Protestant, but he had expected nothing less.

There was silence in the room; his examiners regarded him expectantly, waiting for him to speak.

Finally, gathering his thoughts together, he spoke again. "As for unity, I am glad of it. It is a preserver of all commonwealths, heathen as well as Christian. I would be very glad to come to a unity if it were in the faith of Christ, and according to the Church of God." He sighed, spreading his hands apologetically. "The Protestant faith is often called *The New Learning*. But it is not new. It is ancient. It is the truth according to the word of God. It is the truth practiced according to the disciples of Christ Jesus Himself."

The examination continued in this manner for a couple of hours, with the clergy trying to convince him that the Catholic faith was the one true faith, whilst he tried to convince them otherwise. Unsurprisingly, his arguments were so sincere, and so grounded in biblical texts, that Weston was unable to confute anything the prisoner said. As the session ended, Thomas agreed to take the articles to his cell.

"If you give me leave, I shall study them, although I do believe my reply will not differ," he stated frankly.

To his satisfaction, Weston permitted him to have any books he required to assist him with his studies, and for that, he was immensely grateful. He would need the books, not only for academic purposes, but also for company; after weeks of talking, debating and sharing knowledge together, he and his friends were to be separated. It would be a sad moment, saying goodbye. Their lives had been intertwined for such a long time;

481

they had shared so much with one another, not just during their imprisonment, but over the course of many years.

When the time came, they stood helplessly, looking at each other, realising it was unlikely they would meet again.

"May we have some time to pray together?" Ridley asked of the guards.

His request was granted, and the guards courteously withdrew.

Inevitably, it was Latimer whose spirit upheld them. "We may not meet again in this life, but we *shall* meet in the next. My brothers, I rejoice in that glorious expectation. God bless both of you."

A couple of days later, Thomas was called upon to dispute with a man called John Harpsfield, who was not yet a Doctor of Divinity, but was recognised with respect by his colleagues. Unfortunately for Harpsfield, the prisoner's academic prowess far exceeded his own.

Taking pity on him, Thomas treated Harpsfield with his habitual kindness, prompting Dr Weston to remark, "Your gentle behaviour and modesty is worth much commendation. I give you hearty thanks in my own name, and in the name of my colleagues."

His eyes misted as everyone present stood up and doffed their caps in respect. During the journey to Oxford, as a prisoner, he had expected harsh words, even violence, perhaps. This courtesy was overwhelming.

The following day, Thomas, Ridley and Latimer were declared to be heretics, and would be condemned to burn as soon as the heresy laws were reinstated – which would be in the very near future. When informed of this by Dr Weston, Thomas momentarily felt numb, it was too much to take in. This was what he had dreaded ever since becoming a

Protestant; throughout the reign of King Henry, he had feared it, and now, it had finally come to pass. He would feel the unbearable heat of those flames. The burn of a candle or taper was painful, how would he endure the scorching heat of the fire? The thought of it made his knees tremble. The same fate would no doubt befall all the other Protestants who were crammed into the London Prisons – unless they recanted. It was a distressing thought.

His fate decided, he promptly wrote a letter to Margaret, though he did not know when, or if, she would receive it. He had written to her numerous times since being imprisoned in the Tower but had not received a single letter in return; he suspected her letters had been destroyed before reaching him. She had, at least, succeeded in sending a verbal message to Peter Martyr, who had visited him in the Tower, days before he was removed to Oxford. At least he knew that she and the children were well, and had reached Switzerland safely. Martyr had also revealed that his brother Edmund was also alive and well, and was currently living in Rotterdam. It had been a relief to know his family were safe, even if he was not.

Whilst in the Bocardo Prison, he heard from his gaolers that Protestant priests were recanting in large numbers, and more and more leading reformists were fleeing, including John Knox, who had bolted back to Scotland, declaring that, 'the nation has returned to idolatry'. After spending much of his adult life trying to achieve this one goal, it broke his heart to admit that his precious reformation of the Church now lay in ruins.

As for Queen Mary, now newly married to Prince Philip of Spain, she could not fail to recognise that her early popularity was evaporating rapidly. When she rode through the streets, the cheers were half-hearted, and men did not take the trouble to doff their caps. This was principally on account of her marriage;

everyone knew that Philip of Spain would end up ruling their country, instead of their queen. After all, a woman, once wed, must submit to the will of her husband. Furthermore, it was also known that Philip planned to bring the fearful Spanish Inquisition to England. Queen Mary was becoming more than seriously unpopular. She was close to being hated.

Unfortunately for Thomas and his friends, the heresy laws were swiftly repealed, having been forced through Parliament by Reginald Pole, who was due to become Archbishop of Canterbury, much to the resentment of Stephen Gardiner. On the first of October, in the Church of St. Mary the Virgin in Oxford, the three friends were tried separately: So far, although they had been told they were heretics and would burn, there had been no formal trial. Nicholas Ridley and Hugh Latimer were to be tried for heresy, Thomas Cranmer for heresy and treason. Naturally, all three of them refused to recant; all three of them were condemned to die. Thomas assumed they would all die together.

Two weeks later, John Harpsfield visited Thomas in his cell, as he had been doing since their debate.

"I hear Cardinal Reginald Pole has refused to accept the position of Archbishop of Canterbury, since the position is already filled by your good self. He says he cannot not take it until the present incumbent, yourself, is dead," he explained apologetically.

Thomas merely shrugged. Harpsfield's regular visits were a courtesy he appreciated; the man was compassionate and intelligent, and being in his company was a pleasure, even under the current circumstances. "That does not surprise me." He picked absently at the sleeve of his gown. "We three are all condemned now. It won't be long before we face the flames."

Harpsfield looked uncomfortable. "My lord Archbishop, if the three of you recant, you will be spared. I derive so much pleasure from your learned company, I would hate to lose you." His tone was deeply sincere.

"I thank you for that. I have likewise enjoyed your discourse," Thomas replied honestly.

Harpsfield looked at Thomas solemnly. "There is something else you must know, regarding your current position." He paused. "It is not the same as that of your colleagues. The three of you may have been tried and condemned just over two weeks ago, however, being Archbishop of Canterbury, you have been referred to the Pope in Rome for a second trial."

He regarded Harpsfield with an expression of surprise. This had not occurred to him, though it did make sense. Mary had delivered England once more into the arms of Rome, so it was only to be expected that the fate of the Archbishop of Canterbury would rest in the hands of the Pope himself. "It won't make any difference. I shall still be condemned to die either way," he replied.

Harpsfield shifted uncomfortably in his chair, looking like a man who had bad news to reveal, but did not know how to deliver it.

"Is something wrong?" Thomas asked.

"Your friends..." Harpsfield leaned forward earnestly. "I wish I could tell you otherwise, but they are to die tomorrow."

Thomas felt his mouth go dry, as though all the moisture had been sucked out of it. Searching for something to say, all he could manage was to inadequately murmur, "I pray their suffering will be quick."

"I too pray for that... or else that they may recant," Harpsfield replied quietly.

"I acknowledge your sincerity. You believe their souls shall be saved by recanting. I believe they will be saved by not recanting. I know neither will recant." Feeling his hands beginning to shake, he clasped them behind his back.

His voice was so low that his companion had to lean further forward to hear what he was saying.

He walked over to the small window of his cell, which looked out over the prison courtyard. For some time, he stood and stared, his mind elsewhere. Eventually, he asked, "at what time do they die?"

"Morning." Harpsfield's voice was husky; he dearly wished he could find something comforting to say to this kindly, elderly prisoner. "In the morning," he repeated, his voice a fraction stronger.

After a sleepless night spent in prayer, he heard a commotion in the corridor – the sound of a great many footsteps – and knew it was the guards coming to take his friends away to die. He had no means of looking into the corridor to witness their final departure. Some minutes later, as he was on his knees, earnestly praying, he heard keys rattling, and his cell door opened. A couple of gaolers stood there, with four men at arms. For a moment, he felt faint with shock. They had come for him; he too was to die.

"We are here to take you to the rooftop of this prison, Master Cranmer," the gaoler announced.

His heart was beating rapidly with shock, and the skin on his palms felt damp. "But why?"

"You are to witness the executions of your friends," came the gaoler's brief reply. "It will be taking place in the square near to this building."

Knees trembling, he stood upright. "But I don't want to.."

"You have no choice, Doctor Cranmer. Bishop Gardiner himself has decreed it.' The gaoler extended his arm towards the door, indicating that he was to leave the cell.

Stunned, he obeyed, following them along a bewildering maze of corridors and up several flights of stairs. He knew full well the reason why Gardiner had wanted him to witness the deaths of Latimer and Ridley. It was a terrible way to die; Gardiner would enjoy the idea of him witnessing their suffering, and the council would be hopeful that he would recant immediately upon viewing their grizzly deaths. At last, a door was opened, and he was led onto the roof of the prison. From this vantage point, he could clearly see the figures of his friends being led to the stake, situated near to the north gate of the city. Clutching the stone balustrade, his knuckles white with strain, he watched as they were bound. He could hear the low rumble of the crowd, dogs barking, and children shouting. From such a distance, he could not determine if bags of gunpowder had been fastened around their necks or not. Automatically, he closed his eyes in prayer.

"Master."

He felt an elbow gently nudging his ribs.

"Master, you are to observe. We must ensure that you see it all." The gaoler, not an educated man, but sympathetic nonetheless, looked apologetic.

He heard Latimer's voice, raised in prayer, then the voice of Ridley, also raised in prayer. The morning was damp and cool; not a trace of wind wafted through the still air. With rising nausea, he realised this was not a good day for anyone to burn at the stake. The faggots were likely to be damp, and the lack of wind meant the flames would be slow to rise.

As they began to light the faggots, his gloomy prognostication proved correct; the fire smouldered rather than burned. He flinched as he the screams of agony from his friends, especially Ridley, as the fire began to lick at their ankles. Someone – Ridley's brother-in-law, he later learned – began throwing extra kindling onto the fire, but this turned out to be an unwise decision, for the fire simply began to burn more ferociously around Ridley's legs. . His long-distance vision was poor, but he wished it were worse still; for even from his lofty position, he could just about make out Ridley's face, contorted in pain. Latimer was facing in the opposite direction, but though Thomas could not see his face, he could hear him calling out words of encouragement to Ridley. How typical of Latimer to try and raise his friend's spirits, even in such a situation as this.

It was then that Thomas noticed the behaviour of the watching crowd. They were silent, their heads either bowed in prayer, or facing the front of the courtyard, bravely watching the scene before them, with tears in their eyes and respect on their faces. Men had removed their caps in veneration, women were dabbing at their eyes with their aprons. When Ridley let out a blood-curdling scream of despair, the watching men and women gasped in horror, their faces full of compassion. It was of great comfort to him to know that the crowd were with him; that they could see the injustice of his friends' suffering.

He had no way of knowing how long it took for his friends to die; he only knew that personally he had never experienced such torment. At one point, it seemed Ridley had lapsed into welcome unconsciousness, but he soon revived, and began screaming again. Finally, Thomas could see Latimer sagging, his scorched body only held upright by the chains that bound him. A short while later, Ridley too fell silent, his suffering over. Even from the roof of the prison, he could smell the unmistakable stench of scorched flesh.

488

Shaken and sweating, he was glad to be returned to his cell, and immediately collapsed onto his bed, the trauma of the morning's events playing over and over in his mind. Half an hour later, John Harpsfield arrived, looking pale and sickly.

"I had to attend the burnings," he whispered. "I have seen executions before, but I have never observed a burning... I trust I shall never have to observe one again." His tone was fervent.

"I too beheld them, from the prison roof." Thomas also spoke in a whisper. After a lengthy silence, he finally asked, "Did they say anything?"

"Yes." Harpsfield licked his dry lips nervously. "Master Latimer died relatively painlessly; he was quickly overcome by the smoke. But before he died, he heard his friend's cries and shouted: 'Be of good comfort and play the man, Master Ridley! We shall this day light such a candle, by God's grace in England, as I trust shall never be put out.'. He was a truly exceptional man. They both were."

"I was privileged to know them for a very long time," Thomas choked. It was difficult to believe he would never speak with them or debate with them again.

"Master Latimer gave a devastating attack against the Catholic Church at his trial, you know," Harpsfield informed him, his tone confidential.

"That sounds like Latimer." He managed a brief, sad smile. "When he had an audience, he never wasted the opportunity to proclaim God's word to them. It was ever so. I never knew a man so pure and so fearless."

"Master Ridley walked to the stake wearing a decent black woollen gown." Harpsfield was silent for a moment, then, with a note of awe creeping into his voice, he informed his companion, "Master Latimer, he wore some shabby old thing.

Before he was attached to the stake, he took it off, revealing that he was wearing a shroud beneath it."

"That certainly sounds like Latimer. He had a sense of humour unlike any I have ever known. He never mocked; never aimed to hurt or wound; but he could be so very, very funny." Thomas could barely get his words out.

Tears were streaming down Harpsfield's cheeks. "I am sent to ask of you, will you recant?"

He sat in silence for a while, automatically beginning to pick at the sleeve of his gown. The gown itself had once been black, but during his months of imprisonment, the colour had faded, and the wool was now unevenly mottled with brown. In fact, it was more brown than black. A trivial thought passed through his mind: Margaret would have been so irritated by the state of his attire.

The sight and sound of his friends suffering had been more than enough to make him want to avoid the stake. However, the only way he could honour their memory was to stand firm, and proclaim the faith they so strongly believed in. He shook his head. "I cannot. I have witnessed something this day that will torment my waking and sleeping hours. I pray God will keep me strong and enable me to follow their example, if He wills it."

Chapter Twenty-One

As darkness fell on the day of Latimer and Ridley's executions, he looked towards the lighted candle in his cell. Baring his wrist, he cautiously extended it towards the flame, quickly drawing it back as the searing heat burned his skin. Hastily glancing around for something cool, he held his sore wrist against the cell wall. For a short while, its coolness soothed the inflamed skin. How was he to endure the heat of the faggots if he could not bear the pain of a candle flame? In this brief moment, he had endured only a fraction of the pain his friends had suffered. Especially Nicholas Ridley.

Trying to focus his mind elsewhere, he attempted to pray, but was haunted by Ridley's cries and screams. He did not doubt that such cries and screams would become increasingly familiar to the people of England in the near future, as more and more Protestants burned. It was believed by the Catholics, and various other religious denominations, that burning the body could save the soul. During their imprisonment, this topic had been discussed in depth by himself, Latimer, and Ridley, and they had unanimously rejected these theories. If a soul is impure before God, how does burning the body save it? But their accusers clearly thought otherwise.

491

Two weeks after the deaths of Latimer and Ridley, the Papal delegates arrived from Rome, and Thomas had to once again discuss the accusations made against him. Despite having slept very little since his friends' executions, once he faced the delegates, he managed rally himself to inform them, politely, that he would not recognise their authority.

"I will make my replies to the queen's proctors only," he informed them gently, adding almost apologetically, "I mean no offence towards you, the Papal representatives. However, the fact is, I do not recognise the Pope as Head of the Church, therefore I cannot submit to you, gentlemen."

The Papal delegates, equally politely, explained that their authority came from His Holiness, the Pope himself; but Thomas proceeded to persistently refuse to accept the Pope's authority. Consequently, that first meeting was swiftly concluded, and ended up being an utter waste of everyone's time.

Before he parted company with the delegates, they presented him with a pile of papers, advising him to study them closely once he returned to his cell. The papers turned out to be a list of sixteen charges against him. Once he had read them, then reread them, he put them aside and began to write his defence, working late into the night. He was, he realised, fighting to survive.

First on the list was the charge of treason. This he had expected; he had signed King Edward's Will, paving the way for Lady Jane Grey to become queen. This charge was followed by perjury and heresy, both of which he refuted. 'Recognition of Papal authority is not a natural situation for any queen or king, in any country', he wrote. 'This recognition makes the king or queen the same as their subjects within their own realm, and subject to justice at the hands of a stranger. Therefore, I present my case to the monarch of this realm. Under King Henry VIII, I took an oath to submit to the supremacy of the monarch. I have not perjured that oath. Your Majesty took two oaths at your coronation, one pertaining to the supremacy of Rome, and the other being to uphold the laws and liberties of your realm. It is impossible for any monarch to keep both oaths, for surely there comes a time when one shall contradict the other'.

Adultery was also high on the list, but refuting this was considerably more challenging. He had taken Holy Orders during his early days at Cambridge, which included a vow of celibacy. Although most priests had tended to ignore their vows of celibacy – Cardinal Wolsey was a prominent example –they were considered to be married to the Catholic Church. Upon embracing Protestantism and meeting Margaret, he had deemed those vows of celibacy void. They were part of the Catholic orthodoxy, and no longer relevant to him.

Upon his marriage, he had fully intended to resign his fellowship at Cambridge, but King Henry VIII had changed the direction of his life by making him Archbishop of Canterbury, which had placed him in a unique position. At that time, as a married Archbishop of Canterbury, he could have been executed. Also, if he had refused the position, he could still have been imprisoned, or even executed, should his marriage have been discovered. Instead, he had accepted the position, and used it to guide the Church to the Protestant truth. He explained this ae carefully and coherently as he could.

Finally, he declared himself to be no heretic. 'Truly, I do deny transubstantiation, and would inform Your Majesty that the Lord's Supper in the Eucharistic Service is no new innovation but is ordered by our lord Jesus Christ Himself. I am willing to travel to Rome to defend my cause, although I do not acknowledge Papal authority. I am confident in my ability to argue at length with any theologians in the Papal Courts, for I believe strongly in my own convictions and can plead a suitable case for myself'.

His letter, which was sent to the queen, received no reply. He was not surprised; so far, none of his letters to her had evoked any personal response or acknowledgement. During his years at Court, he had always regarded the then ,Princess Mary, as utterly her mother's daughter, possessing the same single-minded tenacity as Catherine of Aragon. Catherine had refused to look outside of the Catholic faith; she had never permitted herself to even consider the fact that there might be errors in her theology, and Queen Mary followed her mother in this. However, what he had not realised was that there was also a similarity between Mary and her father, the late King Henry.

On various occasions, King Henry had been given the opportunity to spare a life, but had not, because he considered the person in question to be a potential threat to his future as king. Anne Boleyn's revelation that she had been pre-contracted to Harry Percy should have saved her; but had she lived, her very presence might have cast doubts upon the validity of the king's next marriage. Therefore, she had to die. A few years later, Thomas Cromwell, whose life also could have been saved, was publicly executed, to restore the king's popularity. Cromwell had been a hated man; by killing an unpopular minister, the king, whose popularity was waning, regained the love of his people. Once Henry had decided that someone must die, there was nothing that could alter his decision. No signed documents or pleading letters swayed him. Queen Mary was not only the daughter of Catherine of Aragon, she was also the daughter of King Henry VIII. No letters would save Thomas from her now. She wanted him to die; his fate had been decided.

His final condemnation was delivered to him not only in front of the Papal delegates, but also in front of a panel of English bishops and theologians, headed by Bishop Brooks. It was Brooks who opened the trial by informing him that the Papal Courts declared him contumacious for failing to acknowledge them, and for being wilfully disobedient to Papal authority.

The atmosphere during this final examination was completely different to all the others he had endured. From the beginning, there was a chill in the air that had nothing to do with damp, cold weather outside; and every time he tried to speak, to explain himself or defend his position, Bishop Brooks would raise his hand, indicating that this was no time for interruptions.

"You are also to be stripped of your title of Archbishop of Canterbury," Bishop Brooks intoned. "Your final punishment, death by burning, shall be ordered by the English Courts," he concluded gravely.

There was a low murmur amongst the assembled dignitaries.

Bishop Brooks, sensing some people might be sympathetic to the prisoner, solemnly continued. "I will read out your sentence from the Pope." He coughed, clearing his throat. It was November, and his nose was streaming in a most undignified manner. "I, Pope Paul himself..." He bowed his head respectfully. "Sitting in the throne of justice and having before my eyes God alone, who is the righteous Lord, and who judges the world in righteousness, do make this definitive sentence. I pronounce that Thomas Cranmer is found guilty of the crimes of heresy and other excesses, and is found to be wholly unmindful of the health of his soul, having gone against the rules and ecclesiastical doctrines of the Holy Father, the apostolic traditions of the Roman Church and sacred councils, and the rites of the Christian religion hitherto used in the Church. By thinking and teaching otherwise than the Holy Mother Church preaches—"

At this point, Thomas, who had been seated, leapt to his feet and interrupted. "My lords, I have taught only the truth of the most holy gospels!"

His protests made no difference; he was condemned to be burned.

Unbeknownst to him, Queen Mary, Reginald Pole, and Stephen Gardiner, had all decided that it would be excellent Catholic propaganda if the first Protestant Archbishop of Canterbury recanted, and they were determined to go through with this endeavour. He was not to be executed just yet. As a result, two Spanish friars, Father's De Soto and John de Villa Garcia, were entrusted with the task of persuading him to recant of his Protestant heresy. It was hoped they would succeed before the ceremony of degradation took place, which would happen in just over two weeks' time. During this ceremony, Thomas Cranmer, Archbishop of Canterbury and Primate of all England, would be officially removed from office.

Every morning, these two friars visited him for several hours, and had those sessions taken place under more convivial circumstances, he would have enjoyed himself immensely. They were learned men, equally as learned as himself, and their meetings together were stimulating and challenging, not only for him, but for the friars also. All three men began to look forward to these sessions, which regularly continued for hours longer than their allotted time. However, they failed to alter his opinions, and he failed to alter theirs.

As far as the degradation ceremony was concerned, his feelings were in turmoil. He was not angry, nor was he fearful. He had not asked to be Archbishop of Canterbury, but he had fulfilled his duties to the best of his ability, encouraged learning, and setting a good example to other members of the clergy. He regarded himself as a man who would have been content to fill a teaching post in a university; that sort of life would have been one he would have been content to live. Margaret too would certainly have loved that sort of life.

Now, as his position was to be given to another, he could only submit to God's will. If His will was that he should endure what was a ceremony of mockery and degradation, then so be it. Had not Christ Himself undergone terrible mockery and torture? He was enduring nothing more than Christ, his master, had already suffered.

The ceremony required that he should be taken into an anteroom and robed in layer upon layer of clerical vestments, beginning with sub-deacon, then the deacon, priest, bishop, and archbishop, in that order. Each garment was made out of stiff canvas. The result was a multi-layered outfit that was so rigid he could barely move. His mitre was placed upon his head; the pallium over his shoulder, then his crosier was placed in his hand. Clad thus, he was led to Christ's Church for the ceremony to take place. It was a slow journey; his every movement was restricted, and each step was awkward.

Once inside the church itself, a list of the charges made against him was read out by Bishop Thirlby of Ely, with whom he had always enjoyed a cordial friendship. He remained silent during this, whilst Thirlby was moved to tears, his voice at times almost inaudible. Unfortunately, it was Thirlby's task, along with a couple of helpers, to remove the stiff layers of clothing. Thirlby performed the task with some difficulty, his hands shaking visibly, and Thomas' dignity only increased Thirlby's agitation. Ironically, it was he who had to comfort Thirlby. As this was happening, Bishop Bonner preached a sermon against the now former Archbishop of Canterbury. Bonner, he knew, was enjoying this entire proceeding.

The only time he broke his pensive silence was when his pallium was removed by one of Thirlby's helpers. Suddenly indignant, he demanded, "who has the authority to remove my pall?"

There was no one there who was senior enough to perform that duty. Only Reginald Pole, the next Archbishop of Canterbury and Primate of all England, could possibly remove the pallium, the symbol of office. In fact, it was debatable whether even Pole could lawfully undertake this, as he was not yet consecrated. Therefore, under canon law, this ridiculous ceremony could be judged invalid.

"We are the Pope's delegates, so our authority comes from him," Thirlby whispered.

"But I do not acknowledge the Pope," he replied, also in a whisper.

When Bonner began to endorse the validity of the Mass, again he voiced his opinion, refusing to pay heed when told to be silent.

When he had eventually been stripped of all his vestments and symbols of office, his former attire was replaced by the gown and cap of a yeoman bedell, a humble position for someone as educated as he. A yeoman bedell was required to perform minor duties at universities, such as collecting fines occasionally acting as town crier. He might even be required to empty the privies. In short, it was an insult to be thus attired.

Now that his part of the ceremony was dealt with, Bonner was unable to disguise his jubilation. "Now you are a lord no longer," he crowed.

"Those robes I never needed. I had done with them long ago," he responded quietly.

The ceremony continued, with Thomas being pushed into a chair so that a barber could shave his head. The purpose of this practice was to remove his priestly tonsure, but since he had grown this out long ago, it was simply a symbolic act. The tips of his fingers and his fingernails were also scraped, to symbolically erase any traces of holy oil that had been placed there during his consecration. Finally, it was over, and from the sleeve of the coarse shirt he had been wearing beneath the canvas robes, he pulled out a sheet of paper and turned to the officials and bystanders, who had observed the ceremony.

"I appeal to the next General Council," he announced clearly, waving the paper aloft. "Here I have comprehensively stated my cause which I desire may be admitted."

"My lord," Thirlby was visibly agitated. "Our commission is to proceed against you; we cannot admit it."

"It would seem that the cause is between myself and the Pope, since he has condemned me, or at least he has given the authorities permission to do so. It is unjust that I may not appeal," Thomas protested indignantly.

"Well, if it may be admitted, it shall," the sympathetic Thirlby whispered, extending his hand to take the paper. Eyes brimming with tears, he added, "should you wish for a suitor to present a case for your pardon, then I should be honoured to do so." Having taken the sheet of paper, written by the condemned man, he grasped Thomas' hand surreptitiously and gave it an encouraging squeeze.

Thomas' first concern was natural enough. He wished to prolong his life. Not long after the degradation ceremony, he was shocked to be informed that his long-time rival, Stephen Gardiner, had died. The concept of his rival not being alive to rejoice in his own degradation and death, felt strange and surreal.

In a last attempt to save himself, he continued working, desperately trying to complete another treatise against Stephen Gardiner's writings, even though the man himself was dead. At the same time, he also worked on a defence against the Articles of Accusation levelled against himself. He still met with the two Spanish friars on a daily basis, who continued to try all manner of beguiling arguments to convince him of their orthodox beliefs. For his part, he continued to attempt to convince them of The New Learning. So far, it was a stalemate.

"All noblemen bear you good will," De Soto informed him during one of their meetings. "Your release from prison would be highly acceptable to the queen. You could enjoy some dignity within the Church, or else enjoy the quiet life. All you have to do is sign this statement and agree to recant." He indicated towards a nearby sheet of paper.

The quiet life. It was a persuasive statement. Seductive even. He longed to see Margaret again; it pained him deeply to be apart from her and the children. In fact, he had never known a pain like it. But his heart was Protestant; it was a sincere commitment. Whatever he signed, his heart and soul would always be Protestant. He was also aware the queen had no good opinion of him, and very likely she had no intention of releasing him from his prison cell, even if he did recant.

"The queen is determined to have a Catholic Thomas Cranmer, or no Thomas Cranmer at all," De Villa Garcia warned.

He was silent, knowing that he could never be Catholic. If he said he belonged to Rome, it would be a falsehood.

Over the coming weeks he was regularly taken from the Bocardo Prison to Christ's Church, to debate with doctors and priests, and the promise of a pardon was always dangled before him. Several times he felt his resolve weakening, and subsequently buried himself in prayer and study, desperately trying to rebuild his mental resolve. The sight and the sounds of Ridley and Latimer burning – especially the cries of Ridley – haunted him. They could never be erased. He feared burning, yet they had submitted to it and triumphed. Surely, he could do likewise? Why was he so fearful? The pain would not last forever...

After several weeks of work, his appeal was complete, containing the complaint that he had neither been permitted a lawyer during his trial, nor had he been allowed to travel to Rome to launch his defence personally. He denied being a heretic, declaring, 'my only heresy, if it can be deemed such, is to refuse to accept words not accustomed in scripture, and unknown to ancient fathers, but newly invented and brought in by men'.

He was constantly harangued by the two friars, as well as by doctors and priests, who regularly pointed out that his wife and children were in Zurich, and that he might meet with them again, if only he would recant. This was the huge difference between himself and Latimer and Ridley. He had others to think of; it was ordained by God that a husband should take care of his wife and family. It was part of the Christian faith; marriage was a sacred thing and should not be taken lightly.

501

Latimer and Ridley had been single men.   Was Margaret managing to care for the children on her own? Did she have enough money to provide for them? Did they have a roof over their heads? He was the person responsible for their very comfort and wellbeing.

Such was the friars' persuasion, and his concern for his family's welfare, that eventually, after being worn down for weeks on end, he agreed to sign two documents of submission. Seeing these documents placed in front of him, he hesitated. The first was to the Crown, and the second to the Church and Rome. With a feeling of self-loathing, especially where the document of submission to the Church of Rome was concerned, he signed them, hoping this would be enough for the queen.   This was regarded by his accusers as a huge triumph, but shortly afterwards, Thomas was informed that the queen was dissatisfied. The only document she wished to see his signature upon, was the document of recantation.

"I have heard that she is an unhappy woman," De Soto, the most garrulous of the friars, informed him. "She believed herself to be pregnant, you know. She longs for a child, I have heard. But it transpires that she was not pregnant, and meanwhile her husband has returned to Spain. He has no plans to return to England in the near future. Poor dear lady."

"I have heard she loves him deeply." Thomas shook his head. "She is not likely to bear a child if he lives in Spain. Does she plan to join him there?"

"Oh no," De Soto assured him. "She has much to do here. Her sister, Elizabeth... well, the queen is under pressure to have the young princess imprisoned in the Tower. She too is suspected to be Protestant, you know. Also, she is popular."

The unuttered phrase 'Mary is not popular. Not anymore,' hung in the air. The people were looking towards Elizabeth, which was a dangerous situation for the young princess to find herself in. Elizabeth was clever. She was more than clever, she was cunning. He knew that. He deeply hoped this would save her life. He had heard a rumour – which he hoped was untrue – that Catholic Philip desired the death of the Protestant Elizabeth, who, if Queen Mary died without issue, would become queen. Elizabeth had always been popular; even the unfortunate incident with Thomas Seymour had failed to diminish that. As for Mary, he knew from the gaolers that she was hated by the common folk, who called her, 'Bloody Mary', and other such unsavoury names, on account of her willingness to execute her people.

De Villa Garcia wished to steer the conversation back towards persuading the former archbishop to convert to what, he considered, to be the true and rightful faith. "You are still lusty and strong. You might have five… ten… fifteen years left if you recant."

"I doubt it," Thomas objected. "I am nearing seventy now; an old man."

"An old man who does not need to burn. It is a terrible death. The queen has signed your warrant, but she shall gladly tear it up if you recant."

He Thomas eyed De Villa Garcia with suspicion. He was certain the queen wanted him to die. She and Reginald Pole just wanted him to sign that document so they could use him for Catholic propaganda… as an example to the masses.

"You owe your queen your obedience," De Soto added. "And you have told me you believe a monarch rules by God's Will, therefore a monarch must be obeyed. You are disobedient to your own belief."

This was a masterstroke. It had made Thomas uneasy that he was disobeying his monarch. After all, he had been obedient to King Henry, and also to King Edward. Yet he was now flouting an anointed queen. "But my heart tells me that the Catholic faith, which she so adheres to, is not according to the word of God. I will obey her in every other respect. But I cannot deny what God tells me to do. I must obey God first."

The two friars were regarding him sorrowfully.

"I have come to regard you both as friends," Thomas informed them sincerely. "I long for you to become Protestant, so I may save your souls." Seeing them shaking their heads in protest, he half smiled. "I wish you would reject transubstantiation and purgatory."

The headshaking became vigorous. "No, no. That we cannot do," De Soto exclaimed. "And if you persist in your heresy, you shall burn."

"But if you recant, you shall be reunited with your wife and children," De Villa Garcia added.

"But I would be recanting without deeply, sincerely, accepting Catholic doctrine. It would be a false recantation," Thomas objected.

"Well, yes..." De Soto hesitated for a moment. "But you can sign the document, go away with your wife and family, then try your best to accept Catholic dogma. One day, realisation will come to you, and you will understand that you do actually believe it." De Soto leaned back in his chair, looking well-pleased with this statement.

"It would be a pity for your intellect to be wasted," De Villa Garcia added.

"And for your vow of obedience to your monarch to be perjured."

"As we have said, if you recant, you shall have much time to study the true, Catholic doctrines, then accept them."

"If you study our doctrines, your recantation shall not be farcical. For you would at least be trying to accept them."

Thomas' lips were moving as if in prayer. "But I don't believe in purgatory," he protested.

Again, the friars regarded him sorrowfully.

There was silence in the room. His lips were still moving, but no sound came from them, until he whispered, almost inaudibly, "may God forgive me, but I will recant." As soon as he had spoken the words, he wept bitterly. The recantation was truly false. He did not believe or accept any of it. He was betraying not only himself; ultimately, he was he was betraying God! But he could not face those flames.

*****

Word was immediately sent to the queen that the former Archbishop of Canterbury had agreed to recant. A document had already been drawn up, and it was agreed Doctor Thomas Cranmer would sign it on the eighteenth of March. The Spanish friars informed him that there was great rejoicing for the salvation of his soul. When he died, he would now go to heaven.

Heaven. In order to spare himself from those flames, he had imperilled his soul. He could only pray that God would have mercy on his weakness. Alone, in his cell, he wondered if he would immediately be set free. He had an urge to flee with Margaret to somewhere very quiet, then change his name so no one would know it was he who had done such a great disservice to the Protestant faith. Although, of course, this was exactly the reason the Catholics had so eagerly urged him to recant. Glancing at the table in his cell, which also served as a desk, he saw the articles he had written against Stephen Gardiner. They were Protestant, totally Protestant. If anyone read those, they would certainly realise his signature on the recantation document was a means of saving his own life, and not a true recantation of faith.

On the eighteenth of March, at Christ's Church, several documents of recantation were placed in front of him. The intention was that a copy should be placed on the doors of a number of prominent places, including Christ's Church, Oxford; St. Paul's, London; and Canterbury Cathedral. As he signed them, a priest called Dr Cole, whom he vaguely knew as being Provost of Eton and a staunch Catholic, preached a sermon, the content of which he was too distressed to take notice of. The signing of the documents was witnessed by a joyful De Soto and De Villa Garcia. The whole ceremony was over in less than an hour, and without preamble he was returned to his cell.

Later, the two friars visited him. In tones of disgust, they informed him that people were already reading the copy of the recantation that had been placed on the door of Christ's Church, Oxford. They were claiming it was a forgery because his signature had been witnessed by Catholic friars. The supposition of the friars was, that wherever copies were placed, people would believe they were false. Learning of his, Thomas felt a certain sense of satisfaction, and prayed to God that the people would continue to believe that he had never signed those documents.

Unsurprisingly, he did not sleep well that night. He prayed; he wept; he tried to write a letter to Margaret, but his words were tear stained and illegible. He felt so ashamed and confused, the letter hardly made sense anyway. After ripping it up, he took to pacing backwards and forwards. By daybreak, he was exhausted. When the Spanish friars arrived, around mid-morning, his head ached.

The friars, at least, cheerfully rejoiced, and congratulated him that his soul was safe. When he died, it would rest with God.

"There is certainly a great deal of jubilation in Heaven at this moment," De Soto sincerely declared, his eyes misting with tears of joy.

"My signature is false," he admitted. "I do not, in my heart, accept Catholic doctrines. Take purgatory for example. Do I believe in it? No, absolutely not."

"Oh, you will in time." De Soto smiled happily. "It will come to you."

De Villa Garcia was less optimistic. "You can deceive us, but not God. He knows your heart. He knows your soul. Take care, study, and accept the truth. I will keep praying to the Blessed Virgin and the saints in Heaven. May the doors of your heart be opened." Bowing his head, he genuflected.

"I am praying for forgiveness for my weakness," he rubbed his brow wearily. Changing the subject, he enquired, "When shall I be freed?"

The friars exchanged glances. "I have heard nothing," De Villa Garcia stated, whilst his companion nodded agreement. "But I see no reason why it should not be very soon. After all, there is no reason why you should stay here."

"God willing, it shall be soon," Thomas sighed.

That day, he received no other visitors, and he began writing what he hoped was a coherent letter to Margaret. Once again, he tore it up. He felt ashamed to tell her he had recanted. Yet she, he knew, would understand; she had always understood and supported him. The following day, the friars did not visit, but he was surprised to receive Dr Cole, the Provost of Eton, who had preached as he signed his recantation.

"I am here to ask if you intend to remain firm in the faith of Rome?" Cole, a gentle, refined man, looked strained and anxious.

Thomas wondered if the friars had been passing information to Cole, telling him that he was still Protestant at heart. "I will do so," he replied, feeling sheepish for the statement was utterly untrue.

"And what of money?" Cole looked more than anxious now. He looked downright uncomfortable. "Have you any left that can be dispersed?"

He felt the blood rush from his face. This was a question usually asked of a prisoner who was condemned. It was customary to give coinage to the executioner. Or, in the case of burning, to the persons who would light the fire. Also, it was anticipated that well to do persons would distribute alms to the poor too, as a final act of kindness. "I have no personal money," he whispered through lips that were stiff and all but paralysed. He had been promised a pardon, why was he being asked this?

Cole, looking nearly as shocked as his companion, began, "I will give you some crowns to disperse amongst the poor before you die. You see..." He stopped and tugged at his collar, as if it were strangling him. "You see... you are... you are to die tomorrow. At the same place as the heretics, Latimer and Ridley. You must prepare a final statement of contrition to be read before you go to the stake. As for myself, I must preach a sermon." He looked utterly miserable.

Thomas digested this information, sitting stock still on his prison bed, his face pallid, his mind numb. What a fool he had been. The promise of life was false; it had always been false.

What wonderful propaganda it was, to burn a   former Protestant Archbishop of Canterbury, who had recanted of his faith. The two Spanish friars... perhaps they had known all along that he was to die... perhaps they had not. But they had certainly been persuasive, and he had optimistically allowed himself to be persuaded. He had wanted to be persuaded. He had wanted to live. How could he have been so foolish to believe that they would allow him to do so?

Cole did not linger for very much longer; he hardly knew what to say. After waiting in silence for a few more moments, he quietly departed, leaving the shocked prisoner to prepare his final declaration.

Left alone, once he was able to move, he paced his cell, his mind still numb. He had hoped to live, yet a logical part of his mind – which he had optimistically ignored – had always whispered that Queen Mary could not, would not, permit this to happen. She was King Henry VIII's daughter; she would not pardon him. All he had done was lengthen his life by a few months, damaging the Protestant Church in the process. Slowly, as his mind cleared, it began to dawn on him that he could at least do something to strengthen the cause. It was still possible that he could die a Protestant; he could let people know he despised himself for his weakness. He could, and would, die true to his faith.

As was his way in times of crisis, he resolutely began writing. Whenever anyone knocked upon the door, he would hastily hide his speech in his sleeve, lest it should be confiscated, but the only other visitors he received that day were his gaolers. He also wrote to Margaret; his last letter to her. He wondered if she would receive it? It was a difficult letter to write, even more difficult than his final declaration. He settled for something short. A genuine proclamation of his love for her and the children, and his thanks for the happiness their union had brought to him. Finally, he commended them to the love and care of Almighty God. It was enough; it was too painful to write any further sentiments to her. She and the children were in God's hands now.

His last night on Earth seemed to pass more swiftly than any other. Early in the morning, the friars appeared with yet another recantation for him to sign. He was about to refuse, then suddenly realised if he did not sign it, he might be taken directly to the stake and given no opportunity to address the crowd, for there would surely be a crowd. An execution brought people from their homes in droves. Almost cheerfully, he gave what he knew would be his last ever signature on a document, then, shortly afterwards, he was escorted to St. Mary's Church.

As he departed from prison, his heart sank. It was raining steadily, meaning the faggots would be damp and would take time to ignite. Crowds had gathered in spite of the inclement weather, as he had known they would. The church was so full of people that they were spilling out onto the steps outside. The crowd was sympathetic; even those who were inclined towards Catholicism were compassionate. It was a dreadful way to die; they had witnessed the deaths of Latimer and Ridley, and most people were aware that the number of Protestant martyrs was growing by the day. They could lose friends and relatives who were sympathetic to The New Learning. Watching a martyr burn was totally different to watching a felon perish. Most people did not regard Martyrs as criminals. Criminals were a totally different spectacle to watch; their deaths were as entertaining as bear baiting and cock fights.

The smell of damp garments greeted him as he was escorted to the front of the church, where a platform had been made for

510

him to stand upon. Suddenly, he realised that he no longer feared the flames; such was his determination to refute that obscene document of recantation, his dread had totally vanished. Praise be to God.

Dr Cole stood up to preach his sermon, the substance of which was not dissimilar to that which had been preached by Bishop Bonner at the degradation ceremony. It was a declaration of the Church of Rome, the authority of the Pope, and the necessity of every person to submit to this. He heard a rumble of muted, discontented voices, as Cole preached. In a moment of triumph, he realised that some members of the congregation were Protestant. Then, at last, it was his turn to speak. Having knelt and prayed before Cole's sermon, he briefly knelt again, then stepped onto the platform.

For a brief moment, he was silent, taking in the atmosphere, the tension of the crowd. Then, taking a deep breath, he began to speak, reciting the Lord's Prayer in a voice that was melodious, calm, and steady. It was as if he were back in Cambridge, or Canterbury, addressing his clergy and students.

"Every man desires, good people, to give some good speech at the time of his death that others will remember after he has passed, and be better for hearing it."

The church was silent, apart from the occasional smothered cough or clearing of the throat. A sea of faces was turned towards him, their eyes steadily fixed upon him, waiting to hear his words.

"So, I beseech God to grant me grace, that I may speak something at this, my departing, whereby God might be glorified, and you edified." He began to warn the congregation against loving false things of the world, instructing them to love each other – even their enemies – as brothers and sisters. He

511

also advocated that they love and serve their monarch and learn and profit from scripture.

Turning his head slightly, he noticed De Soto and De Villa Garcia exchanging glances with Dr Cole. This was not the script they had expected. However, so far, he had said nothing controversial; they anticipated he would shortly proceed to proclaim his recantation.

"I have come to the end of my life, and upon this hangs all of my past life, and my life to come, either to live with my Saviour Christ in Heaven in joy, or else to live in pain forever with the wicked devils of Hell. Now I see before my eyes either Heaven, ready to receive me, or Hell, ready to swallow me up." He paused briefly, glancing at congregation in front of him; the fact of each individual was turned towards him. "I shall therefore declare to you my very faith, without colour or dissimulation, for now is no time to deny anything I have written in the past."

Again, he caught a glimpse of the Spanish friars and Dr Cole. They were gaping at him with consternation.

"I believe in God the Father Almighty, maker of Heaven and Earth, and every word and sentence taught by our Saviour Christ, His Apostles, and the prophets in the Old and New Testaments."

The features of Cole and the friars were now a strangely frozen. However, as he continued speaking, their expressions became masks of outrage.

"The great thing that troubles my conscience more than any other thing I have said or done in my life..." He leaned forwards, his words tumbling forth. "Is the setting about of writing contrary to the truth. Here and now, I renounce and refuse those things written by my hand contrary to the truth which I thought in my heart, for those things I wrote for fear

512

of death and to save my life, if that was possible. I also renounce all such notes that I have written with my own hand since my degradation, wherein I have written many things that are untrue." There, it was said, and his spirit was at peace for uttering this confession.

He continued, raising his voice several decibels. "My hand offended in writing contrary to my heart, therefore my hand..." he raised his right hand. "shall be first punished. For when I come to the fire, it shall be first burned. As for the Pope, I refuse him as Christ's enemy and Antichrist, with all his false doctrine."

"Be silent!" The shout reverberated throughout the church. Cole had risen from his seat and moved to face Thomas, who regarded him with an air disconcerting tranquillity.

He had said all he needed to say; he was ready to face his maker. It was time to end this proceeding, and make the ultimate sacrifice, like his friends, Latimer, Ridley and others who had gone before him. Ignoring protests from the crowd, who wished for him to continue speaking, he descended from the platform and strode from the church, followed by the friars, their robes fluttering as they scurried after him. The friars, in turn, were followed by guards and warders. Despite his humble attire, his was the only dignified figure.

The stake was prepared, piled high with faggots. He stepped onto it, his feet slipping upon the unstable kindling. Somehow, he managed to stand with his back to the stake, permitting himself to be chained to it.

De Soto was standing directly in front of him, looking agitated. "Think of your soul, I implore you, think of your soul!"

"You recanted; you are a fool to revoke it!" shouted De Villa Garcia.

"I am Protestant. I will die in that, the true faith," he calmly assured them, his voice clearly audible to the watching crowd.

As the faggots were lit and the smell of smoke assaulted his nostrils, he recited aloud a brief prayer, then inwardly asked for God's blessing upon his wife and children. In spite of the rain, the faggots did burn quickly, and the flames rose, sweeping towards him.

Feeling the heat upon his face, instinctively he closed his eyes tightly as he extended his right hand into the flames and cried aloud, "this hand has offended! Into your hands, oh God, I commit my spirit!"

Watched by a large crowd, the former archbishop's agony was soon over. He did not cry out or scream, but kept his arm extended until he lost consciousness. Then, in peace, he went to meet his God.

*****

Thomas Cranmer, former Archbishop of Canterbury and Primate of all England, died on the twenty-first of March 1556, knowing that the Protestant faith, which he had worked long and hard to introduce into England, had been brutally suppressed by England's deeply unpopular Roman Catholic monarch, Queen Mary the first. It is estimated that, between 1555 and 1558, two hundred and seventy-five Protestants were burned at the stake, and the prisons were full to capacity with others who were awaiting the same fate. Queen Mary died on the seventeenth of November 1558, at the age of forty-two. Though she for a child, she never managed to conceive. Mary was succeeded by her half-sister, Elizabeth, who herself had been imprisoned, suspected of being a heretic. One of Queen Elizabeth's first acts was to reinstate Protestantism in England,

and since then, every reigning monarch has been tied to the Protestant faith. Thomas Cranmer and his fellow Protestants did not perish in vain.

BV - #0055 - 230222 - C0 - 198/129/29 - PB - 9781803780153 - Gloss Lamination